CONFUSING HEARTS

A Westin Pack Novel

By

Julie Trettel

Confusing Hearts
A Westin Pack Novel: Book Four

Cover Art by, Desiree Deorto Designs
Editing by, Sara Meadows of TripleA Publishing Services

Thanks and Acknowledgments

So many people have helped me along the way with this series that early on I decided to not do dedications and instead just do thanks and acknowledgments. We're four books in now and for the most part, those that stepped up and started this journey with me are still here. I will be eternally grateful for each and every one of you.

There are 2 special ladies that I would like to give an additional shout out to, though. First, Rachel Young. I love you like one of my own daughters, and I am so thankful to have you in my life. Rachel befriended my Hope years ago. They are inseparable in most of life's adventures. It has been a privilege to watch her grow into the amazing young woman she is becoming. Rachel is one of my biggest cheerleaders; my stylist for all book events; and my only Alpha reader for Westin Pack. Thank you for all you do.

Finally, I need to throw a huge thank you out to a very special lady. She likes her anonymity, and I will respect that by not mentioning her specifically by name. You know who you are! When things started to fall apart, and issues arose with this book, she stepped up to the plate and went above and beyond for me. Thank you, thank you, thank you. Without you, this would have been a much harder and longer path, but we did it!

Chase

Chapter 1

I dropped my bag on the floor and collapsed onto my bed. Three weeks at home had been enough. I loved my family, but they had tried to cram so much into my Christmas vacation that I was exhausted. I knew they loved me and didn't want to waste a second of it, but I was ready for the break.

I had an easy semester of classes planned. My roommate was studying abroad, so even though I lived in the frat house with thirty-four other shifters, mostly wolves, I was looking forward to the space and the quiet. Okay, as quiet as a popular frat house could be.

Archibald Reynolds College, jokingly called the ARC, was a college specifically for shifters, all kinds of shifters. Archibald Reynolds had been a big proponent of shifter integration at the turn of the century. He had worked closely with our Grand Council that governed the wolf shifters to bring peace among all shifters, yet only in the last five years had there ever been a place to truly encourage that philosophy.

My brother, Liam, had been one of the first graduates of the ARC. I was in my third year now and loved everything about it. I had been raised in a wolf pack, like most wolf shifters. Going to the ARC had opened my eyes to so much I had never been aware of, or even thought about, if I were being honest.

The pack gave us securities that other species simply didn't have. I had known my pack, the Westin Pack, was better off than most. I just didn't realize how much so, until I went to college and got to know people with very different backgrounds from my own.

I groaned at the knock on my door. "What?"

"Hey man, heard you were back," Matt Williams, one of my

frat brothers, said, walking in and plopping down on my roommate's bed.

Matt was a jaguar shifter, and while it was rare for felines and canines to mix, he had insisted on rushing Delta Omega Gamma his freshman year. We were in the same class and despite our differences, we'd hit it off immediately. He had put up with so much more as a pledge than I had endured. They even nicknamed him Kitty, and yet it never seemed to faze him. I asked him once why he was so determined to be a D.O.G. and he said that he had always admired the sense of group, of family, that was instilled in the wolf packs. Felines tended to be loners, and he craved that bond with other people like the canines had.

"What do you want, dude?" I asked him.

"There's a new sorority that opened up two houses down. They're having an open party tonight. You're going, right?"

"I just got back. I don't know if I'm up for a party tonight."

"Chase Westin not up for a party? What happened to you, man? You're the ultimate party animal. I've never seen you turn one down. Never."

"My nephews kicked my ass. You try keeping up with a one-year-old and a seven-year-old hellbent on spending every waking moment with you. I love them, but I don't know how my brothers do it. I'm exhausted. Need a vacation from my vacation."

"You can sleep when you're dead. Now get dressed and let's go," Matt told me, throwing my own phrase back at me. I had told my pledge class that every single day freshman year. It was what got us through to become full brothers of Delta Omega Gamma.

I kicked him out, grumbling in protest as I got dressed for the evening. A few minutes later I met up with Matt and two of our other brothers as we walked down the short distance to the new sorority.

"D.O.G.'s in the house!" Matt announced as we entered. Our friends scattered to check out the new place.

A tall, thin girl with long, straight, black hair approached us with her arms crossed and a scowl on her face. She was sleek and sexy as hell. Despite the off-limits vibe she was sending, my interest in the night immediately piqued. I was up for a little challenge.

"Dogs are not welcome here," she said with complete arrogance.

I grinned just enough that I knew my dimples were showing. Most girls found them irresistible, but this one seemed completely unaffected.

"You must be new here, 'cause I'm sure I would have noticed you otherwise."

She rolled her eyes. "Don't waste your breath. Your kind is not welcome here. My sisters and I just transferred. Most of us were forced to come to discourage this sort of nonsense and fraternization between species."

"Oh, now, come on, darling," one of my brothers, Brett, said, approaching and putting on his best Southern charm. "This is the ARC, where we encourage interspecies relations." He waggled his eyebrows and for a brief moment the ice queen thawed.

Game on, I thought. "Ignore the coyote. What's your name, gorgeous?"

She frowned at me. "You are clearly nothing but trouble." She turned to Brett with a look of disgust. "Coyote?" She whipped her long, shiny hair as she turned and stalked away.

"Come on, Chase. What was that all about?" Brett demanded.

"Dude, you totally cut in on my game."

"What game?" Matt laughed. "Hey, Ayanna." The ice queen turned and cocked her head in interest. "Don't be such a bitch."

She hissed as she turned and stomped off.

"Dude, you know her?"

"Chase, my man, you are aware that jaguars and black panthers are basically the same species, right?"

"Why would I know that?"

Matt laughed. "Well, we are. Ayanna and her *sisters*"—he emphasized with air quotes—"are all black panthers—a bunch of elitist snobs. They even frown at fraternizing with my kind, even though the only difference is the color of our coats. Trust me, I did you a favor. Let's go grab a drink and find something better to distract you with tonight."

Much of the remainder of the night passed in a blur, and my next fully coherent memory was waking up naked in bed and thankful I was alone. It wasn't like me to get that wasted, and I didn't like it. It made my wolf uncomfortable when I drank, and I could feel my skin crawling with the sensation I knew as the sign that I needed to shift.

I threw on an old pair of shorts and used the bathroom before grabbing a cold bottle of water from the fridge and heading for the woods. One of the things I loved about the ARC was the massive one hundred and eighty-seven acre forest surrounding the college. It was the perfect getaway, and since everyone on campus was a shifter, I didn't even have to hide when I needed time in my fur.

Once inside the cover of the trees, I started to discard my shorts.

"Chase Westin," a sexy voice purred behind me, and I nearly tripped in surprise. Turning, I saw a girl that I didn't recognize at all.

"Um, hi. Have we met?"

"Chase, you rocked my world last night. I'm Anita, remember?"

Shit! I wracked my brain for any memory of the previous evening.

She started laughing. "I'm just messing with you. You were pretty wasted last night, though. I really am Anita. You and some of your friends partied at my house last night?"

"Oh, you're a panther?"

"You say that with disgust. I suppose my sisters' reputations have preceded us. I really shouldn't be surprised."

There was something different about the girl and I liked her immensely.

"And, you're not like your sisters?" I asked.

"Oh God, no! I'm not a pampered princess, or think I'm the greatest thing ever to walk this earth. I actually love the interspecies policy here at Archibald Reynolds. My sisters are just a bunch of snobs and our king strongly encourages keeping our line pure, if you know what I mean."

"And you don't? By the way, we call it the ARC. Archibald Reynolds College. A-R-C—kind of a pun from the, well, the ark." I shook my head. It sounded stupid trying to explain it, but she laughed.

"I like that. And no, I don't. Well, I'm not against finding my true mate, of course. I just think it's okay to friend other shifters. I don't see the issue there. How about you?"

I shrugged. "Never much thought of it. I assumed I'd find my one true mate someday and settle down. In the meantime, I wasn't going to stress it. My brother went to school here, so I was exposed to all sorts of shifters before coming here. My nephew is half tiger. I guess I just didn't think it was really that big of a deal anymore."

"You have a half-breed nephew?"

"It's a long story, and not really mine to tell."

"I didn't even know that was truly possible."

"Why not?"

"Well, what is he going to be when he grows up?"

"Not real sure. We have a theory that God only gives us one animal spirit, so I guess he has a fifty-fifty chance of getting either a tiger or a wolf."

"Wolf?" she shrieked. "I thought you were a jaguar. You were hanging out with Matt Williams last night."

"Yeah, he's my brother. My fraternity brother."

"Matt's in a fraternity with a, a dog?" She must have seen the look of surprise on my face because she immediately began backstepping and talking really fast. "I didn't mean that like it sounded. I'm just surprised. Until yesterday I had never even met a shifter that wasn't a black panther, or the occasional jaguar, and we were discouraged from even talking to the jags. So yeah, other species are kind of new to me. I guess I just assumed Matt hung out with other cats."

I snorted. "Nah, Matt was insistent he was going to be a D.O.G. Trust me, he took a lot of shit when we were pledges, but now, he's just one of the brothers." I smiled enough to flash my dimples. Unlike the ice queen Ayanna, Anita reacted to them.

"Wow, this is, well, kind of cool. I've been excited to meet other kinds of shifters, just wasn't sure my sister was going to let me out of her sight long enough to make any friends here. Ayanna can be a little, well, okay—I'm not really sure how to describe her without it sounding horrible."

I laughed. "Ayanna is your sister? Like real sibling sister or sorority sister?"

She sighed. "My real sister."

"Wow, it must really suck to be you."

She grinned. "You have no idea. So, what are you doing out here anyway? I was just getting ready to go for a run."

"As was I. Want to join me?"

"A wolf? You want a panther to run with a wolf?"

"I promise not to eat you, and I'll even go slowly enough for you to keep up."

"In your dreams, dog-boy!"

I wasn't sure why, but I turned away from her when I stripped out of my shorts and shifted. She was still in human form, staring at me in shock. She put her hand out like one would when meeting a stray dog. I quirked my head to the side.

"What? I've never seen a wolf this close before. Okay, I've never seen a wolf in real life before. You're all black, just like me." I nodded and finally gave in and walked towards her outstretched hand. "Wow, your fur is so soft, too. Okay, so turn away or go over there or something while I change. I can't believe you just stripped right in front of me like that. Clearly dogs have no sense of civility."

I laughed, and she jumped. I had no doubt it sounded creepy coming through my wolf. I ran a short distance away, and keeping my back to her, I waited for her to shift. My heightened animal ears let me easily track her even without seeing her.

I was surprised to find she was as large as my wolf. I nodded my head towards the woods and took off. She easily kept pace with me. When we heard movement approaching, she disappeared into the treetops. *That is definitely not something a wolf could do,* I thought.

Recognizing a small pack of my brother wolves running with Matt in his jaguar form, I nodded and barked, then joined them on their run. Anita would find her way back home, of that I was certain.

Jenna

Chapter 2

Half my closet was strewn across my bedroom. It was my first day of classes and I had no idea what to wear. I had never been allowed to meet anyone outside the family and panther community, and an occasional jaguar or other big cat. My parents had kept my sister and me close to them. Even my old school had been only panthers in every class.

I was just a kitten when the panthers organized. Felines were already at a disadvantage because of our loner personalities. We didn't run in packs or even prides, like the lions, but as our numbers dwindled, particularly the black panthers, we banded together and formed our own unit. My father was the king and my sister and I were considered the princesses.

It wasn't easy growing up as part of the royal family. While Tessa had rebelled starting in our early teen years, I had never even considered it. I was the epitome of the good girl. It was exhausting at times. I just wanted to be me, and sometimes I wasn't even sure who that was.

When I had applied to Archibald Reynolds College, it was the only act of rebellion I had ever displayed. I hadn't considered Daddy would send Tessa and relocate our entire sorority to the other side of the United States just because I wanted to attend a different school. I tried not to resent them all. It wasn't their fault. When the king issued a command, everyone followed. That's just the way it was.

I finally settled on a pair of jeans and a dark-green shirt. I grabbed my backpack, shoving my new books inside, and stepped out into the hallway. Tessa was there. I stared at her, noticing she had on nearly the exact same thing, like my own reflection in the mirror staring back at me.

"Dammit, Tess. Now I have to change."

"You don't have time, we're going to be late for our first class," she scolded.

"Wait, we're in the same class?"

She shrugged. "Daddy's really worried about you, Jenna. He wants me to keep an eye on you."

I sighed, knowing it was pointless to argue. We headed across campus to our first class. I was excited despite the bomb my sister had dropped on me.

"Wait, I have calculus this morning, Tessa. How did you even get in the class?" I loved my sister, but Tessa wasn't exactly known for her brains. I had always been a nerd. I loved learning and got good grades. Tessa, well, she liked to cook, play sports, and was a phenomenal singer. Basically, she hated all core classes, and only excelled in the electives in high school.

She grinned back at me. "I'm pretty much banking on you doing all the work for us in this class."

"Tess, I can't take two tests at the same time."

"Why not? It's not like we haven't done it before."

I looked at her like she had two heads. "That was high school. This is college. It's not that simple. Plus, we weren't in the actual same class. Remember?"

There were definitely benefits to being an identical twin, at least for Tessa. Okay, that wasn't entirely true. The only class I almost flunked was PE in the ninth grade. I wasn't really the athletic type, but that was Tessa's department. She was great at all sports, but especially volleyball. I didn't really envy her. I had my art, and loved seeing the world through a camera lens, but unfortunately physical education was still mandatory in high school.

You'd think that a panther, sleek in movements with great agility would excel in sports, but not me. I could dance. That was about the closest thing to an actual sport as I got, and that wasn't offered as a high school course alternative to gym class. The funny part was, while Tessa was extremely athletic, she had no rhythm and couldn't dance to save her life.

At that time, Tess had been failing algebra, and fortunately for us, the classes were on the same block. So she would pose as me and downplay her athletic skills just enough to get me a passing grade, and I attended her algebra class to do the same for her. It had been beneficial to the both of us.

It wasn't the only time we had changed places over the years, either. Our own parents had a hard time telling us apart, so it had always worked in our favor.

"Okay, you're right. Why didn't I think of this before? We can't both be in the class. I'm going to go over and see about transferring. Same classes, different schedules, and no one ever has to know, especially Daddy. He'll just see that we had the same classes and assume we were in them together. Right?"

"I guess so," I said doubtfully. We were nineteen years old, sophomores in college, and hundreds of miles away from the man. Why did we still care so much?

"Okay, have fun, take good notes for us," she said, giving me a quick hug as she headed off to student resources in the hopes of changing her class schedule.

I looked around me. Alone. I was alone, or as alone as a person could possibly be on a campus of eight hundred students. I couldn't stop the smile spreading across my face as I walked to class.

"Tessa, over here." I saw my friend Anita waving near the door to my class.

"It's Jenna," I told her.

"Oh, sorry. I thought Tessa said she was going to be in this class."

I tried not to laugh. "Tessa? In calculus?"

Anita laughed along with me. "Yeah, it sounded like a long shot to me too. I should have known."

"She actually did sign up, and then realized I couldn't do her work for her if she was in the same class with me, so now she's working on getting her schedule changed."

"Okay, that sounds much more like Tessa," Anita said.

I followed her into the classroom to empty seats at the front of the room as she chatted on. Anita was a true friend. I had always liked her, unlike her sister, Ayanna, who came across as condescending. I didn't have it in me to be as mean and calculating as Ayanna. She would definitely make a far better princess, and if I could give her the job, I would in a heartbeat. Who was I kidding? I just wanted to be left alone.

As the teacher entered and called the class to order, I took in a deep breath. It was something I always did to calm myself before class, but as I inhaled, I was assaulted by an unfamiliar woodsy scent. No, I had smelled it before at the party we hosted over the weekend. It had caused such a tingling sensation across my skin that I had retreated to my room and locked myself in for the night.

I had heard of such a feeling. It was very much like my mother had described as the call of true mates. No, no, no, no, no, that couldn't happen here. I knew for a fact there were no male black panthers attending Archibald Reynolds. It was one of the things that had attracted me most. There were some male jaguars, though. I said a quick prayer under my breath that my true mate was not a jaguar.

Daddy was very insistent on the purity of the family line. Black panthers were rare enough without polluting the gene pool. I had always assumed my one true mate would be a panther, just like me, but technically there were several species of compatible cats to my kind. I sunk down in my seat, hoping the sensations I was feeling were nothing more than first-day jitters.

As we were settling into class, Anita turned and waved to someone at the back of the room. I wasn't surprised to find she was already making friends. Most panther shifters were loners. We didn't naturally run in groups like other shifters. Anita was somewhat of an exception. She loved people and was a quirky sort of extrovert.

"Did you know Matt Williams is in Delta Omega Gamma? The D.O.G. frat. Seriously, I'm not even kidding. I met one of his brothers yesterday and I couldn't believe it. I mean he was cute and all, but I just assumed he was a jag. Imagine my shock when I went running with a wolf."

"A wolf? Anita, they're dangerous, you can't be hanging out with their kind," I reminded her.

She just rolled her eyes at me. "Jenna, we're at the ARC. Why else are we here if not to mingle with all sorts of shifters?"

Because they have the best photography program of any college Daddy would approve, I thought honestly. I wouldn't dare confess it, though.

The teacher started class before I could answer her, and I got out of there quickly the moment class ended. The scent had continued to haunt me throughout class until it became uncomfortable to just sit there. It had taken everything in my power not to turn around and search out the source of that delicious smell that caused goosebumps to rise on my skin. I just couldn't do it, though. If my true mate was nearby, and he wasn't a black panther, it would be best if we just never met at all, because Daddy would never approve.

Keeping our family line pure was more important to him than the bond of true mates. I had always known it, but until that moment, I had never given any thought to how that could affect me. I even briefly considered switching classes. One thing was certain: I needed to stay as far away from that smell as possible.

Chase
Chapter 3

The last thing I had expected when coming back to college for a new semester was to find my one true mate. Walking into calculus, I was paralyzed by the overwhelming urge to go to her. But who was she?

I sat at the back of the room. My skin was pebbled in goosebumps and my heart thumped hard in my chest. My hands were clammy, and I didn't hear a damn word the professor said.

I scoured the room, looking for any sign of reciprocation. Nothing. There were plenty of females that made eye contact and checked me out, but none were her. Still, I knew she was close. I waited in the hall outside the room as it cleared, closely watching every female as she exited. Still nothing. Walking back into the empty room, I slumped back down in the chair. She had been there. I was certain of it, and suddenly I was consumed with a need to find her.

I couldn't sulk for long. My graphics design class was starting in fifteen minutes. With a sigh of frustration, I headed out and walked two buildings down to Wagner Hall.

The remainder of the day passed in a blur, as did the rest of the week. My senses stayed on high alert, but there had been no further signs of my mate, and I soon began wondering if I had just imagined it. Calc on Monday morning would be the final test to that theory, because she hadn't been there on Wednesday and I didn't sense her in class that morning either.

Matt knocked on my door as I lay there after my classes were done for the week, thinking through what to do for the weekend. He didn't wait for me to answer before opening the door. He never did.

"Hey, man, the panthers are having another party this weekend. Want to go?"

I rolled my eyes. "Didn't we have enough of them last week?"

"What? They're hot. And what do you know? You could barely remember the party last weekend you were so wasted."

"Touché. I guess Anita will be there at least. She seems cool."

He quietly observed me with interest. "Anita? You've been talking to Anita?"

I shrugged. "We went running together last weekend, you know that day I met up with you guys in the woods? She took off as you approached. She seemed cool. Easy to talk to."

Matt sat down on the foot of my bed. "Look, Chase, panthers are off limits. Even to me, if I'm being honest. They are mostly loners, but governed by a dictator who insists on keeping their line pure. Jags and panthers are really the same breed, just different colorings, and my kind isn't good enough for them, if you get what I'm saying. They are beautiful and fun to party with, but absolutely hands off."

I laughed. "Dude, they're cats. I mean, no offense, but hardly my type."

"Okay, just checking. I wouldn't want to see you get hurt."

I shook my head. "I'm interested in having a good time. Nothing more."

"That's what I'm saying. Party, dance, even flirt with them, but that's it."

"I got you. Don't mess around with the panthers. So, why are we still going to party there?" He grinned and shrugged. "Dude, am I getting this lecture as a way of reminding yourself?"

He shoved me off the bed and grumbled. "Just get dressed already."

Before long we were on our way to the panther sorority house. Ayanna was working the door. She rolled her eyes but let us pass anyways. Once inside I immediately spotted Anita and waved. She was with a striking woman who had straight, jet-black hair and a sleekness to her moves. She had to be panther. It was literally like watching the large cat move in human form. I had never been so mesmerized in all my life, and found myself drawn to her.

"Hey, Chase." Anita's voice cut through the haze induced by the beautiful creature.

"Hey, Anita," I said, giving her the nod. I looked around, but the woman was gone. She just vanished before my eyes like a mirage. "I could really use a drink."

She laughed and took my arm to guide me to another room with a fully stocked bar. All I wanted was a beer, but she gave me a whiskey on the rocks instead. Who was I to argue? I shot it back and slammed it down for another round.

"Last one for a while. You were pretty messed up last weekend. You are far too pretty to look at to be a drunk."

"I'm not a drunk. That was one time."

"And well on your way to round two." She nodded towards my glass.

"Alright, I'll savor this one, just for you." I winked at her and she blushed and giggled. She was fun to flirt with and easy to talk to. I knew I should heed Matt's warning and not get involved beyond that, but I was curious to see where the night would lead us.

We sat and talked for a bit and she seemed a little distracted, looking around.

"Is everything okay?" I finally asked.

"Um, yeah. I was just hanging out with a friend and she sort of disappeared on me. I just hope everything's okay. I wanted to introduce you. She's about the closest thing to a sane panther as they come, especially for a princess."

"Is that panther code for bitch?"

Anita laughed. "No, she really is a princess."

"Seriously?"

"Seriously. Oh, there she is," Anita said, jumping up and waving.

I turned just in time to see the beautiful creature I'd been watching, wave back. She was in the middle of the dance floor and her movements weren't quite as sleek this time. I was grateful to find that her hold over me seemed to be a one-time thing.

"Never mind, that's just Tessa . . ."

I nodded, but kept my thoughts to myself.

"So, looks like calculus is the only class we have together this semester," I said, changing the subject. I didn't want to think about the girl who had put a spell on me. No, not a girl, she was all woman.

"Yeah, Tessa's in that class too. At least I think she still is. She was trying to get her schedule changed, so I'm not sure. Her sister Jenna is, though. You should sit with us. Jenna's cool, you'll like her. She's not like some of the others."

"So not a pampered princess?"

She laughed. "No, definitely not."

As the night wore on, I considered my options for hooking up with Anita. Matt's warning wasn't what was holding me back, though; it was the memory of smelling my mate. I had convinced myself it was only in my mind, but my wolf did not seem onboard with moving on. Then again, I had never chased a cat before, so maybe it was just that.

Before I could even make my decision, Anita shot me down. Even though we were both verging on drunk, and had been dancing close and flirting much of the night, nothing was going to happen.

"I'm calling it a night, pup. And no, that's not an invitation to join me. Honestly, I'm going to catch enough crap just from hanging out with you. Friends?"

She offered me her hand, and I smiled, flashing her my dimples as I accepted. "Friends."

I hadn't realized the party had died down until Anita had left. I found Matt and told him I was heading home. He was wrapped up in some chick I recognized as one of his regular hookups, but couldn't remember her name.

Stepping outside, I took a deep breath of fresh air, letting it fill my lungs. Goosebumps popped up across my arms and the hair on the back of my neck stood up.

Mate.

She was near. I could smell her, and this time I was certain. With the sweet aroma surrounding me, I realized I had smelled it the previous weekend, too. I suddenly remembered the reason behind my extreme intoxication. I had smelled my mate and it had freaked me out.

Looking around, I saw no one. I let my wolf come to the surface just enough to channel my full smell capabilities and walked around the building. There was a window open to one of the bedrooms and I could hear laughter coming from inside. Feeling like a perverted stalker, I peeked into the window. Anita. A shiver ran down my spine and my wolf tried to surge, but not in a positive way.

I knew Anita wasn't my mate. I had just spent most of the night with her. I would know. My wolf had clearly not been pleased with my new friend.

"Hey, is someone out there?" I heard her yell from the window. I took off at a full sprint, not wanting her to see me. "Pervert!" she yelled at my retreating shadow.

Jenna

Chapter 4

Anita had waltzed into the room smelling exactly like my mate. I didn't understand why. Panthers weren't exactly known for a keen sense of smell, but I'd know that scent anywhere. I had tried everything to erase it from my memory, permanently, but the second he had walked into the house, I knew it. I had been dancing, lost in all coherent thought and swaying to the music, and that scent had hit me like a ton of bricks. I freaked and spent the rest of the night in my room.

One thing I learned from extensive research that week, there was definitely not even one male, black, panther at Archibald Reynolds. Not one. I had triple-checked. That could only mean one thing: my mate was not a panther. And if he wasn't a panther, he couldn't be my mate. Daddy would never approve. I had sulked, cried, and mourned all week the loss of a true mate, but it didn't seem to matter when his delicious woodsy fragrance hit me.

I had also spent the week trying to rearrange my schedule, even skipping calculus on Wednesday and again on Friday, which was not like me. Knowing my mate was not a panther meant it was best if we tried not to cross paths, but he was in my calculus class. Unfortunately, it was the only one that fit my schedule and was a requirement for most majors I was considering, so I would have to endure it and brace myself for an inevitable face-to-face with him.

The only positive of the week for me was that two classes I had desperately wanted came open after dropouts. I had successfully gotten into both advanced graphic designs and a photography class I had been praying for. They met Monday, Wednesday, Friday, and along with calculus would make for a full morning on those days, but I was ready and excited for the new challenges.

Daddy wasn't going to be happy. Neither would Tessa when she found out that after all her scheming and course changes, we still wouldn't be taking the exact same classes this semester. I hadn't found the courage to tell either of them when Daddy had called to check how our first week had gone. This was my time, and selfishly, I wasn't ready to explain myself. I was doing something I loved, something that made me happy for a change, consequences be damned.

My new feeling of empowerment had me flying high and not even concerned with the whole true mate thing, until I walked into calculus Monday morning and froze. Taking a deep breath, I let his scent envelope me, but didn't dare look left or right for the source of that delicious smell. I walked to the front and took a seat next to Anita.

"What's wrong?" she asked.

"Nothing," I assured her.

A pleasant tingle shot up my spine just as Anita jumped up from her seat and threw her arms around the source of said tingle. I bit back a hiss, swallowing hard to grasp some kind of hold on reality.

Mate. The word kept playing on repeat, echoing in my ears.

"Chase, this is . . ." Anita was cut off before she could finish the introductions as the professor called the class to order.

I knew I was being rude, but I was just so shocked I didn't know what to do. Chase. His name was Chase. The last thing I needed was a mental image of what my mate would have looked like, but I stiffened, stood tall, and pulled my shoulders back, not thinking of what it would do to my breasts until I heard his sharp intake and somehow knew he had noticed.

I slowly turned to meet chocolate-brown eyes shining with confusion. I heard him sniff the air around him and saw his forehead crinkle. Dark eyes searched mine for any sign of . . . recognition? Answers? I wasn't sure what he was hoping to find, but it felt as though he could see all the way to my soul. My palms began to sweat and I knew my heart rate increased, no matter how much I willed it not to.

"Chase Westin," the professor called, and it seemed to jolt us both back to the present.

"Yes, sir," said a deep voice that rumbled through my entire body. It wasn't until the edges of my vision began to darken that I remembered to breathe.

"It is quite the honor as always to have you in class. Would you care to assist today?"

He turned to me and smiled. Two swoon-worthy dimples popped out as he got up and walked to the front of the class.

"Sure," he said, grabbing up a marker and scribbling numbers on the white board as fast as the professor could read them off.

I'm not sure I heard a lot of what was said and I struggled to follow along, doing more staring than taking notes.

At the end of class, Chase was held up and I found my escape, but not before I heard the teacher ask him—no, beg him, really—to be his TA for the semester. *Great,* I thought. He's gorgeous, panty-melting dimples gorgeous, and he's got to be smart, too. Why couldn't he be a panther? Life would have been so much easier for us both.

I headed to my next class, which was now computer graphics. I was really looking forward to it. I didn't have a lot of artistic ability, but I had taught myself how to manipulate and change my photographs to better enhance them. I knew it was a more advanced class than I was probably prepared for, but I was up for the challenge, excited, and ready.

The room was lined with computers, two to a table with about a dozen tables in all. Most already had two people sitting at them, and a few with only one, but I chose the single entirely open table instead. I wiped my sweaty palms on my jeans as I took my seat.

Not five minutes later, the tingling sensation returned. Shocked, I couldn't stop myself from turning to look for the source.

Chase Westin strolled in. He stopped and looked around until our eyes met. He flashed his dimple-perfect smile my way and headed right for me. My eyes widened, and my heart raced as I looked around for an escape.

"Hey, it's you," he said, his eyes still looking worried and unsure. I got the impression that Chase was not the kind of guy who was used to being unsure of himself. "I didn't know you were in this class, and I would definitely have noticed." He ran a hand through thick brown hair and I sensed he was as confused by what was happening between us as I was.

"There was a dropout last week, so I was able to grab the last spot." For some reason, I felt guilty, like some stalker invading his space as I said it. I contemplated grabbing my things and fleeing the room.

Then he smiled at me again. "Well, Friday the dropout abandoned that very seat, so looks like you and I will be partners this semester."

"What?" I asked a little too sharply. It was the way he said 'partners' with a cocky expression that unnerved me. I couldn't be his partner, not in the way my body was already craving. I suddenly realized it was going to be a very long semester.

Chase didn't mention anything about the bond, though I caught him looking at me in that way that made me feel raw and exposed, like he was searching for answers eluding him. I understood that look.

I wasn't sure what Chase was, but I knew he couldn't be panther. Could what I was feeling not be the bonding call after all? I had all the symptoms I'd been told about, but it didn't really seem possible. Could we react similar to just desire? Chase Westin was a very handsome man. Could that really be all it was?

Then I remembered I had felt him before I ever saw him. That threw a kink in my rationale.

"You going to stare at the screen all day, or work on the lesson?" Chase's deep voice jogged me from my thoughts. He was grinning when I looked over and my cheeks burned.

"Um . . ."

He passed me his notes and my stomach rolled. I was in over my head. None of it made sense. It was like staring at a foreign language.

"Hey, it's okay. Don't worry. I'm only taking this class for fun. Click here," he said, pointing at an app on the screen. "Do you have a picture on your phone you can use?"

I shrugged, because I didn't know what kind of picture was needed. Our hands collided as he reached for my phone. For that brief moment, everything else in the world faded away. We stared at each other, seemingly locked into the same shrinking universe where only Chase and I existed. He blinked and the moment was gone.

Scrolling through my phone, he laughed and smiled at the pictures he found.

"Wow, this one is really good. We'll use it."

I glanced down to see a picture of me. I was in the woods, twirling while taking a selfie. My hair was wild and fanning out around me. I had done it for fun, never planning for anyone to see it.

"Not that one," I whispered, horrified. "Can't we use one not featuring me?"

"No, that defeats the term 'selfie.' Sorry, it's the assignment, which you'd know if you were paying attention." He wasn't scolding me, and I didn't even feel judged. He seemed more amused than anything, like he knew he was the source of my frustrations, but not in a self-assured cocky manner either.

"Okay," I conceded. "What are we supposed to do?"

"Fade, add a glow, and pop a color."

"That's it?" I asked him, surprised by how simple the assignment was. I actually did know what he was talking about and my entire body started to relax as I set about doing as he instructed.

"Wow, I'm impressed. That's really good."

My heart beat harder and my palms sweated at his praise. I wiped them on my jeans subconsciously, and chewed my lower lip, a nervous habit I had given up trying to break.

"Thanks," I managed, though my voice sounded a little huskier than usual, causing his pupils to dilate. I was glad to see a real sign that I was affecting him in some way. "I've dabbled a little on my own."

"You've never taken a formal class?" he asked, sounding surprised.

I shook my head, continuing to trouble my lip, until his eyes lowered, entranced by the sight. I sucked in a breath and forced myself to stop.

"What other classes are you taking?" he asked, changing the subject.

"I still haven't decided on a major, so I'm taking mostly basic classes, too. Okay, so I know what I want to major in, I just don't think it will be allowed," I confessed, shocking myself by my admittance. I had never told another soul about my desire to go into photography and maybe expand to a business with graphic design work as well. I didn't even know if I was good enough.

"Don't keep me in suspense, what is it? And why wouldn't it be allowed?"

Sadness consumed me. "Daddy would never allow it. It's a pointless major. No real career path, at least not befitting a princess." I hadn't meant to tell him that either. There was just something about Chase that made me spill my guts when he asked. It was a habit I was going to have to find a way to break quickly.

"So, what is it? No, let me guess… basket weaving? No, too cliché. How about underground Russian music management?"

"What?" I laughed. "Is that even a thing?"

He shrugged, but continued. "Nude model? I hear they pay really well, and since I'm taking three art classes this semester, I won't deny I'm onboard with that one."

The heat that had resided in my cheeks spread to my ears and chest quickly. I had to change the subject. "You're an art major?"

"Minor. Business major. Kind of a family thing, not my first choice."

"Oh, yeah, I know how that feels. Wait, you don't need calculus for a business degree, do you?"

He shrugged and flashed his dimples at me. "I'm not really sure I need any of the classes I'm taking this year for a business degree, but what fun would college be if we only studied the mandatory stuff?"

"Won't that put you behind for graduation though?" It had been my biggest worry when I had signed up for the graphics design and photography classes on a whim.

This time I noticed his cheeks blushing and he ran a hand through that thick brown hair of his. I wondered if that was his nervous habit, like me chewing on my bottom lip.

"I, uh, I only need two classes to graduate in my major." He looked around like it was some big secret. "But I'm only a junior and don't want to graduate early, so I picked up a few minors. This semester I'm focusing on art, specifically graphic design, which is something I enjoy."

"Oh, wow, you must be really smart."

"Shhh, don't say that so loud." He looked around the room like he was making sure no one heard us.

I laughed at him. "There's nothing wrong with being smart, Chase. I heard our calc professor practically beg you to be his TA, so it's not exactly surprising. Why'd you turn him down?"

"Damn, you heard that? I hope you were the only one. It's just, it's not my reputation around here, and I prefer to keep it that way."

"So, you're a closet nerd and don't want your friends to find out?"

"Um, basically, yeah. Okay, it's exactly like that."

"Then why are you telling me?"

"I don't know. I don't even know why we're talking about me when you were about to tell me what you really want to major in, and since I just shared one of my deepest darkest secrets, you're totally confessing it."

I looked at him, wondering how much truth had just spilled out. Had he just shared an intimate secret with me? I made a mental note to do a little research on exactly what Chase Westin's reputation consisted of.

"Photography, maybe even graphic design." My heart lightened at the admittance. Then I thought of something he had said. "Wait, you're taking calculus for fun?"

He looked sheepish and shrugged, like a little kid just caught doing something wrong.

"And your friends never notice? Business major does not equal calculus."

The tips of his ears were bright red as he lowered his voice and cupped my ear to whisper closely, sending shock waves through my body.

"I tell everyone a different major. No one knows for sure what I'm majoring in or what I'm studying." He pulled back and stared at me with that troubling look again. "Except you. And I don't know why I told you, so let's forget it ever happened."

Chase was still watching me with his puzzled look when the professor strolled by.

"Mr. Westin, I assume you're finding this partner much more sufficient than the last?"

Without even breaking eye contact he responded. "Definitely."

"And I assume that you and Ms. Lockhardt actually managed to finish the assignment today?" the professor asked.

Chase turned his laptop around to face the teacher, then

reached over and did the same to mine.

He nodded his approval at Chase's but stopped and considered mine first. "Ms. Lockhardt, did you do this yourself?"

"Um, yes, sir. Chase picked the picture; the rest of the assignment was all me." I wiped my sweaty palms on my jeans and fought not to bite my lip.

"Very impressive. Very impressive indeed. I'm confident the two of you will make a fine pair this semester. You just may have met your match, Mr. Westin."

"Perhaps I have, sir." Chase beamed with pride, and I realized that pride was for me.

As we packed up and headed out, I couldn't help but inquire as to what Professor Stone had meant. Chase looked down at his watch and grumbled.

"What's your next class?"

"Oh, I have photography in ten minutes. I guess I should go."

Chase beamed, seeming less stressed. "Great, I'll walk you. And to answer your question, it's my third class with Stone. I don't always play well with others, or at least my standards tend to be higher than the rest of the class. He doesn't go easy on me, but he likes team projects. He's a penguin shifter, you know. Group work is kind of his thing. I didn't mean to run the girl off last week, she was just, well, subpar. I can't say I'm sorry for it. I think my new partner will be a far better match."

I blushed as he held open the door for me, and then he followed me into my classroom.

"Oh, um, you don't have to . . ."

He laughed. "Actually I do. It's my next class, too."

"Oh," I said, trying to filter the shock.

Chase

Chapter 5

I loved the look of surprise on her face. She was so damn beautiful. Everything screamed *this is your mate*, but it didn't make any sense. I knew she was a panther, a damn cat. That couldn't even be possible. Plus, I had seen her just that weekend dancing and there had been no recognition, yet my wolf had practically leapt out of me the moment I saw her eyes for the first time. Her gorgeous, unique, violet eyes. I could have stared into them forever and been perfectly content.

How did the girl have that effect on me? I had never been smitten by a female before. Sure, I had hooked up with plenty. Okay, more than I'd like to confess. But this was so different than that. Plus, she was really easy to talk to. I had already told her things I'd never told anyone, and I didn't even know why. It was like she had me under some spell or something.

That must have been it. I was bewitched. She'd cast some sort of feline spell on me to cause such confusion and give signs of the mating bond. I thought it would be best to steer clear of her. Nothing good could come from me even dating a damn cat, and yet, I knew, I just knew, there was no way I could stay away from her. Tessa Lockhardt had stolen my heart and I didn't even know how.

I had a few good friends taking photography this year, so to give myself some space, I left her side and went to say hello to my friends. From the corner of my eye I saw her panic, but more than that I could have sworn I actually felt her nerves. She was chewing on that damn lip again. God, it was the sexiest thing I'd ever seen and desire to replace her teeth with mine spiked again. It had been so hard trying to concentrate in class when she had done that.

"Hey, looks like we got a new classmate today, and she is hot," Damon, one of my fraternity brothers, said. I fought back the urge to rip his throat out. Violent need to protect the girl had me seeing red.

"That's Lockhardt. She's on the volleyball team, and she is absolutely amazing!" Kaitlyn, another friend of mine, gushed. I had heard rumors of the new volleyball star, but I was having trouble reconciling it to the girl I had just spent the last two classes trying to get to know. "Hey, Lockhardt, come join us. We have room for one more, and I could definitely use some more estrogen up in this group."

"Yes, please," Damon said, as I took a deep breath, trying to calm myself. He was my friend. He was my brother. I shouldn't have to remind myself of such things, but at that moment, it was necessary.

"Hey," she said almost shyly.

"Hey," Kaitlyn said. "I'm Kaitlyn. This is Damon, Chase, and Neal."

Neal, another one of my frat brothers and overall super cool dude, high fived her. "Hey, awesome spike on Windsor last weekend. You have a killer serve, too. Can't wait to see how this season plays out. You guys are on fire!"

"Oh, uh, I. You see, that was . . ."

Tessa was cut off in mid-conversation by our teacher. He issued an outdoor assignment, and I was thankful there was no more talk of volleyball. For some reason it seemed to make her nervous and I didn't like it.

We weren't supposed to talk on the assignment. We could only take pictures and communicate by sharing them with others. It was a fun assignment that gave us all some good laughs.

I peered over Tessa's shoulder as she scrolled through her pictures. She was really good. Better than me, if I was being honest. She had such a good eye and unique way of capturing just the right angles.

I heard her quick intake of breath at my nearness. I watched as her eyelids fluttered shut and she sucked in her lower lip. God, I wanted to kiss her so bad it hurt.

"Okay, class is dismissed, but remember, I want a portfolio of your pictures from today's assignment uploaded before

Wednesday's class. I will be picking a few select ones to showcase in our next lesson," Professor Jordan announced.

If I had known I would get to spend all morning with this incredible woman, I would have arranged to have lunch with her, too. I could kick my own ass for agreeing to meet up with Matt at One Eyed Jacks.

One Eyed Jacks was a popular eating hole just off campus. A lot of students rarely went into town, even though many shifters lived in the surrounding area. Jacks was owned by a wallaby shifter from Australia. It was mostly a bar, but they served good wings, too, and Matt was addicted to them.

Saying goodbye to Tessa was hard, a lot harder than it should have been. It wasn't until after she had walked away that it dawned on me too late, that I should have got her phone number. I couldn't stand the thought of not seeing her for an entire day. I briefly wondered if maybe we had more classes together after she had rearranged her schedule, but the odds of that were slim. My Tuesday/Thursday schedule consisted of Russian lit and ballroom dancing. I had quite the eclectic schedule.

I walked into Jacks and waved when I spotted Matt.

"Hey, just the two of us?" I asked him, looking around and expecting to see more of our brothers.

"Yeah, the pansies all bailed. Thanks for coming."

"What's going on?" I asked.

"Nah, nothing, just settling back into a new semester. Contemplating what I'm going to do in life when this place is over. The usual."

"Still haven't committed to a major?"

"Nope, though my options are quite limited at this point if I want to graduate on time."

"Sounds like someone's been talking with the counselors."

"Yeah." He sighed. "I need a good party to drink away real life."

"Dude, that's not the answer and you know it."

Matt grinned back at me. "Yeah, but come on, it's a hell of lot more fun! Hey, this weekend, let's hang with the Theta girls. I'm over the panthers."

Something in his expression made me think there was more to it.

"You sure?" I challenged. "Those kittens are starting to grow on me."

"Oh please, you couldn't even name two of them."

"Anita and Tessa. There's also Ayanna, but she really doesn't like me."

We both laughed. "Anita's sweet, I can see why you'd know her, but Tessa? Tessa Lockhardt? Way out of your league, my man. She'd eat you for dinner."

I looked at him seriously and shrugged. "Actually, we have several classes together. She seems nice." I tried to keep it as casual as I could muster. Nice was definitely not a word fitting of Tessa Lockhardt.

Matt pointed across the bar and I turned to see a group of dark haired ladies. In the middle was my raven beauty. Her long, sleek, straight black hair stood out from the others, and when she turned, beautiful violet eyes stared back at me, but she had a look of confusion, even more than I had seen that morning when we had first officially met.

It felt like a wall had gone up between us and my wolf growled in my head. It was freaking me out, but Matt was watching me closely, so I slowly nodded.

I wasn't fully engaged in conversation from then on, but Matt was too self-absorbed to notice. Lunch ended, and I paid the bill just as Tessa was leaving. I said a quick goodbye and ran to catch up to her.

"Hey, Tessa," I yelled.

She turned, surprise in her eyes. "Hey, it's Chase, right?"

Ouch. That sucked. I suppose the signs I had seen and felt earlier were only in my head.

"Yeah. Hey, about the graphic design assignment due next week. If you need any help, just give me a call."

I handed her my business card with my contact information and grinned wide enough to pop out my dimples. I knew the ladies loved them, and always used them to my advantage. Tessa melted just a little and I was relieved to see I wasn't entirely going crazy.

"Thanks," she said, motioning towards the card in her hand.

"Tessa, come on," her friends yelled from a car at the corner.

"Gotta go," she said, and then she was gone.

I stood there wondering what had just happened. It was

Tessa, my Tessa, but everything felt so wrong. I was losing my mind. I had been planning to go for a run after lunch, but instead headed straight home. I needed to talk things through with someone who wouldn't just laugh in my face.

The walk across campus helped clear my head some. I let myself in the house and was glad to find it quiet for once. I headed to my room and plopped down on the bed after tossing my backpack on my desk.

Hitting the silencer button on the dampener my oldest brother, Kyle, had given me as a graduation present to help with the noise of dorm life, and later fraternity living, I picked up the phone and dialed my other brother's number. Liam was four years older than me, but we had always been close, and I respected his opinion. Plus, he was the least gossipy of all my siblings.

I was the youngest of five. My father had been Alpha of the Westin Pack until an injury had passed powers on to my oldest brother Kyle. Fortunately, with a little help from Kyle's mate, Kelsey, Dad had made a full recovery.

I called my brother on his cell, even though I knew he would still be in the office at that time of day. His secretary, Christine Canine, liked to talk and I wasn't in the mood for her chit-chat.

"Hey little brother, what's up?" Liam answered after only one ring. "Not like you to call in the middle of the day. Everything okay?"

"Yeah, sure. You busy?"

"Never too busy for you. Hold on one second." I heard him lay down the cell and speak. "Chris, hold all my calls till I say otherwise . . . yeah . . . okay . . . thanks." Then he returned to me. "You never call this time of day. What's wrong?"

"Nothing's wrong. Can't a guy just call his brother without it being a big deal?" I suddenly wasn't sure I wanted to confide in him.

"No, so spill it."

I opened my mouth to tell him again there was nothing wrong, but everything just came pouring out. "I met this girl, and we sort of connected. It feels like I'd imagine finding a mate would feel, but she's not a wolf, Liam, and I'm not sure she feels the same. Then one minute I'm certain, this is my mate, and then I see her again and it's like, nothing. I mean nothing, nothing. I spent all morning with the girl, and my wolf was acting all possessive and content at the same time, then we ran into each other at lunch and she acted like she barely knew me, and it pissed off my wolf so now I feel like I'm losing my freaking mind!"

I expected my brother to laugh, but he didn't. "Why do you think she's your mate? What are you feeling?"

"Seriously? You want to talk feelings?"

"Do you want my advice or not?"

"Fine. When I'm near her it's like the rest of the world just fades away. It's only her. I recognized her the first day of classes. I realized later, it had been even sooner, but it had freaked me out so bad that I had gotten drunk and didn't remember till we went back to the same sorority a week later and I smelled her. But then it was like I'd see her and just, you know, know. And then I'd see her again and nothing. Today I met her face-to-face for the first time. She's so easy to talk with and just be with. I find myself just blurting stuff out to her that I don't tell anyone. Then at lunch today after spending three classes in a row getting to know each other, she acted like she barely recognized me, and my wolf tried to growl at her, and it's got me so freaking messed up, I don't know what to do, dude."

"I dunno man—that recognize her one moment, but not the other—it doesn't sound like a true mate. Your wolf would never try to growl at your mate. Honestly, it sounds like you really like this girl and it's probably just wishful thinking."

I didn't think that was the case. Regardless of how it seemed, I just couldn't accept that, but I conceded just the same. "Yeah, I guess you're right."

We moved on to other topics and chatted for a bit before he put me on hold.

"Ok," he said when he returned to the call. "Just spoke with Maddie and I'm going to drive on up and hang out this weekend. Is that cool? I haven't been up to the ARC in too long anyway, and you just sound like you need some brother time. Your roommate is abroad for the semester, right?"

"Yeah, come on. It would be great to see you."

As we hung up, with plans for the weekend, my heart felt a little lighter. No matter what crazy curveball life threw my way, I always knew my family had my back.

Jenna

Chapter 6

I caught myself looking for Chase all day Tuesday. We didn't have any classes together and I had been in a sour mood all day. I was shocked to realize how much I missed him. How could I miss someone I barely knew?

Tessa walked into my room without bothering to knock and flopped down on my bed. I was grateful she had insisted we not share a room, and even more so that there was one available that I didn't have to share with anyone else either. Since panthers liked their solidarity, the house was chosen because of its extra rooms and with a lower number of girls living there, almost all of us were granted some space.

"Hey Tess, what's up?" I asked, trying to sound cheerful.

"Tell me about your dog friend. He's pretty cute, but well, he's a dog, Jenna. You know better."

"What are you talking about?"

"Chase Westin. He stopped me yesterday and gave me his card in case I had any issues with our graphic design homework. Since when are we taking graphic design?"

"Sorry, a couple classes I was interested in came open and I grabbed them. It was a selfish whim, Tess. I wasn't thinking."

She shrugged. "It's okay, the same thing happened to me and I already called Daddy and told him. He was fine with it."

She held out the card, but snatched it away as I went to grab it.

"Tessa," I scolded in frustration.

"First, tell me about Chase. He's very cute, and flirty. Those dimples are to die for." I bit back a hiss as she continued, watching me closely. I knew she was testing to see my reaction. I wouldn't give her the satisfaction. "He called me by my real name though, which seemed weird, like he really thought I was in his class. Threw me off guard."

"He did?" I asked sadly, but she didn't seem to notice. Did Chase think I was Tessa then? I wracked my brain to try and remember him ever using my name. I couldn't. Had I told him I was a twin? I didn't think it had come up and I was so used to people knowing, that it hadn't really dawned on me.

Tessa seemed distracted by something on her phone, so I snatched his card away. Was Chase just being nice to me to get to Tessa? It had happened before, but it didn't explain the feelings he invoked in me. I had been so certain he was my one true mate.

"Wait," I said, remembering something Tessa had said. "Did you say Chase Westin was a dog? Like the D.O.G. fraternity or an actual canine?"

Tessa laughed. "Both, actually. You didn't know?"

The look on my face must have given her the answer because she doubled over laughing.

"Sweetie, Chase Westin. Westin, as in the Westin Pack. He's a wolf, a highly sought after man-whore of a wolf, if rumors are even partially true."

"A wolf?" I wasn't sure anything she could have said would have shocked me more. "But he hangs out with Matt Williams, so I just assumed he was a jag."

"Nope."

I groaned. "Anita told me she met a wolf and then she introduced us in calculus yesterday. I just didn't put two and two together. A wolf?"

Tessa got up, still laughing. "At least I don't have to worry about you getting any crazy ideas now."

"I don't know what you're talking about."

"Let's just say Chase was a little too happy to see me, or rather, you."

Happiness blossomed in me. He was happy to see me? Even if it had been Tessa and not me, if he had thought it was me, then that had to be good. I was still in shock to hear he was a wolf. It couldn't be true.

I tried to finish my homework, but I couldn't stop picturing large snarling wolves, and had a tough time reconciling the images with Chase. Tessa had to be wrong. Then there was the issue of the bond. Could I really have been that off base? There's no way a feline would be mated to a canine. It wasn't possible.

I struggled against the urge to call him all night long. I had never felt that need with anyone, not even guys I'd actually dated.

Waking the next morning after a long restless sleep, I dragged myself to the shower and made a small effort to prepare for the day. In the end, I threw my wet hair up in a messy bun, and donned jeans and a school sweatshirt.

I had always had a quiet, passive rebellious side. I knew I was down dressing, part in exhaustion, but more as a statement. Tessa had called Chase a man-whore. If looks were all he was interested in, he wouldn't give me a second glance today. Looking in the mirror I sighed, but with no time to fix it, I grabbed my backpack and headed off to my first class, calculus—with Chase.

I knew without looking around that he wasn't there. Anita was, though, and gave me a quick wave as I headed down to the front row. I one arm hugged her as I took the seat next to her. She looked me over.

"Rough night?"

"Something like that," I mumbled just as the now-familiar wave of goosebumps hit me. I closed my eyes and took a deep breath, preparing myself for something, though I didn't know what. I had somehow convinced myself that I imagined his effect on me, after hearing he was a wolf shifter.

"Good morning, ladies," he said, and the shudder that wracked my body from hearing his voice made me angry.

"Morning, Chase," Anita said cheerily.

"Morning," I grumbled.

He sat down next to me and stared until I couldn't stand the heat any longer and looked up at him. He genuinely smiled—dimples and all. I melted inside. Warm fuzzies fluttered in my stomach. *Mate*, a small voice in the back of my head sighed, and I wanted to lay my head down and cry. I bit my bottom lip, letting the shock of sharp pain stall my tears.

Chase didn't say anything, and I couldn't decide if I was grateful or infuriated.

At the end of calculus, I said goodbye to Anita and headed to graphic design class. My entire body was hyperaware of Chase.

"Hey, wait up," he said, rushing to catch up to me. "You okay today? You seemed a little off at lunch the other day. I've been worried. Plus, you didn't call me."

My mouth fell open, but I didn't know what to say. It was obvious he thought Tessa had been me, but how? He clearly didn't know, but why couldn't he tell? He either didn't feel the same things I was feeling or . . . I didn't want to think of it. Tessa and I were identical twins. Identical! Did that mean our own mate couldn't tell us apart? Would he feel the same for both of us? The thought made me sick to my stomach and I gagged as I rushed to the nearest bathroom, ignoring his concerns.

I didn't throw up, just dry heaved a bit. I washed my mouth out anyway, gargling water and spitting it into the sink. I splashed some water on my face and added a little lip gloss.

Walking out of the restroom, I was surprised to find Chase waiting for me. He didn't say a word at first, just wrapped his arms around me. I froze, and then relaxed into him with a sigh. I let his scent wash over me in a moment of indulgence.

"Are you okay?" he asked, sounding very worried. I nodded against his chest but couldn't find the words to speak. "Do you want to skip graphics today?"

"Yes, but I'm not going to," I said, starting to pull away from him. It was a lot harder than it should have been. My entire body was on fire and my panther pranced happily in my mind, purring. My panther would only purr for her mate. It was a million times clear to me in that moment, that despite all odds or the impossibility of the situation, Chase Westin really was my one true mate.

"Come on then. I'll deal with the professor."

"Mr. Westin, Ms. Lockhardt, so nice of you to join us today," our professor said, and my cheeks heated as I dropped my head and slid into my seat, knowing all eyes were on us.

Chase dropped his things and walked up to the professor. He whispered something that I couldn't make out and the teacher looked at me, then back at Chase and nodded. Professor Stone slapped him on the back and pointed to his seat.

I knew from the syllabus that being late to Stone's class meant an automatic ten point deduction for the day. I looked over the notes on the board and began to panic. Checking the time on my phone, I grabbed my laptop and started to get to work, panic rising inside me.

"Relax," Chase leaned over and whispered. "He's not going to deduct points from you today. The assignment isn't the easiest, but it's not that hard. I'll show you, just follow along."

He turned his laptop towards me and pointed out everything he was doing as he did it.

"Isn't this cheating?" I asked.

He smiled. "No, actually, that's why we're partners."

The way he said "we're partners" warmed me all over. I looked around to distract myself from the sensation, and noticed several tables had their heads together discussing the assignment.

"Okay," I said, relaxing.

We worked mostly in silence, side by side. It was nice and just being with him felt right. I didn't let it freak me out, just enjoyed the moment. Photography class was much of the same. We were indoors this time, but Chase invited me to sit with him and his friends.

The professor used one of my pictures to highlight in the class. At first, I was terrified and embarrassed, until I realized he was using it as a good example of what should be done, not what shouldn't. Pride flared within me, but it also showed on Chase's face and brought back that warm sensation that always seemed to come when he was near.

The rest of the week was a whole lot of the same. Thursday, I didn't see Chase and I couldn't get out of my funk. My sisters had all taken notice of my mood, but I had blown it off as if it were nothing. I couldn't explain what was happening to me, let alone share it with them. They'd never understand, and they certainly would never approve.

To make matters worse, Daddy called while Tessa was at her game.

"Hi Sweetie," he said.

"Hi Daddy. What's up? Tessa has a volleyball game today, remember?"

"I know. I know. Can't I just call and check on you?"

His unexpected sweetness was off-putting. It wasn't that my father was always mean, but he just wasn't that nice either. He was calculating, highly opinionated, and his expectations were often exhausting. He never called without a reason.

"Your mother and I were thinking of coming for a visit. She misses you both. I'm not so sure it was a good idea to let you go so far away."

I rolled my eyes, certain it wasn't my mother struggling with the distance, but him.

"When were you thinking? We're really very busy with classes, Daddy."

"I know. I don't want to interrupt your studies, so we were thinking over spring break. Tessa said you weren't planning to come home, so we'll just come to you."

His tone left no little room for argument. I normally would have sighed, smiled pretty, and said "okay Daddy," while changing our plans to accommodate his wishes. That was the expectation when my father made up his mind about something, but I was changing. I felt stronger and less intimidated by him.

"That's probably not a good idea," I told him, biting my lip surprised by my own candidness.

"Is that so?" he asked using the condescending tone that often made my panther and I both cower in his presence. Lucky for us we weren't in his presence, so I pushed on.

"Yes Daddy, Tessa and I are going to Cabo with the sisters for spring break. It's already been arranged."

There was silence on the other end and I had a rush of nausea. I had never been the daughter that questioned him. I had always subjected no matter how much I hated it. I knew my place and the expectations placed on me and I had never once let my parents down, though they always looked at me like they were waiting for me to fail them. It wasn't in what they said exactly, it was in how they acted. I had never understood it, but had grown to resent it. I was the good girl. I didn't give them reasons to doubt that, ever.

I also somehow knew that Daddy was testing me. I would bet he'd already had the same conversation with Tessa and was looking for validation that what she had told him was true. It was the kind of sneaky thing he did with us.

"Well, very well then. I'll let you go. Your mother will be greatly disappointed to hear this, but I'll break the news carefully to her. I'll talk to you on Sunday as usual." He hung up without saying goodbye.

I slept restless thinking over the conversation. He was a regimented man and it was unlike him to call mid-week like that.

Friday, my world seemed to right itself again the moment I stepped into calculus. Chase was already there in the seats that had quickly become ours. He was chatting with Anita but had left the seat between them open for me. I couldn't keep the smile off my face or the happiness from my heart.

He walked me to our next class and we just talked and laughed. I was fiddling with my phone and Chase grabbed it from me. I watched him snap a picture of himself, then type in his number before handing it back. He then offered me his. I hesitated, but finally took it and programmed my number into his phone. He frowned when I returned it without a picture and chased me the rest of the way to class trying to get one.

That sort of easy banter seemed so natural with us. It felt right and comfortable. It was no surprise we had fallen into a routine that I loved, and I was dreading the weekend. Two days where I might not see Chase seemed like a chasm too big to cross.

"Um, Chase?" I asked at the end of our last class, not wanting our time together to end.

"Yeah?"

"We're having another party tomorrow night. I was just, um, wondering if you were going to be there." I sucked in my bottom lip and waited for his response.

He seemed happy I asked, but there was also a sadness to him.

"Matt's making a push for all the guys to go to Theta Saturday night. Not sure why, but I'll probably have to at least make an appearance. And, one of my brothers is coming to visit. I'm not sure what he'll want to do, but I'll try to swing by. He's mated now, so not likely going to want to hang around Theta for long." He laughed like there was some obvious reason, but I was still new and didn't know much about them.

"Yeah, sure, well, have a good weekend then."

The disappointment was bad, but as I started to walk away, the crushing blow from his next words was so much worse.

"Tessa, wait. How about lunch?"

Tessa? He really did think I was my sister? The pain that

realization caused was almost crippling.

"I-I can't," I said turning to flee.

"Tessa?" I heard Chase yell behind me, but I couldn't turn around. The piercing pain going through my heart was too much to bear. If he wasn't my true mate, why did it hurt so much? Tears stung my eyes and burned from the cold wind against my face as I ran across campus to the safety of my room.

Locking the door, I collapsed on my bed and sobbed. Chase calling me Tessa felt like such a betrayal. The logical part of my brain reminded me I couldn't have him anyway, no matter what he was or wasn't to me. The emotional side was taking over though, and I wanted to scream out in frustration.

My phoned dinged with a new text. On auto-pilot I picked it up and looked.

CHASE: I'm sorry. Whatever I did or said to upset you. I'm so sorry.

Chase

Chapter 7

My mate was hurting. I had seen it in her body language as she turned and ran from me. I felt it in my soul and somehow knew she was crying. I wracked my brain for hours replaying every second of the conversation leading up to her fleeing in tears. Nothing stood out or seemed odd. I couldn't understand it.

I wasn't a man used to chasing a girl. Girls had always come and gone easily for me. I had rules, they either abided or I didn't waste my time. I didn't date. I didn't see the point. I always knew someday I'd meet my one true mate, so why waste time getting attached to anyone else? I had needs though, and I wasn't always proud of it, but I had acquired a bit of a playboy image while at the ARC.

That thought was a harsh reminder that I hadn't had sex since before the Christmas holiday. It had been almost two months in reality. That was a record for me, and yet, I couldn't bring myself to just run out and hook up with the first girl I saw. Sure, I'd done that in the past, but I couldn't now, not after meeting my mate.

In truth, I was little more than an easygoing nerd. I was super smart, so school always came easy to me. Actually, everything came easy. My wolf spirit helped me excel in most sports. I was strong and agile, and could have gotten a full scholarship in several different areas had I chosen athletics in college. I hadn't; I didn't want to be the jock in college. I played that game enough in high school, but I learned quickly that nerds didn't get laid. So, I hid the fact that I was on a full academic scholarship. I lied about my majors to the point even my closest friends still didn't know what I was majoring in, and I downplayed my love of video games, except with my fraternity brothers.

My natural good looks got me out of more trouble than I could remember. I didn't have my brother Liam's charm and I didn't have my brother Kyle's commanding alpha presence, but I had the dimples and was more laid back than either of them, and that brought on its own charismatic charm. I had mastered the untouchable, untamable persona that had girls fighting for their chance to try.

Since the first moment I smelled Tessa, none of that mattered. I had told her more truths about myself than I'd admitted to anyone at Archibald Reynolds. She knew I was a nerd. She didn't seem to care. Maybe it was our bond, maybe not. I didn't really care. I could be myself with her and I loved how she made me feel. It was becoming addictive and my mood took an instant sour turn the moment she had fled from me.

All my other rules regarding dating were null and void when it came to her. So, I didn't hesitate when I grabbed my cell phone and texted her. Any other girl I wouldn't dare text first. It set up too high of an expectation and gave them hope that I wanted more than a quick booty call. In fact, I waited a minimum of four hours before ever returning a girl's text. But with Tessa, none of that mattered. The rules simply didn't apply to her.

The fact that she was a feline should have bothered me. If I stopped to think about it, it made my head spin. My entire life I had been told I had one true mate, and if I was lucky enough to find her, then that was all that mattered. God didn't make mistakes. How many times had my mother told me that? If God didn't make mistakes, and Tessa was my true mate, then that was that. I was ready to accept it.

The only hesitation about us I still had was the few times when things had felt so off, like at lunch when I ran into her at Jacks. It had confused me when my wolf had tried to growl at her, but it hadn't happened again since. I had spent quite a bit of time with Tessa that week and each moment I was with her only solidified what my heart was telling me. She was my one true mate.

I stared back at my phone. Thirty minutes had passed since I had texted her and she hadn't responded. Impatient, I picked up the phone and dialed her number. It rang through to voicemail.

"Tessa, this is Chase. Just wanted to make sure you were

okay. Please call me back."

I didn't care that I sounded needy. God, I had always hated women like that. If I didn't answer the phone it was because I didn't want to talk to them, but the thought of her not wanting to talk to me was unacceptable. It angered my wolf and made me restless.

Deciding I needed a run, I changed into shorts and a T-shirt and headed out for the forest. It was already February, but my wolf was too worked up for the cold air to affect me in any way. I was numb, emotionally and physically.

When I reached the edge of the woods, I stripped without even caring who was around to see and shifted. A shrill female laugh sounded from the trees above me.

"Chase Westin, I'm getting to see far too much of you as it is," purred a voice that made me smile.

I looked up to see my friend Anita. She was flirty and fun, but harmless. My wolf was completely indifferent to her, and as long as she kept her paws to herself, he was okay. I suspected if she ever tried to make an advance on me, it would become a different story.

I hadn't even been able to look at another woman without my wolf stirring in aggravation. We had our mate. The rest were irrelevant. Anita, for some reason, had landed quickly in the friend zone. My wolf responded the same to my good friend, Kaitlyn—happy to see her and tolerant, as long as she didn't touch me.

I had growled at Kaitlyn once already this week when she had tried to hug me. It was perfectly innocent and not out of the norm, but my wolf didn't want any other scent on us besides Tessa's. Kaitlyn had laughed it off and teased me about it. She even suspected that Tessa was the cause, but Tessa and I hadn't even discussed it yet, not once; it remained the big, fat, white elephant in the corner, so I wasn't comfortable talking to Kaitlyn about it. A mating bond was too sacred to share with anyone but my mate, and my family if I had any questions or concerns.

I didn't know how long I had been running. Deep in thought, I had lost myself to my wolf, so I wasn't surprised when I looked up and saw the panther house just ahead. Catching the scent of our mate, my wolf veered off to the left and headed back into the woods. He sniffed the ground and gave chase, stopping abruptly at the base of tree, and howled into the sky.

Looking up, I spotted a beautiful, sleek black panther

lounging on a thick tree limb above me. I knew it was Tessa, but she wouldn't come down. My wolf scratched at the ground and whined. Rolling those stunning violet eyes, she jumped down, landing silently beside me.

My wolf leapt around her in excitement, wagging his tail. Our combined emotions made me feel like a kid given free rein in a toy store at Christmas. He strutted before our mate who looked unimpressed, before inching up on her. Before I could stop him, he was rubbing up against her, ensuring his scent covered her.

I could still feel confusing emotions pouring off her, but the look of shock in her wide eyes when her panther began to purr contentedly told me she was at odds with her animal spirit, too. I tried to stop my wolf from prancing excitedly before her at the sound, but he wouldn't listen. I rolled my eyes, knowing what an idiot we must look like. I felt out of control, which was rare. My wolf and I had never really struggled to find peace. He had an aggressive side I had tamed early on, but this was entirely different.

I wanted to shift back to human form and talk to her, but then I remembered Anita teasing me about my lack of decency. Panthers were much more private animals. They didn't run in packs and Tessa probably wasn't used to seeing naked men.

My wolf growled, and she jumped. I looked around for the threat, before realizing it was the thought of her with any other naked man, or any other man period, that had set him off. He nudged her with his snout back towards the tree and barked for her to climb it. I could feel aggressive protective instincts overwhelming me as my wolf set up camp beneath the tree, growling at anything that dared to come near our mate. Even a poor unsuspecting grasshopper felt his wrath.

It wasn't long before I heard movement high in the tree above, but my wolf didn't have any aggression toward it, he just whined, continuing to sniff the air and paw at the ground. Tessa jumped down from the tree, fully clothed and in human form.

She sat down next to us and hesitantly held out a hand like one would when meeting a stray dog. My wolf sniffed it, and then proceeded to lick it. I rolled my eyes in apology as he danced around like an idiot once again, before breaking into her personal space and nuzzling up to her. When he licked her cheek in a sloppy kiss, she pushed us away, laughing.

"Okay, okay, enough already," she said and to my surprise my wolf instantly calmed. I considered shifting so we could talk, but it was like she had read my mind, which I knew was impossible. It was far too soon for that. "Don't shift, okay? I'm not ready to talk about it. I'm okay though." She got up and started to walk away, then stopped. "Thanks for the text and call. It's just—" She shook her head like she was deciding how much more to say. "It doesn't matter," she finally said sadly. "I'll see you on Monday."

My wolf lay down on the ground before her and whimpered. As she walked away we followed at a distance until she safely arrived back at her house. I knew there was no way in hell I could wait till Monday to see her again. The more time I spent with her, the more overwhelming the need to be with her had become.

I ran full speed back to my clothes, shifted and changed before walking back to my dorm. My door was cracked open. I couldn't believe I would have left it that way. I slowly entered, my hair standing up and my wolf on alarm.

"Loser!" my brother, Liam, yelled.

I opened the door, fully surprised to see Patrick O'Connell sitting on my gaming chair next to him in the middle of what sounded like an intense round of Call of Duty.

Patrick was my sister Elise's mate. He was also one of our pack Betas, but to me, he was another brother I was blessed to have. It was good to see them both. They rose and hugged me.

"I hear you may have found your mate," Patrick said in his thick Irish accent. Despite a year in the States, it hadn't changed any.

I punched Liam in the arm. "I thought you weren't going to tell anyone."

Liam shrugged. "I wanted company on the drive up and it was the easiest way to convince him to tag along."

"I can't believe E let you off the leash long enough to make the trip," I ribbed Patrick, all in good humor.

He laughed, but didn't even bother denying it. "Liam says you aren't quite sure she's your mate," he challenged.

"Oh, I'm sure," I insisted.

"But when we spoke earlier this week you said . . ."

"I know what I said. And that was weird, but I've spent more time with her this week. Our animals even got to know each other today, and I don't know how it's possible, but I'm telling you, she's the one." It felt good to confess it to them.

"Liam says she's not a wolf?"

I shook my head. "No, why?" I could feel myself getting defensive.

"What is she then?" he asked with no judgement in his voice.

"She's a gorgeous black panther," I said proudly. "I know it doesn't make sense, and yet, it just feels right. I'm telling you, she's the one."

My brothers shared a look that I recognized as not good at all.

"You're certain she's a black panther? Not a really dark jaguar?" Patrick asked.

"According to my buddy Matt, there's not really any difference there, but yeah, she's definitely considered panther. She's actually a panther princess," I said proudly. No way would I ever be embarrassed about my mate.

They shared that look again.

"She's a Lockhardt then?" Patrick asked. "Truly, a fecking Lockhardt?"

I gulped, not liking his tone and nodded, wondering what I had missed. "Tessa Lockhardt," I confessed.

"King Lockhardt will never allow it, Chase. He believes in absolute purity. I'm shocked the girl would even give you a second look, true mate or not. I'm sorry. He's even more ruthless than my own father," Patrick said.

Patrick's dad was Alpha of the Irish Clan. He had sent Patrick to Westin Pack during the mating challenges to battle my brother Kyle for his mate Kelsey and take over as Alpha of Westin. The plan had gone awry when Patrick had smelled my sister, Elise, his true mate. He had reneged on the challenge and been disowned by his own father. I had thought it was an exaggeration, until Patrick and Elise's mating challenges began and his father had sent Patrick's own brother to challenge him for my sister. It was all kinds of screwed up.

In the end, things hadn't gone that far. Since we were at war with the Bulgarian Pack and the Irish Clan had sided with them, my brother Kyle, as Alpha of Westin, had stepped in and rejected the challenge, citing some code of war. I couldn't even comprehend the thought of battling one of my own brothers for my mate. Disgusting!

I didn't like what Patrick was saying, but it wasn't the first time I had heard as much. Maybe not quite as candidly, but I was aware of her father and his stance on pure bloods.

"I can't help who my mate is," I said defensively. "And I won't give up on us just because of her father. If she won't accept me, that's one thing, but that's going to have to be her decision alone to make."

They both nodded. They were mated, so they had to understand I'd do anything for this girl. Anything.

"What's going on around this place this weekend?" Liam asked, changing the subject.

I shrugged. "Matt is rallying for a Theta party tomorrow night. Panthers are also having one. Not sure what's going on tonight."

In truth, I had no desire to go to a Theta party. The girls there represented all sorts of shifters. They had no exclusivity whatsoever. I had slept with nearly all of them over the course of my two and a half years at the ARC. In hindsight, knowing my mate, the mere thought of going near that place made me want to puke.

Matt peeked his head into my room without knocking.

"Liam? What the hell are you doing here? I thought you were all mated with a family now."

Liam beamed proudly. "I am."

He proceeded to pull out his phone and show off pictures of his mate, Maddie, and her son, Oscar, whom Liam had officially adopted. He went on to tell Matt that they were expecting a second child. I was happy for them, but I could tell Matt was as far removed from that as possible, and it made me laugh.

Wolves were pack animals and much more family-oriented than many other species. Being a jag, Matt just couldn't comprehend it all. Plus, we were in college and he wasn't thinking about settling down anytime soon.

I had a momentary panic when they began to discuss plans for the night, and Patrick asked about the panthers. I hadn't warned them that no one knew about me and Tessa yet. Thankfully, he must have seen my fear and didn't press.

"Yeah, I think the panther house is having a party. Aren't they always? It's like they got out from under Lockhardt and they just want to go wild. Not wild enough to actually sleep with anyone.

Unfortunately for them, there aren't any male panthers here, so I'm just biding my time till one of them caves."

I bit back the growl threatening to erupt from me at the thought of Matt and Tessa.

"How about we go grab a beer at Jacks and head on over there? Those girls do know how to throw one hell of a party," Matt suggested and my brothers agreed.

I took a moment to clean up and prepare for a night out. I knew I should take a shower, but I wore my mate's scent from our time in the woods. It was faint, but I wasn't ready to wash it off.

I had three beers at Jacks, nervous at seeing Tessa after the way things had ended. It took the edge off a little, but not enough. My body was hyperaware that she was near when we finally walked into her sorority house. Ayanna had rolled her eyes as we entered, but she didn't stop us. It was no surprise she hated the D.O.G.s.

Once inside, Matt headed for the dance floor. Liam went off in search of more beer, and Patrick hung back with me. He asked which one she was, and I knew she was close. I could feel her. My eyes scanned the room and my heart sank at the site I found.

In the middle of the dance floor was Tessa, surrounded by four guys dancing intimately close to her. I gritted my teeth waiting for the possessive need to arise within me, but I felt nothing. I was entirely numb. Disappointed, but not freaking out over the image before me.

Perhaps that shocked me more than anything. Just that afternoon I had gone alpha-level protective over her, and now nothing?

"I swear I'm losing my mind here, Patrick," I yelled above the music. I pointed her out on the dance floor and Patrick's eyes widened in surprise. "My wolf attacked a freaking grasshopper this afternoon for getting too close to her, and now he's perfectly calm at *that*? What is going on? It's like that's Tessa, but it's not. I don't know how to explain it."

"I'm sorry, man, but there is no way your wolf would tolerate its mate dancing like that." He waved towards them in demonstration. "You should be losing your shit right now, but not in confusion. She can't be your mate. Trust me."

I stared at the girl before me. Nothing. I felt nothing. The emptiness it created was crippling. Yet I still smelled her.

"Patrick? How can I look at her and feel nothing, but her scent is still here and affecting me? I'm so confused. One minute my heart tells me she's my mate, the next she's not? I can't stay here. I'm sorry. I'm out."

As I turned to leave, Patrick grabbed my arm.

"Holy shit!"

"What's wrong?" I asked him.

He pointed to the other side of the room, and then looked back at Tessa on the dance floor. His headed whipped between the two sides and I turned to look in the direction he pointed.

When my eyes landed on my beautiful mate, my entire world righted itself. Shocked, I jerked my head between the two. They looked the same, but they weren't.

"Twins?" Patrick asked, voicing my own question. "Identical twins? Can you tell which one is which?"

I nodded. "That one," I said, pointing to the girl leaning against the wall talking to Anita. "That one's mine."

I breathed a huge sigh of relief and doubled over to steady my breathing. Twins. Tessa was an identical twin. Pieces of the puzzle began falling into place.

The moment Anita left her side, I headed straight for her. Predatory instincts were on high alert. I didn't say hi, I just stared at her, then back towards the dance floor.

"Why didn't you tell me you were a twin, Tessa?"

She cringed, then stiffened her shoulders and raised her chin in defiance. "That's Tessa," she said, pointing to the girl on the dance floor. The pain in her voice and the hurt in her eyes felt like a kick in the groin. "I'm Jenna."

Jenna
Chapter 8

I couldn't help the hurt I felt every time he called me Tessa, but he was here, questioning me, and not her. That had to mean something. Didn't it?

I wasn't sure I could have said anything to shock him more. The confusion in his eyes was real. He really didn't know.

"Jenna," he said reverently, letting it roll off his tongue. It caused a warmth to bloom in the pit of my stomach.

"All this time. Why didn't you tell me? Why didn't you correct me?"

I looked around in panic. We weren't safe to talk openly here. "Not here," I told him.

He nodded like he understood and walked away. Pain shot through me at his retreating back. Just like that? He'd give up on us so easily? I should have been relieved, but instead it felt as though my heart was on the verge of shattering.

My phone dinged with an incoming text and I checked it.

CHASE: Woods in 5.

I gasped for breath, trying to rein in the whirlwind of emotions he had just caused. I went to my room and grabbed my coat. I quickly reapplied my lip gloss. I tried my best to compose myself and paste on a smile. I didn't feel confident walking through the house and out the back door, but I didn't seem to draw any attention either, so I hoped I at least looked the part.

Heading straight for the woods, I looked around. Channeling my panther, I called on her eyesight to help me see in the dark. It took no time at all to find Chase. He was about fifteen feet into the woods and I knew that even my sisters wouldn't see us from the house.

The moment I reached him, Chase grabbed me by the waist and pulled me flush against him. I gasped in surprise, but it was muffled as his lips crushed down against mine. Need and desire heated my skin and I purred against his mouth, greedily kissing him back. Shocked by my own response, I pulled back, breathless and wanting more.

"You have no idea how crazy you made me. One moment I was certain. The next, I felt nothing. I've been going out of my damned mind trying to figure out what the hell was going on between us." He paused and looked at me in wonder. "Twins? You may look the same, but you definitely don't feel the same."

His hand framed my face and he breathed in my scent. When I didn't pull away, he closed his eyes and pressed his lips to mine once again. This kiss was softer, sweeter, and held so much promise it simultaneously mended and broke my heart all over again.

"Jenna," he said with a sigh against my swollen lips.

A tear ran down my cheek and he gently swiped it away as he pulled me into his embrace. Warmth, love, and belonging. That's what I felt in his arms.

"When you called me Tessa today, I didn't think you could tell us apart," I sobbed into his strong, muscular chest.

"I may have had the wrong name, but I never had the wrong girl."

We stood there just holding each other. I knew I shouldn't let myself indulge, but my heart was in control now, no matter what my head told it.

He kissed the top of my head and pulled back to look at me.

"I'm sorry I hurt you earlier. It'll never happen again," he said sweetly.

I wanted to believe him, but there was simply no way things could ever work between us.

"Chase, you're a dog."

"And you're a beautiful black cat," he interrupted. "So what? I know you feel it too, Jenna. I can see it in your eyes. You are my one true mate."

My back stiffened and I pulled away. "Don't say that."

"Are you denying it?"

"I didn't say that," I confessed, unable to deny the bond

between us. "But we can't. You don't understand. Nothing can ever happen between us."

The pain was evident on his face. "I don't understand it either, Jenna, but you are my mate. I don't know a lot about panthers, but to a wolf, that means everything. Nothing else in this world matters to me, but you."

"My father, he'll never allow it. You can't possibly understand."

"Actually, I can, to an extent. I'm an Alpha's son, and the Westin Pack is unarguably the largest and wealthiest of all wolf packs. That kind of makes me a little like royalty too, princess."

I appreciated what he was trying to do, but really wished he hadn't brought the dimples into the conversation when he smiled at the end of his speech. It made my body go from stubborn confidence to complete mush in zero to five seconds.

"It's not the same. Before coming here, I had only ever met a few jaguar shifters. I had been sheltered to only black panthers my entire life. We don't live in groups the way you do. I don't even know if I could. I like my space. Yeah, my family's close, but Daddy's very strict about no fraternizing outside the panthers, but outside my species? A canine? It would kill him if he ever found out, and trust me, the sisters will be equally against it."

"Anita's our friend. Don't you think she just wants to see us happy? You happy?" he argued.

I shook my head. "No. Sure, she may feel sorry for me, but she would never support us either."

"It doesn't matter. I can support us. I will take care of you. You'll never want for anything," he told me, offering me the world, yet it remained too far out of reach.

I started to cry again. I had never been much of a crier, but I had never experienced emotions like Chase Westin invoked in me before.

"Please don't cry, princess. I don't know how we're going to make it work, but we will. I'll find a way for as long as you'll have me."

I hiccupped. I couldn't drag it out. "The more we're together the harder it will be on both of us, Chase. It'll be best if we just end it now before it's too late."

He took my hand and laid it against his chest.

"Do you feel that?" I nodded as the soft rhythm of his heart steadily beat against my open palm. "That's not my heart you're feeling. That's yours, because it already belongs to you."

My breath caught in my throat and I nibbled on my lower lip involuntarily as I stared into his eyes. His gaze dropped to my lips and I saw raw desire in his eyes, and a tiny bit of mischief. He pulled me closer and covered my mouth with his, sucking my bottom lip into his mouth, his teeth grazing against it as he nibbled. The world was starting to spin when I remembered to breathe again. He kissed my lower lip as it escaped his teeth and he planted a light kiss against my full lips before pulling back with a smile.

"You have no idea how crazy it makes me when you do that."

I knew he was referring to my nervous habit of chewing on my lip. He had definitely made his point, but I couldn't help but stare in wonder and surprise he'd even noticed.

"I don't know if I'm strong enough to do this, Chase," I admitted, wanting him more than I had ever wanted anything in my entire life.

"One day at a time," he said, as he leaned his forehead against mine. "Just give me one day at a time."

I nodded. I could do that, as long as no one found out. "My sisters can't find out. They'll never understand. I don't even understand. But they'd tell Daddy and he'd have me removed from here faster than you can blink an eye." There was no doubt in my heart it was true, too.

"Okay, but you have to promise me something."

"What?" I said, even knowing I'd agree to anything he asked.

"Promise me I can see you on days we don't have class together. It can be a quick run in the woods, lunch, studying in the library, I don't care what. It's just really hard on the days I don't see you."

He looked so vulnerable, raw even, that I instantly melted.

"I don't like Tuesday and Thursday either, or most of the weekend. My sisters have even noticed I get very moody on those days," I confessed.

I looked up at him shyly to gauge his reaction. I should have known my confession would make him happy.

"So, I can see you more often? I mean we wouldn't want

your sisters suspecting anything, so we should definitely not let you get moody like that."

He grinned, his adorable dimple-filled smile that brightened my day each time I saw it. Those dimples took away every fear, every pain, every concern I had. Weapons like those should hardly be legal. I had the incredible urge to swirl my tongue inside each of them, but I kept it in check, or so I thought.

"What?" I asked him, knowing he was trying to mask something from me.

"Um, Jenna, how well do cats smell?"

It seemed like a random question to me, but I answered honestly. "We have really sensitive noses, but I don't think we have like super smelling powers or anything. Why, do you?"

"Um, yup. Wolves have a very heightened sense of smell."

"Why?" I asked, suddenly panicking. "Do I smell bad?"

His grin turned smoldering as he leaned in and whispered in my ear, tickling the sensitive spot there. "You smell delicious, and quite aroused. It's driving me crazy." He pressed himself against me and I felt exactly how crazy I was driving him. He kissed down my neck and across my collarbone as I struggled to breathe normally.

Pulling back, he was still smiling, and then he wasn't. A low growl rumbled in his chest and he pulled me behind him.

"Relax, pup, it's just us," a strange voice said from the dark.

Using my panther vision, everything cleared and I saw two tall men walking towards us. I was certain I had never seen them before and my heart started thumping in my chest.

Chase relaxed immediately, but I couldn't. My body was strung tightly with emotions and panicked from the two strangers.

"A few of her sisters are looking for her. Best to return now. Tessa, is it?" the redhead spoke, surprising me with an Irish accent.

"It's Jenna, actually," Chase said. "I was wrong. I'll apologize for the rest of my life for it. Tessa is her twin sister. Identical twin. So, I'm not going crazy after all."

I watched the two men closely even with Chase still shielding me.

"Dude, you screwed up her name?" the blonde razzed him.

"Sure, laugh it up. If Maddie had an identical twin sister what would you have done?" Chase questioned.

Both men laughed. "We wouldn't have been as fecking daft

as you," the Irish one said.

Chase just shook his head. "I was there when both of you mated. Remember? Laugh it up all you want. I still haven't screwed up as bad as either of you."

My eyes widened and my heart raced. "You told them?" I demanded.

Chase cringed. "Jenna, meet Liam and Patrick. My brothers. Not like my frat brothers; these are my actual brothers. Remember I told you they were coming in for the weekend? Okay, so Patrick is technically my sister's mate, but we claim him just the same."

Patrick smiled affectionately. "You're either a Westin or you're not. Keeps things pretty simple."

"How many others know?" I asked, horrified. I couldn't afford for it to get back to my family. I could never be this open with my own family. I was surprised how much that thought pained me, but it was the truth.

"I only told Liam," Chase said. "I swear, but he told Patrick, which means Elise already knows, and if E knows then Lily knows, and if Lily knows the whole damn pack probably knows by now."

The world was starting to spin around me. His whole pack already knew about me?

"Do they know what I am?" I whispered into Chase's ear.

"Yup, we do, and you should probably know, we have heightened hearing, even in our skin. Chase has a device in his room that dampers everything if you need to talk without fear of others hearing. Use it," Liam advised.

"Best device ever invented," Patrick added.

"It doesn't bother you that I'm not wolf?" I asked incredulously.

Liam shrugged. "We just want the kid to be happy. We've both been blessed to find our true mates, and if you're it for him, then great. I mean, who the hell am I to judge anyone? My kid's half tiger."

I wasn't sure I heard him right. "Excuse me? Half what?"

"Tiger," Liam said definitively. He pulled out his phone and Chase rolled his eyes and shook his head.

"Now you started it," he warned.

Pictures of an adorable boy with dark hair and dark eyes flashed across the screen.

"This is Oscar," Liam said proudly. "My son. He's half wolf and half tiger. So, sure, cats and dogs, not exactly the norm. Not everyone will get you two, but that doesn't mean it can't work."

"You really should be getting back. I can hear them starting to look more aggressively for you," Patrick said.

I wanted to stay. I had a million questions for Liam after hearing his mate was a cat, too, but I couldn't risk being caught with them.

"Okay," I said, and started to walk away.

Chase grabbed my arm and pulled me back to him. "Try actually responding to my texts or calls once in a while."

He gave me a quick kiss on the lips right in front of his brothers and I turned in shock, feeling the heat rising in my cheeks as I walked away.

"Pup's never actually texted or called first, and he sure as hell hasn't been ignored by a lady before, so give his poor bruised ego a break and answer him next time," Liam said to my retreating back.

When I reached the edge of the woods I dared to look back. Patrick had Chase in a headlock, giving him noogies as they harassed him. No doubt they were talking about me. I still couldn't believe he so easily told his family. The more people who knew, the less we could be together. I made a note to discuss the importance of keeping this to ourselves the next time I saw Chase.

Chase

Chapter 9

I lay awake staring at the ceiling and thinking of Jenna. I grabbed my phone and texted her, but first I corrected the name on her number. Erasing Tessa, I added Jenna as the new contact and marked her number one on my speed dial.

CHASE: Sweet dreams, beautiful

I didn't expect her to answer, but my phone dinged almost immediately.

JENNA: Can't sleep

CHASE: Me neither

CHASE: You actually texted me back □

JENNA: This is crazy

CHASE: □ life's crazy

On the next ding of an incoming text Liam groaned. A pillow hit me hard across the head.

"Go to sleep or at least silence that thing," Liam complained.

I tossed the pillow back to him. Nothing was going to dampen my mood. The most beautiful woman in the world was my mate and she was texting me back. I was on cloud nine. I silenced my phone and looked back at the screen.

"I'm getting too old for this shit," Liam grumbled as he rolled over, away from the light my phone was shining. I turned down the brightness as much as I could, but it still lit up the room.

JENNA: No one else can know. Promise me.

CHASE: I promise.

I couldn't help the stab of disappointment in her insistence to keep us a secret, but I did understand it. My family might be surprised, curious, even concerned, but they would support us no matter what. I was confident in their love and unconditional acceptance. It saddened me that Jenna didn't have that in her life, but she would from now on, because I would give her that.

JENNA: Thank you.

CHASE: Can I see you tomorrow?

There wasn't a reply for a long time and my mind started conscripting all sorts of negativity. We were doing so well, and then she just went blank? I cursed myself for feeling so needy, but dammit, it was one simple question. When I couldn't take it any longer, I texted her again in the most pathetic way that always ensured I would never respond again when a girl did it to me.

CHASE: Jenna?

JENNA: Sorry, Tessa came in to say good night. She's drunk.

I waited to see if she would answer my question. It felt like another small eternity passed, before it dinged again.

JENNA: Maybe on tomorrow. If I can get away. But aren't your brothers still here?

CHASE: Yeah, we're going hiking tomorrow. Join us?

I knew I'd get some grief for bringing her along, but I was desperate to spend more time with her, even with them in tow.

JENNA: Probably can't. Let you know in the morning. What time and how long?

CHASE: 7am, back by lunch.

JENNA: Seriously?

CHASE: yes

JENNA: um, raincheck?

I laughed out loud.

CHASE: Not a morning person?

JENNA: It's 3am and I'm wide awake, what do you think?

CHASE: LOL Is that a cat thing?

JENNA: It's a Jenna thing.

JENNA: but yes, panthers tend to be more nocturnal

CHASE: Good to know

CHASE: Picnic lunch afterwards?

JENNA: I can probably swing that

CHASE: I'll send coordinates

JENNA: Very 007

CHASE: Isn't that the plan?

JENNA: LOL
CHASE: Get some sleep, princess
JENNA: You too

I sighed and closed my eyes, remembering what it felt like to kiss her. I drifted off to sweet dreams of my beautiful mate.

Morning came too soon. My alarm didn't go off because I silenced my phone, but Patrick woke me up. I grumbled but jumped in the shower and felt a little more human afterwards. The drive to the trail was short, and a light layer of fresh snow covered the ground.

It hadn't been snowing when we got back to my dorm. It must have started in the wee hours of morning. The snow had already stopped, but it was beautiful, and I loved the smell of the crisp, clean air it brought with it.

We debated on human or animal forms, finally settling on our original plan to hike in our skin. We all agreed if it got too cold we'd shift for the run back.

Patrick had never been up to the ARC, so it was all new to him. He was quiet, observant as he took in the unforgettable mountain views. I had expected them to give me a hard time about last night, but each of us seemed content to be lost in our own thoughts as we hiked up the mountain to the most beautiful overlook imaginable.

Sitting there in reflection with my brothers I felt fully at peace.

"Thanks for coming this weekend," I told them.

"We'd probably have had to commit you by the end of the semester if Patrick hadn't been observant enough to sort out the twin thing."

Patrick laughed. "Yeah, you must have had tunnel vision not to have noticed, but I get it. I'm glad it's all sorted now, though I still worry. She's a panther, Chase."

"Does that bother you guys?" I asked earnestly. "That she's not a wolf, I mean."

Patrick shook his head. "I don't care what she is or isn't, it's more of who she is. I just don't want to see you get hurt. You've found your mate. I know how life changing that is, but her father . . . I just hope it works out for you."

"But you don't think it will?"

"It definitely isn't in your favor," he said.

I growled, and he put his hands up in surrender.

"He's only keeping it real, Chase," Liam said in Patrick's defense. "We aren't saying we don't support you. Of course we support you. If she's your true mate, then we want that for you, more than anything."

"If? If? I told you she is my mate. Why would you question me on that?"

"She's a cat, Chase. It's just hard to take in. And it's not just that. Patrick's right, she's a panther—a royal panther even. It's not going to be easy for you, and we're worried about you."

"Well, don't be. I'm a grown man. I don't need you guys worrying about me. I just need you to support me!"

They looked at each other and both nodded.

"We'll always support you, Chase," Patrick assured me.

"We've got your back, no matter what," Liam added.

I knew they wouldn't stop worrying, but I needed to hear they were on my side, even if I had basically forced them to say it. I had enough to deal with worrying about her family without stressing over mine too.

We chatted about lighter things on the walk back to the car. They were both starving when we got back but I had to apologize and tell them I had plans for lunch.

"Just, be careful," Liam asked.

"I will."

I dropped them off then swung by the grocery store to pick up what I needed. The snow was still blanketing the ground and judging by the thick coat Jenna had worn the night before, I assumed panthers weren't as warm as wolves.

As a full member of Westin Pack, money was of no issue to me. My family had started the Westin Foundation several generations back and it not only funded our pack but gave each of us a sizable monthly income. I was expected to work in the Foundation in some capacity after graduation. Business had been pressed upon me at a young age, but graphic design was where my passion lay. I had dreams of updating our website and redefining the look of the Westin Foundation. I hadn't discussed that with Liam yet. As the current CEO, it would ultimately be his decision. I wanted to prepare a thorough portfolio and give it to him closer to graduation time.

I picked up the food, then swung by the hardware store to buy a small, portable propane heater that I hoped would keep Jenna comfortable outdoors.

Hiking to the spot I knew well, overlooking the lake, was easy, even with the added weight of my items. When I arrived, I checked the exact coordinates and texted them to Jenna. I hoped she could find it okay.

JENNA: Now?

CHASE: I'm waiting.

JENNA: On my way

While waiting, I first set up the heater, and snow around me began to quickly melt away. I laid down a tarp to keep the wet ground from soaking through and covered it with a thick plush blanket. I had another one to cover Jenna if she needed it.

Next, I pulled the food out of the basket. I had kept it simple; I wasn't exactly gourmet, more meat and potatoes, and I really didn't know what panthers preferred to eat. I set around trays of sandwiches, hummus and chips, and chocolate-covered strawberries.

Checking the champagne in the cooler bag, I realized it was only cool, so I took it out and wedged it down into the snow, along with two glasses. I stepped back to examine my work and was pleased with the effect. I had wanted to buy her flowers, but didn't want her to have to explain them to her sisters, so this would have to do.

When I heard movement in the trees, I took a deep breath, scenting the air around me. *Mate*, a small voice in my head confirmed.

I turned just as Jenna reached the clearing. She stopped short and gasped. I could hear her heartbeat quicken as she looked around, taking in the views and my handiwork.

"When you said a picnic, I didn't think you really meant it. You really did all of this?" I nodded. "This is incredible," she whispered.

She squealed as she hugged me and sat down to check out the treats. My wolf and I were more peaceful than I could ever remember. We had pleased our mate and the high it gave me was indescribable.

"I wasn't sure what you like to eat, but I hope there's something here that will work. I'll do better next time."

"Better? Chase, there's a heater! We're literally having a picnic in the snow and not freezing to death."

I grinned. "I noticed you like thick, warm coats. I assumed you don't handle the cold as well as my kind."

She considered it. "I have noticed you're prone to T-shirts, or at most a sweatshirt. That's really not fair. Super smelling, super hearing, and a built-in heater?"

She was teasing, and I loved it. It was a new side to my mate I had only seen glimpses of.

"Well, I don't see as well in the dark, and I can't climb trees," I offered.

She laughed as she grabbed a chip and dipped it in the hummus. She sighed contentedly as she ate.

"Do you have enormous appetites too?"

"Yes. Yes we do. Why?"

"Because there's like a dozen sandwiches here." She laughed at the massive pile I had stacked on the tray.

"There's more in the basket, and it's not because I plan to eat them all, though." I laughed. "Okay, I will actually eat them all, but it was because I had no clue what you liked, so I just grabbed one of everything they had, and two of my favorites, just in case you chose those."

I flashed my classic boyish grin and saw her sigh as she stared at my dimples. I had never before been so happy to have those stupid birth defects.

"Meat," she blurted out. "I eat a lot of meat. I like veggies and other foods more than most of my kind though, so really there isn't much I won't eat."

"Well, we definitely have that in common then." I didn't always know why I told her the things that seemed to fall out of my mouth, but once again I found myself oversharing. "My sister, Elise, is borderline vegetarian. I mean she does eat meat, she just really loves vegetables, and I don't know if your kind ever eats raw, but wolves do sometimes. Not E. She throws up nearly every time. She throws up even if she sees another wolf eating raw. Lily, on the other hand, will eat anything and everything in sight. She's on the petite side, but dang—don't ever challenge her to an eating contest. She out eats me and my brothers."

"She's another sister?" Jenna asked, sounding genuinely

interested.

"Yeah. I'm the baby. There are five of us. Kyle and Elise, and then Liam and Lily are twins. Then me. What about you?"

"Just me and Tessa," she said. "We may be identical, but we couldn't be any more different. She's athletic, the star volleyball player currently. I'm sure you've heard all about her." I watched her flinch. "You're probably going to be very disappointed to hear I don't have an athletic bone in my body. Dance was the closest thing I've ever been good at when it comes to sports."

I brushed her hair back, letting my hand run through it and marveling at how silky it felt. "Why would I be disappointed by that?" I asked almost absentmindedly.

She shrugged. "Well, you thought I was Tessa, which means you had to have heard all about her. She tends to be a big deal on campus and loves the spotlight. Popular and fun. Everyone loves Tessa. But that's not me."

I looked at her like she was crazy. Did she really think I cared about any of that? "I had a difficult time reconciling the image of Tessa Lockhardt with the Tessa I knew." I ran a hand through my thick hair. "Now we know why. It was never Tessa I was interested in and I don't care about any of that."

"Oh really? Because Anita friended a couple of Thetas, and I have to admit I'm having a hard time reconciling the Chase Westin everyone talks about, with the you I know."

"Thetas?" I groaned, covering my face with my arm and laying back on the blanket. It was inevitable my reputation would catch up to me, but I was honestly embarrassed that Jenna had heard about it.

"Let's see," she started. "The rules of Chase. Number one: no dating. Period." She looked around. "I'm afraid this looks suspiciously like a date. Number two: one night stands are one night stands. No repeat sex within the same month." She cut her eyes at me and reveled in the fact that I was embarrassed. "Number three: no cuddling, no crying, and absolutely no sleepovers."

I pulled her down next to me and tucked her into my side so that her head rested on my shoulder.

"Chase Westin, I do declare, this feels a lot like cuddling. Are you breaking rule number three?" she asked in her best Southern belle interpretation.

I kissed the top of her head in response, ready to silence her with a real kiss, but she pulled back and continued. "Number four: Chase will not initiate texts or phone calls, and something about a minimum four-hour delay in all text responses, and then some crazy time limits on returned calls, too. Yeah, you've broken that rule a lot already. Finally, rule number five: no attachments. Chase Westin will not be tamed, so don't bother trying, and if you do, you're culled from the list forever. What is up with that one?"

I laughed, then rolled to my side to look at her seriously. "Those rules were all in place for you."

"What? That's insane. How is it, that how often you screw someone . . ."—her face scrunched up and she had to take a deep breath. I could sense she didn't like thinking about me with other women and it made me crazy happy to see her jealousy—"how is that for me?" she finally blurted out.

I kissed her, keeping it light despite the desperate need I felt to mark my mate.

"All those rules ensured no attachments. I didn't date or have recurring . . . relationships"—I decided that was a better word to use—"with anyone, because I knew one day I'd find you—my one true mate. There was no reason to ever get emotionally attached to anyone when I was just biding my time waiting for you to come into my life."

Jenna

Chapter 10

Chase spoke so openly and honestly with me. I wasn't used to anyone talking to me like that. I was a princess—even my closest friends didn't dare speak so candidly. Yet, I found myself doing the same with him. I had learned at an early age to keep things to myself. Even my twin sister couldn't be trusted with my inner thoughts, but things just had a way of popping out of my mouth before my brain confirmed them, when it came to Chase Westin.

"I don't even know what to say to that," I told him, shaking my head. "On the one hand, that's actually very sweet and romantic even, but on the other, you've slept with a lot of women. I mean a *lot,* if even half the rumors are true."

I liked that he had the decency to blush. Okay, so he wouldn't admit it was a blush, but color definitely brightened his cheeks and his body stiffened next to me.

"I'm sorry," he said quietly.

Surprised by his apology, I felt bad for making him feel guilty. I had been more curious if the rumors were true than concerned that they might be.

"You don't need to apologize," I assured him, regretting ever having brought it up at all.

His warm hand was back on my cheek, forcing me to look at him.

"If I had known I'd feel like this, I'd never have even looked at another woman. I'm sorry."

My heart fluttered wildly. I didn't wait for him this time. I closed the gap between us and pressed my lips against his. I didn't feel I had the right to ask him not to see other people, but I knew it would rip me to pieces if he did.

As if sensing the sadness that came with that thought, he pulled back and stared into my eyes.

"You don't have to worry about all that. There can never be another for me now that I've found you."

His words made my heart soar, but I had to keep enough restraint to face reality.

"I can't see how this will ever work, Chase."

"One day at a time, beautiful. That's all I'm asking for. One more day."

I giggled. "And you'll ask for one more day again tomorrow?"

He flashed me his dimples in a classic Chase grin. "That is what one day at a time means."

We lay there talking longer than I had meant to stay.

"Shoot," I said, looking at the time on my phone and realizing I'd been gone for over four hours. "They'll send out a search party soon if they haven't already. It's nearly five, Chase."

He sat up and shrugged, noticing the champagne still wedged in the snow.

"I forgot the champagne," he said regretfully.

"Save it for next time."

He grinned and pulled me into his lap. "So, you're saying there will be a next time?"

My breath hitched from his smoldering look, and my mouth went dry as I nodded. I recognized his movements and knew I was about to be kissed. It didn't surprise me this time, but the moment our lips met, a new kind of energy jolted us. It was stronger than a static shock, but pleasant and warmed me all over. God, that boy could kiss.

I was lightheaded when he finally ended it. It all felt so dream-like, and I didn't want to leave the peaceful cocoon we had formed in the middle of the snow overlooking the beautiful lake and the mountains beyond. The day had been more perfect than any fantasy I had ever read or dreamed. Going back to reality wasn't going to be easy.

"Are you coming to the party tonight?" I asked him as we started packing up the picnic basket he'd brought.

I saw him cringe and knew the answer was no before he even

spoke.

"Matt's insisting on hitting up Theta tonight, remember?"

Theta? After everything he'd confided that was the last place I wanted him to go. A hiss escaped me before I could stop it. I was too embarrassed to even look at him, so I just continued packing as fast as I could.

"Hey," he said, stopping me and taking both of my hands in his. "I'm only making an appearance for my frat brothers. I know you have no reason to believe me after everything we talked about, but I swear to you, you have nothing to worry about. I am yours. Only yours. Even if I wanted to be with anyone else, which I absolutely don't, my wolf would never stand for it. You're it for us."

"I don't have the right to even ask that of you." I truly felt that way too. I knew we couldn't be together in the end, so all of this was just torturing the both of us.

"You're my mate. You have every right to ask, and if you don't want me even stopping by the Theta house tonight, I won't."

"No, that would probably just cause rumors and questions anyway. Go, have fun," I said. A terrible wave of hurt washed over me. "Okay, not too much fun," I admitted.

"Can I walk you back?" he asked.

I looked to the woods. "Not all the way back. Here, let me help you with that."

Chase was loaded down with the two large baskets and the portable heater, but he brushed it off and refused to let me carry anything.

"I've got it," he insisted.

We were mostly quiet on the walk back, but just before the clearing that would lead to my house we stopped. He dropped the stuff to the ground and hugged me.

"Can I see you tomorrow?"

"I have to study tomorrow. Calc test on Monday, remember?"

"Library at two? I do believe I have to study for that same test."

I pulled back and gave him a look. "You could take that test with your eyes closed, Chase. You may have everyone else fooled into believing you're some dim-witted playboy, but I know better."

He threw his head back and laughed. "Caught on to that, did

ya? Well, I can help you study for the test at least."

I knew I should have said no, but the idea of not seeing him for an entire day did not sit well with me, or my panther. "Okay," I agreed.

"Tomorrow then," he said, kissing me playfully on the nose. It did all sorts of things to me on the inside. I could tell he had no idea, either. Cats were hypersensitive on the nose, and until then, I had no idea that it could cause such pleasurable sensations. I was hyperaware of my mate, and my skin was tingling all over as I turned and headed for the house. At the edge of the woods, I looked back and gave one final wave before disappearing.

Back at the house I plopped down onto my bed, still in a dreamlike trance. Chase had a way of doing that to me. He was a dog. None of it made sense. Daddy would never approve, and yet there was something so romantic about a forbidden love affair. Even knowing my heart would someday be crushed, when I had to give him up, I was walking right in with my eyes wide open.

Anita knocked on my door, and peeked her head in. "Hey girl, sisters meeting in the lounge in five."

I sighed. I wondered if love was written on my face. *Love?* I thought. I couldn't be truly in love with Chase. I examined my feelings thoroughly. *Oh boy*. I was already falling in love with Chase Westin.

"Jenna, let's go," Tessa yelled from the hallway outside my room.

Begrudgingly I got up, checking myself quickly in the mirror before walking to the lounge on the other side of the house. All my sisters were already there waiting.

"Finally," Ayanna grumbled as she called the meeting to order. "As you all know we are eleven gorgeous, exotic, sophisticated women who have never had this much freedom. King Lockhardt made certain we attended a school with absolutely no eligible mates. Not one male, black, panther attends the ARC. So, what are we going to do?"

"Interspecies challenge!" Louisa yelled, and all the other girls cheered.

"What's that?" I whispered to Anita, though it must have been loud enough for others to hear, because Ayanna rolled her eyes at me.

"It means that we are tired of being virgins, Jenna. We may not be able to find suitable mates here, but we can certainly have a little fun in the bedroom."

I blushed as the other girls all whooped and hollered in excitement.

"We all," she said, glaring at me, "must agree. What happens at the ARC stays at the ARC. Nothing can ever get back to our families and especially to our King."

Heads nodded all around and Anita nudged me until I was nodding, too.

"Great, so I've come up with a list of eligible hotties and we're going to draw names. Several are listed multiple times, so we'll see who can bed them first," Ayanna continued.

"Hold up, we're all chasing after the same guys?" I asked.

"Yes. That's the challenge, Jenna. Keep up," Tessa said, glaring at me.

I really didn't have a good feeling about this.

"If you don't want to participate, fine, but you have to swear not to say a word about it outside this group. Not to anyone."

I nodded. As the bowl with the names was passed around I took one and glanced at it.

Matt Williams, the paper read.

Anita peeked over my shoulder. Looking around to make sure no one was watching, she snatched it from me and gave me hers. I turned to question her, and her eyes pleaded for me to accept. I nodded, wondering if Anita had a thing for Matt or something.

I opened the new piece of paper and my heart dropped.

Chase Westin.

Ayanna had said that there were multiples of each name. I looked around the room wondering how many of my sisters would be throwing themselves at my mate for this challenge. It took everything in my power not to roar in anger.

"Now, we're going to go around and each of us reads off the name so we know who our competition is."

Four others claimed Chase before it finally reached me.

"Chase Westin," I said.

A few snickered. Tessa and Ayanna both had Chase too. So did Louisa and Chloe. I wanted to throw up.

"Um, Chase is a wolf. You know that, right?" I said wanting

desperately to dissuade them from this madness.

"Jenna, we know that. It's called the interspecies challenge," Tessa said, clearly getting irritated with me. That wasn't anything new.

"But Matt Williams is on the list and he's not really a different species," I protested.

"If you had been here from the beginning you'd already know we made an exception for him. He may be feline, but he's still forbidden by our King, and he's hot, so he's in," Ayanna said, sharing Tessa's annoyance with me.

"It's not like you really stand a chance anyway, Jenna." Chloe laughed. "I wouldn't even bother trying if I were you."

A few of the other girls laughed too, but Anita grabbed my hand and squeezed, giving me strength and encouragement.

"When the boys arrive tonight, it's game on!" Ayanna squealed excitedly.

I couldn't believe this was even happening. It was insane.

"What if more than one of us gets our man?" Louisa asked.

I ground my teeth to keep from lashing out at her "our man" comment. He was mine. Only mine. The fierce possessiveness that overcame me nearly knocked me backward.

"Well, that is why we chose these particular guys. I mean, come on, Chase Westin? Super hot, super easy. Once he knows the panthers are available, he'll be sniffing around here all the time. Won't be able to help himself from what I've heard," Ayanna informed them.

I took a deep breath in through my nose and slowly exhaled through my mouth. When I felt calm enough to speak, I raised my hand.

Tessa shook her head in embarrassment for me.

"This isn't second grade, Jenna. Speak," Ayanna said in her cattiest voice.

I was fighting back my claws threatening to turn loose. "Are we still having the party tonight? 'Cause the D.O.G.s aren't coming," I informed them. Shock was evident on their faces.

"And how exactly would you know this?" she demanded.

"Because Chase told me. We have several classes together. Matt insisted they party at Theta tonight." I smirked.

"What?" Tessa shrieked. "We have to go to Theta then."

"Cancel our party?" Louisa asked.

"Yes. This starts tonight. If they aren't coming here, then we go there," Tessa said, not once doubting I was telling the truth.

"How do we know this isn't some sort of trick so Jenna can get a head start on Chase?" Chloe asked.

The rest of the room dissolved into laughter. Even Anita laughed, though to her credit she did try to rein it in.

"Whatever," I said. "Are we done here?"

I got up and went to my room. I wasn't sure, but I thought I might be hyperventilating. How could this be happening?

Then another thought occurred to me. I'd just been given a free pass to openly flirt with my mate. Maybe the challenge wouldn't be that bad after all. I still hated the fact that at least four of my sisters, including my identical twin, would be throwing themselves at Chase, but I had to trust that he was telling the truth when he said I had nothing to worry about.

Game on.

Chase

Chapter 11

"He looks smitten," Patrick said as I lay on my bed staring up at my ceiling.

"Smitten for a kitten," Liam said, laughing at his own joke. "I take it you had a good lunch?"

"Yeah," I said. "How did I get so damn lucky?"

My mate was the most incredible woman in the world. Maybe all mated males thought that, but I knew it for a fact.

"What's wrong with him?" Matt asked, barging into my room, unannounced as usual.

"Nothing," I said, sitting up and pulling my shit together. "What time are we leaving?"

"Ten minutes, so get your ugly ass up and ready."

I stood and checked myself in the mirror. I wasn't out to impress anyone, so didn't see the point in changing.

"You guys ready?" I asked my brothers.

"Yeah, let's do this," Patrick said.

We walked as a pack with my D.O.G. brothers over to the Theta house. I hated every step of it. It was true I had slept with nearly every one of the Theta sisters in my time at the ARC. I wasn't proud of it, and I especially hated knowing that Jenna had heard about it. I didn't want to be there, but an appearance was necessary.

Walking in, I immediately felt the familiar tingle signifying Jenna was nearby. Before I could find her, Tessa found me.

"Chase, dance with me," she pouted, pulling me onto the dance floor.

"I'm really not in the mood, Tessa. Hanging with my brothers tonight," I said, quickly introducing Liam and Patrick.

Kaitlyn came over and stared her down until she backed off. Giving me a big hug, she whispered. "I'm sorry. They found out you guys would be here, cancelled their party, and crashed ours. I've heard some disturbing rumors they're out to bed some D.O.G.s, so heads up. The interspecies challenge, they're calling it."

I stared at her in confusion. "Seriously?" I mouthed, and she nodded.

I introduced Kaitlyn to my brothers all the while scanning the room in search of Jenna. I could feel her presence, so where the hell was she?

Half a dozen Thetas stopped by, most with offers for the evening, but I declined them all. Ayanna cornered me and practically purred as she too propositioned me. *What the hell was going on?* I wondered.

Liam, Patrick, and I grabbed a couple beers and headed for a corner.

"There's some weird shit going on around here. Kaitlyn said the panthers are on the prowl and setting their sights on me and few of the boys," I told them.

Looking around, Liam commented, "I certainly don't remember the ladies looking quite so sexy when I went here." He pointed out a few. They were all panthers.

"Damn. They definitely didn't look like that at my college either. Makes me feel guilty just being here, like I need to go call Elise," Patrick confessed.

We all laughed and teased him for being so whipped and losing his man card. Then I spotted Jenna and a low growl rumbled through me.

"Bloody hell," Patrick said, following my gaze.

She was wearing a much-too-short mini-skirt with a button-down tank top that had one too many buttons undone at the top. The outfit was paired with high-heeled black leather boots that shined like her hair, which was brushed straight down her back. If we weren't in a room full of males trying to catch her attention I'd think I'd died and gone to heaven just looking at her, but that wasn't the case, and my wolf and I were not happy with this turn of events.

Liam grabbed my arm as I started to stalk off. "Do not cause a scene. Remember, no one's supposed to know."

I took a deep breath. "I'm good."

"We should leave," Patrick said smartly.

"Not without Jenna," I growled.

I walked slowly and cautiously toward my mate. Anita grabbed her arm and whispered in her ear.

"See, I told you that outfit would work. He's ignored the others but headed this way. You've got this," she told her excitedly.

"Anita, Jenna," I said, acknowledging both girls.

Jenna blushed furiously and tried to wiggle her skirt down lower, but it just exposed her lower stomach and I couldn't stop my eyes from drifting to the sight of her exposed skin. I swallowed hard.

"What are you two doing?" I asked, including Anita, who was wearing even less than Jenna.

"We're just here to party," Anita said unconvincingly.

"Bullshit. Please don't tell me you're in on this interspecies challenge shit. You two are better than this," I told them, trying to maintain my cool.

Anita sighed, but Jenna couldn't even look me in the eyes.

Some girl I hadn't met before came over and draped herself around me.

"Hello, Chase," she purred. "Want to dance?"

I saw the barely concealed fury in my mate's eyes and I felt the anger rolling off her.

"No," I told the girl, physically removing her arm from around me. "Jenna, Anita, let's go," I said, leaving no room for argument. "We're leaving," I told the new girl.

Anita giggled when we were out of earshot. "Oh my god, Chloe is going to be so pissed!"

Matt came over to me. "Hey, where are you off to?"

"We're leaving. We'll be back at the house. Come over if you want. I'm done here," I told him as I stalked out. My hands balled up in fists to keep from protectively covering Jenna from every male eye in the room. Fortunately, Patrick and Liam closed in the gap behind the girls and shielded them from view.

"Thank God. I'm really getting too old for this bullshit," Liam said.

I snorted.

It wasn't until we were halfway back to the house that I turned around to face them. Jenna's teeth were chattering. I yanked off my sweatshirt and covered her with it. Anita watched curiously, but didn't comment.

Once we were safely inside the doghouse, I grabbed the remote and turned on the TV. It was already fired up to the Xbox.

"Yes!" Liam and Patrick said in unison, high fiving each other. They sat down on the couch and quickly grabbed for the controllers.

"Make yourself at home, Anita. Kitchen's through there," I said, pointing. "I'll be back in a few. You and I are going to talk," I told Jenna, taking her by the arm and leading her down the hall to my room.

"Told you that outfit was going to work. You've so got this," Anita told her as Jenna turned to her with wide eyes, pleading for her to shut up.

I didn't say a word. I led her into my bedroom and confirmed the dampener was on.

"Chase, I'm sorr—" she started, but I moved quickly, pinning her against the wall and claiming her with a kiss.

She wrapped her arms around me and moaned into my mouth. I reached down, cupping her ass and lifting until her legs locked around my waist.

"Mine," I growled, nipping at her ear and kissing across her jawline until I found her mouth again. I couldn't have stopped the urgent need in my kisses if I'd wanted to, and I did not want to.

I pressed my desire against her and she purred in my arms. It was the sexiest thing I'd ever heard. It made my canines elongate and I had to pull back and break her spell on me, lest I claim her right there. I knew she wasn't ready for that and I fought to rein in my own desires.

Setting her down on her feet, I stepped back and ran a hand through my hair. Shit, I wanted her so badly it physically hurt. I worked on controlling my breathing and regaining some semblance of control.

"Chase?" she said breathily.

"I just need a minute, princess," I said, still trying to catch my breath. One glance at her in that sexy outfit with her hair mussed and lips swollen from my kisses and lust consumed me again. "Shit!"

I walked over to my dresser and pulled out a pair of sweatpants and handed them to her.

"For the love of all things holy, please put these on," I all but begged her.

She giggled, but did as I asked. "Better?"

"Damn, you're even sexier in those. What the hell am I going to do with you?"

"I'm sorry. I really am. It's, well, I guess you already heard about the challenge." She bit her lip nervously and it took every ounce of willpower not to close the gap and stop it.

"Tell me about this challenge," I demanded.

Her eyes widened and she blushed furiously. "I thought you already knew?"

"Kaitlyn warned me the panthers were on the prowl, but you? Anita? What the hell, Jenna?" I wanted to give her time to explain, but my wolf was still far too agitated from seeing our mate in so little surrounded by other men.

"Okay, I'll tell you. Ayanna made us all draw names, and we're supposed to, um, try and seduce him."

I didn't bother trying to contain my growl. She didn't frighten—quite the opposite, I could smell her essence in the air. My alpha side turned her on. It was almost more than I could handle just then.

"So, you each have one person you're targeting?"

She nodded.

"Tessa, Ayanna, that last chick that asked me to dance. Did they draw my name?"

"Yes," she confirmed, not quite meeting my eyes. That would be normal in wolf culture, especially in my aggressive state, but this was Jenna and she only did that when she was nervous or hiding something.

I ran a hand through my hair again, not sure I wanted to know the answer, but needing to at the same time. "Whose name did you draw?"

Her eyes flashed to mine. "Matt."

I started to curse and began to pace, a clear sign of my wolf's displeasure.

"But," she said, and I saw a twinkle of mischief in her eyes, "Anita wanted him and traded me before we had to announce our draws."

"Okay, so Anita is trying to seduce Matt?"

"Yes, and I suspect she may have a crush on him. I mean, she yanked that paper from my hands almost faster than I could read it and shoved hers into mine."

I took a deep breath. "And who did she draw?"

"You, Chase. She drew you."

I stared at her and my mouth fell open. I closed it, but no words came out at first. Slowly my brain started to comprehend. "So, if Anita now has Matt, that means I'm your challenge?"

She grinned happily and closed the gap between us as she wrapped her arms around my waist and planted a quick kiss on my lips. "Yup. And I don't think I'm sucking at this challenge nearly as much as my sisters thought I would."

I threw my head back and laughed. "That's hardly fair. You're a cheater."

"Am not," she said, playfully smacking my chest.

"You totally are, but seriously, that outfit was not playing fair." I sucked in a sharp breath. "Next time you wear jeans and a turtleneck. Save this thing, for my eyes only." I had wicked images of what I'd like to do with her in that skimpy little outfit.

"Anita insisted we go all out tonight. Some of the girls were giving me a hard time about it, saying I was too much of a goody-goody to even bother trying, so she thought this would show them."

I laughed. "You definitely showed them. How many am I going to have to avoid from now on?"

"Four," she confessed. "Well, five if you count me."

As if I would ever avoid her.

"And how far exactly is this seduction challenge supposed to go?" I kissed her forehead. "This?"

She shook her head no, so I kissed her lips.

"This?" I said breathless, pulling back.

She shook her head no again. A combination of lust and curiosity spurred me onward. My hands glided up the sides of her slight hourglass figure and I reveled in the shiver that shook her body. She didn't try to stop me as I cupped her left breast, filling my palm as I explored. I let my thumb drift lightly over her nipple, feeling it pebble at my touch.

"First base?" I said in a voice deeper than I expected.

She bit her lip and shook her head no once again. I smiled and let my hand drift further south down her body. She let out a soft sigh as I reached the top of the sweatpants I had insisted she wear. Staring into her gorgeous violet eyes, I pushed the pants gently down her hips. They were too big and loose on her, so it took no real effort. Still, she didn't stop me.

The look of sheer lust radiating from her eyes was nearly my undoing. The high of knowing my mate wanted me was better than anything I had experienced in my twenty years of life. The smell of her essence filled the room and I wasn't sure I had the willpower to stop.

I leaned in and kissed her as my fingers pushed aside the soft cotton of her underwear and began to discover her intimately. I knew she was a virgin. I wasn't sure how I knew since she had never told me, but I knew it was true. It drove my wolf crazy and made us overprotective of her. No other man would ever touch my beautiful mate and I rejoiced in that knowledge.

Her breathing came out in quick pants and she pulled out of my kisses as my hand mercilessly explored her, memorizing each place that caused her to moan, or, better yet, purr. I watched her as her body convulsed under my touch, never losing eye contact. The emotions swimming in her eyes told me far more than words ever could.

Finally, as her breathing started to even and her cheeks flushed as she came back down to reality, I grinned proudly.

"Second base, then?"

After the moment we had just shared, I don't think I could have said anything more surprising to her. She giggled and buried her face in my chest, still shaking her head no.

My forehead creased as I forced her to look at me.

"Just how far does this challenge go?" I asked. I already knew Jenna was not the only virgin among the panthers. They all were. It was the number one reason my fraternity brothers continued to frequent their house. That many virgins in one place had started a sort of frenzy for domination.

"Home run. Nothing less," Jenna told me. I sucked in a sharp breath.

Everything in my being screamed to take her right then. I didn't think she'd resist either, but her first time should be more than a quickie with my brothers down the hall waiting for us to join them. Channeling every ounce of resolve I could muster, I pulled the sweats back up to her waist and kissed her forehead.

"Not happening tonight, princess."

I could feel her disappointment hit me like waves in the ocean. Relieved to know she wanted me as much as I wanted her helped ease the transition away from the bedroom.

"Trust me, it's not that I don't want to, I definitely want to, I just don't want my brothers and Anita waiting for us down the hall when that happens. I plan to take my sweet time and enjoy every second of it."

Her skin flushed, but a new kind of confidence seemed to blossom before my eyes. She moved with cat-like grace, mesmerizing me. It reminded me of the trance she'd put me in watching her dance at that party. I thought maybe she'd be embarrassed walking out of my room with the others forming assumptions about what had happened between us, but that was absolutely not the case.

She took a moment to smooth down her hair and check her appearance in the mirror. Satisfied with the results, she curled into my side as we headed back to the main den. I left her at the door for only a moment to run back in and grab a second set of my sweats.

She did pull away as we entered the main area, just out of reach of my touch, but she carried herself with the new confidence I was seeing evolve before my eyes. Just before we reached the others, she grabbed my arm and leaned in to whisper in my ear.

"I know what home plate is, but if that was only second base, what's on third?"

I doubted she had ever been as candid with anyone in her life, but she didn't even blush asking me. I leaned back and whispered, "A whole lot of the same, but next time I get to use my mouth."

Her body stiffened, and I smelled her arousal.

"Oh," was all she could say.

I chanced a quick look towards my brothers. Yeah, I was certain they had heard and smelled her too. If they were anyone else, my wolf would not have been happy, but two mated males were no threat to us.

Anita was watching us suspiciously but didn't say a word. I saw her check out the new outfit Jenna wore and laugh.

I threw her the second set of sweats and left no room for

argument. "I can take you home now, or you can put these on. You two are better than this."

Anita sighed and put the sweats on right over her clothes. "It was only in good fun," she said, then dropped down into a chair and sulked. "What's wrong with dressing up and prowling for guys?"

"What's wrong is that you deserve better than that, both of you. You really want your first time to be some meaningless booty call?"

"This coming from the biggest man-whore on campus? And you told him we're virgins?" Anita asked Jenna, turning fifty shades of red.

I was glad the heat was off me, but her "man-whore" comment didn't sit well with me.

"I didn't have to, he already knew. Says it's some sort of wolf thing. They smell really good."

Anita's lips formed a straight line and she closed her eyes, holding back a laugh.

"That's not what I meant." Jenna looked at me and shrugged. "Fine, you do smell good, but I meant wolves have a heightened sense of smell, and well, they noticed. That's why all the D.O.G.s, have been sniffing around our place."

I think Anita was more shocked at Jenna's frank comment regarding my scent than anything else. I didn't have to really know her at all to understand Jenna would be facing a full inquisition later. Luckily for us, Matt came back at that moment and slunk down on the oversized chair next to Anita.

"You're back early," I commented as I joined my brothers on the couch and picked up a controller. Jenna hesitated for a moment, and then joined us.

"You bailed on me, and a fight broke out between Theta and the panthers. I'd had enough. What are we doing? Call of Duty?"

"Yup, room for one more," I offered, but felt Jenna stiffen. Somehow, I knew she wanted to say something, and when I looked at her she was biting that damn lip. "Would you like to play?" I asked her curiously. She nodded, and a mischievous grin broke out across her face. I handed her a controller. "Sorry, dude, you and Anita can be on deck to play the winners if you want."

"No, thank you," Anita said. "That's Jenna's thing. I hate those stupid games."

"Jenna's thing, huh?" I asked, turning towards my mate with open curiosity. She blushed and shrugged. "Okay, so me and Jenna, against Liam and Patrick."

My brothers high fived each other happily.

"Easiest battle ever," Patrick said.

"You're going down, little brother," Liam added. "And Jenna, FYI, he hates to lose."

I laughed, knowing it was true, but the thought of my mate actually enjoying video games and wanting to play with me brought more pleasure than winning ever could. It only took minutes into the game to realize Jenna knew how to play, too. We pulled ahead quickly.

Anita laughed. "Jenna's only competitive in two areas: academics and video games. She's competed in Worlds the last four years."

"Damn," Liam said. "If I wasn't already mated, I'd marry you."

The growling bubbling out of me was cut off when my brother nudged me in the side. I pushed him back and soon we were play fighting, flipping over the back of the couch onto the floor as we wrestled.

Patrick shrugged. "Wolves. What can you do?"

Jenna gave one quick glance our way and then turned her full focus back to the game. "Just you and me then, leprechaun."

Patrick laughed heartily. "You're on, princess."

A few of my frat brothers started trickling back in. And at some point I hadn't noticed, Anita and Matt disappeared. The brothers all cheered on the game as Liam and I joined in. It had felt good to wrestle with my brother. So much felt like it was changing fast, but my family was one thing that I knew would always remain constant.

It was a close matchup, but in the end, Jenna easily defeated Patrick all by herself. Pride welled within me. Others were already forming teams and claiming next challenge. A few tried to take on partners with Jenna, but she was firm with them.

"Sorry, Chase is my partner. He just got a little distracted"—she gave me a stern look—"but I'll give him another chance. Do it again and I'll be hunting for a new partner," she threatened half-heartedly.

We spent the next five hours taking on team after team. She was relentless, amazing, probably the best Call of Duty partner I'd ever played with, and she was mine. She held her own with all my brothers, both family and fraternity.

Anita and Matt had snuck back in at some point, and I couldn't help but wonder if the stupid challenge was already over. They seemed quite cozy together, and happy. It didn't go unnoticed that she was no longer wearing the sweats I'd given her.

"In your face, Damon!" Jenna yelled, taking the final shot to end our closest game yet.

She had been on her feet, fully invested in the action, for much of the match. Her victory dance was the most adorable thing I'd ever seen.

"You're a nerd," I said as she sat back down next to me.

"That's really no big secret," she admitted. "But you, Chase Westin—who knew you were such a nerd?"

My brothers all laughed.

"I don't think we've ever had a chick over to play with us, so it's a well-kept secret. You'll have to sign a confidentiality agreement. We can't have it get out that our most eligible bachelor and campus ladies' man is a closet video game junkie," Damon teased.

I hated the title, and I really hated that I couldn't claim my mate before them. Even my fraternity brothers couldn't know about us. So, I kept my mouth shut and took the ragging while chancing a sad look at Jenna. I could see the emotions swelling in her eyes and knew she felt the same.

Looking at the clock, I realized it was 3 a.m. already.

"We should get you girls home, it's getting late," I said, not really wanting her to leave, but not wanting to press my luck, either.

"Jenna, you're welcome anytime. Xbox is always open," Neal told her.

"My purse is in your room," she whispered as we stood up and I led her back to my room. The second the door closed, I pulled her in for a kiss, but I knew we couldn't indulge. The last thing I wanted was the others thinking that my mate was easy and available.

She took off the sweats, showcasing the sexy little outfit she had chosen to wear to the party. It felt like that had been ages ago. My stance on the thing hadn't changed. Alone, in my room, for my eyes only, it was the sexiest sight in the world, and I loved it. Knowing she was about to walk past most of my brothers in the skimpy little thing, set my wolf on edge.

"We still on for the library tomorrow?" I asked hopefully, trying to distract myself.

"Not sick of me yet?" she teased.

"Never," I said, giving her another heated kiss before forcing us to leave the room.

"Anita, you ready?" Jenna asked as we got back to the main room. Another round of games had started, but mostly the group had broken up.

Anita begrudgingly followed, but so did Matt. We walked the girls back to their house. I gave Jenna a quick hug, daring a kiss just below her ear that I knew turned her on. She swatted at me and shot a warning glare my way. I flashed her the dimples and watched her melt.

We really didn't need to be concerned about Matt and Anita. They were so wrapped up in making out with each other that they never gave us a second a thought.

"Matt," I said, smacking him on the arm to break them up. "Give the poor girl some air already."

There was something about Anita, my first panther friend that made me protective of her. I didn't want to see her get hurt and knew she and Matt couldn't be together long-term. *Hypocrite*, a small voice in the back of my head said.

The front door opened just as he released her.

"Where have you two been?" Ayanna demanded.

"Sorry we kept them out so late," I told her, giving Jenna a meaningful look and squeezing her hand before letting go; though, knowing about the challenge, I leaned in and kissed Jenna on the cheek. Her skin flushed and her eyes swore retribution, but I couldn't hold back the joyful grin from my face.

Matt was far more in-your-face obvious as he kissed Anita one last time, before nodding at Ayanna.

"See you tomorrow, babe," he said as we turned to leave.

Back home, my bed was covered in the scent of Jenna. It caused equal parts pleasure and torture. I longed for the day she could just stay.

Jenna

Chapter 12

The second the door closed, I noticed my sisters waiting on us, arms crossed and claws ready to come out.

"How dare you, Jenna!" Chloe squealed.

Confused, I asked, "How dare I, what?"

"How dare you monopolize Chase Westin like that!" she said.

I laughed. "Really? The stupid challenge wasn't my idea."

Louisa spoke up next. "No one thought you'd actually play along."

"Well, you thought wrong. Chase is a good guy. He doesn't deserve to be a target for this insanity." I tried to defend him, and they laughed in my face.

"Called it!" Ayanna said. "You totally pulled the friend card to get him away from those of us actually taking this seriously."

"You wish," Anita said. "Chase was all over her tonight. They may not have gone all the way, but I know for a fact that they made it to second base."

I glared at her. I couldn't believe she'd just announced that. The last thing I needed was eleven sets of eyes tracking me and Chase.

"I don't believe it," Chloe said. "Were you there? Did you see it?"

"No," Anita said, "but Jenna doesn't whisper very well, either."

I blushed furiously.

"Well," Ayanna said, hands on her hips while glaring at me, "you all know the rules, and unless you have proof that you went all the way, then game's still on."

"Actually," Anita said, pulling out a Ziploc bag showcasing a used condom and grinning from ear to ear, "challenge complete."

Mouths dropped, including mine. I knew she and Matt had been gone for a while. How long, I couldn't say, because I was too absorbed in the game. But, wow! Just wow!

"No way!" said Cameron, another one of our sisters.

"Woohoo, Anita, you little slut. Who did you have again?" Tessa asked.

"Matt Williams," she said proudly.

"They were still making out when he dropped her off," Louisa pointed out.

"What does this mean now?" Chloe pouted, asking Ayanna.

"I guess Anita wins the challenge."

I could see Ayanna was shocked. Her younger sister had bested her in her own game. I couldn't even fathom what would come next because of it.

"Come on ladies, it's late and it's been a crazy night. I think everyone needs to get some sleep and we'll talk about this tomorrow."

As the girls broke up and headed off to their respective rooms, Tessa followed me to mine. She sat at my desk chair and stared at me.

"You really made it to second base with Chase?" she finally asked, breaking the silence.

I found I couldn't lie to her and nodded.

"How, um, how was he?"

"I can't even describe it, Tess. He was incredible." I wanted so badly to tell her everything, but she had hurt me in the past and I couldn't fully trust her. It saddened me. She was my twin. There shouldn't be anything I couldn't share with her.

"Just be careful. I'm worried about you."

"What?" I asked, confused. Why would Tessa worry about me? "What are you talking about? There's nothing to worry about."

"The other girls, they've been boy crazy forever. They fall in and out love like it's nothing. But you? Jenna, I know you. Tonight was a big deal, and I just don't want to see you really fall for him only to have your heart broken. You can never truly be together. This is all just supposed to be fun. Please don't lose sight of that."

It had been a long time since Tessa and I had a sister moment of any kind. She had been resentful of my change in colleges, even more so when Daddy forced her and the others to follow me. When she wrapped her arms around me, it took every ounce of willpower not to hold on and cry at the truth in her words.

"I'll be careful," I promised with as much conviction as I could muster.

When she left the room, I found solace in my pillow and cried myself to sleep. Chase was mine. My heart already belonged to him and it wasn't just the bond. I couldn't believe that. It was him, Chase Westin, so confident and cocky on the outside, but a closet nerd, gamer, and romantic, fiercely loyal to those he cared about. He had already stolen my heart. I loved him, but I also knew I could never have him, not in the way I so desperately wanted.

The next morning felt like a hangover. *A Chase hangover*, I thought.

I got up and checked myself in the mirror. I had mascara streaks down my face from where I had forgotten to wash my face. I was a hot mess. Heading straight for the shower, I was again grateful I didn't have to share a bathroom.

Most of the rooms had a conjoined shower, two rooms shared one. The original sorority that built the place had two people per room with four people that would share a bathroom. We didn't have enough members in our elite group for that, so everyone got their own room. Two had private baths. As princesses, those were assigned to me and Tessa. I didn't always appreciate the perks of being a princess. They set me apart from the others, an outsider, but in this case, I was eternally grateful.

Feeling almost human again—well, as human as a shifter can feel—after my shower and fresh clothes, I grabbed my phone to check the time. Stunned, I saw it was already after one o'clock. I checked my texts but hadn't missed anything.

I messaged Chase.

JENNA: Slept in. Grabbing some lunch. Still on for 2?

Within seconds my phone dinged.

CHASE: What's for lunch?

I smiled to myself.

JENNA: grabbing something at the café.

CHASE: see you in 5?

JENNA: ok.

My heart raced with anticipation. I hadn't planned on seeing him outside of the library. Speeding up departure, I practically plowed over Anita on my way out of the door.

"Oh, hey," I said in surprise.

"Where are you off to in such a hurry?"

"Study group at two and I need to grab some lunch first."

"Oh, what study group?"

"Calculus," I said, without even thinking she was in the class, too.

She perked up immediately. "I'm really struggling with a couple of the questions on the practice test he gave us. Can I tag along?"

There was no way I could say no. "Sure."

We headed over to the café. Chase was already there waiting, and Matt Williams was with him. I looked at him curiously. Anita squealed happily when she saw him. Anita hugged him and he kissed her right there in front of everyone as they went off to find food.

"Sorry," Chase said. "I didn't know Matt was struggling with calculus when he asked my plans for the day. I told him I had a calculus study group at the library, so he invited himself along."

I threw my head back and laughed. "Anita's crashing, too. Same exact scenario."

He grinned. "Guess we suck at sneaking around."

"Guess so."

"Come on, let's grab some lunch at least. I'm starving. And my treat, no arguments."

I didn't want him wasting his money on me. I knew how tight budgets were for college students. Money had never been an issue for me; my father was wealthy and I was raised with every advantage, but I didn't want to bruise his pride by saying no. I vowed to discuss it with him later.

I picked up a tuna sandwich, some chips, and grabbed a water. Chase looked at my meager lunch and added a fruit bowl and side salad to it.

"You expect me to eat all of this?" I asked him, even knowing I could polish that off and then some. I was starving.

"Yes, I do," he said definitively, and that was when I noticed the heaping pile of food he had on his own tray.

I shook my head. "Wolves."

He grinned and pulled out a black Amex card to pay. It was crystal clear I didn't know as much about Chase Westin as I thought.

The girl at the register glared at me behind his back.

"Thanks, Kelly," he called over his shoulder.

I sped up to keep up with him.

"You totally slept with her," I accused before I could stop myself.

He turned to look at me in surprise. "Uh, why would you say that? And it was a long time ago."

I laughed. "She's clearly not over it, though, from the glares she was giving me."

He cringed. "She was one of the clingy ones. Nice girl, but definitely not the girl for me."

The smoldering look he gave me made me blush.

We joined Anita and Matt at the table. I immediately noticed Matt's plate was piled high, too, while Anita had a small chef salad. Her eyes widened at the amount of food on my tray.

We were large cats, so our appetites probably rivaled the boys on most days; however, as ladies we did not show that to the opposite sex, especially guys we liked. I don't know if it was the human television influence that caused us to hide it, or what, but all the girls did. Those that dated would practically starve themselves, then come home and ravish an entire turkey.

I happily ate my lunch, grateful for the bit of extra food, but still hungry when I was done. I hadn't eaten breakfast, which made it worse.

I'm not sure how Chase knew, but as we talked, he casually dropped a slice of pizza on my tray. I tried to ignore it, but the longer we sat there the more it taunted me. After I ate that, he shared half his fries, and then a full slice of cheesecake. I sighed contentedly as I polished off the last bite. When I looked up, Matt hadn't seemed to notice, but Anita stared in envy at my now empty plate.

On the walk to the library, Anita held back and pulled me with her. The guys talked as they walked ahead.

"I can't believe you ate all that food in front of them," she scolded.

"I was starving. I slept through breakfast."

"You put way more food on your tray than you normally eat

in public," she pointed out.

"I didn't, Chase added some of it," I confessed.

"And then he just kept giving you his, too?"

I shrugged. "Wolves have like super hearing or something, you know. He probably heard my stomach still grumbling, and for sure they're listening in on this conversation," I pointed out realistically.

Chase laughed, confirming my suspicions.

"If you were hungry, why didn't you just eat?" Matt asked Anita as the guys waited for us to catch up. "I may not put away quite as much as a wolf, but Chase knows we eat almost as much as they do. I may not be black, but still the same species, remember?"

"Why do you guys do that?" Chase asked.

"Do what?" Anita asked innocently.

"Pretend like you don't actually eat. Buy a small salad and swear it's enough. That's such a human thing to do. We're animals, we eat, and our metabolisms require much more food than an average human, so why bother hiding it?"

Anita and I both shrugged. "It's a girl thing, you wouldn't understand," she finally said.

The guys shook their heads, but dropped it. We reached the library and settled into a study room on one of the upper floors.

"Who else are we expecting?" Anita asked.

"Huh?" I asked.

"You said it was a study group. How many more are we expecting?"

My eyes flashed to Chase's for help.

"The other two texted earlier and couldn't make it, so it's just us," he lied without even flinching.

"Oh, well, I guess it's a good thing I tagged along, or you'd be stuck here with just these two," Anita said.

"Good thing," I agreed.

We opened our books and got down to work. Chase took the lead and walked through several problems, answering all our questions.

"Wait up, so you're like some kind of math whiz?" Anita asked.

Matt laughed. "Shh, it's his biggest secret. He's a closet genius."

I was pretty certain I was his biggest secret, but I'm sure that was a close second.

Chase shrugged. "No one will believe you if you try and tell anyone."

She looked confused. I was, too, if I were being honest.

"Why would you care if people knew you were smart?" Anita asked.

"Not a match with his reputation around campus. Nerds don't get laid," Matt said.

I had to bite back a hiss. My panther did not like hearing about Chase's reputation with the ladies. Neither did I.

I was still stewing about it an hour later when we took a break. Matt and Anita disappeared quickly, leaving Chase and me alone in the room.

"Hey, are you okay?" Chase asked me.

I nodded and pretended to study the question we had just gone over. I hated feeling jealous of the girls he'd been with before me. I knew it wasn't rational, but that didn't stop the hurt and disappointment every time it was mentioned.

He reached over and took my pencil, and I looked up at him. He relaxed and smiled. "Better."

"Give me back my pencil, Chase," I said sternly. "I'm still trying to work out the last of this problem."

His smile faltered and I saw uncertainty for the first time. Chase was always larger than life and so sure of himself, always in control. Worry consumed me. What was wrong? I couldn't stop my hand from reaching out to him. I stroked his arm reassuringly.

"Are you okay?" I asked him.

He shrugged. "You feel . . . off today. I don't know how to describe it." He toyed with the ends of my hair. "Are we okay, Jenna? Did I do or say something to upset you?"

My heart cracked a little more. "No, no, I'm fine," I rambled. "It's stupid, but yeah, we're fine. It's not your concern, I promise."

He stared deep into my eyes. "You're my mate—everything that concerns you is my problem, too."

I smiled and let go of my frustration. "Sometimes, I just get a little jealous. I can't even seem to help it, no matter how stupid it is. My panther"—I blushed furiously at my admittance—"doesn't like seeing you with other females, or talking to other females, or mentioning anything between you and other females even before we came into the picture. I'm sorry. I'm trying to keep it in check."

"Matt," he cursed under his breath.

I laughed. "It's not his fault. It really is me."

"Listen to me, beautiful. While I can say a million times a day that you have nothing to be jealous of, I am one hundred percent yours, I do get it." His cocky grin was back. "I won't lie, I love knowing you're jealous."

I smacked him. "Chase," I scolded.

He laughed. "I'm serious. It lets me know you really do care. I feel so damn much it's overwhelming at times. I struggle even having Matt in the same room with you, and he's one of my best friends."

He was so open and honest. I made a point to remember that in the future and talk to him instead of letting things fester. I wasn't used to having someone I could trust with all my thoughts, or my heart.

My heart pounded as he leaned in and kissed me, deepening it quickly. My breath hitched and I pulled back, looking around. We were alone in the room, but one wall was entirely open to the main library.

"People will see. We can't," I reminded him.

When his dimples flashed at me, I knew he was either up to no good, or knew something I didn't know. In this case, I suppose it turned out to be a little of both.

"Never noticed how they're mirrored on the other side? We can see out, but others can't see in. It's why I reserved this particular level for us."

He wrapped one arm around my waist and the other under my legs and lifted me easily out of my chair and settled me into his lap. I yelped in surprise.

"Matt and Anita could still return at any time," I reminded him.

"Then stop talking and let me kiss you before they do."

I liked his logic and we were soon lost in our own world. My chest was heaving and my body was tingling all over when he again surprised me, by dumping me back into my chair and walking to the other side of the table.

Hurt and confused, I looked at him in disbelief, but he just winked and blew me a kiss. He started talking aloud and pointing out the problem I had been focusing on earlier, seconds before the door opened and Matt and Anita returned.

I looked at him in shock, my cheeks warming, and he just smiled back and casually pointed to his ears. I burst out laughing.

"What's so funny?" Anita asked.

"Um, uh, I finally understand what Chase was trying to say." It wasn't even a real lie. I may have been insinuating to her it was regarding our practice quiz question, but he got it.

He high fived me and said, "That's my girl."

I glared at him, warning he was taking it too far, but he turned to the white board behind him and scribbled down the last of the problems. To my surprise, I really did get it. The part I had been struggling with somehow clicked right at that moment.

When I was no longer flustered from Chase's complete one-eighty on me, I tuned in to my friend. Her cheeks were flushed and her hair was slightly askew. I suspected they'd been making out in the stacks. As if confirming my suspicions, they couldn't stop making eyes at each other, and barely a half hour passed before they both made excuses to leave.

They left separately, but the moment the door closed behind Matt, Chase grabbed my hand and pulled me over to the window. We pressed our cheeks against the cool glass and watched. Sure enough, Anita was waiting for him at the first stack of books.

I laughed. "Do you think we suck that badly trying to sneak around? I mean, they were so obvious."

He shrugged. "We haven't put that much effort into hiding it yet."

Horrified, I realized he was right. "That stupid challenge definitely had helped with that somewhat. Now that it's over, we're going to have to be extra careful. If any of my sisters found out, they'd tell Daddy, and then he'd have me on a plane out of here in thirty minutes flat."

Sadly, I wasn't exaggerating. I could feel waves of anger rolling off Chase. I knew if it came to that, he wouldn't let me go without a fight. I had not yet allowed myself to consider that situation. When it came down to it, would I follow my family, or do anything it took to stay with my mate?

"What do you mean the challenge is over? Who? When? It

sure as hell wasn't me."

I tried to hide back the smirk. "Matt and Anita, at your house Saturday night."

"Seriously? I mean I knew they disappeared, but you said home plate and nothing less."

"Yup, and she had to show proof too, or it didn't count. I think the other girls are really disappointed, and considering letting it continue anyway. The ones who drew your name are all pissed at me for hogging you. I'm not sure they're ready to give up," I hissed angrily, turning away from him so he wouldn't see how much it bothered me.

He wrapped his arms around me and pressed his lips to my neck, trailing light kisses down and across my shoulder.

"They can try. It won't work. Wait, how exactly does one prove something like that anyway?" he asked curiously.

I scrunched up my nose. "She brought back the used condom."

"Damn. You girls are ruthless. That's disgusting."

Chase

Chapter 13

Jenna and I fell into an easy routine, but it was never enough. Monday, Wednesday, and Friday we had classes together, all morning, and then lunch together afterwards. Friends almost always joined us.

On Tuesdays and Thursdays, we met in the library for study time. The problem was, as others heard of our study groups, more and more people began joining us until we were actually studying. I felt terrible about it too. The initial guise was that Jenna was tutoring me in calculus: only Matt and Anita knew the truth about that, and as partners in two classes we tried to dissuade others from joining us, but someone always seemed to tag along.

Saturdays were hit or miss. Sometimes we'd see each other at a party. Sometimes we could carve out a few hours in the morning or around lunch to sneak away, just the two of us, but my brothers and her sisters often kept us busy with expectations on the weekends, so we didn't always get that time in either. I would never dare go to her sorority house—that was opening a can of worms we weren't ready to address. She was always welcome at my house, but my brothers treated her like one of the guys. They always fought over who would partner up with her for video games, and I felt like I was in constant competition with each of them.

Finally, Sunday would come around. We had our room on constant reserve at the library, but without a lock on the door, it was never the best place to be alone. We did somehow manage to keep that time somewhat sacred and free of intruders, but overall there didn't feel like there was any place on campus we could just be alone.

Six weeks had passed since I'd met my beautiful mate. I couldn't complain about how things were going, even if my wolf was unsettled and anxious for us to complete our bond. However, I selfishly just wanted some alone time with her. I wanted more than just a few stolen kisses, and I was a man used to getting my way. Maybe it was the spoiled brat syndrome of being the youngest, maybe I was just too stubborn to hear the word no, but as I began formulating a plan, I realized it was the best thing for the both of us.

It was early on a Saturday morning and I awoke to a ringing phone. I snatched it up without even looking at it. Only one person would call me at that hour.

"Good morning, beautiful," I said in a deep, sleepy voice.

"Well, good morning to you as well," a much too chipper voice returned. I pulled back the phone and saw my realtor's face pop up on the screen. "Probably not who you expected, but two new properties just hit the market. We gotta move fast. They won't last."

I groaned. "Okay, give me twenty."

"Great, I'm texting you the first address now."

I got up and took a quick shower, shaved, and dressed in record time. I grabbed my coat and was out the door before anyone else in the house even stirred. It didn't take long to drive over to the address she sent.

"This better be good, Collette, for you to drag me out this early on a weekend," I grumped as I opened my car door to find her already waiting.

"We can go right up," she said, handing me a cup of coffee. I took a deep sip, surprised to find it exactly the way I liked it.

It had been two weeks since I had gotten the brilliant idea to buy my own place off campus. I hadn't told Jenna, and it was getting exceedingly difficult to keep it to myself. My thoughts were that if we had our own place, we could finally get some time alone.

When I had confided my plan to Kyle, he had laughed. "That's pretty extreme for a little booty action," he had said, and I growled and threatened to come through the phone and rip his throat out. It was a good thing he was my brother and only laughed harder. As my Alpha, if I had been anyone else making such threats, I'd be lucky to still be alive. We had ended that call with a reminder: "Mom never said there was anything sane about a mating male."

It was true. Kyle, Patrick, and Liam had all had their fair

amount of insanity during their mating periods, and they didn't have half the battles Jenna and I were facing.

Collette led me up to the fourth floor of a high-rise apartment building. It was small and tight inside, and my wolf was uncomfortable. Still, it had all the basics and it was literally the first place available in weeks. I had no doubt, if I waited until May to buy I'd have my pick of anything, but I didn't want to wait that long. Archibald Reynolds wasn't the only college in the area, so housing was limited.

"No," I said sadly. "It makes me feel claustrophobic in here."

Collette smiled. "I knew you'd say that, but I'm not sure another rental will come available before May."

I groaned in frustration.

"But—"

She got my attention, I liked 'but' in this case.

"—how do you feel about buying?"

I hadn't really considered that as an option.

"Now," she continued, "just hear me out. There's a hunting cabin nearby. It's only five minutes from the campus' main gate. It's secluded, with an open floor plan and five bedrooms. I realize that's way more than you need, but your mortgage would still be in the range we discussed. First floor has everything you're looking for, just with an added second level."

"Okay. I hadn't really thought about buying, but I like the sound of the place. Let's take a look."

She led the way back downstairs to the cars, and I followed her the short distance to the next place. When she turned off the main road onto a hidden driveway, my interest increased tenfold. We drove another quarter of a mile before it opened to a clearing where a log cabin sat. I felt an overwhelming sense of calm and knew this was going to be my first home. I didn't even care how much it would cost me. There was a swing on the front porch where I could already see myself with a cup of hot coffee, a blanket, and my mate tucked into my side.

"It's perfect," I said.

Collette laughed. "Would you like to at least look inside first?"

"Yeah, okay. How many acres does it come with?"

"Three acres for just the house, then there's another parcel of thirty acres they're selling off the back, but you'll have about half an acre buffer from the back of the house to the property line," she explained.

"How much for all of it?"

Her eyes rounded in curiosity. "Two hundred and fifty thousand. Just the cabin is only one hundred forty-seven thousand, which is a steal. Owner died, and his grandkids just want money fast."

"Great, offer them two twenty-five, cash, for both lots," I said.

"Cash? And sight unseen? You don't want to even see the inside?" she asked.

"Oh yeah, well, we can look, but I'm going to have this place," I assured her.

Inside was even better than I imagined. It was a little musty smelling, like it had been closed up for a long time, but it had a big open floor plan, a loft that would make the perfect study area, and two bedrooms on each side. Another large master bedroom was on the main level. I knew Jenna was going to love the master bath with the large soaking tub. The kitchen had a nice island I could see us eating breakfast at, and everything we would need conveyed, even a washer and dryer. It was perfect.

"Make the offer," I told Collette.

She whipped out her phone and got down to business before I could change my mind. It might have seemed like an impulse buy to her, and maybe it was, but I knew I wouldn't regret it and couldn't wait to surprise Jenna.

The owners accepted the offer on the spot. Since it was a cash transaction, closing was scheduled for fifteen days later. I could hardly wait to tell Jenna, but I was determined to keep it a surprise.

Two more weeks dragged on and Jenna showed signs of equal frustration, since we had not had a single moment alone. It weighed heavily on both of us, but I knew it would be coming to an end soon.

Collette dropped off my new keys the day before closing. The money was already secured in escrow and closing was essentially a done deal.

"The last of the stuff the owners wanted has been removed from the property. Anything remaining conveys to you," she informed me.

"Can I get in tonight even though closing isn't until tomorrow?"

"Yes, it's all yours. Tomorrow's just a formality of signing the paperwork, since it's a cash transaction."

We said goodbye and I thanked her profusely, staring down at my house key in disbelief.

It was Wednesday morning and I was late for class. Worry hit me as I entered the room, only it wasn't coming from me. I should have sat in the back, sneaking in as inconspicuously as possible, but Jenna needed me. I made my way down to the front, as the professor's back was to us as he worked a problem on the whiteboard.

I was already sitting in my usual seat, next to my mate, when the professor turned around. He simply nodded my way and kept teaching. Getting through the next two classes was going to be hell. I was so excited to take Jenna home, our first home together.

She wrote something on a piece of paper, and then slid it over to me that asked, *are you okay?*

I wrote back, *never better,* and added a little smiley face then slid the paper back to her.

Anita was watching us closely, so I ignored further attempts at interrogation.

When the class finally ended, I headed out and Jenna ran to keep up.

"What is with you today?" she demanded. "First you're late to class. Now you're ditching me?"

My eyes widened as I turned to her. I wanted desperately to pull her into my arms, but I saw Anita walk out of the class and look curiously in our direction.

"Just keep walking," I told her. I made no attempt to reach out to her as I wanted. I didn't even talk to her again until we were in our class. Then I turned to her. "I'm so sorry. Anita's been hinting to Matt that she thinks something's going on with us. I didn't think you wanted even her to know."

"That's why you were late this morning?"

"No, I'll tell you all about that at lunch," I assured her. "But that's why I was trying to rush out of our last class and not linger. I didn't mean to make you feel it was because of you."

She relaxed visibly. "My afternoon class cancelled today. Maybe we could actually get away for a little bit today?"

I grinned from ear to ear. My mate was missing time alone with me, too, though little did she know I had already solved that problem. Now I just had to wait and count down the seconds until our classes ended. Of course, that meant they both dragged on for what seemed like forever.

With five minutes left in our photography class, the lights dimmed as the professor showed us pictures from the Renaissance period, I checked the time on my phone one last time. There were five minutes left in class. I grabbed up my things and headed out, sending a text to Jenna as I did.

I heard her phone ding and chanced a look back at the confusion on her face when she answered it before leaving the room and then sprinted across the campus.

CHASE- faculty parking lot at the back, as soon as class ends.

Jenna sent back a thumbs-up emoji. By the time she arrived, I had made it across campus, picked up my Jeep, and was waiting. She came out and looked around, standing on her tiptoes and straining in search of me. I honked the horn and waved her over.

"Whose Jeep is this?" she asked as she slid into the passenger seat.

"Mine," I told her.

"You've had a car this whole time? Why are we just now using it?"

I really hadn't thought about that previously. There were many places off campus we could have gone to get away. I just shrugged guiltily.

"Sorry, until now I just didn't think about it."

"Why were you late this morning? I was worried."

I waited until we were off campus and stopped at a red light to pull her towards me and steal a kiss. "I love that you worry about me, and if you can just be patient, I'm going to show you why."

"Okay, okay. I'm not really good at surprises though, just so you know."

"Now you tell me?" I asked incredulously.

We drove in silence and she felt nervous. I wasn't used to her being nervous around me, not since the early days of our mating. I hadn't felt it like this then though. It was a sign our bond was strengthening.

I pulled off the road a short time later and down the long drive. *Our drive*, I thought. I could see the confusion on Jenna's face as I pulled up to the log cabin.

"What's going on, Chase?" she asked.

I got out and walked around to get her car door. I pulled her up by the hand and squeezed it reassuringly.

"Come on, I'll show you."

We walked to the front porch and I opened the door, then scooped her up in my arms and carried her inside. She giggled and punched me until I let her down.

"What is this place?" she asked.

"Well, first, what do you think of it?"

"Huh? It's amazing. Look at it. Needs a little cleanup and some new furniture, but it's great. Where are we?"

"Home," I said simply, wrapping my arms around her waist and pulling her back against me. "Our first home. We close on it tomorrow, but since the money's already in escrow, they gave me the keys a day early."

"Our home?" she asked slowly, her faced flushed. She turned to look at me to make sure I was serious.

"If you really don't like it, I'll put it back on the market tomorrow after closing and we can keep looking."

"Not like it? Are you kidding? Look at this place." She wandered around checking out each of the rooms, then the back yard. "It's huge. Why do we need so much space?"

I shrugged. "I liked the solitude. I'm tired of sharing you and worrying about getting caught all the time. We can just be together, be ourselves, here."

"You bought me a house just to spend time alone together?"

I nodded. "Yeah, basically."

"Chase, that's insane! How can you even afford this place? We're in college."

I looked at her oddly. I hadn't considered that we had never really spoken about our finances. It felt like we talked about everything.

"Have a seat," I told her, pointing to one of the rocking chairs that had been left on the back deck. I took the one closest to her.

"How much do you know about wolf packs?"

She shook her head. "Not much. I mean, I know you tend to live in groups and instead of a King, you have an Alpha. I think that's right, at least."

"That's true. Westin Pack is one of the largest packs in the world. My however-many-greats-grandfather started the Westin Foundation as a way to fund our pack. It deals with a lot of charities and investments. It sets us apart from other packs. We were civilized earlier. We carry no debt. Everything in San Marco, where I'm from, is a front or hobby for the town itself. The Foundation pays a monthly stipend to all wolves in the pack equally. It starts when your wolf surfaces. For me, I was sixteen. I was an early shifter," I told her proudly.

She rolled her eyes. "Why am I not surprised?"

I laughed. "Basically, that means I've been accumulating money for the last four years and just banking it in savings and personal investments. I've never really touched it, till now. Don't worry, though, this place is only about three months of earnings."

I let that sink in for a minute.

"You're, like, rich? Like, really rich?"

"I don't know what your pack, or family, or whatever you call it, is like, but with me, princess, you will never want for anything. I have more than enough for the both of us, and when we are bonded, you will become a full pack member and receive your own monthly allowance from the Foundation."

She snorted as she laughed. "Chase, I'm a panther. I'll never be pack. They won't just turn over all that money to me. It's a sweet thought, but let's be real here."

"They will actually. My bonded mate will be accepted into the pack, period. It doesn't matter what you are." I begged her to understand that.

"That's a nice thought, but I live in the real world. Cats and dogs, they don't mix."

"Are you saying we don't mix? Are you saying we're not right for each other because my animal spirit happens to be a canine and yours is a beautiful feline?" I let my fingertips drift lightly up her arm and watched in satisfaction as a shudder wracked her body. I let that sink in and changed subjects abruptly on her. "What are you plans for spring break?"

"What?" she asked, sounding a little dazed and I knew it was from my touch. "Oh, um, the sisters are heading to Cabo for spring break."

"And you?" I asked.

"I'm expected to go with them," she admitted.

"Can you get out of it?"

"I don't know, to be honest."

"Will you try? I'd really love to take you home with me for spring break. You can meet my family and my pack and see how it goes."

Tears welled up in her eyes. "Chase, you don't understand. Even if your family and pack opened their hearts to take me in, Daddy would never allow it. My family will never accept you."

I pulled her over to my lap and held her while she cried. I honestly hadn't thought about that. I could give a shit if her father accepted me. I could easily provide for the both of us, and if he was that insistent, we didn't need him in our life, but I hadn't considered how that would affect Jenna.

"Shit, I'm sorry," I said, stroking her hair and toying with the ends. "I've been so busy working out things on my end to ensure you had everything you could need or want, and I hadn't stopped to think that would include your family."

"He'll disown me, Chase. Panthers aren't like your kind. We're okay alone. Being banned isn't as devastating a thought as you'd think, but still. He's my father. He won't let me see or talk to Tessa and Mother once this gets out. I'm not saying he's a complete tyrant. He's a very good man and a strong leader, but he's very elitist and insistent that we protect the purity of our breed."

"What do you want, Jenna?" I asked, knowing I'd do whatever it took to give her what she wanted or needed most. If that was her family, it would hurt like hell, but I'd back off and give her that.

She shivered, so I got up and led her back into the house. We sat on the leather couch that had been left. The cabin was mostly furnished. The few things the owners had taken seemed to be artwork and personal items instead of the big stuff.

She seemed to be deep in thought, so I stayed quiet. She rubbed her hands down her pants. It was another nervous tick I had noticed. The confusion and frustration on her face seemed to disappear and I could see her resolve strengthen. I wasn't sure I really wanted to hear the outcome.

Jenna reached over and took my large hands in her small ones, and when she focused those beautiful, exotic eyes on me, I felt more vulnerable than I ever had in my life.

"Chase," she started, and I had found I was holding my breath in anticipation. "My entire life I've known what was expected of me and what would happen should I find my one true mate was anything but a black panther. Meeting you has been more than I could ever have imagined. I don't care what you are. I care who you are, and I know you, Chase Westin. You're a good man with strong family values. You are protective of those you care about and you let your heart guide you. Your positive outlook makes me want to believe everything you paint of a future together, but we don't come from the same places. I don't trust everything will just be okay, and I know I can't have everything I want in life. That brings me to a crossroad. It's the biggest decision of my life and I've been sick to my stomach for weeks over it."

I squeezed her hands to encourage her to continue. This woman held my future in the palm of her hands. Wolves were different than other shifters in many ways. One of those was our fierce allegiance. I had given my heart to Jenna and it could never be occupied by anyone else. I didn't want to put that added pressure on her decision. It had to be hers alone to make. If she chose not to accept me, I knew she would go on and find a compatible mate and live a happy life. If that was best for her, I could live with that, but I also knew my life would always be hollow without her. I would never take another mate. It was her or nothing for me.

A tear slid down her cheek and I reached to wipe it away. I wanted so badly to fix everything and tell her it was all going to work out, but I couldn't know that with certainty, and it wouldn't be right to give her false hope. If she chose me, I would do everything in my power to make her life happy, filled with laughter and love, but that's all I could promise her.

My family was everything to me. I didn't know what decision I'd make if I were in her shoes. In the moment I'd say I'd always pick Jenna over anyone, that my true mate was more valuable to me than anything or anyone else, but I didn't have to truly make that decision. Even if my family wasn't happy about it, or couldn't understand it, they'd still love me, unconditionally.

"I know what I'm supposed to do, Chase, but I can't."

My eyes stared deep into hers. Was she saying what I thought she was saying? Her spine straightened, and she raised her chin in defiance.

"I never expected to meet my true mate. There aren't a lot of male black panthers, so the odds of finding one and being my true mate, was low. I always figured if I met him, he'd be a jaguar, maybe a puma, something compatible but still unacceptable. Daddy kept us sheltered to avoid situations like this. Maybe he was right."

My heart plummeted. She was going to break our bond. I couldn't speak and vowed to stay and hear every heart wrenching word first. I already knew I would never return to this cabin, as it would hurt too much. I looked away, unable to fully meet her eyes any longer.

"Maybe he was right to shelter us in order to preserve our breed, because meeting my true mate—" She paused, and her small hand caressed my cheek until I stared back into her eyes. "Meeting you, I know without a doubt or hesitation that I could never settle for anyone less."

My mouth dropped open as my heart soared. I let out the breath I was still holding. The anguish I had felt only a moment earlier melted away like the snow on a warm day.

"I love you, Chase Westin, and I don't have a freaking clue how this is going to work, but I'm all in. I'm yours and could never be anyone else's."

My lips were on her with a possessive growl. She roared in response and my entire body lit with pure need. I was a little surprised to feel my canines elongate. Breathless, I pulled back and smiled, showing her exactly what she was doing to me. She grinned widely, proudly showing me her fangs for the first time.

She repositioned so she was straddling my lap. I knew I was already rock hard and there was no way she didn't know it, too. When she tilted her head and brushed her hair back to expose her neck to me, I could barely control my breathing and excitement. I wanted her so badly.

"You're certain? There's no turning back after this," I reminded her.

She gave me a wicked grin. "I'm yours, so claim me already,

in every way possible."

I growled and sunk my teeth into the smooth ivory column of her neck. It was quickly followed by a pinch on mine as she bit into me. For one brief moment, a calm I never knew existed washed over me, and then came the frenzy.

Jenna

Chapter 14

Of course I'd been told about the bonding process, but I hadn't expected it to feel that way. I thought it would hurt; it hadn't. I thought the taste of his blood would make me gag, but it had quite the opposite effect. As my fangs began to retract, I was a little disappointed. That one perfect moment seemed to end much too quickly. I licked at the spot I'd just left on Chase's neck, watching it seal shut. The mark of our bond.

I kissed the spot and felt his entire body tremble. When I pulled back to look at him, a shyness set in and I couldn't fully meet his eyes. Bonding was far more intimate than sex, or so I had heard. I was still a virgin, so I had nothing to compare it to.

The warmth and completeness we just shared was overwhelming me. My body was on fire with this sort of buzzing sensation I didn't recognize. Was that normal? Did he feel it, too?

I finally made myself meet his eyes, and what I saw there took my breath away. His pupils were dilated and there was something wild about them. I could feel his wolf in a new way and he was close to the surface. It called to my panther.

I wasn't aware of how heightened my senses were until Chase's hand brushed up my thighs where I still straddled his lap. His fingers left a trail of heat behind and I shivered at his touch. Desire welled up deep within me, as a growing warmth spread out from the pit of stomach.

I leaned down and kissed him, watching him watch me closely. I knew he was waiting to see what I'd do. My handsome mate looked so incredibly sexy with an unabashed wild expression in his eyes. Mine didn't leave his, until they closed of their own accord as our lips touched. I moaned as I opened myself to him.

Chase Westin was a man who knew how to kiss. As my lips parted, his tongue began a sensual dance with mine, as if we both knew all the right movements to please the other. A possessive growl reverberated through his entire body, igniting a fire deep within me.

With a feverish frenzy I began removing my own clothes, breaking our kiss to pull my shirt over my head as he watched. Next to go was his shirt, as our clothes were thrown without care throughout the room. I didn't stop until we were both gloriously naked, and I rose and stood before him, letting my eyes roam over every inch of his body with open curiosity. I saw his manhood twitch under my scrutiny and it gave me more confidence than I ever knew existed.

"You are so beautiful," he said reverently. "Come here." He pulled me back down onto his lap.

The sensations of my soft, sensitive skin brushing against the hard planes of his body was almost more stimulation than I could handle. My senses were going into overdrive, but something wild and untamed within me was aching to burst free.

It wasn't the first time Chase and I had shared an intimate moment. I knew what he could do with those hands, but it had in no way prepared me for what that man could do with his mouth. My head was spinning, and bright lights flashed behind my eyelids. I cried out his name as he brought me to the peak of ecstasy.

He was grinning in satisfaction as he kissed his way back up my body. Slowing the pace with gentle, sweet kisses across my cheeks, nose, and finally my mouth, I sighed into him, feeling elated and relaxed as my convulsing body began to still.

"Living room officially christened," he said.

With quick reflexes, Chase was off the couch faster than I knew possible. The cool air against my abandoned skin barely had time to register before he scooped me up and carried me to the only closed door in the room. Balancing me against the doorframe, he freed a hand and turned the knob, kicking the door open as we proceeded forward.

"Wow," I said in surprise. A beautiful king-sized log bed filled much of the room.

"Do you like it?" he asked, sounding a little nervous.

"It's gorgeous," I told him honestly, but the thought of sleeping in someone else's bed was like tossing cold water on the fire within me.

Guessing the source of my distress, Chase said, "I wanted to pick everything out together, but I really wanted a bed for us. Don't worry, it's brand new. My realtor oversaw the delivery this morning."

He really had thought of everything. Carefully he lowered me to the bed and I knew I would have a tough time ever leaving it. The mattress was firm, yet so very soft, almost like laying on a cloud. I had never seen such a luxurious bed before. I moaned in satisfaction as I stretched out, testing it.

Chase gulped hard, but smiled so big his dimples popped out. I sat up and tugged him towards me. Since the first time I had seen those dimples I'd had an irrational desire to taste and explore them. My tongue delved into the crevices, first on one cheek, then the next, as I kissed my way between them. On my second pass, he nipped at my lips, causing me to giggle in delight.

He joined in with his own playful explorations and soon the fire that was still simmering within began to ignite once again. Our carefree caresses soon had us both panting. I reached for him, feeling his manhood for the first time as his eyes rolled back and he groaned in pleasure. He didn't let me explore long, even as my confidence continued to grow.

Soon I found myself pinned beneath him as he positioned himself between my legs. My breathing was erratic and my body burning from within.

Chase leaned down and nipped, then kissed the mark he had left on my body that signaled to all that I was his.

"Are you ready?" he whispered, pushing himself up on his arms to stare into my soul.

I could only nod.

I had thought the invasion of my first time would hurt. It didn't. There was a slight sting followed by a fullness that left me feeling whole, complete. I didn't need to worry or feel uncomfortable around Chase. He was patient and gentle, but mostly my body instinctively knew what to do and soon was matching his rhythm until a sort of convulsion took over me.

"Chase!" I screamed out, feeling myself so close to the edge.

"Jenna," he growled, and that was all it took to push me over. He joined me soon, as his weighted body collapsed on mine and jerked violently through his own release.

Still huffing hard and trying to catch my breath, he rolled off me and disappeared through one of the doors in the room, returning shortly with a warm washcloth that he used to clean me up. I saw a small amount of blood on the rag when he pulled it back and quickly looked down. It wasn't as bad as I had imagined. I should have felt embarrassed, but I didn't. He already knew I was a virgin, and I only bled a little, but the fact that he even thought to care for me in that way made my heart overflow with love.

"I love you, Chase," I whispered, and his hand stilled as his eyes flew up to search mine.

He gave me the sexiest smirk I'd ever seen. "I love you too, Jenna." He followed up those beloved words with a heart-melting kiss. "You are mine. Always. Whatever happens, whatever life throws our way, we're in it together from now on." His warm hand on my face gently brushed a tear from my cheek. "Mine," he growled before giving me one more unforgettable kiss.

He took his cleanup efforts back to the bathroom and pulled down the covers when he returned. I slid beneath them, crisp and cool, but only for the brief moment it took Chase to join me, then they instantly warmed.

He pulled me to him, rolling me towards him so that my head rested on his chest. We didn't speak. His hand lightly rubbed my back and my eyes became heavy and I began to purr softly. Contentment soon lulled me into a deep sleep.

My next coherent memory was of Chase's hands on my breast. I took a deep breath and smelled that unique scent that was only Chase before any fear could possibly set in. It brought me such comfort. He smelled like home to me, like safety, like all things good, like the promise of our future.

All the memories of the day before came rushing back to me. I hesitated a moment to let them sink in. Was I scared? Was I upset? Had I done the right thing? No. No. Yes. I was consumed by love for my mate.

"You are nearly impossible to wake," he protested as his hot breath tormented my hard nipples before taking one into his mouth. I moaned as I opened my eyes to complete darkness.

"What time is it?" I asked sleepily, feeling the new sensations of arousal flame within me.

"Who cares?" Chase said in a deep, husky voice that caused goosebumps to break out all over me. "I need you. Mine," he growled.

"Yours," I confirmed, sleepily, though my body was waking up faster than my foggy, now lust filled, brain.

He moved over me and peppered my chest and neck with light kisses till he reached my mouth. I growled into him as he entered me slowly and began a seductive rhythm so very different from our first time. He whispered sweet words and told me he loved me as he held me close, never changing pace until the very end. His own climax caused mine to trigger and I had tears in my eyes as my body and breathing began to still again.

It was the most beautiful moment of my life and felt like a dream I never wanted to wake from.

He tucked me close to him again and kissed the top of my head as my exhausted body pulled me back to sleep.

The next time I awoke Chase was still asleep, but his alarm was going off on his phone. A brief moment of fear set in. It was morning and I hadn't made it home yesterday. As soon as my sisters found out all that had happened, I was going to be kicked out anyway. Anguish filled me. It was too late to reconsider the consequences. Chase and I had sealed our bond. I waited for the panic to rise . . . nothing but sheer happiness followed at the thought. It was a true sign that I had made the right decision.

"Hey, sleepyhead, I thought you didn't have class till after lunch today," I said, poking him in the side.

"I don't," he murmured.

"Well, your alarm isn't going to turn itself off."

"My alarm?"

"Yes," I told him.

He finally seemed to register the sound for himself and grabbed for it on the nightstand next to us without even opening his eyes. It shut off immediately, but he opened one eye to look at it.

"Shit," he said, sitting up quickly and taking the sheets with him.

"Hey," I protested.

"Sorry, beautiful, but we're going to be late if we don't hurry."

Suddenly Chase was out of the bed, fully awake, and still gloriously naked.

"I really hadn't meant to sleep all night here. Are you going to be okay in yesterday's clothes?" He shot me a killer grin filled with mischief. "It's not like you were in them that long."

I threw a pillow at him, laughing. "What are we late for? I don't even have classes today, my only one canceled."

"Even better, but we do have a closing to get to in an hour. Come on," he said, tossing me over his shoulder and carried me caveman-style into the bathroom. I kicked and squealed the whole way, until he set me back down in front of the shower.

A part of me thought I should feel embarrassed to be standing there naked in front of a man, but Chase wasn't just any man, he was my mate, and I didn't need to feel self-conscious; if anything, being naked before him had the opposite effect.

I did have to pee, though. "Um, can you get out so I can use the bathroom?" I finally blurted out.

He laughed. "I'll get the shower started and promise not to peek. Just go already, I still have to, too."

I groaned. Okay, being naked, having sex, that was one thing, but peeing with him in the same room did feel awkward. In the end, his stubbornness won when he turned on the water and I really had to go. True to his word, he didn't peek.

I asked if I could shower first, knowing my hair was going to be a hot mess, so the more time I had to try and fix it, the better.

I jumped in and quickly realized we had nothing but water to wash up with. No soap, no shampoo, nothing. I let the hot water pour over me anyway. The damage of wet hair was already done. I closed my eyes and let the spray massage through my hair. When something brushed across my arm I screamed and almost fell before strong arms wrapped around my waist to steady me.

"What are you doing?" I asked Chase. "You scared the life out of me."

"Good thing you have nine lives then," he said, looking proud of himself.

I rolled my eyes. "That was terrible, and quite racist, you know."

He just laughed. "It'll be quicker if we shower together." He grinned, letting his eyes wash over me.

When his head lowered towards mine, I pushed him away, laughing. "No, we don't have time for that. And we have nothing here. Not even a bar of soap to wash with."

His grinning face frowned. "Sorry, I forgot. Here, let me just wash you up," he said, smirking and holding up a clean washcloth.

"I can handle it myself. We'll never get out of here if you start touching me."

He looked torn on that decision. I agreed that the thought of hot shower sex appealed to me too, and then I burst out laughing at the thought. Who was I? Just twenty-four hours earlier I probably would have died of embarrassment at just that thought.

"What's so funny?" he demanded.

"Nothing. Just wash up so we can go," I said sternly.

He didn't stop trying to reach for me, but each time I playfully swatted him away, promising next time when we didn't have a closing to get to. I finished up first and left him in the shower, pouting. Finding my clothes in the living room took a little effort. Things were thrown everywhere. I blushed, remembering how bold I'd been.

When I heard the shower turn off I quickly started dressing. I had on my bra, my shirt, and my socks, and was holding my pants when Chase came into the room still drying off with a towel.

"I can't find my underwear," I confessed.

He shrugged. "So, go commando."

"I can't do that."

"Sure you can. Look, if it makes you feel better, I'll go commando, too."

"What? How would that make me feel better?"

"Well, you'd know you weren't alone."

"Yeah, but all I'd think about was how much less there was between the two of us. Not conducive for an important meeting like this." With hands on my hips I demanded he help me find them.

He was fully dressed and we were still looking for my underwear when he burst out laughing. He pointed up and I followed his gaze. Hanging from the rafter beneath the loft were my panties.

"How the hell did you manage that?" he teased.

Chase

Chapter 15

Collette was waiting in the parking lot when we arrived at the address she had texted me.

"Wonderful, wonderful, you're both here. Thought for a moment you were going to stand me up," she said dramatically.

"Collette, this is Jenna. Jenna, this is our realtor." I quickly made the introductions.

The ladies seemed to size each other up. Jenna felt tense, and Collette seemed disappointed. I wondered briefly what the two women saw in each to cause those reactions, but I didn't dare ask. I had sisters, I knew better than to get in the way of a female territorial dispute.

I put my arm around Jenna's shoulders and pulled her to me, kissing her temple. "You ready to go buy a house?"

She took a deep, calming breath. "I'm ready."

Collette seemed to snap out of whatever her issue was upon hearing that. Clearly dollar signs won.

On the ride up to the lawyer's office, I wanted to make sure we were all set. "No surprises, right? You had no issues drawing up the amended files to include Jenna?"

"Everything is written exactly as you requested. The owners have already signed their part. This is truly just a formality. The cabin and all thirty-three acres are yours."

The process went quickly, the papers were signed, and we were soon shaking hands and being congratulated as keys and copies of the documents were being thrust our way.

"How about an early lunch to celebrate?" I asked, including Collette in the offer.

"Sorry, I have another closing in ten minutes. It was nice to meet you, Jenna," she said a little coldly, shaking my girl's hand. "And Chase, as always, the pleasure is all mine."

I laughed. "Sure it is, but really, thanks for everything Collette."

We said another round of goodbyes in the parking lot and I opened the door for Jenna to get in, but she turned and hugged me, pressing her lips briefly to mine.

"This is insane, you know that, right?"

"What?" I asked innocently.

"A house? Chase, we're homeowners!" she squealed in delight and I knew that there was absolutely nothing in this world I wouldn't give or do for this woman to keep her that happy forever.

We drove over towards the mall to grab some lunch. It was nice being able to touch Jenna, put my arm around her waist as we walked in, or hold her hand, waiting on our order without concern that someone would see us and say something.

With our stomachs full we headed off for Walmart, the big supercenter kind. I figured we could probably find most things we needed for the house there. Jenna was adorable with how excited she was to shop together for our home. It warmed my heart watching her and knowing it was the start of our life together.

I grabbed a cart and immediately turned towards the home goods section, while she made an abrupt left for pharmacy and personal care. I raised an eyebrow at her in question.

"First things first. There is no soap or shampoo at the house. I can't even believe I'm out in public looking like this," she said, holding up a strand of her hair in disgust.

I laughed. She looked gorgeous to me, but if it meant that much to her, conditioner here we come.

I watched her fill the cart with all her favorite products before asking me what my preferences were. We stocked up on not just soap and shampoo, but deodorant, toothbrushes, and more toothpaste than I thought we'd consume in a year. I teased her, causing her to blush.

When she was certain we had enough to survive, because, you know, the store was only ten minutes from the house, so who knew when we'd get back there, we headed towards home goods.

"Did you take inventory of what was in the kitchen?" she

asked.

"Not really. There are some mismatched dishes and small appliances. I'm sure it's enough to get by on, but we can donate whatever you don't want and buy new," I assured her.

She bit her bottom lip, causing my body to stir. I couldn't help it. She was mine now, and I didn't hesitate as I leaned in and sucked her lip out of her mouth and into mine. She was breathless and her cheeks were heated when I pulled back. She quickly looked around to see if anyone had seen us before smacking me playfully and scolding me about PDA.

I laughed at her as I grabbed two toasters off the shelf, one in black, one in stainless steel.

"Decision time," I said, juggling them back and forth. "Pick a toaster."

She surprised me by reaching for the black one.

"Black, huh?"

She nodded without hesitation. "All the appliances are already black, but stainless picks up fingerprints so easily it always looks dirty to me."

"Black it is," I said, adding it to the cart before pulling a matching black microwave off the shelf.

"I'm pretty sure there's already a microwave there," she informed me.

I crinkled my nose in disgust. "There's just something wrong about a used microwave."

She laughed. "If it's dirty it can be easily cleaned, you know?"

"No, just no. Sorry. I'm not giving up mine in the dorm, and I refuse to use the one left there. You have a fallout shelter's worth of beauty supplies, so I can have a new microwave."

She laughed and nudged me, shaking her head. "You're so weird sometimes," she teased.

We got through the kitchen aisle before attacking the linens. I left most of that up to her, insisting I didn't care. She picked out blankets and a new comforter for our bed, an extra set of sheets, towels, and even throw pillows for the couch. She fell in love with a particular lamp and so I added two to the mix.

When she reached the candles aisle, I had to tell her no. Apparently the smell of candles was not as awful for panthers as it was for wolves. She looked a tiny bit disappointed, but said she understood before heading off for my second biggest nightmare, cleaning supplies. We made some compromises there, but in the end, it seemed to work out.

We wandered through the food aisles, discussing our favorite and least favorite foods. It turned out to be a wonderful way of getting to know Jenna.

With an overflowing cart and one last stop in women's clothing for her to pick out a few items to keep at the house, we headed for checkout, paid, and headed home.

On the drive back to the house, Jenna's phone rang. She sighed heavily and I could feel her nervousness when she looked at the screen.

"Hey, Tessa," she said, answering the phone. "Yeah . . . uh-huh . . . I know, sorry to worry you . . . I'm not on campus right now . . . Yes, I'm fine . . . No, you have your game tonight and I've got plans out of town this weekend and won't be back till Sunday evening . . . I understand what's expected of me, Tess, but I'm telling you I'm not going to make it to the party, I have other plans . . . It doesn't matter. Look, I'll talk to you on Sunday, have a good weekend."

She hung up the phone and stared at it for a moment. "I wanted to tell her, Chase, but I'm not ready to lose her just yet. We're going to have to keep things a secret a little while longer."

I felt a stab of disappointment, bordering on rejection, but mentally I understood where she was coming from. As I pulled up in front of the house and killed the engine, I pulled her towards me and kissed her temple.

"I know it's not always going to be easy for us. You take however long you need to tell her. We'll be careful on campus, but here, you're all mine." I waggled my eyebrows up and down causing her to snort as she laughed. "Come on, we've got, um, a few bags to take in and put away."

We both turned to look at the overflowing pile of bags in the back of the Jeep and groaned.

The next four hours were spent moving in and getting the place settled. Jenna scrubbed the floors and bathrooms, I hung new pictures she'd picked out and took down old ones we didn't want to keep. We rearranged the furniture the way we wanted it and stocked the kitchen. The pile of donations kept growing as we found more and more things stashed around the house neither of us wanted to keep, especially in the loft. There were four more bedrooms up there and one of them was crammed full of miscellaneous stuff. What the hell were we going to do with four extra bedrooms? My mind began to wander to all sorts of delicious thoughts.

"Look at this," Jenna said, interrupting a scene playing out in my head. I turned to see her holding up an old typewriter.

I laughed. "Guess if the power ever goes out, we can still get our papers written."

When we'd done as much as we could, we both collapsed onto the couch, exhausted. I was starving and suggested ordering pizza, but she was determined we were not wasting all the food we had just bought, and she stubbornly managed to drag herself into the kitchen to cook.

Watching my mate barefoot in our kitchen preparing our first meal in our first home overwhelmed me. I thought my heart would explode with happiness. I knew deep down that life wouldn't always be this simple and perfect, but it didn't stop me from wishing it would be.

My cell phone rang, and I smiled as I saw Kyle's face pop up on the screen.

"Hey, big brother," I answered.

"Hey, yourself. Haven't heard from you in a while, just wanted to check in to make sure you're attending classes and keeping your nose clean."

"Ha ha ha, very funny. I'm the least troublesome of the entire family."

He laughed, but conceded it was the truth. "Seriously, everything's good?"

"Yeah, why?"

"Just been worried about you. You ever sort out that issue with the feline?"

"Jenna, Kyle. Her name is Jenna."

"Jenna, huh? It's serious, isn't it?"

"Yup."

"How serious?"

"Kyle, she's my true mate."

"So, panther, is it?"

"Yeah." A sinking feeling hit my stomach. "You got a problem with that?"

"Dude, if she's your true mate, you know I might not understand it, but of course I wouldn't have a problem with it. I'd never deny anyone their one true mate."

I let out a breath I hadn't realized I was holding. "Good."

"That serious? You thinking about completing the bond with her?"

"I'm not thinking about it, Kyle," I said, trying to relay to him the full impact of what I was trying to say.

"Shit, you already bonded? I'm your Alpha and you didn't think to call and tell me?"

I laughed. "Technically, Alpha,"—I exaggerated the name—"I have seven days to tell you, and it just happened."

"Something like that doesn't just happen, Chase."

"I don't mean it like that, I mean literally, Kyle, it just happened yesterday." Before the shock of my words could fully sink in, I figured I might as well disclose it all. "Oh, and we bought a house, so we've been a little busy the last twenty-four hour."

"You what? You seriously bought a house? Why? I thought you were just looking for a place to rent."

"Because I want to spend time with my mate," I said matter-of-factly. "And I didn't like any of the rentals available."

"Then you put a sock on your doorknob. You don't run out and buy a house."

"Well I did, and I'm happy for it. If you have some free time you and Kelsey should drive up and check it out. It's a nice place and we have plenty of room. We'll be here another two years, Kyle, it just made sense. Plus, her family isn't exactly going to be thrilled with her taking a wolf for a mate."

"You're telling me. King Lockhardt is pretty vocal on his stance of interspecies dating, let alone mating. He's going to flip when he hears one of his panthers bonded outside his circle—pure bloods and all that."

I flinched. "Yeah, about that, it's a little worse than that."

"What?"

"Um, okay, so Jenna isn't just some panther, she's Jenna Lockhardt. Her dad is the King." There was silence on the other end. I gave it a moment and nothing. I thought maybe the call had dropped, but looking down, it still showed connected. "Kyle? You still there?"

"Tell me this is a joke, Chase."

I growled. "I would never joke about something like this."

"Chase, please tell me you did not mate Lockhardt's daughter without seeking permission first."

"Why would I do that? We both know he wouldn't have granted it."

"Chase!"

"Don't Chase me, Kyle. She's my one true mate, so I have every right to bond with her. There's nothing he or you can do about it. If you can't support that, then fine, we don't need you in our lives."

I had never once considered that my family wouldn't back us one hundred percent. The pain and hurt that caused was almost unbearable.

"Simmer down, pup. That's not what I meant. It's just, dammit, Chase, do you have any idea the interspecies shitstorm this could stir up?"

"She's well aware her father will likely disown her. We're keeping things quiet through the remainder of the semester, or as quiet as possible to give her some more time with her sister."

"I'm not talking about disowning—I'm talking about an all-out war, Chase."

I hadn't even considered that as an impact. "I'm sure you're just overreacting, Kyle."

"Just, keep a low profile, while we come up with a plan, okay?"

"Yeah, okay, if that's what you think is best. I had planned on bringing her home for spring break. Is that okay? I want to introduce her to the family."

"Yeah, man, of course that's fine. And Chase?"

"Yeah?"

"Congratulations man. You must have balls of steel to go through with this, but I'm really happy you found your true mate, even though she is a cat."

I laughed. "Thanks, bro," I said, hanging up the phone.

Jenna looked at me sadly. "Not as happy about our bonding as you expected, huh?"

I looked up at her, knowing she had been listening to my conversation. “It’s not that. Actually, he was happy for us. He’s just worried about your dad.”

“My dad? Why?”

“Kyle seems to think he could cause some trouble and take it out on the pack.”

“What? He wouldn’t. At least I don’t think he would do anything that extreme. Never speak to me again, yes, but beyond that?” She chewed on her bottom lip.

“Hey, don’t worry. Jenna, I’m serious, you can’t stress over what he may or may not do. If anything happens we’ll deal with it, one step at a time.”

She nodded and collapsed onto the couch next to me, snuggling into my side. I knew that as long as we had each other, everything else would work itself out.

I skipped my Thursday classes and when we got word that our graphics class had canceled, we blew off our Friday classes, too. I knew we couldn’t make a habit of it, but right then it was what we needed.

The remainder of the weekend seemed to fly by and by Sunday afternoon we were both in denial that we had to return to school. The cabin was far better than I had ever hoped. It was secluded and quiet. We had enough land to roam freely in our animal forms whenever we felt like it, as we had the night before with only the crest of the moon to light our way.

If I didn’t want to dress at all, that was okay. I had spent most of the weekend naked as the day as I was born. No fear of someone walking in on us, or even coming to the door. We resided in our own perfect bubble without prejudice or worry and we would always have it as a safe haven to just love openly and freely.

I knew the life we were creating together would be wonderful, but we also still lived in a world that wouldn’t always see past our differences. My fraternity brothers loved Jenna and enjoyed having her hang out at the house, but even they thought we were only friends, because in our world, cats and dogs didn’t mix beyond that.

A part of me didn’t want to return. I had tasted something sweeter and I didn’t want to give it up. Sleeping without Jenna tucked into my side or sprawled out across my chest seemed cold and empty. I wanted to be with my mate.

We could have petitioned for a mated room. We weren't the first couple at the ARC to bond before graduation, but to do so would be to confess what we'd done. I was okay with that. My family knew, and they were the only people I truly cared about. I knew if my frat brothers couldn't get past it, then that would be okay. I'd be okay without them, but Jenna wasn't ready to risk losing her sister.

I didn't know how we were going to pull it off. Our combined smells alone would tip off anyone near us. My wolf would naturally put off a scent alerting other male wolves that I was newly mated. It warned them of potential instability and aggression. How would everyone not see it just in the grin I couldn't keep from my face? I knew I'd do anything Jenna asked, but hiding our bond was going to require Academy Award-level acting skills I wasn't sure I possessed.

Jenna's phone rang again as I was locking the door behind us.

"Tessa," she said. "That's the eighth time she's called today. I know she's just worried about me, but she's driving me nuts."

"It's not like you to run off alone for a long weekend, or skip classes. After a couple weeks, hopefully she'll get a clue and calm down."

"Or she'll never let me out of her sight again," she groaned.

"Not an option," I said adamantly. "Keeping to ourselves during the week will be hard enough. There's no way I'll survive through the weekend without you."

She grinned and rose up on her tippy-toes to plant a kiss on my lips. "I won't last that long either, though it does help knowing you will be just as miserable."

I groaned. The woman was going to be the death of me.

We got in the Jeep and drove mostly in silence. I held her hand, not ready to let her go. When we pulled up to the lot closest to her house, I parked.

"Promise you'll call me tonight when you're settled. I know Tessa will drill you hard before then and I get you need time with your sisters, too, but call me before bed, regardless of how late it is."

"I will. I promise." She looked out the window sadly, then, sighing, she leaned over and chanced one last kiss before leaving the

Jeep. At the edge of the woods and the path that led to her house, she turned and waved before disappearing.

The moment Jenna was out of sight I felt an emptiness that I hadn't expected. My chest ached at her loss. "Pull it together, Westin," I scolded myself aloud. "She's been gone less than a minute."

Still, I knew that even that short of time was too much. How was I going to survive most of the week? I was already counting down the seconds until calculus class when I could see her again.

I parked the Jeep in my usual spot as close to the house as possible and walked the short distance. Opening the door and entering, I saw some of the guys were strewn out across the living room couches playing Call of Duty. I didn't see Matt, and felt bad for being grateful for it. I knew he'd be the one to make a big deal of my disappearance.

"Hey, Chase is back. Missed you this weekend, man. Epic party with the panthers!" Damon said.

I just nodded and quickly headed for my room. Opening and closing the door behind me, I moved to collapse on my bed when I heard rustling to my right.

"What the hell?" I yelled, seeing a chubby new kid on my roommate's bed quickly shoving bags of chips into the nightstand drawer.

"Hey," he said when the drawer was closed, though he kept looking at it and then back at me like he thought I'd make a move for his chips or something. "You must be Chase. I'm Chad. I just transferred here. I'm your new little brother. We're going to be roommates!"

Jenna

Chapter 16

I was struggling to keep the smile off my face even though nerves were fluttering in my stomach as I approached the house. I had this vision of being ambushed and questioned the second I walked in. Could I keep it to myself?

Bonding with Chase made me feel like an entirely different person. Still me, just more. I was stronger, more alive and confident than ever. Would they notice? Did it show on the outside as much as that change felt on the inside?

My heart was pounding in my chest as I reached the front door and slowly turned the knob to enter. To my relief, or maybe even a little disappointment, no one was around in the main living areas. Realizing I could just slip into my room undetected, I quickly made my way down the hall. As I opened my bedroom door I was grateful I didn't have to deal with it all just yet.

I had taken a shower that morning, but Chase and I had made love three times since then and I was certain to be covered in his scent. I didn't want to wash his scent off, but I knew it was the prudent thing to do. I threw my backpack on the bed and started to head for the bathroom.

"Where have you been, Jenna? I've been worried sick." Tessa said as I screamed. I hadn't seen her sitting at my desk when I walked in. My heart was suddenly pounding even harder in my chest than it was before I entered the house. I didn't know that was even possible.

"Tessa, you scared me half to death!"

She looked slightly remorseful, but she still radiated irritation.

"It's not like you to just disappear like that. You're supposed to be the responsible one here."

I snorted. "Me? The responsible one? Tessa, no one cares what I'm doing. I'm not up to something devious or bad. I just wanted to get away from this place for a few days. And look, I'm really tired, I still have some homework to finish up and I desperately want a hot shower first."

She crinkled her nose as I passed. "You do need a shower, but we will be talking about this more. Daddy is video calling at six. Please don't miss it. You've been skipping them a lot lately. He always worries about you so much. And truthfully, Jen, I like it here. I don't want him relocating us again if he feels he can't trust you. Don't worry, I won't say a thing about this weekend. Next time you want to just go off by yourself, please just at least tell me first. I really do worry about you."

As Tessa exited my room it dawned on me that my sister assumed I had been alone all weekend. She had not even thought to question that. I had always been a loner and needed my downtime to recover in solitude. Maybe getting away with Chase on the weekends wouldn't be that hard. I'd just let Tessa know I needed some alone time.

I quickly showered, feeling refreshed. As I dried off I noticed a few faint bruises on the inside of my thighs. My muscles ached, but the heated water had helped. I knew I was coming down from my Chase Westin high and I realized I was sore all over. I had gotten the workout of my life and knew I'd be paying for it over the next few days, but I couldn't help but smile back at the memories we'd created. Yeah, it was worth it. He was worth it.

Chase's optimism about our future was contagious. For now, he was going to remain my little secret, yet a part of me wanted to scream from the rooftops, "Chase is my mate, so back off, ladies!"

I glanced at my clock as I dressed. Five thirty. I didn't have long before Daddy would be calling in. I grabbed my backpack and pulled my books out to get to work. By the time Tessa knocked on my door I was feeling back to my normal self and two questions away from finishing the last of my calculus assignment.

"Hey, is it time?" I asked.

"Yeah. Can we take it in here?" she asked. "My room's a mess and I don't want to hear about it."

I laughed. "Sure."

Relieved, she settled onto my bed with her back against the wall and her feet dangling over the edge. I finished the question I was working on before joining her. Her laptop sat on her lap with the program already open and waiting. She placed her head on my shoulder and sighed.

"How're your classes going?" she asked me.

"Mostly fine. Calculus is a little tougher than I had expected, but I'm managing. I absolutely adore my photography class and graphic design. I know I shouldn't. It's not in the plan." I rolled my eyes above her head. "But I really love them."

"Daddy's wrong on that, you know. I'm happy you found something you love. I'll admit, I was pretty upset when he forced me to uproot and follow you here. All the girls were, actually."

"Tess, I never asked—"

She cut me off. "I know. We all know. We may be identical, but Daddy's always been more worried about you. He's always watched you closer, made certain you had more security. You never ask for anything, so when you asked for this, it wasn't a surprise he granted it. I've acted out for years trying to get his attention, but it's always been you he pays the most attention to. 'Tessa, watch after Jenna. Keep her away from boys, especially those lions. Remember, she's your charge,' he had said, before we left to come here. He checks in every week to see how you're doing. I'll admit, sometimes I'm resentful about it, but mostly I just feel sorry for you. I'm glad you're taking your life into your own hands. Screw him! You live for you and be happy, Jenna."

There were tears in my eyes and I hugged my sister close. She had no idea how much her words meant to me. I had always known they put the pressure of watching me on Tess. It had been a thing when we were little. "Tessie, watch after Jenna. You're the big sister, it's your duty," anytime we went anywhere.

I had even felt sorry for her because of it. It strained our high school years and I was well aware of the resentment towards me from all the sisters over the transfer to Archibald Reynolds.

"I never asked to uproot any of you, Tessa. I'm so sorry. I know you hate the responsibility of watching out for me. And it shouldn't be your job. I'm a grown woman capable of making rational decisions, even if they aren't exactly as Daddy would like."

I grimaced, thinking of Chase. Would Daddy blame Tessa for allowing it to happen on her watch? I hadn't thought about that as a possibility. I knew the consequences of my decision for me, but I hadn't given any thought as to how they would impact her.

"It's okay, Jenna. I am your big sister."

I groaned. "By two minutes, Tess! Two minutes. For all we know, they could have mixed us up in the hospital or anytime afterwards and I'm really the oldest."

We both laughed. It was true. Our parents had been terrible at telling us apart our whole lives. As two distinctive personalities evolved it was harder to mix us up, but as babies and little girls, it was a frequent occurrence.

"You are not. I am. I will always be the oldest even if you are the more mature and responsible one." She elbowed me in the side and grinned.

The computer flashed and a phone jingle started. We both stared at each other and took a deep breath. Daddy. Tessa hit the connect button and we plastered identical fake smiles on our faces.

"Hi, Daddy," we said in unison as our father's face filled the screen.

"There're my beautiful daughters."

Edmond Lockhardt was a tall, thin man, graying with a receding hairline. He wasn't extremely overbearing to look at, yet his eyes always held a lethal quality to them. He was observant and sharp as a whip, probably the smartest person I'd ever met. Fully grown men cowered under his scrutiny.

I had never been afraid of my father, but I was now afraid of the impact my mating Chase would bring to my family. Tessa and I had a strained relationship, largely because of our dad, but she was still my best friend.

"Jenna, I hear you switched a few classes?"

"Yes, Daddy, I did. I'm studying photography and graphic design. I love it!" I tried to infuse as much excitement as I could muster. I would not have had the courage previously, but I was still riding a bit of my Chase high, plus the nearly three thousand miles of distance helped boost my confidence.

His nose scrunched up and I fought back a hysterical laugh. I knew that was a sign of how displeased he was. It was one I rarely saw, though I had seen plenty of others shake in their boots at that same face. It both terrified and elated me. I was going to piss my father off when he found out what I'd done, just knowing that had a weird sort of freeing elation. I didn't have to please him any longer.

"Well," he finally said. "I suppose it could be worse. I assume you're doing okay in your 'real' classes too?" He put major emphasis on the word "real" that had me cringing.

"Yes, Daddy, I'm doing well in all my classes." I couldn't help but emphasis "all" in the same manner. Tessa shot me a glare with questioning eyes, wondering what I was doing and begging me to shut up.

"How about you, Tessie?" Daddy had always called her Tessie. I knew she hated it, said it made her sound like a little girl.

"I'm doing surprisingly well in all my classes too, Daddy," she confessed.

I realized she hadn't once asked me to cover for her or do any of her assignments since we started the semester. I had been so wrapped up in my own drama that I hadn't even realized that I had missed hers.

Fortunately, Daddy was interrupted and had to end the call early. He told us he loved us and hung up. We both stared at the screen in silence. I got the feeling Tessa felt as relieved as I had that the call had ended. I think we both got off the hook a little easier than expected.

"I can't believe you told him about the new classes and how much you enjoy them. Way to go, Jenna," my twin said proudly.

A warmth started low in my stomach. A very different warmth than Chase usually invoked. I tried not to blush even thinking it. This one spread and filled me with pride.

"And you," I added, trying to quickly change the subject, "you're actually going to class and keeping up okay? You haven't once asked me for help here."

She blushed. "There's a really cute TA in my history class who is tutoring me. I don't know. He's different, Jen. I don't want to be the normal dumb rich girl around him, so I'm actually trying." She laughed. "Who'd have thought, but I'm understanding everything just fine. I have B's in all my classes right now, and aside from his guidance, no one has helped me get them."

I could hear the pride in her voice and I reached over and hugged her. We weren't exactly the touchy-feely kind of family, so my gesture surprised her, though she didn't pull away.

"I'm so proud of you, Tessa! I always knew you could do it. If I'd had any doubts, I'd never have helped you to begin with."

She laughed, "You little brat, you did not."

"Did too, you just needed to believe in yourself. That's all."

"When did you get to be so smart?"

We both laughed. I had always been the smarty pants of the family.

"Hey, did you hear? Anita is dating Matt Williams," Tessa told me.

"What? Seriously? I mean, I knew they liked each other and had, um, messed around."

"Sex, Jenna. It's called sex," she said, laughing at me. "It's okay to say 'sex.' Actually, several of the girls are having sex. If Daddy only knew. He'd be furious! There's not one single male panther at this school. What was he thinking?"

I blushed at how candid she was being and she rolled her eyes at me.

"Jenna, we're all adults here. What's really the harm in it?"

"I know that, Tessa. I'm not judging. I think Anita and Matt are great together. I'm just wondering what happens if they decide to mate."

I was testing the waters with my sister. I knew it was a dangerous game, but I couldn't seem to help myself.

Tessa sobered. "Jenna, you know what Daddy expects. Not just from you and me, but all of us here. He would demand Anita return home if he found out about Matt, and he's a freaking jaguar. Same species, different colored fur. But Sidney, she's seeing a lion, and um, the TA I was telling you about? He's uh, he's a tiger."

My eyes widened in shock and my mouth dropped open. Of all the felines, my dad hated the lions the most, but tigers were a close second. I had heard whispered rumors of why over the years, but it had never made any sense to me.

"A tiger? Tessa, are you sure that's what you want?"

She nodded. "He's a really sweet guy. I mean, don't get me wrong, he's not like my true mate or anything. I'm not going to bond with him, but I really like him and we get along great. I'm hoping he asks me out, and maybe we could go to spring formal together." She stared at me with her big eyes looking so vulnerable. It was like looking in a mirror at myself, or how I'd imagine I would look when I finally got up the nerve to tell her about Chase.

I smiled and she slowly relaxed. "Tessa, I think that's great! I know everyone here thinks of me as some goody-goody, but honestly, I just want you to be happy. I don't care if this guy is a tiger, a lion, or a camel, or a jackal even. As long as he treats you right and it's what you want."

"Thanks." I thought she genuinely meant it, too, but then she laughed again. "A camel? A jackal? Really Jen? A freaking dog? Even I have some standards."

I cringed. "Anita's dating a D.O.G," I pointed out.

"Not the same."

"No, but all of his fraternity brothers are canines, and they've been sniffing around this place since we arrived."

"Sure, they're pretty to look at and fun to flirt with, but I can't imagine any of the panthers actually falling for one of them. Can you even imagine?"

I faked a laugh alongside my sister. Yeah, I could definitely imagine, but I wasn't ready to tell her that. I wasn't sure if I ever would truly be ready for that confession.

Tessa finally said good night and left me alone in my room. It wasn't even seven yet and had only been about two hours since I said goodbye to Chase, yet I missed him terribly and wanted to talk to him. I picked up my phone and texted him.

JENNA – Miss you already.

My phone dinged almost immediately.

CHASE – Miss you more.

JENNA – Dinner?

I bit my bottom lip as I waited for his response. I knew I was pushing my luck and we were bound to get caught, but I couldn't help myself. I wanted my mate.

CHASE – On campus or off?

I rolled my eyes and grinned. I could already imagine where his thoughts were headed… home.

JENNA – better make it on.

CHASE – Fine, but I have a study date in 30min. □

I smiled. I hadn't thought about that. It was Sunday and we did have a standing study date in the library every Sunday evening.

JENNA – Subs?

CHASE – Perfect. I'll pick them up and see you there.

I put down the phone, still smiling, but jumped at a knock on my door.

"Who is it?" I asked

The door opened, and Anita peeked her head in without asking.

"Hey, Anita, what's up?"

"Where were you this weekend?" she asked in a hushed voice as she closed the door behind her.

"I just needed to get away," I lied.

"I saw Tessa leave earlier. Did she, um, tell you?"

"Tell me what?"

Her eyes filled with worry. "Oh, uh, sorry, I thought she'd have told you. You see, I, um, I'm sorta, I'm sort of seeing Matt Williams," she finally blurted out.

"Oh, yeah, that. She told me."

Before I could continue, she started talking a mile a minute. "I wanted to tell you first, but you weren't here, and it sort of slipped out at the party last night. I had one too many beers and I blabbed. Plus, he was here, and he just looked so yummy, I couldn't keep my hands to myself. Oh no," she said, her hands flying to her mouth. "I'm sorry. I didn't mean to give too much information. I can't imagine what you're thinking right now. Do you hate me?"

I laughed. "Slow down, girl. I could never hate you. I think you and Matt make a really cute couple, and as long as you're happy, I'm happy for you."

She let out an exaggerated sigh of relief and collapsed on the bed next to me. "Thanks, Jenna. I didn't really care a ton about what the others thought. Ayanna is furious, tainting the family name and all that, but the rest I could care less. I just really hoped it wouldn't screw up our friendship."

"Anita, that's crazy. Why would it?"

She shrugged. "I don't know. I mean you'd think people would be more open-minded at a place like the ARC, but really, we've both been cold-shouldered by people already, and I know your dad will flip if he ever finds out."

"I wouldn't sweat it. I mean your sister is one thing, but the others are just jealous, Anita."

"What do you mean?"

"Oh come on, Matt Williams is hot, girl. There's bound to be plenty of girls mad he's off the market. I wouldn't take it personally."

"Wow, um, thanks, Jenna. I really hadn't thought about it like that."

I started packing up my backpack and glanced at the time. I needed to hurry to meet up with Chase.

"Hey, where are you going?"

"It's Sunday," I reminded her. "Study group with Chase. Are you and Matt coming tonight?"

She blushed. "Um, yeah, about that. No, we're not. We were only really using the time to see each other."

I laughed, knowing that's the only reason this study group ever got started, so Chase and I could spend time together without questions.

"But hey, if you don't want to be alone with Chase, of course we'll come."

I snorted. "Why would I care about being alone with Chase?"

I was glad my back was turned to her when I realized what I'd just said. Luckily, she didn't seem to take it that way at all.

"You're right. Chase is a great guy and I know he'll watch out for you. You know, there are plenty of ladies on this campus who would kill to be in your shoes."

"Huh?" I turned to face her, trying to understand what she was saying.

"I know you and Chase have fooled around a little bit at least for that stupid challenge, but then again, what ovary holder on campus hasn't?" I struggled to bite down the roar threatening to escape me at the insinuation about my mate as she continued. "But really, I mean you guys are like actual friends and you spend a lot of time together. I'm just saying. I know you don't think of him like that, but Chase is pretty hot, too. Not as hot as Matt, but still h.a.w.t., hawt! Most girls would be super excited to spend some alone time with him in the library." She waggled her eyebrows up and down comically and I laughed, shoving her aside and leaving on that note.

Shaking my head, I left her sprawled out on my bed. "See you later Anita."

"Where are you headed?" Tessa called after me as I was

leaving the house.

I turned to see her. "Oh, hey, Tess. Nothing exciting, it's Sunday night, I have study group."

"Oh right, I forgot. Well, have fun." She waved and closed the door as I turned and walked across campus.

Chase was already in our regularly booked room with subs, chips and sodas laid out on the table for us. He looked over my shoulder as I closed the door behind me. I never felt like we had privacy in the room because you could see out into the library so clearly, but I did know we were entirely alone and those on the other side of that two-way mirror couldn't see us.

"Where're Matt and Anita? I grabbed extras figuring they'd be here."

"Apparently she and Matt went public."

"Public what?"

"They're dating, Chase. As she put it, they don't need to pretend they are studying to see each other now, so she'd rather not even bother. Anita hates the library, she only ever came to see Matt."

"Oh," he said, a wide grin breaking out across his face. He reached over and snagged me around the waist and pulled me into his arms. "That is great news to me." He leaned down and kissed me. I was already breathless when he pulled back, still grinning.

We sat next to each other at the table, close enough to touch, and started to eat. The need to be near him was so much stronger than I had ever imagined it would be. Just sitting there in the same room, our knees touching under the table while talking amiably, made me feel so peaceful.

That peace was interrupted by a knock at the door seconds before it flew open.

Chase

Chapter 17

"What the hell?" I said as my head whipped around towards the door as Matt and Anita walked in, with Chad behind them.

"I thought you guys weren't going to make it," Jenna said.

Matt gave me a sincere apologetic look. "We weren't, but um, Chad needs some calculus help. One of the guys told him about our Sunday night group and he asked to tag along."

"Is one of those for me?" Anita asked, eyeballing the two uneaten foot long cheesesteaks on the table.

"Are you going to pretend you don't want it?" I teased, taking out a salad from the other bag. "'Cause I grabbed a salad just in case."

"Oh God, no! Leave that rabbit food for the other panthers who want to pretend they're human stick figures. I'm past that," Anita assured me.

Matt put his arm around her and grinned. "We had a long talk about that. She's done trying to starve herself on my behalf."

Anita punched him in the arm. "It wasn't on your behalf, exactly."

"Hi, I'm Jenna. Are you Chad?" Jenna asked sweetly.

Shit! I hadn't even thought to introduce them. Feeling like an ass, I made the introductions. "Sorry. Jenna, this is Chad, my new little brother and roommate for the rest of the semester. He just transferred here from somewhere out east. Chad, this is Jenna." I bit my tongue to stop myself from adding *my mate* to the end of that.

"Hi Chad, it's nice to meet you. I just transferred too, at the beginning of the semester. Welcome to the ARC. I hope you find it as awesome as I have."

"Thanks," Chad said. "It's definitely taking some getting used to, but I'll adapt. My family just relocated out here and my dad wanted me to stay close to the family. I wasn't supposed to start until next fall semester, but they made an exception for me. I'm a freshman. I rushed Delta Omega Gamma in the fall and they were able to transfer my membership here. It's certainly been different. D.O.G. isn't really comprised of actual dogs back East."

Anita snorted and Jenna laughed. "Really? I thought Matt was the only non-wolf shifter crazy enough to rush D.O.G. So, what spirit animal are you?"

Chad looked around nervously. I saw him eyeballing the chips and already guessed he had a bit of an obsession with them. I handed him one of the unopened bags and he quickly snatched it from my hand with a thanks.

"I'm, uh, well, I'm a squirrel," he finally confessed.

"A squirrel? Really?" Jenna asked.

"Aww, that's the cutest thing I've ever heard," Anita gushed, causing my new little brother to blush furiously.

"Squirrels are a lot tougher than people think," he said, huffing out his chest in a show of manliness. I bit the inside of my cheek to keep from laughing.

In the brief time since I walked back into my room earlier that day, I had learned plenty about my new roommate. First, he loved chips and he squirreled food away, which I suppose was only natural given he was a damn squirrel. Second, that kid could talk. I didn't think I'd ever been around a person who talked as much as Chad. But, I also found him to be a truly good guy. He might not be the coolest dude on campus, and he was quirky as all heck, but there was something nice and easygoing about the kid, too.

I may not have been thrilled with the interruption to an evening alone with my mate, but I hadn't exactly planned on having her all to myself anyway, so I tried not to let it disappoint me.

"Chad, have a seat. Join us. There's extra subs and a salad," I told him, grinning at Anita.

"You really wasted money on a salad?" she said.

I laughed. "That's all you ever eat," I argued.

"Fine, but no more. I'll eat the stupid salad. Chad can have the other sub." She pouted.

"It's okay. If you don't mind, I'd prefer the salad. I don't eat a lot of meat," he assured her.

"Oh, well, okay then," Anita said, passing Chad the bag with the salad.

"So, what spirit animals are you all?" Chad asked.

Jenna answered for all of us. "Matt's a jaguar. Anita and I are panthers, and Chase is a wolf."

I liked the way she said wolf, more assertive than the others. I noticed a touch of pride in her voice. The thought of her being proud of my wolf sent an extra jolt of thrill through my body. I was very thankful we were seated at the table in that moment. It was pathetic how even something so minor registered as acceptance and excited me. It was even more embarrassing how much I craved any signs of approval from Jenna. I could just see my damn wolf in my head wagging his tail happily.

I couldn't let my emotions get away from me. Being so close to Jenna in front of others was dangerous, especially one of her sorority sisters. I switched subjects and got down to business. For the next hour we concentrated on calculus as I pushed aside every bodily urge that came from being so close to my mate and not touching her. Every now and then she would brush her leg against mine or squeeze my leg under the table. Just the knowledge that she felt that need to reach out warmed me all over and got me through an exhausting hour of study.

In some ways, being bonded now helped calm my wolf; in others, it made things so much worse. I didn't feel the aggression towards others that I had felt during our mating. I didn't want to rip Matt's head off when he accidentally bumped into her, and I had faced those demons previously. No, now I just wanted her on a deep level, all the time.

As if the desires weren't bad enough to keep tamed without embarrassing myself, my brain chose the most inopportune moments to flash up pictures of Jenna naked beneath me in my mind. I blamed it on my wolf, on my animal instincts that only wanted our mate in that way, but it probably wasn't fair to blame it entirely on him. I felt like a horny teenager who just couldn't get enough of her.

It had been more than an hour since I last tasted her sweet lips and I was going to lose it if our friends didn't wrap up and leave soon. I couldn't let myself think about the long cold night I was about to face alone.

I don't know if Matt got some sort of brotherly hint or it was just time, but a few minutes later he rose and stretched and admitted he was done for the night. Of course, the others followed his lead as he and Anita left with Chad in tow.

The second that door closed behind them and I was certain they had left, I scooped Jenna up in my arms and kissed her. It was like breathing fresh air. She eagerly kissed me back as my hands roamed to the hem of her shirt. I needed to feel her soft, warm skin beneath my hands.

The opening door didn't register in my brain until I heard a gasp and a throat clear behind me.

"Um, sorry, Anita forgot her purse," Matt said, grabbing it from the chair and trying to pull her from the room as quickly as possible. I opened my eyes just in time to see the truly apologetic look in his eyes.

"But . . . What . . ." Anita was trying to talk, but was obviously shocked by what they'd walked in on, as Matt was busy shooing her out, away from the room.

"Wait," Jenna finally said. Her voice was solid despite her racing heartbeat. "Anita, come back. We need to talk."

"It's okay, Jenna. I got this," Matt assured her.

"Uh-uh," Anita said, pushing her way back to the room. "Girl, spill it. I thought you just messed around with him that one night to screw with our sisters." She perched on the top of the table and waited with unabashed excitement.

"Where's Chad?" I asked Matt.

"He said he was heading on home."

I let out a breath of relief. "Good, thanks. Make sure the damn door's closed."

"Did you know about this?" Anita asked, turning on Matt.

"Um, no. No, I didn't. Okay, so I sort of suspected, but I didn't actually know."

"Jenna? What's going on?" Anita asked, turning her attention back to my mate.

I couldn't help the overwhelming need to protect her as I stepped between the two girls to shield Jenna from her friend.

"Whoa." Anita clearly noticed my aggressive stance. "Calm down, dog-boy, this is girl talk time right now."

"It's okay," Jenna said, sounding far calmer than I certainly felt. This was the one thing she absolutely did not want to happen, at least not this soon.

"You're sure?"

"I'm sure," she said, and then shocked me back down a peg as she rose up on her tippy-toes to press a kiss to my lips before taking a spot on the table next to Anita.

"Please promise me you won't tell anyone about this, Anita. Not yet. I know it's all going to come out before the end of the semester, but I'm not ready to lose Tessa or any of you just yet. I need some time to prepare for it."

Anita laughed. "Jenna, you're not going to lose us. To be honest, there're a few of our sisters that will be relieved to hear this. I mean, come on, you're Jenna Lockhardt! No offense but you've never done anything wrong or disobeyed your father even once in your entire life."

Jenna flushed red in her cheeks. I started to protest, but she held up a hand to stop me. "She's right. I've always done whatever it took to please my parents and everyone else."

"Exactly." Anita turned to me as if to say "I told you so." "So what makes him worth going against your dad's orders to not fraternize outside our kind?"

I watched Jenna turn beet red, but she raised her chin in determination. "I don't know how to say this any other way. Anita, Chase is my true mate. My one true mate."

I'm not sure anything had ever shocked Anita more. Her face started to turn an odd shade of purple and her eyes nearly bulged out of her head, then it contorted and she started to laugh.

"That can't be," Anita said with certainty.

"I know it sounds crazy, but it's the truth," Jenna said.

Matt was eyeballing me, equally as shocked as his girlfriend.

"A feline and a canine? True mates? I've only ever seen that happen one other time," Matt said solemnly. "It didn't end well, and it won't be easy, Chase, if you decide to pursue it."

"There's no "if" to it, Matt. Jenna's my true mate. That's it. You know how my family feels about true mates," I reminded him, since he knew how I felt on the issue already.

"Do they know?" he asked.

"Yeah. They haven't met her yet, but my family is well aware of the situation and looking forward to seeing her over spring break. The pack has been notified too and so far, so good," I told him.

"Wait, you officially notified your pack?" Matt asked, even more shocked than before, and I just grinned and nodded.

"What does that mean?" Anita questioned.

Panthers didn't follow the same rules as wolves. She didn't understand the pack or our customs. I grimaced slightly, realizing Jenna needed more information on that too—on the off-chance someone challenged her. I didn't expect to go through the trials. What other wolf besides me would want a panther for a mate? But I hadn't thought about it from her side. Someone could challenge Jenna for me. I bit back a growl at the thought just as Matt yanked my shirt collar down. He and Anita gasped simultaneously at the sight of my bond mark.

Anita reached over and revealed the same on Jenna. "Are you insane?" she shrieked. "Your father is going to kill him, and probably still disown you after he's dead."

Jenna turned white. Clearly, she hadn't thought things through from my side regarding her family situation, either. We still had some talking to do. I vowed to do just that over the weekend at the cabin. We were so distracted and wrapped up with each other and settling in that we didn't exactly do much talking about that sort of stuff.

"It's going to be fine, Anita," I said, trying my best to sound confident.

"I can't believe you're bonded, and to a dog," Anita said to Jenna. I didn't take it personally. We already knew the prejudices we'd have to face.

"You won't tell anyone?" Jenna asked hesitantly.

"Who would believe me?" Anita laughed. "Of course I won't tell anyone."

"And, we're cool?" she asked.

Anita rolled her eyes. "No, never." Both girls cracked up laughing as I frowned. But they hugged, so I could only assume it was some sort of inside joke. "When? Where?"

"Oh, that, well, it sorta happened this weekend," Jenna confessed, blushing.

"But you were gone this weekend," Anita challenged.

Matt cleared his throat, grinning. "So was this guy."

"Where did you go?" Anita asked.

"Home," I said, smiling.

"But you said you weren't introducing her to your family till spring break," Matt pointed out.

"Not San Marco. Our home."

"Could they come over sometime?" Jenna asked.

I gave her a look that caused her to snake her arm out and smack me in the stomach. I didn't bother dodging it. She never had to ask me for permission to invite someone over to our home. Her face told me she heard what I was thinking loud and clear.

"Where?" Anita asked.

"We have a cabin only about ten minutes off campus. It's gorgeous and amazing. I can't wait to show you." Jenna squealed with delight as she told Anita about it.

"You bought her a house?" Matt asked, rolling his eyes. "Dude, you are so whipped."

"You have no idea," I confessed.

"Damn, I hope Anita doesn't think I'm buying her a house, too."

Jenna

Chapter 18

I couldn't believe how well Anita was handling everything. It gave me unfounded hope that maybe things would work out after all. Still, I scolded myself every time my mind went there. Thinking like that would only lead to more heartache down the road. I knew without a doubt that Daddy would never accept my mate.

Throughout the week she even covered for me on a few occasions so I could get some extra time in with Chase. Anita and I had always had a sort of friendship. With our sisters being best friends, we were constantly thrown together. I guess I had never really seen what a true friend she was to me until all this came out.

"Hey," Anita said as we were sitting in the café having tea between classes on Thursday. "Some of the girls are heading out of town this weekend, some conference or something. I wasn't really listening. Are you going?"

I shook my head. I knew what she was talking about. Tessa had mentioned it to me, but I had just seen it as a weekend at the cabin with Chase that wouldn't be scrutinized.

"Did you already make plans?" she asked.

I shrugged. "Not really any plans, just hanging out at the cabin this weekend. Why? What's up?"

"Oh, nothing really. I just wanted to see if you and Chase wanted to do something with me and Matt. I mean the girls know about me, but I figured with most of them away we could go out and do something together. I think it would be fun."

"We could do that, but off campus. Too many eyes and way too many people know him for on campus," I sighed. *And too many gossips around*, I thought.

Just in the few days since our bonding, word had spread that Chase Westin was off the market. Apparently he had gone to some social with his fraternity on Tuesday night and a couple girls tried to come on to him. He had repelled them, explaining he wasn't interested, but they weren't taking no for an answer. One of them tugged on the collar of his shirt and exposed his neck, and my bond mark. It had been the talk and shock of the entire school, but he hadn't once mentioned who his mate was, just confirmed he was mated and off the market.

A part of me was grateful he had abided by my request to keep it to ourselves, but a part of me wanted nothing more than for him to claim me publicly and let every female in a hundred-mile radius know he was mine.

It had been a tough week just being apart from him, but to have to listen to "Chase Westin this . . ." or "Chase Westin that . . ." or "Did you hear about Chase Westin?" everywhere I turned was grating on my last nerve.

Our last Friday classes had been cancelled. Calculus was a study session only class, which I didn't need thanks to Chase. Graphic design was an online assignment while Professor Stone was snorkeling in the Bahamas. And the photography instructor was currently on bed rest with complications due to pregnancy.

I was ready to get away from the ARC and thought for a minute about seeing if I could take the Jeep and head to the cabin a day early. Then I remembered Anita had a car too.

"Hey, you're done with classes for the day, right?"

She nodded.

"Want to get out of here?" I asked.

"Sure, what do you have in mind?"

"I've just handled as much of this place as I can take this week. I'm ready to go home." Anita's eyes widened, trying to assess the situation. As if on cue, a group of Thetas sat down in the booth behind me.

"Still no word on Chase Westin's mate?" one of them said.

"No, we think maybe she doesn't go to the ARC. He was out of town all last weekend," said another.

"I just can't even believe it. He was always so much fun to play with," the third added as the others agreed.

Anita got up. "Come on, let's get out of here." As soon as we were out of earshot she added, “I don’t know how you’ve put up with that all week.”

“It hasn’t been easy,” I confessed.

We walked the short distance to the lot where her car was parked. Once we were settled in and on our way, she cranked up the music and we jammed along with the radio. It felt carefree, and tension started rolling off me as we headed for the cabin.

As we turned off the road and drove up the long driveway, something felt off. Anita looked over at me with concern, feeling the shift in my emotions. I couldn’t quite put my finger on it, but my panther was suddenly very agitated.

She parked the car, but I stopped her from turning off the ignition. I looked around. Nothing was obviously out of place, or at least that’s what I thought at first—on closer inspection, I noticed the front door was cracked open.

I didn’t hesitate. I picked up the phone and called Chase.

“Hey beautiful, what’s up?” he said, and I could hear the smile in his voice.

“I think someone’s in the cabin, Chase. The door is cracked open, barely, but it looks like it from the car at least. Everything here feels wrong. I don’t know how to explain it, but it’s creeping me out.”

“You’re at the cabin?” he questioned.

“Yes, Anita and I wanted to get away for some girl time, so I thought I’d show her around.”

“Do not get out of the car, Jenna. I need you to listen to your panther. If she’s giving warning, there’s a reason.” He sounded calm, but there was an edge to his voice I didn’t recognize. “Help is on the way. Just stay in the car. Drive over to the mall or something if you need to. I’ll be there soon to check it out.”

As soon as we hung up the phone, Anita asked, “What’s going on Jenna?”

“I don’t know. Probably nothing. I’ve never been out here by myself and I’m sure I’m just spooked,” I confessed.

“So, this is the cabin?” she asked.

I nodded.

“Jenna, this place is huge. It’s not a cabin—it’s a really big house, and literally feels like we’re in the middle of nowhere. How many acres came with it?”

"Thirty-some. They were selling it with three, I think, but Chase wanted the raw land surrounding it, too. It gives us a place to run if needed, without worry of being seen, like the forests surrounding the ARC."

"So cool! I swear you have the coolest boyfriend ever," she squealed. "He bought you a house, Jenna."

I was starting to relax, not seeing anything alarming. Her words rang true to my heart and made me happy.

That feeling was short-lived, though, as the front door of my house opened and a man I didn't know walked out. He walked right up to the car and knocked on the window, motioning for me to roll it down. I only cracked it, not even enough for him to stick a hand through.

"Hey, can I help you? You ladies lost or something?" the stranger asked, and the tone of his voice and the way his sharp eyes washed over me caused goosebumps to break out over my skin, and not in a good way.

"No," Anita said. "We're just waiting on a friend."

I shot her a glance of warning.

"Here?" the man asked, and I could see him shift uncomfortably from one foot to another and look back towards the cabin.

I took in a deep breath, smelling the air around me. Shifter. I knew this guy was a shifter. That thought on a normal day would have provided at least a little comfort, but in that moment, it only heightened my anxiety.

"My friends and I are meeting a buddy here, too. Why don't you ladies come on inside and wait where it's warmer?" the stranger said with a gleam in his eyes.

I glanced back to the front porch and now saw four other large and equally strong men watching curiously. I shuddered, realizing we were dealing with a small pack of something—my panther told me they were dangerous.

I needed to warn Chase.

"It's fine. We're good here. Chase should be here anytime," Anita told him, and I wanted to punch her, or duct tape her mouth shut.

"Chase called a few minutes ago and said he was running late," the guy added, not missing a beat. "Come on inside. I'm sure he won't be long."

"It's okay, really," I assured him. "We're fine here. And"—I looked down, grabbing my backpack and pretending to look for something—"shoot, I left my calculus book back at the house. Do you think we could run back and grab it?" I asked Anita, pouting.

At least she finally seemed to catch on. "Again?" she asked dramatically as she rolled her eyes. "So, what's your name?" she asked the stranger. So much for her catching on.

"Stan," he said, only hesitating slightly.

Anita strained to look at the men on the porch. "Is that Jack?"

That seemed to really throw Stan off. He stuttered as he finally managed to get out a "Yeah."

"Tiger, right? He's dating one of our sorority sisters I think. He's a TA over at Archibald Reynolds, right?"

I vaguely remembered Tessa mentioning she was dating a tiger, a TA from one of her classes, which suddenly made me stop and rethink things. Could these guys really be that bad then? But what were they doing in my house?

The man that must have been Jack walked over curiously. He stared down at me with obvious shock.

"Tessa, what the hell are you doing here?" Jack asked.

"What the hell are *you* doing here?"

Jack turned red in the face and uncomfortably shifted from one foot to the next. "I'm meeting a few friends here, that's all."

"Well, I'm meeting some friends here," I told him.

Stan seemed to have wandered around the other side of the car towards Anita. Jack motioned for me to roll the window down as he squatted next to the car. Against my internal warnings, I did.

Jack leaned in through the now-open window and moved to kiss me on the lips. I turned my head at the last second so he got my cheek instead. I couldn't stomach the idea of any other man's lips on me. My panther roared in my head, but I fought back for full control. It disgusted us both, but he thought I was Tessa and something told me that was a good thing.

He appeared to nuzzle against my cheek as I clearly heard him whisper, "Babe, I don't know what you're doing here, but take your friend and get the hell away from here. I'll call you as soon as I can. You just have to trust me on this."

I pulled back and stared into his eyes and nodded.

"I have to pick up my books. No sense in a study group without books. We'll be back in a few," I assured him. "Come on, Anita."

I plastered a smile on my face and waved at both him and Stan as I whispered hurriedly "Go, go, go"s to Anita, who I was relieved to see obeyed as she put the car in drive and headed back the way we came.

"What is going on?" she demanded.

"I have no idea," I admitted. "I don't know who those guys are, but they're up to no good. I can feel it, and that Jack guy thought I was Tessa and warned me to get away from there. I need to call Chase back."

I picked up the phone and dialed his number. He answered on the first ring.

"Hey, any change?" Chase asked, sounding out of breath like he'd just been running.

"Yes. There is a pack of at least five tigers camped out in the cabin. Tessa is dating one of them and he thought I was her and warned me to get Anita and get out of there. Something's not right with them, Chase. I don't know how to explain it. It's the way that guy named Stan was watching us, like we were the tastiest steaks he'd ever seen."

A loud growl erupted through the phone. "We're coming, Jenna. Get out of there and I'll let you know when it's clear to return."

"Okay, okay, are you sure? Should I just call the police?"

"No, sweetheart, this is something I need to handle."

"Chase, please, no! There are five of them at least. I don't want them to hurt you." I was fighting back hysterics as tears pricked my eyes.

"Have a little faith in me, mate. I'm coming fully armed. By the time the sun rises, you'll never question your safety in our home again. I promise you that. Now go, and wait for me. I love you."

"I love you, too."

Chase

Chapter 19

After Jenna's first call I had made a few of my own. I met my brothers back at the fraternity house. Not one of them questioned me, they all just acted. I explained the layout and perimeter and that Jenna was really spooked by something that I needed backup to investigate.

After Jenna's second call, I decided we needed to go in with fur. We had almost arrived before her final warning. Tigers. And they were trespassing on my territory. They were about to learn a lesson they wouldn't soon forget, but first I made a quick call to Kyle to explain the situation. He had enforcements arriving by helicopter, but they would be about an hour out. I already knew they would miss the action, but needed their help to secure my land.

We parked the cars at the front entrance, eight in all. If they had come by car, there was no way they were leaving by my driveway. All Delta Omega Gammas were there and ready. When you went after one of us, you got the whole pack. Never in my time at the ARC had the call of brothers been invoked for anything more than a meeting or party. I knew I'd have to tell them all about my mating to Jenna, but that was a small price to pay for the loyalty and support they each had already shown me without question.

"Okay, so word is there's a pack of at least five tigers camped out at my house," I told them as they gathered around.

"Your house?" Brett asked.

"Yes, I bought a cabin. I'll explain all that later, but right now there is a pack of tigers that spooked my girl and copped a squat on my place. I don't have a good feeling about this," I explained.

"Your girl?" Brett asked again. "The rumors are true?"

"Look, I promise to explain everything once my territory has been secured. This is happening with or without you guys. Are you in or not?" I asked in frustration. I didn't want to tell them that I needed them to watch my back before I killed someone, because both my wolf and I were pissed. Jenna should never, under any circumstances, be afraid in our territory, and I had heard the fear in her voice through the phone.

Damon stepped in. "Calm down, Chase. We're here. We are Delta Omega Gamma. We are brothers, and we have your back no matter what." Heads all around started to nod and a little of my tension eased.

"Thank you, my brothers." Next, I gave them information on the layout of the house and the surrounding land.

"Let me take the lead, Chase," Chad requested. To say I was shocked would have been an understatement. "People always underestimate the little guys. I can get on the porch undetected. If they open the door, I can get inside and wreak havoc in record time. Even get them all out of the house for you guys to surround. Let me help. Let me do this."

I didn't need to be asked twice. I nodded. "If you're sure, man, we'll take your lead on that and wait for them to exit the cabin."

Chad grinned and there was an unsettling hint of mischief and evil there. "No one does wild squirrel better than me."

The rest of us divided into small groups. Everyone began to strip and leave their clothes by the vehicles before shifting into their respective animals. All but Matt and Chad were some form of canine. Matt's jaguar was impressively bigger than several of our brothers, and then there was Chad.

I had never seen Chad in his animal form, but even knowing he was a squirrel shifter could never have prepared me for the sight before me. Chad was the fattest squirrel I had ever seen. The kid was chubby in human form, but I didn't even know how he could stand on his tiny squirrel feet because he was so fat, let alone fight.

Even more shocking was when he turned and nodded my way before taking off so fast I had trouble tracking him when he hit the trees. How in the hell did that roly-poly creature move so quickly?

Brett, already in his coyote form, started to laugh. He

sounded and looked more like a hyena, but soon others were laughing, too. Shaking our heads, we started to part. Two groups were heading to the back of the house in case the tigers came out that way, while two more groups were setting up on either side of the front of the house. Basically, we had groups spread out around all four corners and ready to close in.

I was at the front and to the right, closest to the front door. I watched as Chad jumped up onto the front porch. He scurried around and scratched at the front door just enough to get the tigers' attention. It seemed like an eternity, but finally the door cracked open and a head peeked out. I didn't recognize the man, but he was big, easily six foot two and I'd guess pushing two-fifty. Five of them that size and I'd have been on the losing end by myself, but there were thirty-eight of us now and we'd easily take them down.

"It's just a squirrel. A fat, lazy squirrel looking for food," the man yelled back into the house. "Hi, there. Shouldn't you be hibernating, little fella?" The big guy spoke to Chad like he was a small child.

The next thing I saw was when Chad leaped into the air and wrapped his fat arms and legs around the dude's face. He screamed, and Chad jumped off of him, flying in the air and through the open front door. There was lots of banging and squealing and soon four more men came running out the front door.

It wasn't even two minutes later that Chad, back in his chubby human form and entirely naked, waved from around the side of the house. No one else was inside. He signaled the others at the back to close in. Five large canines and one fierce-looking jaguar came walking in a line of battle. Five more rounded the corner on the far side, when the tigers finally noticed.

They started to rush back into the house, but Chad in all his naked glory stood on the front porch with a baseball bat in hand. The sight was so comical, it was downright scary.

"I really wouldn't if I were you," he warned, but two of the men turned and took off at a full sprint heading for the driveway.

I howled and the rest of my brothers moved in to surround them. The two who made a run for it, didn't get very far before rejoining their brothers. Four of the guys shifted to tiger form, shredding their clothes in the process. The fifth put his hands up in surrender and backed up to the porch.

"I'm tired of their games. I don't want any part of this," the man said, sitting down on the porch steps.

"So why were you guys even here?" Chad asked him.

"This place has been abandoned for a long time. I've settled into the area here, but the others are just passing through. They use this place to crash whenever they're in town. I told them something smelled different this time. So why are you guys here? And what the hell is a squirrel doing with this pack of mutts?"

Chad laughed. "Can't you see the resemblance? These are my brothers!"

The man shook his head in annoyance.

"I'm serious," Chad continued; "My fraternity brothers. We all go to the ARC. Chase just bought this place last week and you and your buddies apparently upset his girl. Wolves are pretty territorial, and he's really pissed."

"I teach over at the ARC. My girl showed up here with a friend earlier. I told them to get out of here. These guys, well, they tend to find trouble. We've done a lot of terrible things over the years. Some really bad, I won't lie. Then we were incarcerated for years and—" He shook his head as a shudder wracked his body. "I don't want to talk about it, but I'm never going back there again. My brothers, they just don't seem to have learned anything and are running wilder than ever. I don't know what to do about it," he confessed. "Which one is your friend who owns this place?"

"Big, black, scary wolf taking the lead." Chad pointed to me and I briefly shot him a look. Having to stand there and listen to the two of them prattle on was not helping the situation.

I stared down the biggest of the tigers as they all walked in circles within the perimeter we held. I could see from their movements they were used to fighting together. They were trying to intimidate us, but it wasn't going to work.

I tried to calculate the time. Kyle was coming with even more reinforcements and judging by what I'd just heard from Chad's conversation with the tiger that surrendered, we needed to not only get them off my property, but contain them.

For the first time in my life, I wished there was a jail for shifters. Sending them to a regular prison seemed like the cruelest punishment possible, as they'd never be able to shift while there. That alone could drive a sane shifter crazy, and I suspected these tigers weren't entirely on the sane side.

I had thought I was overreacting by calling in all my favors to run off a couple tigers squatting on what had been a mostly abandoned cabin in the woods until a week ago. My agitated wolf and my heightened temper, knowing how scared they had made Jenna, led to this. I hadn't thought they were going to fight back. I simply wanted to intimidate them off my land and ensure they wouldn't consider returning.

I had been wrong. These guys were looking for a fight. The gleam in the eye of the biggest one told me he would enjoy it, too.

He lunged in my direction, but I held his gaze and didn't budge. He tested a few others and to my relief, none of my brothers backed down, though a few began to snarl. When they moved towards Matt, his jaguar roared, causing one of the tigers to back up. It was their first sign of weakness. I could work with that.

Studying them more closely, I noticed that the two milder ones kept looking back to the man on the steps. I still wasn't sure if he was setting a trap I'd regret, or genuinely wanted no part of it. I only hoped that if it came down to it, Chad would keep him occupied long enough for us to snare him within our circle and not take an attack from behind.

In the blink of an eye, everything changed. The lead tiger lunged my way, but this time he didn't stop. He went straight for my throat, but I was too quick for him as I rolled us both sideways until I was on top with the advantage. It was clear he did not like being pinned on his back.

The circle tightened and despite protests and attempts, my brothers would not let the remaining three pass and assist. I snapped my teeth and snarled then I growled in warning when the tiger tried to squirm from under my hold.

I didn't want to hurt the guy, but neither would I back down if he persisted. We were in another standoff. I felt him loosen his grip and relax beneath me. I knew it was a trick and pretended to let up some, too. The second I did, he pushed back full force, as I had expected.

He was stronger than I estimated, and managed to get to his feet. We circled each other. He roared, but all it did was piss off my wolf even more. I had to fight to maintain control and not fully give in to my wolf. If I did, I knew I would kill this tiger. I growled back and watched the fur on his neck stand up.

He made his move to attack and I sidestepped him. He shifted direction and knocked me to the ground, but I was back on my feet before he could advance further. He tried to come in low, but despite the incredible size of my wolf, his tiger was much larger, giving him no advantage there. He tried to go high and come at me from above, but that was easy to roll away from.

Steadily and slowly I moved us towards the house, cornering him at the porch and protruding bay window. He spit and snarled when he realized what I had been doing, and then he made his first direct attack. I barked for the others to hold back, leaving him to me, even as his large paw swiped at my hind leg and made contact that caused me to howl out in pain.

The fight was on. I bit out, catching his front right arm as he moved to strike again. He snarled, pulling back. That gave me time to steady my feet. My leg was throbbing, but I pushed aside the pain and instead channeled it towards the tiger.

He was injured from my bite, so I went for his left side. I missed his arm but landed a chunk out of his side. He growled and hissed back. Still cornered, he had nowhere to go. The fear in his eyes was evident and my wolf had tasted blood. I gave a menacing growl that had him backing up even further against the house.

That's when I noticed the commotion around us had stopped.

"Stan? Just give it up, man, we'll find a new place to hang," said one of the three tigers my brothers had trapped who was now standing naked—still surrounded, but surrendered.

The tiger I was fighting roared in anger. He was alone, trapped, injured, and scared. I took a step back to give him a little space. He seemed to be more subdued, but I didn't know how much of it was for show.

The standoff finally ended when his body shook and he shifted back to human form. My leg was injured pretty badly, so I didn't want to shift back yet, as we heal faster in animal form.

"Who the hell are you?" he spat out, obviously still in anger.

So much happened all at once in that moment—whirring sounds from above indicated helicopters arriving which were Kyle's reinforcements, and lastly, out of nowhere, a beautiful panther appeared. Of course I knew instantly it was Jenna. Her violet eyes gave her away, but more than that, I'd know my mate in any form.

Seeing me injured didn't sit well with her. She roared and hissed at Stan, positioning herself between us to protect me. She was the scariest beast I'd ever seen, and even Stan cowered in response.

Boots on the ground came running.

"Stan," I heard a stranger's voice say from behind me, and I watched the large man fold in fear.

"No, please, no. Don't let them take me," he begged.

"I think it's time you and I had a little visit," Jacob Winthrop said. I had never met the man before in person, but I had spoken to him briefly on the phone over the holiday break when he'd called the house looking for Maddie, Liam's mate. The man had a very distinctive voice, one you didn't forget.

"Chase," another voice boomed from behind me. I turned around quickly, putting my back to the tiger for the first time. I knew that voice; it was Kyle, and I was safe. Even still, I felt Jenna guarding me from behind as she continued low hisses at the man.

My fraternity brothers were mostly scattered now. I saw several walking back towards the cars, some in their skin and some still in their fur, no doubt going to get their clothes.

I stared at Kyle and motioned my head towards the house.

"Go on, we've got this," he told me.

I turned back to Jenna and nuzzled the side of her face. She stopped hissing and looked at me. I nodded my head towards the door. She reluctantly followed. Chad opened the door for us and we walked in and headed to our bedroom before shifting back to human form. Most shifters were perfectly comfortable with nudity, but I had absolutely no desire to show off my mate in that way to all my brothers, both of blood and fraternity.

"You really did bring in the full cavalry, huh?" she teased as she opened a drawer and took out an outfit we had bought the previous weekend to leave there. She grabbed some clothes from my drawers too and tossed them on the bed.

"I thought I told you to stay away until I gave the all clear," I scolded.

"I tried. I just couldn't sit there and do nothing and think about what may or may not be happening. I was envisioning the worst, and from what I walked in on I'd say it wasn't too far off. What if something had happened to you? What if you'd been hurt? I would never have forgiven myself."

I hadn't thought about it from her perspective, I just needed to know she was safe. I took a step towards her and grimaced as pain shot up through my leg. I looked down. The wound had already closed and looked like it was days old, but it was still red and very sore.

"You're hurt?" she questioned, rounding the bed quickly to examine my injury.

"Jenna, it's fine, really. Another few hours in wolf form and it would be entirely gone."

As she looked around the cabin, I could tell she was questioning more than just my injury.

"Princess, don't. Don't overthink this. I know I overreacted. I just couldn't stand the thought of anyone scaring you in our home. This is our territory and I had to defend it. I didn't really expect them to fight back. I'm glad now I did overreact. That big one, Stan, he knows Jacob Winthrop. He was terrified of him, Jenna."

"I noticed. Who's Jacob Winthrop?" she asked.

"I don't really know, aside from that he and his wife took Maddie in when she ran away. That's Liam's mate, wife, whatever. I remembered Maddie as Lily's friend growing up. She's from a different pack so I never saw her all that often. They're four years older than me, so I never really hung out with them. I got to know her and her son over Christmas break. Not all of her story made sense. Like, I know Jacob was basically her adopted father and they were close, but Jenna, he's human. I'm certain of it, so how does he know Stan? It doesn't make sense."

"He came with your brothers. I saw him get off the helicopter with the one you called Kyle, Chase. I'm assuming that's your brother, at least. You guys sorta look alike."

I smiled and nodded. "Yeah, Kyle's the Alpha of our pack now. He'd definitely have his reasons for bringing Jacob Winthrop with him. Right now, I don't much care, as long as you're okay."

She closed the gap between us and wrapped her arms around my waist. "I'm okay as long as you're okay."

Jenna

Chapter 20

I regretted leaving the property almost immediately. Anita had refused to take me back and instead, drove to campus despite my protests. I sulked for only a few minutes before heading back out and walking to the far side of the campus where the woods began. I had faith that once I'd shifted, my panther would know exactly how to find our mate.

I had been right. We kept mostly to the trees where we could, or silently racing across open spaces, when certain the coast was clear. It hadn't taken nearly as long as I'd thought it would to get back to the cabin.

I was shocked at the sight I saw there—so many shifters all in one place. They were in their fur and a group of canines were surrounding three large tigers. Jack was sitting on the front porch casually watching and chatting with a very naked Chad. Scanning the area, I recognized Matt's jaguar mixed in with the canines. There were several solid black wolves, but I couldn't determine exactly which one was Chase.

Then I heard a howl that caused my stomach to drop. I knew it was my mate. There was no question about it. I raced across the field, and as I rounded the side of the house, I saw him. The large man who had scared me earlier was now cowered in the corner. Another man stood over him and Chase was limping as he guarded this new stranger. Anger I didn't know I was capable of surfaced. I hissed at the naked man and bared my fangs at him.

When Chase turned his back to the man, I kept my eyes glued on him. It felt right guarding my mate. It made me feel powerful with Chase by my side, just like it felt right to be enveloped in his strong arms now.

I knew there was no place I'd ever feel that safe. I squeezed him closer, trying to reassure myself and my panther that he truly was okay. The smell of desire filled the room and I laughed, smacking his backside. He was definitely okay.

"Chase, there are dozens of men outside waiting for you. Don't even think about it."

"What?" he said, pulling back and looking down at me with an innocent grin. "Honestly, I can't help it. Their smell is in our house. They invaded our territory. I have this all-consuming need to mark every inch of this place, starting with you, my beautiful mate."

A knock at the door made him tear his gaze away from my eyes. I wasn't sure how much longer I could have handled his scorching look of desire before acting on it, so in a way, I was grateful to whomever interrupted, but on the other hand, I was quite simply irritated by it.

"Come in," Chase said.

The door opened. "Jesus, Chase. Can you at least try to control it?" Kyle said, referring to the scent my mate was filling the room with.

"No," he said seriously. "I really can't, Kyle."

Kyle just laughed at his discomfort. "Well, you have quite a mess out there. I think we've got it all sorted but need you to confirm a few things and let me know what you want my guys to do."

"Yeah, okay," Chase said, looking reluctant to leave me.

"You must be Jenna," Kyle said, extending his hand to me.

I hesitated only a second before loosening my grip on Chase and meeting him halfway. "I am. You're Kyle, right?"

"That would be correct." He studied me for a moment. "You have a protective nature that's not always common with panthers." He stated this as a fact, not a question. "I noticed it immediately in the way you protected Chase from Stan, even when he was no longer a threat and Chase had his back to the guy."

"Just because he was in human form didn't alleviate the threat."

"You'd be correct, though I fear he posed more of a threat to you than your mate."

I blushed, taken aback by how easily he called Chase my

mate. A noise just outside our bedroom door kept me from dwelling too much on it.

The door burst open as Liam walked in carrying a woman I didn't know.

"Take it down a notch, dude. I need somewhere to lay Maddie down. Can I use your bed?" Liam asked. Chase nodded. I could see he was still battling a territorial thing.

"Hey, Jenna," Liam said. "This is my mate, Maddie. Do you think you can do me a favor, and stay with her for a few minutes while we sort something out?"

"Sure," I said. "What's wrong with her?"

"Panic attack. Sweetheart, I need you to just keep breathing. This is Jenna, Chase's mate. She's going to stay with you, just listen to her voice and breathe. In and out." He encouraged me to continue chanting with him.

"In and out," I said.

He nodded and left her side. "It's them, Kyle. And if we don't get them out of here now, all hell is going to break loose. I will kill them for what they did to her. Do you understand me?"

I shuddered at the lethal threat. There was no doubt in my mind that he meant it.

"Shit!" Chase said. "Are you telling me that one of those guys out there is Oscar's father?"

"Yes," Liam said through gritted teeth as the brothers left the room in a hurry.

I was suddenly alone with Maddie. "Keep breathing, Maddie. In and out, just like Liam said."

She was gasping for air now but starting to calm down. "I'm sorry," she managed to get out.

"Whatever this is, you have nothing to apologize for. I'm certain of that. Those guys creeped me out pretty good earlier, too," I said, holding her hand and stroking her arm in what I hoped was a soothing manner.

She growled, but not in a way that made me jump back. "Did they hurt you?" she asked, no longer struggling for control.

"No, just spooked me a little. They apparently were using the cabin and something about them just creeped me out. They acted like they knew Chase, but I didn't believe it. Jack, one of the tigers, he warned me to get away, so I did."

"My friend Anita was with me and we went back to our sorority house and I called Chase to explain what was happening on the way. He said he'd take care of it, which he obviously did. I just couldn't wait around without knowing he was okay and came back anyway."

She nodded, calming down some. "I'm glad you did that. I don't know why one of them would have warned you, but I'm glad you listened. It's Jenna, right? You're Chase's girl?"

I blushed again and nodded. Anita and Matt were the only ones I'd ever said anything to, so having my mating as basic, everyday conversation was completely foreign to me.

She studied me for a bit and when she seemed satisfied with whatever she saw there, she started talking again. "Those Westins, they love fiercely and with all their hearts. Once you're family, you're family—period—no questions asked. I know that Mary, Chase's mom, worries things will be difficult for the two of you. Don't let that discourage you. She worries about everything for everyone. Westin Pack opened their arms to me and my son, Oscar. He's different, too. Half wolf, half, um, tiger. One of those striped beasts out there is his biological sperm donor. I thought I had seen them once before, a few months ago. Prior to that I had only seen them the one time . . . the, um, night my Oscar was conceived. They left me for dead when they were done with me."

I gasped and tears stung my eyes at what she was telling me—and the things she wasn't telling me.

"Shhh, it's okay. It was a long time ago. I still get, um, anxious sometimes. I'm sorry you had to see that. It was just a shock. I'm only telling you this because I think it's important for you to understand. If they can overlook my past and accept my son as part of the pack, they'll accept you too, with open arms. That's just how those Westins are."

I cried openly as she voiced my biggest hopes and constant fears. "You, you know I'm not a wolf, right?"

She smiled. "I know. And if there were any doubts in anyone's mind that you and Chase belong together, you put it to rest today. I've never seen any animal look as fierce as you did protecting that boy out there. He's lucky to have you."

We hugged, sharing a new unspoken bond. Chase had told me his pack would accept me, but I had never allowed myself to even hope for that. It was just too much to ask for, but here this complete stranger was telling me her darkest secrets and sharing this message of hope. Hope that maybe Chase and I really could have a normal, happy life together to share with family and friends.

The door opened and Liam walked back in. "Sweetheart, how are you feeling?" he asked her. The love and concern in his voice was evident. "They're gone now. Well, all but one. His name is Jack, and even Jacob swears he's not like the others."

"Was he the one sitting on the steps?" I asked. I didn't mean to interrupt them, I was just curious.

"Yes, that's the one. Do you know him?" Liam asked.

"Not exactly," I said honestly. "I'm going to go check on Chase and give you two some privacy, if that's okay."

Liam nodded.

With my hand still on the doorknob, Liam spoke again. "Thanks for looking after my girl, Jenna."

I smiled back at him. "You don't need to thank me for that, Liam."

"Yeah, I do. I really appreciate it."

I nodded and started to leave the room.

"Hey, one more thing . . ."

I stopped and looked back at where Liam sat on the edge of my bed, caring for his precious mate.

"Welcome to the family."

Tears threatened to fall once again as I smiled in thanks and left, unable to speak past the lump in my throat.

I headed for the front porch, finding the rest of the cabin still empty. As I walked out, I saw Jack standing there talking to Chase and a few other men. He pulled away from the group and headed right for me. In my peripheral vision I could see Chase start to move in defense, but he backed up in shock as Jack threw his arms around me.

"What the hell are you doing here, babe? I thought I told you to leave and not come back," Jack said.

He was worried about me. No, he was worried about Tessa. I knew in that moment that Jack truly did care for my sister.

A loud growl from behind him caused goosebumps to break out across my skin.

"Get away from my mate," Chase said through gritted teeth.

There were a few nearby gasps and people started whispering all around us.

I gave Jack an apologetic smile.

"Tessa, what the hell is going on here?" Jack asked.

"I'm, uh, I'm not Tessa, Jack. I'm Jenna. Tessa's my twin sister. My identical twin sister," I clarified.

"What?" he asked, taking a step back to look at me like I had just sprouted horns.

Chase was quickly by my side. When I reached out for him, I felt his body start to relax at my touch. It was a heady feeling, knowing I had that much power over him.

"Chase, I know you've been acting weird all semester, but you really took a mate? She's not even a wolf. Hell, she's not even canine," Brett pointed out.

"So?" Chase responded, like he had just been asked the dumbest thing in the world.

"Okay, so Chase took a mate. It's not like we all didn't suspect it. You can pay up when we're back at the house," Damon said.

"Pay up?" I asked.

"There's been a pool going for three weeks on the topic. We all saw the signs, though no one could figure out whom. It really does make sense now," Neal added.

"What makes sense about a wolf and a panther?" Brett asked, and then covered himself when arms started flying over to smack him.

"Jenna's cool, it's all good. I can see it," Damon said.

"You can?" I asked in wonder.

"Yeah. He's been sniffing around you for the last few months. You're a great gaming partner, and a nerd, like Westin needs that in his life. I just can't believe you've kept it quiet. Why?" Damon asked, and others seemed to acknowledge their interest in that answer, too.

"Look, we have to keep it quiet for now. Her family isn't going to deal well with having a wolf join the family," Chase said trying to keep things light.

"My father will disown me and forbid me from seeing or talking to my sisters. I knew the consequences and still chose Chase despite it all. He's worth it," I said grinning at my mate to a chorus of obnoxious "awws" from his fraternity brothers. "But if you guys could please just keep this to yourselves a little longer, I'd really like to get through this semester with my sisters."

It was the sad truth of the situation. They all nodded.

"I'm invoking D.O.G. code on this," Damon said. "Chase Westin taking a mate or even seeing Jenna Lockhardt is Delta Omega Gamma classified effective immediately. Am I clear?"

"Yes, sir," they all said in unison, followed by a chanting of "Delta Omega Gamma" over and over as they jumped around, hooting and hollering. Chase grabbed me by my waist and jerked me to him. My eyes were wide when his mouth captured mine to the roar of cheers around us. He pulled back and grinned before looking to the sky and howling. His brothers echoed him.

"Okay, okay, now that that's settled, we need to decide what to do about Jack," Kyle said seriously.

"Take him inside and I'll be there in a minute," Chase told Kyle before turning back to his fraternity brothers.

A group of men passed by, as they escorted Jack inside. The man Chase had said was Jacob Winthrop followed, and I shivered. I wondered where the other tiger shifters were, but I didn't dare ask.

Chase walked down off the porch and I followed him. He wrapped one arm around me and pulled me close to his side.

"I really don't know what to say. Thank you. You guys have gone above and beyond our brotherhood today and I appreciate it more than words can say." He looked down at me and smiled warmly. "We both do."

"I have a question," Chad asked, raising his hand to the snickers of the others. "Where are we?"

"Yeah, I've never heard of this place before," Neal added.

I couldn't help but smile, genuinely smile. We were home. Despite everything that happened today, it was still our home, and I had no doubt in my mind that Chase would do everything in his power to ensure that nothing like this ever happened again.

"If everything wasn't still up in the air with my brothers here and all, I'd invite you in. This is our home. Jenna and I bought it last week, as well as the thirty wooded acres surrounding the house. You guys are welcome to come out for a run anytime," he told them.

"And we'll be happy to host a game night soon for any of you who enjoy getting your butt kicked by a girl," I added.

Smack talk ensued, but in the end, they each in turn hugged me and assured me that a challenge was coming soon. It felt good to talk and joke with the guys. They were important to Chase, and the time I had spent over at the doghouse had been good. They were fun, easygoing, and accepting even before they saw me as Chase's mate and not just his friend. In some ways I felt more accepted by Chase's friends than I ever had with my own actual blood.

Chase tossed his keys to Matt as we said goodbye to the others. "I'll swing by with Anita tomorrow afternoon and drop it back off. Call if you need anything in the meantime."

"Thanks, Matt," Chase said. We headed back inside, hand in hand.

The living area was set up much like a courtroom with Jack sitting on one of my kitchen chairs in the center while being grilled by the others. I quickly noticed Maddie and Liam were not present and could only assume they were still in the bedroom. Patrick was talking. I hadn't noticed him amidst the others before. His Irish accent gave him away even before my eyes found him.

"Jack, why are we to believe you've changed? That you're any different from your brothers?" Patrick asked.

"Look, I've kept my nose clean since the escape. I have a job working at the college. I haven't caused any trouble. Jacob, you know me. Tell them, I'm not like my brothers. Tessa's sister can confirm it, too." Looking at me he added, "Sorry, I don't remember your name."

"Jenna," I said.

"Right, Jenna can tell you."

"Actually, I can't. I'm sorry. Tessa's mentioned you a little, but not much. We don't exactly share things like that." His eyes were pleading me for help and something in their vulnerability made me want to reach out and help him. "I can tell you all, he warned me to get away from here today. He tried to help."

"And, when it came down to a fight, he walked away and refused to join his brothers against us," Chase added.

"He's never been a problem. Being the youngest, he was prone to following his brothers, but given an option he always chose opposite them. Without their influence I'm confident he won't be a problem," Jacob told the group.

Liam walked in and right up to Jack. "I need to know if you

raped my mate. I know you were there. I need to know if you participated in it."

I shivered at the menace in his voice. There was no doubt in my mind that Liam Westin could kill Jack with his bare hands. I had never seen anyone so pissed.

"I'm sorry, man, I don't know who your mate is," Jack said, his voice quivering with nerves.

"I am," Maddie said as she walked into the room. She didn't need to continue, because the second Jack saw her face, he turned white as a ghost and cowered. "I'm Madilyn Collier. You and your brothers brutally raped me and left me to die in a dumpster eight-and-a-half years ago. We met at a concert. You all lured me upstairs to a private box seat room and drugged me. I couldn't move, but I was aware of it all. All—Of—It," she said. There was a deadly silence throughout the room.

Jack started to cry. I'm not sure Maddie was prepared for that as she took a step back and leaned into Liam for support. All eyes were on Jack.

"I'm so sorry. I'm so very sorry. If I could take it all back, I would. What we did to you was unspeakable. I was only fifteen years old at the time. I may have looked older, that's normal for a tiger, but I was just a kid. I had to prove myself to my brothers. They terrorized me about it. Said they had the perfect girl for me to lose my virginity to. I didn't know what they had planned. They got me just as drunk before it happened. I didn't want to do it, but they made me.

When it was over, I ran to the corner and threw up. What they did to you afterwards has left me with nightmares. I've never even been with another woman since. Not even Tessa, and she's the only girlfriend I've ever had, and I can't even bring myself to really kiss her," he confessed.

It was heartbreaking to hear his story and realize he had been almost as much a victim of his brothers, as Maddie had been.

Maddie stared at him. "Why didn't you stop them?"

"I couldn't. I wasn't strong enough to stand up to all of them. You can't possibly understand," he told her.

Maddie started crying and Liam wrapped his arms around his mate. The tension was evident in his shoulders.

"I believe him," Maddie finally said. "I don't think he's a

threat to society without his brothers. I do have one request before you let him go," she told the group before turning back to Jack. "I need a vial of your blood."

"What?" he asked surprised. "Why?"

"It doesn't matter why," she said. "A vial of your blood for your freedom today."

He looked around at the others to see if she was serious. They all nodded in agreement. He held out his arm, accepting her terms without further question. Jacob picked up his bag and dug out the necessary medical supplies. After he drew a small vial of blood, he slapped a Band-Aid on his arm, and told him he was free to go.

"I feel like this is some sort of trap," Jack said.

"It's not," Liam told him. "My mate has given you your life back. It's more than you did for her eight years ago. It's more than you deserve as far as I'm concerned, but I will support her decision and will not track you. I do warn you, though—continue living a clean life and do not make me regret this. You will not be given another chance should our paths ever cross again negatively."

Chase pulled me closer to him and wrapped his arms around me when my entire body shuddered.

I spoke up as he moved to leave. "Do me a favor, Jack. Don't tell Tessa what happened today. I need to tell her in my own way."

Jack looked back and forth between me and Chase as if realizing what I was saying, and he nodded. Jacob and another man I hadn't been introduced to said their goodbyes and left behind Jack.

"Is he safe with them following him?" I asked when the door closed behind them.

"They won't follow him," Kyle spoke. "They will address the other four, though."

"I hate the thought of sending even them back there," Maddie said, suddenly looking and sounding exhausted.

"Back where?" Chase asked.

"You don't want to know," Kyle assured him, imploring Chase not to question things further, so Chase shut his mouth, and didn't ask any more questions.

Chase

Chapter 21

Looking around the room, I noticed only my family remained. Having all those strangers off my land helped me finally begin to relax. I turned and hugged Jenna.

"How you holding up?" I asked.

"I'm fine," she told me. I looked her over as she squirmed under my scrutiny and a light blush stained her cheeks. Satisfied she was okay, I nodded.

"You've met everyone, right?" I asked

"Yeah. Hi," she said awkwardly.

"I'm genuinely sorry we had to meet under such circumstances. We've all been looking forward to your visit over spring break. But regardless, it's nice to finally put a face with the name. I'm not sure how much you know about pack life and hierarchy, but I am Alpha of Westin Pack."

The other men groaned and rolled their eyes.

"No one here cares right now, Kyle," Liam teased.

"What? I'm just trying to officially welcome her to the pack," Kyle defended.

"There's time for that later," Patrick said. "Now, where are you hiding the beer?"

Chase laughed. "Dude, we just bought the place last week. You're lucky we have food."

"Ah, so you've at least been to the messages. Tell me you have some crisps around this place. I'm starving."

"Crisps?" Jenna asked. "I'm not sure what you're talking about. What are the messages?"

My brothers and I laughed. "Sometimes he sounds like he's

speaking a foreign language. He's asking if we went to the store and bought some chips."

"Crisps, not chips," Patrick clarified.

"Chips, dumbass," I told him. "He'll argue chips are fries, not chips. Crisps are chips. It can be confusing at first, but you'll catch on and learn to ignore him after a while," I assured Jenna.

She laughed. I led her over to the couch and we sat down. Liam and Maddie sat at the other end while Kyle and Patrick took the adjacent chairs.

I wished Elise and Kelsey could have been there, and even Lily. I missed my family when I was away at school, but I got so tied up in my own life that I didn't always remember that, until I was face-to-face with any of them.

Jenna rose and headed for the kitchen. She fumbled around the cabinets and then came back grinning. From behind her back she pulled out a bag of chips and tossed it over to Patrick.

Grinning, she asked, "Crisps, right?"

"Ah, a lady after my own heart," Patrick said. "She's a keeper, Chase."

"That's the plan," I assured him.

We ended up ordering pizza as we talked, laughed, and caught up. Maddie and Jenna seemed to hit it off quickly. I was grateful for it and thanked Liam for bringing her even though she hadn't given him a choice.

I was still curious as to why humans were brought in to help, but I didn't dare ask. I didn't know everything that Maddie had been through, but I knew it was bad. Hearing her confessions to Jack had rattled me, and I couldn't stop thinking of Jenna and what I'd have done if they'd have tried that with her. I don't think I would have had the restraint Liam had. I'd have wanted blood. Hell, I wanted blood for Maddie. I knew I'd see nothing but red if that had been my mate.

It was getting late. I watched Jenna stifle a yawn.

"You guys came by helicopter, right? Are you planning on spending the night? It's kind of late to head back home now," Jenna said, thoughtfully.

"I don't think we even thought that far ahead. The helicopter already headed back with the others. We'll pick up a rental and drive back tomorrow. Do you guys have room for us to crash? We can get a hotel if you want to be alone," Kyle said. I appreciated his understanding, as Jenna and I were newly bonded, after all.

"We have plenty of room." She got up and walked over to the laundry room, returning with an armful of freshly laundered sheets and towels. "Let me just change the sheets and make up the beds. There're four bedrooms upstairs. This place is crazy big, much more than we need, but we like the peace and quiet out here. Well, it was peaceful and quiet our first week here, at least before today," Jenna said, exasperated after the day's events. My brothers all laughed.

Maddie jumped up. "Let me help you with that, Jenna."

"Sure," she said, gratefully.

The girls disappeared up the stairs. I watched them go, talking amicably. I felt a sense of peace wash over me. Jenna and I were going to be okay. Any concerns about my family that had tried to infiltrate my brain, were being put to rest seeing the two girls already becoming fast friends.

"She's nice, Chase. You did good, baby brother," Kyle said.

I didn't need his praise, but it sure felt good to have it. "Thanks, she's the best."

"I'll admit, I was a little concerned when we were here last," Liam confessed, "but I was wrong. She's really good for you. You've settled. I can feel the change."

"She'll have you neutered in no time, but it's not all bad," Patrick said, and we all grimaced at the analogy.

Shaking my head, I threw a pillow at Patrick's head, laughing as Kyle and Liam clearly had the same idea. Pillows went flying in his direction.

"How're Kelsey and Zander doing?" I asked Kyle, changing the subject.

His entire being brightened as he went into a ramble about how amazing his mate and son were. I started tuning him out immediately. He was still talking when the girls returned.

"Who's Zander?" Jenna asked, joining in the conversation.

"My nephew. Kyle's kid. He's one year old. You've seen his picture taped to my computer back at the doghouse," I said absentmindedly.

"The little blonde with the curls?" she asked.

"That's him," Kyle said proudly.

"He's really cute. So, the older kid with the dark hair, that's Oscar?" she asked, remembering the pictures I kept taped to my monitor.

"Yes," Maddie said. "That's our little boy, or not so little these days, I guess. He'll be eight this year. It's unbelievable."

I could see Jenna calculating, and putting things together.

"Oscar's the greatest kid on the planet," Liam said matter-of-factly. "Z's a cool kid, but he's still got big shoes to fill."

"I can't deny that," Kyle conceded.

It was nice catching up with my brothers, but I was thankful when they finally decided to call it a night. It had been a long day and I was ready to settle down and be alone with my mate, or as alone as one could be with four sets of wolf ears nearby. I wished I had thought to bring the dampener with me, but why would I? That was supposed to be the great thing about the cabin. No need to be quiet or worry about anyone hearing a thing.

I took Jenna's hand as she said good night and led her back to our bedroom. It stunk of Liam and Maddie, and I had another urge to go mark every inch of the place. It left me restless, and I knew I wasn't going to go to sleep until it was done.

"Sorry," I said. "I really have something I need to do." I didn't want to tell her what I was up to. It wasn't that I was ashamed, but I knew panthers didn't have the same urges and territorial nature as wolves.

I walked outside and stripped, leaving my clothes on the back patio, and shifted into my wolf. My leg had been aching all night and this would be a benefit to help it heal faster, too. I took off at a full sprint to the marker at the edge of the property line. I peed on it and every 500 feet around the property from there. Then I peed a trail back up the driveway and all over the house. I wasn't proud of my actions, but it sure helped to calm my wolf and give me the satisfaction that if any shifter came near my property again, they would know this land was taken. It was something I should have done the second we bought the place.

It had taken longer than I thought and when I shifted back to my skin, I noticed immediately how much better my leg felt. I didn't bother putting my clothes back on, just quietly crept into the house and to my room.

I expected Jenna to be asleep, so she startled me when she

spoke. "Is your leg all better now?" she asked sleepily.

"Much," I said.

I could still smell my brother and his mate on my blanket. Knowing the wild smell of wolf was still strong on my skin, I rolled around on the top cover until their scents were only a memory. Content, I crawled under the sheets and pulled Jenna to my side. She sighed and rested her head on my shoulder.

My pulse sped up the second I realized she was naked and waiting for me. I pulled her further up my body until our faces aligned and I kissed her. I meant to keep it sweet and loving, but my wolf had me in an agitated state for much too long. I had marked my territory and I desperately needed to mark my woman.

She moaned into my mouth as I aggressively ravished her.

When I pulled back to catch my breath, she giggled. "Did you mark the entire perimeter?"

I stared at her, my mouth slightly ajar before dropping my head back on the pillow. Busted. "No comment."

"I'm not sure you should try marking me, too, with so much company and sensitive ears around," she told me.

I stared back at her and laughed. I rubbed my body against hers until my scent covered her. I could smell her arousal when I was done and as I leaned down and kissed my bond mark on her neck and blew my scent on to her sensitive skin, it spiked, filling the room and combining with my own.

"Hopefully they'll be leaving first thing in the morning," I whispered.

We snuggled back down and tried to go to sleep. Much to my surprise, after a bit of restlessness, my body finally relaxed and I was out like a light.

The smell of fresh eggs, bacon, and coffee woke me the next morning. To my disappointment, the bed was empty and Jenna was nowhere in sight. I went to the bathroom, dressed, and followed the scent of coffee.

"Morning, sleepyhead," Jenna said, giving me a quick kiss on the lips and handing me a mug of steaming coffee.

Grateful, I took a long sip, letting the heat seep through my body and slowly revive me. I closed my eyes and sighed.

"Damn, it's been a long time since a cup of morning coffee and a night with a sexy woman was that satisfying," Kyle teased.

"Speak for yourself," Patrick said. "Elise is . . ."

He was cut off with a synchronized chorus of, "Nooooo!"

"She's our sister, you freak. We don't want to hear about your sex life," Liam told him.

Patrick shrugged, completely unaffected. "Your loss."

"Gross, man. It's bad enough I lost my office chair, don't make me lose my breakfast too. Jenna, this looks amazing," Kyle said, trying to change the subject.

It disturbed me that I knew the exact chair they were talking about. I had noticed over winter break that it now resided in E's living room. *Ewww*, I thought. Way more information than I ever needed to know.

Maddie handed out plates that Jenna dished up, and we all sat around our kitchen table. After discovering what Patrick had done in Kyle's office, I wasn't too sure he'd want to hear about what Jenna and I had done at the exact spot his breakfast now sat.

I chanced a look at my mate and when our eyes met, she blushed furiously and I knew she was thinking the same thing. We both cracked up, ignoring the inquiries from the others.

Jenna
Chapter 22

Meeting Chase's family wasn't as weird as I'd expected. I'd already met Liam and Patrick before, but only very casually. That whole night had been a bit of a blur. It was the night Chase realized I was a twin and that he wasn't going crazy, just mixing us up.

My life had been such a whirlwind since then, but getting to spend time with Maddie and his brothers, gave me hope that our future would work out okay. I was envious of their closeness. A part of me wished Tessa and I could be that close.

Kyle and Patrick spent most of the morning securing the land and installing a surveillance system around the house. Liam stayed close to Maddie, who I now realized was pregnant. I wasn't sure how I had missed her protruding baby belly sooner, but they were ridiculously cute together.

Kyle walked back in just in time for lunch. "Damn you, pup. Did you have to mark the entire property line? You're disgusting. I told you we'd secure it for you."

Chase shrugged. "Had to do what I had to do."

After lunch, they said their goodbyes when an Uber car arrived to take them to the rental car they had booked, to return home in. Maddie hugged me close and told me she couldn't wait to see me again. We made plans to get together over spring break.

"Take care of that boy," Kyle told me as he hugged me, too.

Wolves were far more touchy-feely than panthers. It would take a little getting used to, but it didn't feel awkward or uncomfortable, either. Their scents were comforting with similar smells to Chase's, but not exactly.

"Why do you all smell similar?" I finally asked Chase when

everyone had left.

"I'm actually surprised you noticed. Your nose is more sensitive than you let on. That smell is pack. All Westins have a similar scent; it's one of the ways we recognize each other as pack."

"Will I smell like that too?" I asked curiously.

Chase leaned in and sniffed, sending shivers through my body. "Yup, it's a little faint, but I'm pretty sure it's not just me." He trailed kisses down my neck, tickling my skin and making me giggle.

A knock on the door interrupted things before they could escalate. I went to answer it.

"Are we interrupting something?" Anita asked. "You're looking a little flushed there."

I knew I was blushing, but I didn't care. "Come on in. His brothers just left, so no, you weren't, for the record."

"Wow, this place is huge!" Anita said, looking about in awe. Matt was with her but had kept quiet so far.

"Hey, who is it?" Chase yelled from the kitchen as he worked on washing the lunch dishes.

"Matt and Anita are here," I hollered back.

"Hey, man, welcome to our humble abode," Chase said, walking around the corner, then stopping to shake hands and bro hug Matt.

"I still can't believe you bought her a house. You said a cabin. This is not a cabin," Matt said, shaking his head.

I left the two guys and grabbed Anita's hand. "Come on, I'll give you the grand tour."

We started upstairs, four bedrooms plus the office that we already set up with desks and work areas for both of us in the loft. We originally considered each taking one of the upstairs bedrooms for offices, but neither of us wanted to be that isolated from the other.

"I really thought there was no way we needed four extra bedrooms, but we filled three of them last night, so I guess they'll get some use after all," I confessed.

"This is amazing, Jenna. I can't even believe it. I'm so proud of you," Anita said, getting a little emotional.

"You are?"

"Yes. Look at you, you're following your heart instead of

your head. I never thought in a million years you'd defy your father like this."

"I'm not trying to defy anyone, Anita," I said sadly. "I just—I just can't do what's expected of me. It's been kind of freeing actually, not living up to anyone's expectations, but mine."

Anita hugged me. "I just don't want to see you get hurt. Chase Westin isn't exactly the model image of boyfriend. I'm worried about you."

I laughed. "He's not my boyfriend, Anita. He's my mate."

"I know. I think I'm still in shock."

It seemed odd to me that I was more comfortable with Chase's brothers and Maddie than I was with Matt and Anita's visit. My panther was restless while they were there and when they suggested going to see a movie, I quickly encouraged them to go but said I had a headache and wanted to rest instead.

"What was that all about?" Chase asked as our guests left. "Are you okay?"

"Yeah, I'm fine. Sorry. If you really want to see the movie, we can go. I don't know I was just done. I don't know why, but having them here was stressing me out," I admitted. "I don't understand why having virtual strangers here was perfectly fine. I enjoyed having your brothers and Maddie stay, but Anita and Matt just felt off. She's my best friend, Chase, what's wrong with me?"

"Nothing is wrong with you, princess," he said lovingly. "Remember that smell you were asking about? You said my brothers smelled a little like me."

I nodded.

"That's because they're pack, sweetheart. That smell should always bring you comfort. Being part of a pack is very different from what you're used to, but I can already see the signs of your panther reaching out and accepting it. Over the semester you've gone from tolerating my fraternity brothers for an hour or two, to pulling all-nighters playing video games. It's not quite the same there, but wolves do lean towards each other. They are my pack away from home, I guess you could say. That feeling of comfort is only magnified with our actual pack. You'll see when we go home for spring break."

"About that," I hesitated. "Do you really think that's a good idea?"

"Uh, yeah, I do. I think it's really important for us, for you," he said.

"I don't know how to get out of going to Cabo with my sisters," I admitted, biting my lip in frustration.

Chase started to speak and then hesitated. "Is that what you want? Be honest with me, because I can sense when you aren't, you know. Would you rather spend the week in Cabo with Tessa and the other girls?"

I looked up into his beautiful brown eyes and slowly shook my head. "No, I would rather spend it with you."

He grinned, popping out those dimples. "So, are you saying you'd rather just stay home and hang out here alone with me all week instead of going to my parents'?"

I knew he was teasing me, and it made me blush anyway. I also knew the answer was a most definite "YES!" When his grin deepened, I knew he knew it, too, without me having to make the confession.

"Okay, so how about this, a compromise. I already know our Friday classes are cancelled, again, so we'll head out Thursday night and make the drive back to San Marco. We'll stay through the weekend, and then play it by ear. If you want to come home early, we'll drive back on Monday, though Mom may harass us to stay for her Tuesday night family dinner. Just leave her to me if she starts to guilt you."

"Okay, I can do that, except that the girls aren't leaving until Friday and it may draw even more attention my way if I leave before them."

"Fine, we'll leave on Friday as soon as the girls make their exit for Cabo. Deal?"

I nodded, feeling a little relieved. On the one hand I was excited to see his family again, at least those I had already met, but on the other hand I was terrified to meet his parents, especially his mother. I couldn't imagine any mother being happy her wolf son would choose a panther for a mate.

"Don't worry so much. They're going to love you," Chase said, and my eyes shot up to meet his.

"Can you hear my thoughts?" I asked. I knew it was a stage of bonding, but I didn't think it should happen that quickly. Then again, I'd been able to feel his emotions and his location since almost the beginning and that was one of the final stages of a fully bonded pair.

"No, I can't. I hope to someday, but that's one of the final stages of a sealed bond," he told me. I looked at him like he had two heads.

"No, it's not. And we're already exhibiting signs of a sealed bond, Chase."

"We are? Like what?"

I hesitated. Could he really not feel it? "Um, I can feel your emotions, Chase. I can sense your presence and always know where you are. It started happening even before we met, and it totally freaked me out. That's one of the final stages of the bond."

Chase laughed, "Um, maybe we should go through the stages. I think maybe they are different for different animal shifters. That's the only thing that would make sense. For a wolf, emotions and presence are among the first signs of a bond beginning."

"Really?" I said curiously. "Panthers are more touch driven. Our first signs can be the feel of presence, too, but also the physical connection."

"What do you mean?" he asked.

I picked up my knife and pressed the blunt end hard into the palm of my hand.

"Ow," he said, staring down at his own hand in disbelief.

I shrugged. "I knew you were injured before I got here yesterday. It's one of the reasons my panther was so aggressive. I could feel it. That should strengthen over time where if you get hurt it physically hurts me too, but that part takes a lot longer. The sensations begin at the start of the bond."

"This is so cool," he said excitedly. "It's like our bond signs are in different orders but we're getting hit with both at the same time. Telecommunication usually takes longer for us, but it typically happens before physical feelings."

"And for panthers it's the emotional connection that comes towards the end," I said. "So, you can imagine that all this really had me freaked out. That first day of calculus I knew you were there. I could feel your presence and I shouldn't have been able to do that."

"I was looking all over for you. I knew you should have felt my presence and yet you didn't react at all. I scanned that entire room waiting for you to turn around or show some sign of recognition and nothing. I mean I could hone in on your general location, but I didn't understand why you wouldn't react to the mating call."

"I guess because I shouldn't have felt it that way. The mating call for panthers, or so I've been told, starts with a physical connection. You usually have to be in close proximity and it's described as feeling a brush across your skin. My mom always called it the shivers. Like when goosebumps break out on your skin for no reason. I do get that with you too, just the added emotional stuff had me weirded out at first, but I guess if we're each experiencing both of our mating signs, that makes sense."

He thought about it and nodded. "I know that feeling you're talking about. I never really attributed it to the bond though. It's kind of cool how our bond is merging both wolf and panther traits."

The rest of the weekend seemed to fly by. I was grateful for every second I had alone with Chase. When it was just the two of us, life was perfect. Once again, going back to the real world Sunday evening was hard on the both of us. Chase dropped me off in the parking lot behind my sorority house and an hour later I met him in the library for our study group. Matt and Anita didn't show up this time, and neither did Chad, which meant no actual studying occurred in the three hours we had the room reserved—and we made use of all three hours.

There was something about doing stuff in a semi-public place that you were not supposed to be doing that made it all the more exciting. After I left, I wasn't sure I could ever set foot in that room again without blushing. It was like all the stress of the weekend finally came to a head and all we could do was hold on to each other for dear life. Even I could smell the scent of sex in the air as we left.

Two stacks away I heard a giggle so like my own it made me freeze to the spot. Tessa? It had to be her. No sooner had I thought it, than Tessa rounded the corner, pulling down her shirt as Jack stepped out from behind her.

Both their eyes widened, guilt written all over their faces. Looked like I wasn't the only one getting a little action in the library that night. It never dawned on me that Chase's arm was still around my waist until Tessa's eyes turned from guilt to shock as she took in the scene before her.

"Jack," Chase said, nodding.

"Chase," he acknowledged in the same manner.

"You two know each other?" Tessa questioned, still looking back and forth between me and Chase. It was obvious she was trying to make sense of what she was seeing—bad boy Chase Westin with her perfect, do-no-wrong sister.

My heart started beating fast in my chest and I feared I might hyperventilate. Taking a deep breath, I turned towards Chase. "Well, thanks for the lesson, and I'll see you in calculus tomorrow."

"Oh, that's right. You have study group tonight," Tessa said, as if suddenly that made far more sense.

Yet Chase hadn't let go of me. I wanted to smack him for it, but I could feel his wolf on edge, probably responding to my own threatening panic attack.

I pivoted to walk away, but Chase moved at the same time and I crashed into the hard wall of his chest. His arms instinctively wrapped around me as he checked to make sure I was okay.

"Ow," I said without thinking.

"Jenna, look at me." His deep voice rumbled through my body. "Jenna," he said again, this time a little more demanding.

I shook my head, still buried in his chest. "I'm fine. I'm not hurt, just a little embarrassed."

To make matters worse, Tessa started laughing. Jack joined in and I could even feel, without looking, that Chase was grinning enough to pop out the dimples, even if he refrained from actually laughing. His arms wrapped around me as his hand rubbed my back. I started to hug him back and then froze.

No one was laughing when I flattened my hands against his stomach and pushed back, giving him a look to tell him to behave.

"Okay then," I said, nervously worrying my bottom lip. "Tessa, see you later. Jack, good to see you again. And you," I said, looking up at Chase, "see you tomorrow."

I turned quickly and walked away.

I didn't even make it to the stairwell before Tessa caught up to me.

"Wait, wait, wait," she said. "Jenna, stop."

I turned around slowly and tried to look as innocent as possible. Fortunately, that was a face I was used to hiding behind.

Hands on her hips, she asked, "How do you know Jack? I didn't even introduce you."

Crap. Of all the things for her to pick on, that was one I wasn't expecting. "I, uh, I met him this weekend. He thought I was you," I said simply. It wasn't exactly a lie.

"Oh." She seemed to ponder my answer. "But you weren't around campus this weekend, and Jack was visiting his brother and just got back, so where did you meet?"

Jack walked up, then quickly turned and headed back towards Chase who laughed at his quick exit.

I looked back at my sister, still waiting on an answer. I knew I couldn't lie to her. Not telling her was one thing, lying just wasn't in my nature. I couldn't do it.

"Not here, Tessa. Please, let's go and I'll answer whatever questions you have."

She looked back at Chase and Jack, and then nodded.

"Let me just say bye to Jack," Tessa said.

"Okay."

While she went to speak to Jack, Chase came over to check on me. We walked into the stairwell for a little privacy.

"I won't lie to her, Chase. She's already questioning where I was all weekend and how I know Jack. My evasive answer didn't appease her, and let's face it, I'm just not any good at sneaking around. I've never been able to really tell a lie."

"Jenna, it's okay. She's your twin sister. You should be able to tell her anything."

I sighed. "It's not the same for us like it is with you and your brothers. We're just different."

"Do you want me to stay with you? We can tell her together. Whatever you want. Just tell me what to do," Chase said sweetly.

"I don't know if that would be better or worse. I guess I should talk to her alone," I said, still not certain of the decision.

"If you change your mind, I'm only a phone call away. And you will call me regardless once you're done talking, right?"

I rolled my eyes. "Do you really think I'd fall asleep without telling you goodnight?"

He grinned and leaned down to kiss me. I wrapped my arms around his neck and pulled him close, channeling his energy to boost my confidence. Of course, Tessa chose that moment to open the door to the stairwell.

"Oh, um, sorry," she said, stumbling back into the library.

"Tessa, wait. It's fine, come on. We have a lot to talk about," I said, feeling a little more confident.

"You got this," Chase whispered, kissing my temple before releasing me.

I gave him what I hoped was a reassuring smile before turning my focus towards Tessa. Halfway down the stairs I stopped. I didn't want the sisters to overhear us. I wasn't sure where we could go to truly have privacy. I briefly thought about going to Chase's room where he had the dampener, but then I remembered Chad was staying there now and that wouldn't be fair.

Turning back, I saw Chase still watching us from the landing.

"We need a place to talk," I said. "Can I borrow the Jeep?"

Chase didn't hesitate as he tossed his keys down towards me. I caught them mid-air.

"Thanks," I hollered back up to him as we turned and walked out of the library.

Tessa and I walked in silence across campus towards the doghouse. Brett was in the parking lot near the Jeep.

"Hey, Jenna. Where you off to tonight?" He looked back and forth between me and Tessa. "I'm not expected to actually know which one is you and which is your sister, right?"

Tessa shot me a side glance. I knew she was used to being the popular one and I was just "the sister." I could only imagine how she must have felt, like she just got pulled into some weird alternate universe.

"Jenna," I said, waving. "This is Tessa. Tess, this is Brett."

"Hi," she said softly, with none of her usual flirtations.

"Where you ladies off to this fine evening?"

"Not sure yet, just going for a drive."

"Chase actually handed over the keys to his baby?"

I jangled the keys for him. Brett laughed and shook his head, but I was thankful he kept his mouth shut from further comments.

"Drive safe. It was nice to meet you, Tessa. See you later, Jenna."

Tessa didn't say a word until we were both in the Jeep. She turned and looked at me as I started it up. There was hurt in her eyes.

"It's like you have this whole life I know nothing about, Jen. How is that even possible?"

I sighed. "I'm sorry, Tess. I know we have a lot to talk about.

And I promise to answer any questions you have."

I put the Jeep in reverse and pulled out of the parking spot. I headed off campus not certain where I was headed. As soon as we were on the road, Tessa turned her full attention on me.

"Okay, clearly you wanted to make certain no one heard us, and I can sort of guess why. So, spill it. What is going on with you and Chase Westin? Don't think for one second that it has gone unnoticed that he too has been MIA the last two weekends. Were you with him? Are you two like together?"

I took a deep breath, started to close my eyes, then forced myself not to since I was behind the wheel of his baby.

"Um, yes," I said, nibbling on my lip. I was so nervous.

"Okay, so where did you go? Were you just at the doghouse all weekend? Matt and a few of the guys said they hadn't seen him."

"Um, no. We weren't on campus," I said honestly.

"So, what, you take off on romantic weekend getaways with Chase Westin? Did he take you to some exotic place?" Tessa laughed at the thought.

"Tess, this isn't funny. If you're just going to poke fun at me, we can head back to campus."

"I'm sorry, Jen. I didn't mean to upset you. You really like him, don't you?" she asked.

I nodded.

"Oh, Jenna. I truly hope you're having a good time, but you're not exactly a fling sorta girl, and this is Chase Westin we're talking about. He's way out of your league and I don't want to see you get hurt."

"Chase won't hurt me," I told her.

"We all want to believe that when it's happening to us. You think I don't dream about a happily ever after with Jack? I know it's not possible. Besides, Daddy would never allow it. But hey, at least he's a feline. Chase is a wolf, Jenna. Daddy will freak."

"Daddy will freak out about anyone who isn't a black panther and you know it. Jack isn't any better than Chase just because he's a cat. The fact is he's not panther and that's all that matters to our father. I'm well aware of what's going to happen when Daddy finds out about me. I haven't told you about Chase because I didn't want it getting back to him. I didn't want him to take you away from me. I'm not ready to lose you." Tears pricked my eyes as I spoke.

"Jenna, don't cry. I don't care what Daddy says. You're my sister. My twin. You're never going to lose me," she said, causing tears to streak down my cheeks.

"You don't know how much I wish that were true. I love you Tessa," I told her honestly.

Throughout our admissions, I wasn't really paying attention to where I was going until I was turning into the driveway of the cabin. I gasped.

"Where are we?" Tessa asked.

"I, um, I don't know what I was thinking. I didn't mean to come here. Shit," I said. "Well, I suppose if we're going to have this talk we're going all in." Suddenly my reserve strengthened and I was ready to face the facts.

"Wow, look at this place, it's amazing," Tessa said, craning her neck to look at the house.

I parked the Jeep and got out, motioning for her to follow.

"Wait, is this where you've been hiding out with Chase?" she asked.

I laughed. "Um, yeah, for the most part."

I unlocked the house and escorted her in, remembering to stop and turn off the new alarm system Kyle and Patrick had installed. I hesitated for a minute to see how I'd react. Home. I sighed in relief, thankful I felt no fear or worries after the incident with the tigers. I was confident in my mate and his ability to protect our territory.

"Want something to drink?" I asked Tessa as she looked around, not even bothering to try to hide her interest.

"Sure. So, does Chase's family own this place?" she asked.

"Um, something like that," I told her. I knew I was terrible at evading questions.

I went to the kitchen and poured us both Cokes. I suspected it was going to be a long night. I only hoped Tessa kept her word and I really wouldn't lose her after this—at least not yet.

I brought the drinks into the living room and sank down on the couch. The familiar smells surrounding me helped calm my nerves. I kicked off my shoes and sat criss-cross-applesauce with my back to the arm of the couch. Tessa came and joined me. I motioned towards her glass.

"Thanks," she said, taking it and looking a little

uncomfortable. "So, spill it, what's going on with you?"

I took a deep breath. I still hadn't come up with an easy way to say it; so, much like with Anita, I just blurted it out.

"Tessa, you don't have to worry about Chase hurting me, because he can't."

"Jenna, I know you want to believe that, but . . ."

"No Tessa, you're not hearing me. He can't hurt me. Chase Westin is my one true mate. Trust me, I know how crazy that sounds, but it's the absolute truth." I waited with baited breath to see how she'd react. The last thing I expected was for her to laugh in my face. Hurt, I recoiled, pulling my knees up to my chest and wrapping my arms around them as if that in some way would protect me.

"Your true mate is a freaking dog?" Tessa asked, laughing even harder.

Tears silently streamed down my face at the pain in her words.

When Tessa finally caught her breath and looked over at me she turned white as a sheet of paper. "Oh, no, Jenna, I didn't mean it like that. Look there's something you need to know that made me find that funny. I wasn't laughing at you. Actually, I was laughing at Daddy, but I'll explain that in a bit. I'm so sorry. I didn't mean to upset you."

Tessa wrapped her arms around me and held me while I cried.

"I know how Daddy feels about mating outside our kind. You don't know how hard this was to tell you," I sobbed.

"Oh, sissy, please don't cry. I'm so sorry," Tessa said, using a pet name she called me when we were small children. "Look, just because Chase is your true mate doesn't mean you have to accept him. That's your decision to make."

"Don't you think I know that? It was my decision, Tessa, only mine, and I already made it."

"Wh-what are you saying?"

I pulled back and dried my eyes. "Chase is my one true mate, and he always will be, Tess. I've already chosen him. This cabin is ours. We bought it last weekend. It's not wolf and it's not panther, it's just ours. A safe place no matter what happens. Chase wanted that for me, for us."

Before she could respond, my phone rang. I looked down and

saw Maddie's face on the screen. My stomach dropped as I tried to think of what could possibly have happened for her to call me.

"Sorry, Tess, I need to take this," I said, grabbing the phone.

"Hello?"

"Jenna? Hey, it's Maddie."

"Hi Maddie, is everything okay?"

She must have heard the panic in my voice. "Oh, sweetie, I'm sorry. I didn't mean to freak you out. Nothing's wrong. Everything's just fine."

"Oscar, the baby, everything?"

"Absolutely everything. I just wanted to give you a heads up about this weekend. We're kidnapping you Saturday for a girls' day! Elise wanted it to be a surprise, but I didn't want to just spring it on you. She and Kelsey and Lily can't wait to meet you. It's going to be fun, I promise and if it's too much, just let me know and I'll tame it down a notch."

"Oh, okay." I couldn't believe they'd be that excited to meet me. It was a little overwhelming already.

"You sure everything's okay?"

"Yeah, everything's fine, but hey look, I'm talking to my sister right now. Family stuff. Can I call you back later?"

"No need, Jenna. We'll talk on Friday."

"Right. Friday. Thanks for the heads up, Maddie."

"Looking forward to hanging out and getting some girl time in."

"Me too. I'll see you soon."

I hung up the phone. Tessa was staring at me.

"What was that? I don't think I know a Maddie."

"No, you wouldn't. She's Chase's sister-in-law. I'm not going to Cabo this weekend, Tess. I'm going to San Marco to meet the rest of Chase's family."

"Oh. Right. So, you're like serious with him then? You're really going to go through with the bond?"

I pulled my shirt down and exposed his bond mark on my neck. "We've already sealed the deal, Tessa."

I bit my lip, waiting for her to yell or scream or do something with the news. The last thing I expected was the loud squeal that came out of my sister.

"Oh Em Gee!!! You're serious? My baby sister is all

properly mated and everything? What was it like? Tell me everything."

I had seen this side of Tessa with friends over the years. Never with me, though.

"Um, what do you want to know?"

"Did it hurt?"

"No, not really. Not like you'd expect. I mean it stung a little, I guess."

"Oh my gosh, you're not a virgin anymore, are you?"

I shook my head.

Tessa pouted. "You, Anita, what's wrong with me? I'm going to be the last of all our sisters to get laid."

I laughed. Of all the things to worry about, Tessa focused on me losing my virginity before her. It was an odd situation I had never considered.

"Wait, you mean you and Jack?" She shook her head. "Never?"

"Never. Hey, you never did tell me how you and Jack really met."

I know my whole face must have changed because I saw Tessa's pupils dilate with concern. I told her about how Jack and his brothers were using the cabin and what went down over the weekend. I explained that his brothers were really bad, but that he was actually a decent guy and set free in the end. She didn't seem quite as surprised to hear it as I had expected.

"You knew?" I challenged.

"Not everything. Jack did tell me how he lost his virginity. It was disgusting and heartbreaking what his brothers did to him. He was forced to rape a girl, Jenna. It's, um, it's why we haven't, you know, sealed the deal and all that. He still struggles with the guilt of it. He was caught with his brothers and held in captivity for years. He only escaped this past fall and has been trying to rebuild his life. He's really not a bad guy, Jenna."

"I know," I said. "And I, um, I knew about the rape, too."

"You did?" she asked, shocked.

"Yeah, it sorta came out this weekend. Maddie, the one who just called…"

"Chase's sister-in-law?"

"Yup, she was, uh, she was the victim he raped, Tess."

"What? Oh my gosh, I think I'm going to puke," she said dramatically. "You've met her? He told me she was dead."

"I think he truly believed that. They had left her for dead, but obviously, she's not. He looked like he was seeing a ghost when she walked in and confronted him. I felt terrible for both of them. And I really don't think he's a bad guy, Tess. He really cares about you, you know? I was bringing Anita over to see the house, and something just felt off. One of his brothers came out of the house and I was terrified of him. Jack came out too, and when he saw me, he thought it was you. He told me to get away and not come back, that he'd call as soon as he got rid of them. He tried to save me . . . or you rather."

"He did? Wait, you told Anita before me?" She pouted.

"Sorry, she sort of walked in on us last week. They said they weren't coming to study group and then showed up anyway, so I had to tell her."

Tessa and I stayed up half the night talking about anything and everything. It was wonderful, and bittersweet. It felt like the bond between twins like the kind you read about in books, but I had rarely experienced in my lifetime until that moment. Despite her assurance that no matter what Daddy said I'd always have her in my life, I didn't dare cling to that hope.

We ended up falling asleep on the couch. I awoke to eight missed messages, all from Chase. I hadn't even heard it ring once. Checking my settings, I realized it was still shut off, because I had silenced it after it started ringing in the library the evening before, when several people had scolded me for it as I was walking in to meet up with Chase for our study group which had resulted in very little studying, unless you count me memorizing the ridges of his abs.

Checking the clock on my phone, I realized I was going to be late for calculus.

"Tessa, you have to wake up. I'm late for class," I told her, knowing it took an act from God himself to wake my sister.

She grumbled while I started brewing coffee, hoping the scent would rouse her.

"Tess, I'm in classes most of the day. You have to hurry." My pleas were only met with more grumbling.

With the coffee ready, I quickly filled two travel mugs and

was surprised and thankful to see Tessa starting to stir. I shoved one of the mugs into her hands and wrapped my arm around her to heft her up.

"A little help, Tess. God, you're heavy," I complained. That was enough to get her moving.

"Hey, I've only gained a few pounds this semester. You don't have to poke fun," she whined.

"I'm not making fun, but I'm literally begging you to move so I don't have to carry you all the way to the Jeep."

She giggled but straightened. "Do I have time to go to the bathroom at least?"

"No. I'll drop you off at the house. You can do the walk of shame and be the talk of gossip all week. You'll love it."

She looked at me and pouted. "Where did you get those clothes?"

"I live here, remember?"

She looked around in a sleepy daze as reality slowly settled back in. "Oh, right. Yeah, that makes sense. Okay, let's go." To my relief, she finally relented.

I made it back to campus, dropped Tessa off, and drove over to my first class. I ran the short distance to the building and arrived breathless just as the professor walked in. He looked at me and shook his head with a look of disappointment, but didn't comment.

Chase and Anita were already there waiting.

"Are you okay? You never called last night," he said, his voice filled with worry while looking me over to see that I was okay.

"I'm fine. Sorry. We went back to the cabin, and then fell asleep after talking until like four a.m. I'm exhausted and didn't think Tessa would ever wake up."

"Tessa knows about the cabin?" Anita whispered, clearly listening into our conversation.

I nodded. "Tessa knows everything."

Chase was watching me carefully, but didn't reach out like I could vividly feel he wanted to.

"And . . ." he asked.

I smiled, genuinely happy. "We're good. She took it much better than I expected."

Chase

Chapter 23

Seeing that Jenna was okay, made me feel like I could breathe again. After everything that had happened over the weekend, I couldn't help but freak a little when she didn't call or answer my calls the night before. I knew she and her sister had gone off to talk and they had likely left campus since she took my Jeep, but that certainly didn't help my sanity one bit. I think it was the first time that I fully understood just how important she was to me.

Jenna Lockhardt was my life. She was my future. She owned my heart and was the only person I wanted to spend my time with. I was glad she had time with her sister, but a part of me was jealous of that, too, because I had missed her so much and I didn't want to miss out on any part of her life.

I scolded myself for being a sap. I was whipped; there was no denying it. Maybe I needed to spend a little time with my fraternity brothers and remember what it was like without Jenna consuming my every thought. Nah. There was no point, because I knew she'd still be there, if only in my mind. I was a goner. I simply couldn't imagine my life without her. Though, I knew the old Chase from even three months ago would be kicking my own ass over it. Even knowing that, with her by my side, I simply didn't care.

Without thinking, I reached for her hand, threading her fingers between mine. I needed that physical contact as much as I needed air to breathe. She looked over and smiled and my world righted itself again. She scooted in her seat a little closer to me.

It wasn't until the end of class, as the whispers began, that I even realized what I had done. My heightened wolf hearing tuned in quickly to the gossip line running rampant throughout the room the moment someone said "Lockhardt."

"Did you see Chase Westin with Tessa Lockhardt? They were looking pretty cozy in class. Can you believe it?" one girl said as we were leaving class.

She was near the aisle and when we reached her, I leaned in and whispered to my eager audience. "That's Jenna, not Tessa. If you insist on spreading freaking gossip, at least get her damn name right." She flushed, as did the two girls with her caught talking about us. I pointed to my ears. "Benefits of being of a wolf."

Jenna was waiting for me at the door.

"What was that all about?" she asked.

"I'm sorry. Seems every eye in the room was watching us today. I shouldn't have reached for you like that."

She looked back into the classroom as the girls I had just spoken to scrambled to look away and pretend they weren't continuing to watch us. To my surprise Jenna just shrugged.

"Honestly, my best friend knows, my sister knows, screw the rest of them. Let them gossip. Who would believe them anyway? Chase Westin doesn't do girlfriends. Haven't you heard?" she said with a straight face. If it wasn't for the twinkle in her eye, I'd have thought she was being serious.

"Girlfriend, huh?" I teased. "You really want to be my girlfriend?"

She gave me a look like she was judging my sanity.

"Let's see, if you were my girlfriend, I'd walk you to your next class."

She laughed, "And where else are we headed right now?"

I shrugged and grinned. "I would hold your hand, 'cause it's the only way I could keep from touching you all the time, everywhere," I said, lowering my voice and watching her pupils dilate to my insinuation. I held out my hand and she took it with a nervous giggle.

"I'd steal a kiss when I could." I brought our joined hands up and kissed the back of her hand as she sighed. "And I'm pretty sure I have my old letterman jacket I could dust off for you to wear. Maybe dig out my class ring. We could even go to the next school dance together."

She stopped and let go of my hand, smacking me in the arm.

"You are not as funny as you think you are," she said,

laughing.

"Yes I am. I'm hysterical," I told her.

The gossip continued to spread around campus. Jenna ignored it. I tried not to encourage it. I didn't realize the news of me having a girlfriend would cause other girls, especially the Thetas, to become even more aggressive. It was like I was no longer unreachable. I think it gave hope to several that if Jenna could tempt me, then they'd have a chance, too. I wanted to scream out loud, "She's not my girlfriend, she's my mate and none of you will ever compare," every time one of them tried to get close to me.

Wasn't it just a week ago they were questioning my mating status? Did they really forget that quickly, or was the thought of a wolf and a panther just too much for them to even consider?

By Thursday I'd had it. After my last class, I went straight to over to the panther house. Tessa answered the door when I knocked.

"Hey, Tessa. Is Jenna around?" I asked.

She nodded and smiled. "It's crazy how easily you can tell us apart. Even our own parents can't do that."

I smiled. "I've got that built-in Jenna-detector that's all. But I'll tell you, you confused the hell out of me at first."

She laughed. "I hadn't really thought about that, but yeah you were acting a little weird that first week or two."

"Yeah well, I didn't know there were two of you," I said.

"There's not," she assured me.

I grinned back at her. "Touché. You are correct about that. So, where can I find her?"

"Come on in."

I followed Tessa down a hallway lined with doors. She knocked on the second door on the left before opening it and peeking her head in.

"Uh, sounds like she's in the shower," Tessa said.

"Mind if I wait?" I asked.

"Go on in," she said. "And hey, Chase?"

"Yeah?"

"You'll watch out for her this week, right? I mean, I know you will, just, she's going into pack territory. It makes me nervous. Keep her safe for me, okay?"

"I'll protect that girl with my life, Tessa. Nothing's going to happen to her. I promise. Besides, you forget, she is pack. It's her territory now, too."

Tessa didn't quite look convinced, but nodded.

"Hey, Tessa, can I ask you something now?"

She turned around at the door. "Sure, what?"

"So, you know that news is spreading like wildfire around this place, right?" She nodded. "And are you aware that I was assaulted by no less than seven girls walking across campus just now?"

She snorted, crossing her arms over her chest defensively. "I'm not surprised. Rumor has it that you are ready to settle down and so they want to break you and Jenna up so they can have their chance, or just seduce you into taking them instead of her."

"Yup, that's pretty much my theory, too. So, we were originally heading out of town tonight, but Jenna wanted to wait until tomorrow after you girls leave, so that we didn't draw any attention."

Tessa laughed. "A little late for that, hon."

I grinned sheepishly. "I know. So, you cool if I take her today instead?"

"She's a big girl, she can make that decision herself, but sure, for what it's worth, it's cool. Just take care of my sister."

"I love her, you know," I said honestly.

She smiled. "I'm happy for you guys. Really. I know it won't always be easy, but I don't have any problems with you, Chase."

"Glad to hear it, Tessa. Thanks. And have a great time in Cabo."

She said goodbye and closed the door. I plopped down on Jenna's bed looking around at her stuff and taking it all in. The water was still flowing in the shower and I was tempted to strip and join her. No sooner had I thought of it, I heard a loud and off-key rendition of We Are the Champions coming from the bathroom. I couldn't help but laugh. My mate was a terrible shower singer.

Shortly after the song ended, the shower cut off. I stayed on the bed and waited until she finally opened the door. She was wrapped in a towel, a second one piled high on top of her head, and steam surrounded her like a vision.

She walked to her desk, picked up the phone, looked at it, and then put it back down. Her bottom lip jutted out in a pout. "Class ended an hour ago," she said to herself.

"Yes, it did. Did you miss me?" I asked, unable to keep quiet any longer.

Jenna screamed and as she whipped around to face me, she dropped her towel. There was no greater sight in the world than my mate naked. Her chest was heaving up and down as she tried to catch her breath.

"I'm sorry." I grinned. "I didn't mean to scare you."

"Scare me? Scare me? Oh, no, I'm completely used to random guys hanging out in my bedroom. What are you doing here?"

The door to her bedroom opened and she quickly reached for her towel to cover herself. Four heads popped through the doorway to make sure she was okay. I had no doubt the sight of her standing before me, completely naked except for the towel still on her head, as she scrambled for the towel she'd dropped, was not what they envisioned from her terrified scream. Four jaws hung open in shock.

Tessa walked by them. "Sorry, sissy. I didn't think you'd freak out that bad."

"You let that boy in her room?" Ayanna asked in disgust. "With all those awful rumors about them flying around?"

"Drop it, Ayanna. Jenna's a grown woman and can do as she pleases. Now close the door. You know she likes her privacy," Tessa told her with some authority in her voice. To my surprise, they listened. A few blushes, and a few mumbled sorry's later, followed by the sound of the closed door, and we were alone once again.

I grabbed the towel from her and pulled her down onto my lap. Wrapping my arms around her, I kissed down her neck until I found my bond mark and paid special attention to the sensitive skin there. Jenna shivered in my arms.

"Behave. My sisters are all home right now," she warned me.

"Fine," I said. "Do you have any plans for the rest of the day?"

"No, why?"

"Can we please just hit the road and get out of here? It's been a rough week."

"Aww, not enjoying being pawed over by every available female on campus?" she hissed.

"I only enjoy being pawed over by one particular, only available to me, female on campus."

That earned me a smile and a kiss. I refrained from deepening it and kissing her the way I really wanted to.

"At the very least can we go to the cabin tonight if you don't want to drive to San Marco now?" I asked.

"Tessa and the girls don't . . ."

"Don't care at all whether we leave today or tomorrow," I interrupted. "Trust me. I asked."

"You didn't," she said, with a threat of punishment in her voice.

I grimaced. "I really did. I just talked to Tessa about it. It's fine."

"Chase, we talked about this."

"Jenna, the entire campus knows we're together. I think that ship's sailed already."

She slunk, her shoulders slouching forward.

"Look, let's just get out of here and forget about it all. Hopefully we'll be old news by the time spring break is over."

"Fine. Let me get dressed and finish packing."

Jenna
Chapter 24

It didn't take me long to throw a few last minute things into my bag and call it good. I'd been packing for days, second-guessing everything I put in there. I just wanted to make a good impression with his family. I was a nervous wreck as we loaded the Jeep and hit the road.

It was already late afternoon and we had several hours of driving ahead of us. It was strange. I mean, it wasn't like Chase and I never talked, but we'd never been stuck in a car side by side for hours on end before, either.

At first there was an awkward silence. When he flipped on the radio, I didn't like the song that was playing, so I changed it. He changed it back and started singing along, so I changed it again. I hit the scan button and we let it roll until we finally came across a song we both agreed on. I sang along with him. I knew I was tone deaf, but I just didn't care. I loved to sing. I saw the amusement on my mate's face, but he didn't comment on it.

As we headed south, the scenery changed around us. I grabbed for the camera in my bag and started taking pictures through the window. It was so beautiful that everything else faded away except what I could see through my camera lens.

I was surprised when the motion stopped. I dropped the camera and saw that Chase had pulled over at a scenic overlook stop. He was watching me and I gave him an apologetic look. I had always been able to get lost behind a camera, seeing the world through its lens in a new light.

"Thought you'd get some better shots here. Plus, I could use a good stretch," he said.

He opened his door, exited the Jeep, then closed the door behind him, and then jogged around the vehicle to open my door for me. I got out in awe of the beauty of nature around me.

"This is one of my favorite stops on the trip," he told me.

I didn't waste any time, or need encouragement, as I grabbed my camera and happily started snapping away. I lost track of time and had no idea we'd been there for almost an hour when I finally put the camera down.

Chase was perched on the stone wall meant to be a buffer between people and the drop-off on the other side. He was watching me. He looked peaceful and content.

"Sorry," I said with an apologetic shrug. "Sometimes I just get lost behind the camera."

In the months I'd known him, I had tried to keep it in check, mostly because I had been so nervous around him, but that had shifted after our mating. I was more comfortable with Chase Westin than I was with anyone else.

I went to put my camera away, but instead I whipped it around in his direction and took a few candid shots before he caught on and started posing for me. He even tore off his shirt and my mouth watered as I eagerly snapped pics of my shirtless mate.

He redressed when I finally put it back in its case.

"Okay, my turn," he said, pulling out his phone. He grabbed me around the waist and pulled me back towards him and held it out in front of us. I buried my head in his chest and shook my head.

"I hate having my picture taken," I confessed.

"Too bad. This is happening. I have like two pictures of you. I need more."

"Why? You see me every day," I said matter-of-factly.

"Come on, smart-ass. Humor me. Please?"

There was no way I could ever say no to that face. I turned my head towards the phone and smiled for real when I saw the two of us together, his strong arm around me, making me feel so safe, with the beautiful forest and rolling hills in the background as the sun shined down on us, was perfect.

I had chosen a dark purple sweater, jeans and boots to wear for the trip down. The effect the color had on my eyes was stunning. I had always considered Tessa beautiful, gorgeous even, but despite knowing we were identical, I had never quite seen myself that way, until now. Through an artist's eye, I could appreciate how truly breathtaking the two of us looked together.

"I want a copy of that," I told him.

My phone dinged and as I went to check it, he leaned down and kissed me. "Already sent. See, that wasn't so bad, was it?"

I rolled my eyes and gave him another peck on the lips. The sun was just beginning to set, and I knew we still had a long way to go.

"We should hit the road. And you shouldn't have let me take up so much time," I scolded, getting back into the car and continued our drive to San Marco.

At some point in the drive, I must have dozed off. I awoke suddenly with Chase's arm around me as I drooled against his shoulder.

"Hey," I said sleepily. "How long was I out?"

"A few hours. We're heading up the mountain now. It's the final stretch. Won't be long now."

"You okay? Do you need me to take over and finish driving?"

"Nah, I'm good. It's still early."

"Sorry, I can never stay awake in the car if I'm not behind the wheel."

He laughed. "Good to know. Are you hungry?" My stomach growled suddenly and we both laughed. "I'll take that as a yes. I'll call ahead and let them know we're almost there so Mom can have some dinner ready."

"Do they know we're coming in tonight?"

"Nope," he said.

"What? You didn't tell them?"

"Relax, Jenna, it's not like we need a reservation to go home."

"You don't, maybe. I can't believe you didn't tell them I was coming."

"Princess, they know you're coming. They are excited to meet you. Everything's going to be fine. I promise."

His hand now rested on my thigh and he gave it a squeeze that sent a jolt of pleasure cutting through my paranoia. I took a deep breath. I could do this.

As we entered San Marco I felt this strange sort of comfort.

The entire place seemed to have that faint scent of Chase. Not Chase, I remembered, but pack. It relaxed me a little, despite my concerns.

We drove through a little town. It was quaint and far smaller than any town I'd ever been in. People were out talking to one another and just hanging around. There was a place called The Crate that seemed to be hopping. Young people were crammed into a cute little ice cream shop. I craned my neck to look, taking it all in.

"Welcome to San Marco," Chase said, pulling off the main road and down a long, wooded path, much like the driveway to our cabin. "And welcome home," he said, pulling up in front a large, inviting house. It was brightly lit like they were waiting for us.

He got out and grabbed our bags. I waited until he came around and opened my door, checking my appearance quickly in the mirror on the back of the visor. I grabbed my lip gloss to reapply before I got out.

I wiped my sweaty palms on my jeans and nibbled on my lip. I loved the taste of watermelon lip gloss, so it in no way dissuaded me from the nervous habit. Chase noticed. Chase always noticed.

He dropped the bags to the ground and wrapped his arms around me, my back pinned against the Jeep. He lowered his mouth to mine and sucked my bottom lip into his. I fought back a grin. He seemed to do that a lot and it inevitably calmed my nerves and caused a different sort of butterflies in my stomach. He deepened the kiss and made my knees shake. I sighed.

He pulled back with a grin. "You have nothing to worry about."

I just nodded. I wasn't sure I could even talk after that anyway. He left one arm around me and led me towards the house.

"What about the bags?" I asked when we hit the porch.

"Don't worry about it. I'll get them later."

He didn't stop, or knock, just walked right in, pulling me with him. I felt so out of place. A crashing noise came from another room and a ball bounced into the foyer right towards us. Chase stopped it with his foot, as a young dark-haired boy in pajamas and socks came slipping and sliding around the corner, abruptly stopping

His eyes were wide with excitement. "Uncle Chase?" He sounded like he couldn't believe what he was seeing. It only lasted a moment before he launched himself into Chase's expectant arms. After a quick hug, Chase set him down and those little arms wrapped around my waist. "Hi Aunt Jenna!" he squealed. "They said you wouldn't be here till tomorrow."

"Surprise," Chase said . . .

I hugged the little man closer. "You must be Oscar," I finally said, happy when my voice didn't crack.

"Yup, that's me," he said, letting go and stepping back to look me over. "Mom, Uncle Chase and Aunt Jenna are here!" he yelled over his shoulder.

I stole a quick look at Chase, who just grinned and picked the boy up.

"You monkey, how can we surprise anyone if you're going to tell the whole house?" He began tickling Oscar, who squealed in delight.

People started coming from all directions. A petite woman with short blonde hair and pink highlights came bouncing down the stairs. Several people came from both directions on the main level. When Maddie came into view, I stopped holding my breath. She didn't hold back but walked right up to me and pulled me into an embrace.

"I know they can be a little overwhelming. Just remember to breathe. Everyone's excited to meet you," she whispered. I already knew that whispering in a house of wolves was pointless, but then again, she clearly made her point as people started taking a step back and giving us some space. A little louder she said, "Come on, let me introduce you around."

"Mom said you weren't coming in till tomorrow," the one with the pink-streaked hair said.

"Surprise," Oscar said, mimicking Chase.

"Oh, come on in to the living room. Maddie show her the way," instructed an older lady who I knew must be Chase's mom. As we rounded the corner to the left, I saw her give Chase a big hug and she had tears in her eyes. They followed behind us, her arm linked through his.

The living room was huge. I'd never seen such a big space. There were at least five couches in just the one room. A monster sized TV hung on one wall, and the back wall was lined with floor-to-ceiling windows that made it feel like you were outdoors. A chess board sat on a table in the corner with two chairs. There was also a card table, and games and books lined several shelves flanking the big screen TV. One corner of the room was stacked high with toys. It was clear this was the hub of family life in the Westin house.

"Mom, Dad," Chase said, drawing my attention back to them. "This is Jenna, my mate."

I blushed at his candidness. "Hi, it's nice to meet you," I said awkwardly before his mother pulled me into a hug, followed immediately by his father.

Chase had explained once before that wolves were very touchy creatures. I don't think it really hit me until that moment just what he had meant. My parents would never hug a stranger like that. Heck, they barely ever hugged me and Tessa.

"I'm Jason, this is my mate, Mary," the older man said, finally letting me go.

"I'm Jenna," I said, then chastised myself for it, 'cause, duh, Chase just told them that.

"Welcome, Jenna," Mary said, misting up.

"Mom, you're gonna freak her out. Pull it together," the pink-haired girl said.

"Don't be rude, Lily," Mary warned. "I'm allowed to get a little emotional. My baby boy just brought home his mate."

Lily rolled her eyes. She pulled me into yet another hug. "Follow my lead," she whispered.

"Hi Jenna, I'm Lily, Chase's sister," she said a little louder. "Oh, was that your stomach? Have you guys not eaten?"

My cheeks heated. I didn't realize my stomach grumbled, but I was starving.

"Oh, let me heat something up real quick for you both," Mary said, smacking Chase on the arm. "You should have called and let me know. I would have had something ready when you arrived."

Chase gave her a grin I had never seen before. Something told me it was the one that he used to wrap his mother around his little finger and get away with anything.

"It was a last minute decision, Mom. I figured we'd surprise you."

I snorted. "Last minute? He had his bag packed and in the Jeep, and was stalking me before I could even take a shower after class."

"I let you take your shower," Chase argued.

I laughed. "You scared the life out of me!"

"I really did," Chase defended. "Then I grabbed her stuff and hit the road before she could recover."

His family was taking in the light bantering we had going on between us.

"So basically, you kidnapped her," her mother pointed out.

Chase shrugged and gave her that grin again. "But I got her here and we have a whole extra day home."

Lily shook her head. "You have serious issues, baby brother."

As Mary turned to scold Lily, Chase made a face at her behind his mother's back. I couldn't believe it and my face must have shown my shock because Mary whipped around and Chase had that damn grin of pure innocence on his face before she saw him. Meanwhile, Lily stuck her tongue out at him. I couldn't even believe it. I would never in a million years act that way to my sister, but especially not in front of our prim and proper mother.

"Do I need to send both of you to your rooms?" she asked them.

"If I can take Jenna with me, I'm okay with that," Chase confessed, and I smacked him hard in the gut and then wanted to crawl in a hole and die of embarrassment for my behavior.

"I'm so sorry, Mrs. Westin," I immediately apologized.

"It's Mary," she told me firmly, "and no apology needed. I've always had a soft spot for my baby. He needs a strong woman to stand up to his shit."

She said it with such a straight face that I fought back the need to laugh, until the entire room erupted. Chase wrapped his arms around me and hugged me close to him. He was laughing, too.

"Mom, you've had a long day. Just relax. I'll take the lovebirds down to The Crate. Maddie, you want to call and have Liam meet us there?"

"Yeah, sure, that sounds great," Maddie agreed.

"That's not necessary. It'll only take a moment to warm up leftovers for them and they just got here, I'm sure they are exhausted," Mary said.

"I slept most of the way, but I'm fine with whatever," I told them.

"Relax, Mom, you weren't expecting us till tomorrow anyway. We'll go hang out tonight. I promise we won't be out too late," Chase said, and his mother conceded.

Lily was on the phone and heading for the door. She started talking and then stopped and turned around. "Mom, Kels is about to call a sitter," she said in a tattle-tale voice I imagined she reserved for her siblings.

"No, she isn't," Mary Westin said. "Tell her to bring that baby over here on her way. Oscar's staying the night, so he and Zander can have a sleep over."

"Yay!" Oscar cheered.

"Thanks, Mom. She'll be by in a few," Lily said, hanging up the phone.

Instead of turning towards the front door, Lily kept walking down the hall and started banging on a door.

"Jesus, what's going on?" Kyle said when he opened the door. "What's the matter?"

Lily nodded my way. "Chase and Jenna got in early. So stop working and come to the Crate with us."

I smiled and gave him a small wave. It was nice to see a familiar face.

Maddie walked up behind me, "Okay, Liam's going to meet us there. Let's go."

"Did you call Kelsey?" Kyle asked Lily.

"Of course I did. She's bringing Z over here to have a sleepover with Oscar, then meeting us there."

"Okay, let me just finish things up and I'll head over with her when she gets here," Kyle said.

Lily rolled her eyes again. I was beginning to think it was just a normal look for her. "Fine. See you there, but you better not bail on us again."

Kyle grinned from ear to ear and I could tell there was definitely a story there, and that it was probably one I really didn't want to know.

We all shuffled out of the house. Chase ran ahead and grabbed our bags that were still sitting in the driveway next to the Jeep. He threw them back into the house and I heard him ask Oscar to take them up to his room.

I climbed into the Jeep as Maddie agreed to ride with Lily and they argued over who would call Elise. I knew that was Chase's other sister, but I hadn't met her yet, or Kelsey.

Their family dynamics overwhelmed me somewhat, and yet it just felt right being there with them all. When Chase climbed into the driver's seat he turned and looked at me.

"Hey, beautiful, what are you thinking about?"

It had dawned on me when he asked Oscar to take our bags up to his room that we'd be sleeping together . . . in his parents' house. I hadn't even considered the logistics of that before.

"Um, are you sure your parents are okay with us sleeping together?" I knew mine sure wouldn't be.

He looked at me with his eyebrow quirked like it was a crazy question to ask. "I'm sure, Jenna; we're mated. Trust me, it's okay. Mated is basically the same as human marriage, only more. They can divorce, but for us, it's forever."

I had never thought about mating quite like that.

"Wait, human marriage?" I asked. "Does that mean wolves don't marry?"

Chase looked at me like I was crazy. "No. Do panthers?"

"Well, yeah, we do." I had dreamed about my wedding day since I was little girl. It had never occurred to me that I wouldn't have one.

"Why?" he asked simply.

"Why? Because that's what people do. They fall in love, they get married, and then they have kids."

"That's what humans do. Shifters find their mate. If they're as lucky as I am, their one true mate. They create an unbreakable bond. It's private and it's beautiful. They create a life together, they have pups . . ."

"Or cubs," I interrupted, correcting him.

"Or cubs," he conceded in our case. "Babies, and grow old together. If the bond fully matures they live until one dies, and the other follows his or her mate into death." He looked at me hard, studying my reaction. "Do you want to get married, Jenna?" he finally asked.

I shrugged. "I guess I always assumed I would. Most panthers don't complete their mating bond until their honeymoon. Marriage first. I guess since we've already done that, it doesn't really matter."

"You don't sound convinced. If you want to get married, we will," he said matter-of-factly.

"You'd do that for me even though it would mean nothing to you?" I asked skeptically.

"Look, it's nothing I would have thought of, but that doesn't mean it would mean nothing to me. Liam and Maddie got married last year. Wedding, dress, the ring, the name change, the whole bit. He even legally adopted Oscar at the ceremony. It's not that we can't get married if we want to."

"Why did Liam go through all that if it's not important to the wolves?" I asked, more curious than anything.

"Oscar," he said simply. "Oscar was raised in the human world. He didn't understand their bonding and called my brother out on it. He took the kid's words to heart and made it right for his family."

"What about taxes and stuff? I mean, you have an entire town, all shifters. If no one gets married, doesn't that look suspicious or something?"

"We have a perfectly legal clerk, of course. She files the paperwork for the government on every mated pair, so I guess legally, yes, we are considered married. In a little less than four months, ours will be filed, unless you want to have a real wedding."

Of course I wanted a real wedding, but I didn't want to tell him that. Did it really matter? I'd have to do some soul-searching at a later date to figure out the answer to that, but right then we were pulling up in front of the bar I had seen on the drive in, and I really hoped they had real food, not just fried bar snacks.

Chase

Chapter 25

Jenna had surprised me with talk of marriage. I made a mental note to discuss the idea with Liam while we were there. I wanted his take on whether it was worth all the trouble weddings seemed to be, or not.

For now, walking into the Crate with my mate on my arm was the best feeling ever. We met Lily and Maddie in the parking lot and walked in with them. Patrick and Elise were already there. E stood and hugged me before turning to hug Jenna.

"Hi, I'm Elise, you must be Jenna."

I loved my family, but I especially loved how they were welcoming my mate.

"Hi, it's nice to meet you," Jenna said. "Hey, Patrick."

"It's good to see you again, Jenna."

Once the pleasantries were over we settled down, pulling three tables together to accommodate all of us. Liam arrived talking to Cole Anderson. Cole was one of Kyle's Betas and on the Pack Council. He also owned a tattoo parlor in town. After introducing him to Jenna, I asked him to join us. Kelsey and Kyle were the last to arrive as Misty came by to take our orders.

"What's good?" Jenna asked. "I'm starving."

"Burgers," my siblings and I said in unison.

"Trust us, they're the best," I assured her.

There was a local band of high schoolers playing on the small stage. Not so long ago that had been me. When they heard I was in the audience, they begged me to sing with them. One even offered me his guitar to play. With my siblings cheering me on, it was hard to say no, but when Jenna leaned over and asked me to please do it because she'd never heard me play, I was on stage as fast as lightning.

Playing with the band, eating Crate burgers, hanging with my family, and spending time with Jenna pretty much meant a perfect night for me. By the end of the evening as we started breaking up and heading home, Jenna was already part of the family. I could feel the shift and acceptance from each of my siblings.

The girls were busy making plans for Saturday and Jenna was being persuaded to at least stay through Mom's Tuesday night family dinner, and she said yes.

I was exhausted and elated as we made it back to the house. Mom was up waiting, as she always did. She never went to bed until she knew all her babies were home safe and sound.

I walked Jenna up to my room, then came down and told Mom goodnight.

"Sorry we were out so late, Mom."

"Oh, it's fine, sweetie. It makes my heart happy to see all my babies together and enjoying each other."

"We really did. It was a great evening," I confirmed.

"I like Jenna. She's good for you. I can see why you love her so much," my mom said.

"Mom." I started to talk, but she interrupted.

"Don't say a word, son. I can see how in love you are, and you best be telling that girl just how much you love her every single day. It's not always going to be easy for you two. You've chosen a different path and not everyone will be accepting of that. All relationships have their hurdles, though, and as long as you have true love, you're going to be just fine."

I hugged my mother tight, thankful to be blessed with such an amazing woman in my life. If it weren't for her and my father's love, I don't know if I would have had the strength to go through with the bond. I had already heard and seen more prejudice in the last week at school, since word of us just dating had spread, than I'd experienced in my entire life. But my parents showed me unconditional love, and I knew that no matter what, they'd be supportive of my decision, which really wasn't a decision at all because Jenna Lockhardt was my true mate.

I headed back upstairs. Nothing further needed to be said. When I got in the room, Jenna was already in her pajamas, sitting on the bed. She looked adorably cute. I went to my suitcase and pulled out the dampener. Best damn gift I ever got. I plugged it into the wall.

"Chase, is that the dampener?" Jenna asked.

"Yeah, best device ever invented."

"Why did you bring the dampener?"

I looked at her like she was crazy. "Why do you think? Liam and Maddie stayed over for Christmas and he leaves his, in his office." I shuddered. "I'm not doing that to Lily or my parents."

She laughed. "You actually think we're having sex with your parents down the hall?"

Instead of answering her, I stripped down to nothing before her eyes.

"Do you really think I even bothered to pack pajamas?"

Her eyes widened, and she licked her lips. The smell of her arousal immediately started filling the room, but there was a stubborn determination lingering there, too.

"We are not doing that with your parents down the hall."

"Wanna bet?" I asked, jumping onto the bed and grabbing her around the waist before she could escape. She giggled and thrashed, trying to get out of my grasp before eventually settling down and conceding. I kissed her softly. "I know we're both tired and it's late, but it's gonna be a long, hard weekend if you insist on being that stubborn, and don't think for a moment I'm not going to try everything in my power to get my way."

It was both a threat and a promise of things to come. We slept peacefully that night in each other's arms.

Each day in San Marco was better than the last. Jenna truly fit right in with my family. I don't think she ever realized just how easy she was to love.

My sisters adored her, spending all day Saturday spoiling and pampering her with a girls' day at a spa in the city. My brothers and I met up with the girls at a nice restaurant when they were done. By the time I saw Jenna, she was glowing and happier than I had ever seen her with anyone besides me. Her hair was sleek and shiny, and her violet eyes accentuated by some kind of makeup on her face. She was breathtaking. And my heart nearly stopped in my chest at the first sight of her walking in.

It had been a surreal moment, one I would not soon forget.

We danced, we laughed, and we celebrated life that night. I didn't want the evening to end, but I also could only stand sharing her for so long before we headed back home.

The door to my bedroom had barely shut behind her before I had her pinned against it, capturing her with a kiss. She gave no resistance when my tongue parted her lips and sought to explore her delicious mouth. Her usual scent combined with a slightly strange but appealing smell. Usually perfumes and smelly stuff hurt my head and made me sneeze, but whatever this was, it seemed to highlight her natural scent and drive me mad.

Breathless, she placed both palms flat against my chest and pushed back. She kept pushing until the back of my legs hit the bed and I sat down hard. She stood before me with a sultry look on her face and desire in her eyes. I tried to stand up and go to her, but she stuck out a perfectly polished finger, and shook it side to side without saying a word, so I sat back down. A new sort of confidence surrounded her actions.

Slowly she turned as I took her all in, devouring her with my eyes. She backed up to me and signaled for me to unzip her dress as she watched me over her shoulder. I wanted to touch her so badly and feel her soft skin under my fingertips, but as soon as the zipper was lowered she stepped away and turned around to face me again. Her stare had me pinned to my seat.

She lowered one shoulder, exposing my bond mark as my breath quickened. With a sly grin, she dropped the dress entirely. My heart nearly leapt from my chest when I saw the black lacy lingerie she wore beneath the dress. It was the hottest thing I had ever seen in my life.

The fabric was nearly see-through and left little to the imagination, not that I hadn't already memorized every inch of her body. Stockings rose to mid-thigh, attached to the upper part with some little clamps. They looked intricate and like potential trouble for my shaking hands. I briefly wondered how disappointed she would be when I ripped them from her body. The hooks attached on the other end to the lacy, see-through material that covered much of her body. The material stopped just above her nipples where her breasts crested the top like an open invitation. And, as my eyes washed back down, my breath caught as I realized the outfit was entirely crotchless.

Unable to sit still much longer, I rose and growled as I closed the gap between us. She didn't push me away this time, but her breath caught with my unexpected roughness when I grabbed her by the ass and lifted her easily. She wrapped her legs around my waist and I carried her back to the bed.

I stood back, my breathing already erratic and I hadn't even touched her yet. Seeing her laying there, dressed up for me, she looked like the embodiment of every sexual fantasy I'd ever had.

Without grace or a care, I quickly discarded my own clothes and climbed into bed with her. When I went to touch, she smacked my hand away, pushing my shoulder until I rolled over on my back.

She climbed on top of me, straddling my waist. "I've been spoiled and pampered all day. Now it's your turn," she said with a sly grin.

I gulped as she started at my bond mark and worked her way down my body, kissing and licking every inch. It felt as if she were marking me in a whole new way. Our eyes locked and I couldn't look away, transported to some other plane of existence that only included Jenna. It was the most erotic experience of my life.

Later, when we were both sated and covered in a light sheen of sweat, before sleep pulled her under, I held her close and told her how much I loved her. My heart was full. I'm not sure what I had expected in a mate, honestly. I was still young enough that I had never given it much thought, but somehow, I knew this was far more than I could ever have hoped for.

In that moment, I knew what I needed to do. Jenna said she'd always imagined she'd get married someday. I had watched enough Hallmark channel movies with my mother over the years to understand what that meant and how girls could obsess over such a thing from even a young age. If that's what she wanted, I would see to it.

Liam's wedding really hadn't been so bad, it had even been a little fun. But it was even more than that, because resting there, exhausted from the best night of my life, holding my mate, I knew I wanted this every day of my life. Yes, she was my mate and that was a greater bond than any human tradition, but I wanted her to be my wife, too. I wanted her to carry my name and someday my children. Closing my eyes, I could see our entire future before me. I drifted off to sleep with a smile on my face.

Jenna

Chapter 26

Coming to San Marco was probably the best decision I ever made. Chase was right! Everyone I met had been welcoming and friendly. I didn't think I ever felt so accepted anywhere in my entire life.

Rumors had already spread about Chase mating outside of the wolves, so there were a lot of strange looks and questions, but nothing rude or unsupportive. Just genuine curiosity.

I had a lot to learn about the wolves, and when Kyle and Chase finally sat me down to discuss their customs and what they called the challenges, I think I took it better than they expected. It wasn't that I was completely naïve to other shifter customs. Wolves, bears, lions, gorillas: lots of the bigger predatory animals had similar archaic rites of passages.

"How long?" I asked calmly, stunning them in mid-conversation as we sat in Kyle's office.

"What?" Kyle asked.

"How long does the challenge period last?"

"Typically four months, but I made notifications the second Chase told me you'd mated and so you're well into month one already. So far, no challenges have been made. I think people are still stunned by the two of you. That'll wear off a little bit since people have met you, Jenna."

I shrugged. "You two look worried. Don't be. The odds of someone challenging Chase are slim. After all, what other wolf would actually want a panther mate?" Chase growled at the thought and I shot him a look. "I can handle your stupid challenges if it comes to it. My panther is as big, if not bigger, than your females.

I've been taught fighting techniques since before I could walk and extensive training once my panther emerged. My daddy saw to it that Tessa and I would always be able to defend ourselves. I'm not fond of the idea of killing another being for sport or placement, but I know it's not uncommon among other animal species and I'll do what I have to do."

Chase's face beamed with pride, while Kyle's jaw dropped a little.

"Okay, well, I'll be sure to warn our females that you are a lethal fighting machine ready to accept their challenges then," Kyle finally said when the shock wore off.

"That's my girl," Chase said, proudly. "Kyle, you and Kelsey had your challenge period lowered. Can Jenna and I get in on that?"

I looked over at Kyle curiously, wondering if that was true and if they made exceptions because of his Alpha status. He looked slightly uncomfortable by the question.

Clearing his throat, he answered. "Chase, there were some extenuating circumstances regarding that."

"Oh, I know. You guys always ignore me since I'm the baby of the family, like I'm too young to understand, but I'm listening. I know all about how your mating signs came on faster and stronger, and why they really shortened the challenges for you," Chase said, staring his brother down.

I found it odd that Chase was looking directly at Kyle, though I saw him squirm a little in his chair. It hadn't gone unnoticed that no one truly looked the Alpha in the eyes, except his mate. Panthers and other big cats averted their eyes to my dad as a sign of respect. To look at him directly was a threat and challenge. I had thought maybe the same was true for wolves, but Chase was clearly staring Kyle down. When his squirming became shaking, I watched him drop his gaze and made a mental note to ask him about it later.

"So, what are you trying to say, Chase? If you really know the details of all that, then you know our bond strengthened faster because of Kelsey's, um, extra circumstances. You and Jenna have a strong bond, it's easy to feel it when you're together, but are you really saying it's more than it should be at this stage?"

Chase grinned back at his brother. "Did you know that the sacred mating signs differ among species?"

Kyle perked up with interest. "Go on."

"For example, talking to my new little brother, Chad, who's a squirrel and rarely shuts up, I've learned that the first sign of a squirrel mating is telepathy."

"How's that possible? That's one of the last stages," Kyle argued.

"Yes, for a wolf, who dominates in the emotional connection phase, first sensing his mate in location and emotional state," he paused, letting it sink in a little as he reached over and threaded his fingers through mine. "Panthers' dominance is in physical connections, Kyle. Whereas that is the final stage of bonding for us."

"Are you saying you can already feel each other physically?" Kyle asked.

"It's not enough to kill him, but if I go into the challenges right now, he would endure every emotional and physical impact I faced from it. As best as we've been able to determine, both of our bonding symptoms are coming on equally at the same time. We're in what my people would call stage two only times two because the signs are different for both of us," I explained.

"If I were to cut you right now, would he feel it?" Kyle asked me, seriously. Chase growled in outrage. "Simmer down, pup. I need to know."

"He would feel the sensation of it, yes. It would hurt him, but if I bled, it's not like his skin would slice, too. Yet. That will come in time, but usually takes a little longer," I clarified.

"Shit. The pain of it might be enough. I'll take it to the Council and we'll make a determination. Thank you for letting me know. I realize it's not exactly easy to discuss your bond—at least it wasn't for me—but this is the kind of information I do need to know. I would never have suspected anything like that was possible, but I'm not exactly up to speed on interspecies bonding, especially for true mates. Until you two, I didn't even know such a thing was possible."

It warmed my heart that Kyle believed we were true mates, and I fought down the emotions welling up inside. I had seen the looks and heard the whispers since word of me dating Chase had gotten out around campus. My hearing had improved significantly since the bond, and I didn't really like it. I hated hearing what everyone was saying about us, but I knew the general consensus was that it was only temporary because a Westin would never settle for a compatible mate, and dogs and cats could never be true mates. They were wrong, but having someone like Kyle acknowledge it as truth caused overwhelming gratification.

That wasn't the only meeting we had with Kyle during our visit. We also met with the Council, which I found a little more intimidating. Everyone was fascinated with the idea that a wolf and a panther could really be true mates. We did find a few skeptics, but nothing like I'd imagined.

We were originally supposed to leave on Monday—that's what I'd agreed to—but Mary had been so welcoming, taking me into her home and her family, that I couldn't disappoint her by missing out on my first Westin family Tuesday night dinner. I could feel Chase's happiness through our bond when I told him I thought we should stay over till at least Wednesday.

Tuesday came much too quickly, and I was surprisingly nervous before dinner. My family only ate formally on holidays. Most of the time Daddy was too busy with work, and Mom was too, with her various fundraisers and ladies' groups, to ever spend much thought on dinner. I liked the idea of big family meals, though. I thought I would be stressed and overwhelmed with Chase's large family, but it wasn't like that at all.

"Jenna, can you help me in the kitchen?" Mary called up to me.

It still amazed me that my hearing had become so sensitive. I was upstairs in Chase's room going through my wardrobe for the hundredth time, trying to decide what to wear, and I knew she was downstairs somewhere. It was the craziest thing.

"Coming," I said in my normal voice, because I knew she'd hear it without me having to yell.

I pulled on a pink sweater with a hoodie and my favorite pair of jeans and headed downstairs in my sock feet. I wasn't sure what she wanted, so comfort trumped style.

Walking into the kitchen, I saw Mary leaned over and waving a hot pad at something in the oven.

"Oh, thank goodness. Can you help me lift this?"

I grabbed two more hot pads from the counter and took the side of the oven opposite Mary. I bent down to pick up a huge cookie sheet from the largest oven I had ever seen in a normal kitchen, and was shocked at how heavy it was.

"Oh my gosh, that is heavy," I commented.

"I can handle the weight okay, it's the size that always gets me," she admitted. "It's just easier with an extra set of hands. Thank you, dear." She kicked the oven door shut with her foot as we lifted. Pots covered the stove top, so I wasn't sure where to go. "Right over there. We'll just set it down on the counter here," she advised. "Perfect," she said, clapping her hands in delight once the enormous pan was safely on the counter.

"It smells wonderful. What is that?" I asked.

"Oh, nothing fancy. It's hams."

"Hams? As in plural?" I questioned.

She removed the aluminum foil cover to reveal six large hams. They were sitting in some sort of orange colored liquid I couldn't quite place.

"Orange juice," she whispered. "Old family secret. Always cook your hams with an inch of OJ. It keeps them moist and the flavor blends amazingly with smoked hams."

I looked around the kitchen in awe of the amount of food I saw. "I thought it was just immediate family at your infamous Tuesday night Westin family dinners?"

She grinned. "Oh, it is, dear."

"Six hams? Isn't that a bit much?"

"My little family has grown quickly. There are thirteen of us now and if you weren't aware, wolves like to eat, especially their meat."

I laughed. "I did know that. I just didn't realize what that would look like for so many."

"Oh, this is nothing. Wait till you see a pack meeting meal."

"I can't wait," I told her, genuinely.

"Well, if you guys stick around through the weekend, we have a pack run on Saturday," she confessed.

"What exactly happens at a pack run?" I asked.

Mary excitedly motioned for me to sit down. "We hold pack runs once a month. Not all packs do them that frequently. The entire pack joins. We have a huge fellowship meal at the pack house. Just before sunset, as the moon is beginning to rise, Kyle will call the pack together, just out back here. He'll say a few words, and everyone shifts, then runs toward the woods. For the first few minutes we're all running as one, then large groups will break off together, and eventually some will separate out and run as couples or even solo on occasion. I really don't know how to explain it, there's just something so magical about pack runs."

She spoke with a dreamy voice like she was remembering some romantic pack runs of her past. I couldn't even imagine what a sight that would be—so many wolves all changing and running together.

"How many wolves are there in Westin Pack?" I asked.

She shrugged. "I honestly don't know for certain, but more than five hundred, probably less than a thousand, though I could be wrong on that. Only the Alpha knows for certain."

"I guess I'd stick out pretty bad in a setting like that. Probably best not to rub it in so soon," I admitted.

"I'm assuming your fur is solid black."

I nodded.

"And you're probably as big as an average wolf, maybe a little leaner." It wasn't really a question, but I nodded again anyway. "Chase's wolf is solid black you know."

"Yes, I've seen it many times."

"I was certain you had. Westin has many solid black wolves. You wouldn't look quite so out of place as you imagine. Maybe if you were a jaguar with defined spots or a tiger, who is much larger and has different coloring, but a black panther isn't going to stand out among us as much as you think. If you were a rabbit or a fox, I might worry about you getting eaten, but I am certain you'll be able to hold your own. Plus, Chase would never let anything happen to you. He would never leave your side on the run."

I shuddered at her words about being eaten. As a large animal of prey, I knew it was a natural instinct, but I could never stomach raw meat like that. On the rare occasion I had given wholly into my panther, she couldn't go through with it either. Fortunately, it was an acceptable custom for my kind to deliver prey to the King, and so that is what I would do with kills. I didn't know if that would be acceptable in the pack, though.

"Um, do you kill and eat small prey often? Do you have hunts? They're like your runs, only for food," I tried to explain.

"No, dear, we don't. There are some who enjoy eating off the trails. No one will think anything of it if you'd prefer that." I must have made a face, because she laughed. "I know that face well. Elise could never stomach a kill either."

"I've not had a choice really," I confessed. "But we thankfully have the option to eat or present it to the King. Daddy always got my kills on a hunt."

"There are some wolves that still believe a hunt is a rite of passage and they take their children out almost as soon as they've shifted for the first time. Others find the practice archaic and unnecessary, much like other shifters find our challenges. Now, have Kyle and Chase properly explained the challenges to you?"

"Yes ma'am. We've had several meetings and sparring sessions. I'm well equipped to hold my own in a battle."

"Wonderful. You don't know how relieved I am to hear it," Mary admitted.

With my new upgraded hearing I heard the front door open. I didn't have to hear the sound of voices though, because Chase's scent hit me like a ton of bricks. I gasped, a little taken aback, and sniffed the air around me.

Mary watched me closely. "Are you okay?"

I shrugged. "Weird stuff has been happening since the bond," I confessed, knowing I was blushing just mentioning the bond to Chase's mom.

"How so?"

I sighed. I really needed someone to talk to. "I'm not talking about the bonding symptoms. Those are normal-ish. It's the other stuff. Panthers don't have super smelling and hearing like wolves, but mine have improved tenfold since we completed our mating. I can hear almost as good as a wolf, and just now when the door opened, I smelled Chase, like smelled him as clearly as if he were right here next to me."

Mary considered my words. "Hearing and smell are extremely important to wolves. It sounds as if, along with the bond symptoms, you're also acquiring our greatest assets, too. Has Chase been experiencing the same?"

I shrugged. "We haven't really talked about it."

"Well then, what would be the most important attributes of a panther?"

I thought for a moment. "Speed and agility, I suppose. Night vision, maybe."

She nodded. "That sounds reasonable. Let's go test this theory."

Mary was up and walking out of the room, heading for the front door before I realized what was happening. I jumped up and ran after her.

"Oh, look, it's the majority of my babies here early. This never happens," she accused.

Liam looked sheepish. "Something smells really good, Mom." He leaned down and kissed his mother's cheek.

"Don't you try to butter me up now. Your father's in with Kyle. Go get them. We have a slight change in plans for Tuesday night dinner. How about a little activity first?" She looked back over her shoulder at me and grinned conspiratorially.

Without question Lily went to get Kyle and Jason. Maddie walked upstairs where the kids were playing.

"I'll call Elise and Patrick if you'd like," Kelsey offered.

"Tell them to stay put, we're heading their way," Mary said.

She directed everyone into vehicles and took the lead in the first car herself. Chase and I had been told to ride with her and Jason. I sat in the back seat next to my mate, looking awkwardly out the window as we drove over to Patrick and Elise's house.

"You okay?" Chase whispered.

I nodded without looking his way.

"Jenna, what's wrong?"

I looked over at him finally and smiled. "Nothing, but I think you're about to be tested. Sorry."

"Tested for what?" he asked.

"Speed," his mother interrupted.

"What's all this about Mary?" Jason asked, so she relayed the information I had told her. He seemed to take it in stride and nodded his approval with obvious interest.

"Why didn't you tell me?" Chase asked me.

I shrugged. "I wasn't sure at first. It was kind of a slow process, not one defining moment. Okay, so the smell thing a few minutes ago took me back a little, but my hearing has been steadily improving. I knew from hanging out at the doghouse what my hearing limitations were around wolves. After we mated it seemed to improve some. At first, I thought I was just used to it and it wasn't really any different, but then little things started happening that I really took notice of, like walking around campus last week with everyone whispering and talking about us."

"Shit, I never wanted you to hear all that," Chase said.

"Language, Chase," his mother said sternly.

"Sorry, Mom."

"Coming here, it was kind of obvious. I think all the new sounds made it a little clearer," I confessed.

"So why is my speed being tested?" Chase asked.

"If Jenna is experiencing heightened attributes of wolves, your mother wants to see if the same is happening for you. Panthers are well known for their speed and agility," his father said.

"Do we have to do this in front of the entire family?" Chase asked.

"Son, there's nothing to be worried about. Your siblings have always been supportive of you," Mary told him, but he didn't respond, just turned and looked at his window.

"Hey, what's wrong? If you don't want to do this, you don't have to. We were just curious," I told him.

Chase nodded. "You might as well know. My wolf isn't as fast as my siblings. Even as a little boy, long before my wolf surfaced, I was just never fast. I was big and tough, just slow. So yeah, speed tests aren't exactly my idea of family fun time. And with a name like Chase, everyone always expected me to be fast. It's just not me. Plus, I run every single day both in my fur and my skin. You know that, Jenna. Don't you think I would have noticed if something was changing?"

"No," I told him. "You run to a steady cadence. I've never seen you just let go and run, so I'm not sure you would have noticed."

He sighed and looked sad. I didn't have to hear him say the words to understand he had been bullied as a kid for not being the fastest. I was certain being an Alpha's kid didn't help any, either.

We arrived at Elise's and they came outside as everyone got out, standing around waiting for instructions. Zander and Oscar were already wandering off to play in the field.

"Okay Mom, we're all here. Now what's going on?" Kyle asked.

"You don't have to do this, if you don't want to," I said to Chase, all eyes turned our way.

He closed his eyes and took a deep breath. "Yeah, I do," he finally said, quickly stripping off his clothes and shifting. His massive wolf rubbed up against me, letting me know it was okay. He always took my breath away, such a magnificent animal.

"Jenna, I know panthers are short burst sprinters, whereas we are more distance runners. What do you think your short burst speed is?" Mary asked.

"Panther animals can hit up to fifty miles per hour, but shifters are much faster. The fastest I've been clocked is zero to seventy-two in ten seconds."

Patrick whistled. "Girl, that is fast."

I shrugged. "I can't sustain anywhere near that speed."

"Okay. Elise, mark off the half mile and one mile marks, take Liam and Maddie with you for that," Mary instructed. Jason sat back, looking amused with his mate. I had a feeling that when Mary Westin set her mind to something, an act of God himself wouldn't stop her. "Kelsey since you hold the record for the fastest known wolf, I'd like you to race him first."

Kelsey gave Kyle a helpless look. He smiled and walked over, putting his arm around his mate and nodding at her.

"I'm sorry, Mary, I can't. You're going to have to use Kyle instead," Kelsey said.

The look on Mary's face confirmed she was not a woman used to being told no.

"Mom, listen to her. She can't," Kyle said, exaggerating the word "can't."

I quickly looked back at Kelsey, wondering if they were trying to say what I thought they were saying. There was only one reason a female shifter wouldn't, or rather couldn't, shift.

Kyle leaned over and kissed Kelsey's cheek before rubbing her stomach. "Mom, she can't shift . . ." he said, trying to make his point, confirming my suspicions.

Mary gasped. "You mean?"

They were both nodding confirmation.

"We were going to tell you all tonight at the family dinner," Kelsey said, happy tears in her eyes as everyone started hugging her and giving their congratulations. Chase howled and Liam, Maddie, and Elise came running back to hear the good news.

Maddie started crying. "Stupid pregnancy hormones," she

said, wiping tears from her face.

I wasn't sure how far along Maddie was, but she was definitely showing. It was crazy. I could see a shift in the size of her belly just since the week before. I didn't have enough experience with pregnancies to even guess when she might be due, but I loved the idea that both she and Kelsey were pregnant at the same time.

Elise walked up next to me and put an arm around my shoulder. "Planning on joining them anytime soon?"

"Oh God no!" I said, a little too quickly. I was still in college. Chase and I had just mated, we needed time together. I wasn't ready to have a baby or even think about it. The horror at the thought must have shown on my face.

Elise laughed. "Same! Lily's not even mated yet, and with her massive crush on Cole Anderson, her true mate could probably walk up and slap her, and she'd be too blinded in lust to notice."

Lily snorted, hearing her, but didn't argue it. "You guys will just have to wait for me then, so our babies will one day have cousins close in age to play with too," she said.

I shrugged. "Oscar and Zander seem close despite the age gap. Our kids will be fine . . . someday," I added, reinforcing that someday would not be anytime soon.

Elise squeezed my shoulder. "Just wait. The pressure hasn't begun yet, but it will. Mom loves the idea of a house full of grandpups."

"Or cubs?" I asked.

"You see our Oscar out there?" She pointed to him. I nodded. "Half pup, half cub. You really think any one of us love that boy any less because of it?" I shook my head as my eyes started burning while fighting back tears. The thought of my kids being loved as much as I'd witnessed these people love Oscar was too much. "Someday . . ." Elise said, causing me to laugh instead of cry.

As the excitement of Kelsey's news began to die down, Mary got back to the issue at hand.

"Okay, well, Kyle we'll use you then instead," Mary finally said. "Now, get on with it, dinner's getting cold."

Kyle stripped and shifted. I averted my eyes. I knew nudity was not a big deal for shifters, but my family was just more private about it. I think felines in general were more prude when it came to such things. And while Mary's earlier description of a pack run had intrigued me, it wasn't until that moment that it dawned on me the sheer number of naked people that would entail if they were all to shift at once.

I looked back up to find everyone staring at me. I forgot, that I would need to shift in front of everyone else, too. I felt awkward and exposed. I turned my back to them and started to remove my shirt. A growl sounded just behind me. I looked over my shoulder just in time to see Elise roll her eyes and start to walk away. All other backs were towards me as my wolf stood watch, giving me the privacy he must have known I needed.

I made quick work of my clothes and shifted to stand in my place beside Chase's magnificent wolf. My panther rubbed up against him and purred.

Mary turned back around at my sounds and froze. She clapped her hands together and smiled. "Jenna, dear, your panther is as gorgeous as you." I nodded my large head in acknowledgement. "Okay, Chase, take Jenna to the lineup. The rest of you, back in place," she instructed.

I followed Chase to where Kyle's wolf stood. I hadn't looked at him earlier and was surprised to find a very large brown wolf. For some reason it seemed odd to me. Chase's was black, so I guess I had assumed all Westin pack wolves were black. I mean, I knew wolves came in a variety of colors, I just assumed those in a pack had similar colorings, or maybe that was just because of all the purity crap my daddy had engrained in us growing up. Coloring was so important to him that it had never once dawned on me that wolves, in the same family, especially, wouldn't all look similar.

Mary instructed us to line up. It was half a mile to Elise and we were told to run as fast as we could to that line, one at a time for accurate timing. Kyle took off first. He was fast, but I knew he was nowhere near as fast as I was.

Next, Mary signaled me to go. With a quick burst of adrenalin, I took off. I loved the feel of the wind running over my short fur. I pushed ahead as fast as my legs would allow and didn't even begin to slow until I flew by Elise. Stopping took almost another half mile, and I could see Patrick just up ahead.

As I turned to head back, Chase blew past me. I couldn't believe it. He was so fast he was practically a blur. He finally slowed around Patrick and headed back. I could see shock in his big brown eyes. The others were talking animatedly when we returned to the starting line, confirming my suspicions. Chase had gotten faster.

"Well, wow, that was really fast, Chase," Lily said excitedly. "I've never seen a wolf that fast. Should he run the full five miles? I bet he's faster than Kelsey even."

"Maybe," Jason said. "Remember, if he's truly getting his speed from his bond to Jenna, panthers are short distance runners."

I nodded my agreement.

"But if she merely enhanced him, and wolves are distance runners, it's possible he'll see an improvement there, too," Mary argued.

"Perhaps," Jason conceded. "Do we want to test him tonight, or head back for that delicious food that has been tormenting me all afternoon?"

"I'm very curious, but I know you all must be starving. Let's head back and we'll do this another day. I think it's safe to say that his speed has definitely received an upgrade."

With the dismissal, Kyle quickly shifted back. I turned away again. Would I ever stop feeling so self-conscious with that? Chase nipped at my shoulder and motioned his head towards the woods. I looked back at Mary.

"Go on, we'll meet you back at the house," she said, picking up our clothes as they all headed for the vehicles.

Chase started jogging for the woods and I followed. When we hit the trees with a low-lying branch, I leapt onto it. Chase stopped and looked up at me. I chirped at him to follow. He shook his head. I chirped again. He sighed—I could see it in his entire body—but he jumped, landing easily, albeit not very gracefully, next to me. I wasn't sure he could actually do it, and yet there he was; a wolf in a tree.

The height must have made him dizzy and uncomfortable, because he waivered and started to fall to the ground. I was relieved to see him land on all fours. The look he shot back up at me was comical. I silently jumped down and licked him before taking off into the woods. We ran and played. I had no idea where we were, but Chase carefully led us through and before I knew it we were exiting the forest just behind his parents' house.

I looked around and started to panic at the thought of walking naked through the house with everyone there. Chase headed towards the back deck, then shifted into his human form. He must have sensed my unease, because he picked up the stack of clothes neatly piled on the top step and grinned down at me.

I let the familiar shiver and warmth roll through me until I was able to stand on two feet again. I knew Chase was watching but standing naked before my mate was a thrilling sensation with absolutely no discomfort.

"Mom must have noticed you aren't completely comfortable with nudity around others," he commented.

My head dropped like it was something to be ashamed of. "My kind's just a little more modest about it," I admitted.

"Princess, it's perfectly fine. Kelsey struggled with it a lot at first, too. She was raised in the human world, so it was a foreign concept to her. She had only shifted privately and never even suspected others like her existed, let alone that she lived among an entire pack of wolf shifters."

I didn't know how that was even possible, but I believed him. I quickly dressed, and we headed into the house.

"Why was Kelsey raised in the human world?" I asked, curious now that he'd brought it up.

He hesitated for only a moment. "Did you know that some shifters can have extra powers?"

"Like the witches?" I asked. My dad had two at his disposal as well as a seer. He used them to help protect us.

"You know about the witches?"

"Yes, Daddy keeps two of them close by. He even had houses built on the edge of our property to both protect and ensure exclusivity to them for years. He has a seer, too."

"A seer?" he asked.

"Yes, you know the power to see into the future? She makes predictions. She's always told me that what she sees isn't necessarily clear and because of free will, visions can change. Only prophecies are bound to absolute truth. I've heard talk of a rumor that Daddy keeps her around because she once made a prophecy on the panthers. Tessa says it's why he's always been so adamant about keeping the panthers pure. I don't know if I really believe it all, but that's what I heard."

He nodded like that made sense. "Kelsey's a witch," he said. "It's why she was raised in the human world. Wolves fear the witches but are especially terrified of females with Alpha powers. Kelsey was born an Alpha, but she was also a triplet. Her sisters each had their own power. It became a problem, and at the age of four the girls were sentenced to death. Her parents couldn't save them all, but they were able to escape with her and keep her in hiding until she was about twelve. I guess the past caught up with them then. They killed her parents, but she got away and lived in the human world all alone until she came here. When her sisters died, she inherited all their gifts as well. She's one super badass witch," he said, proudly.

To say I was stunned would be putting it mildly. My dad protected our witches, but they were always kept at a distance. I think they secretly terrified him. Yet Kelsey wasn't treated any different than anyone else I'd met in San Marco, aside from maybe a slight reverence for being the Alpha's mate.

"Wow, that's an incredible story," I said, still trying to take it all in.

He shrugged. "To us, she's just Kelsey, though I definitely wouldn't want to piss her off."

We walked hand-in-hand, into the house and headed for the dining room. Everyone was there waiting.

"Finally," Liam complained. "We're starving waiting on your two."

Chase and I quickly took the last two empty seats. Mary said a blessing, and everyone dug in. It was a little intimidating seeing the size of plates piled high with food. Everyone was talking over top of each other. It was like some sort of organized chaos. I had never experienced a meal like it before. I waited quietly as large plates were passed around. If it happened to pass by me, I'd take a little, but there was no way I was jumping into the middle of those wolves and their food.

I think Chase noticed I was feeling overwhelmed. He started loading food onto my plate as he filled his own, until I finally had to tell him to stop.

Elise was sitting on my other side. I felt like I'd gotten to know the other ladies well, but Elise had been quieter, distracted, during our girls' day and hadn't opened up like Lily, Maddie, and Kelsey. It made it a little more awkward having her so close.

"So, Jenna," Elise started. "What are you majoring in?"

I shrugged. "I'm not sure anymore. My father gave me two options, science or business. I picked science, but I don't really know what I want to do."

"Yes, she does," Chase said. "She just isn't ready to admit it."

I looked at him in confusion. "And what is that?"

"Photography," he said simply.

I almost stopped breathing. I had never truly vocalized my desire to be a professional photographer, had I?

Elise nodded. "That could be a great choice if you're interested in working for the Westin Foundation. Did Chase explain to you about the family business?" I nodded. "Good, then you should know that we need graphic designers, and a fulltime photographer would work great with that position."

I chanced a look at Chase, feeling his tension on the rise. He shook his head slightly, not enough to draw attention to himself, but enough to tell me he didn't want to discuss it. I frowned and crossed my arms over my chest. "Seriously?" I whispered to him. He shot me a look.

"What?" Elise said.

"Tell her," I whispered to Chase.

He shook his head. "Just drop it, please."

I sighed. "It's nothing, I guess," I told Elise, but I knew she didn't buy it for one second.

"Spill it, pup, or there will be a twin team up on your ass," Elise told Chase.

That got the attention of Liam and Lily.

"Did someone say twin team up?" Lily asked excitedly.

"Chase is hiding something," Elise said.

"I'm not hiding anything," Chase demanded. "Just drop it, E."

"I'm sorry," I whispered. "I didn't know it was a big deal."

"Um, Jenna," Kyle said, trying to hold back a grin. "There's no such thing as a whisper in a house of wolves. You might as well just say it out loud, 'cause everyone is listening."

I blushed. "Sorry. I keep forgetting that."

"So," Lily said, dramatically cracking her knuckles, while Liam rolled his eyes and shook his head at her. "What's the extraction?"

"Chase is hiding something. Don't know what it is," Elise said.

"It's really not that big a deal," I defended.

Lily and Liam both began to rise.

"Not at my dinner table," Mary said. "Now take it on into the living room."

Oscar laughed, and Maddie shot him a "mom look" that had him stuffing another piece of ham in his mouth to keep from getting in trouble.

"Cut it out," Chase said. "It's really not that big of a deal. If you must know everything, I picked up extra minors in graphic design and network security. Over the summer Dad told me to consider my place at the Foundation, and I did. I knew there was a need. I want to bring our online presence into the twenty-first century, because it's very archaic, simple, and needs better security."

"Chase, that's awesome," Elise said. "Why didn't you just say that? We have room for more than one position. You can head up the department at your discretion. I still think a photographer would be great, though. If that's where Jenna's passion is, the two of you can work together."

"And if you're that good, Jenna, you could open a studio in town, too. We could use a photographer around here. I have to drive Z almost an hour to get professional pictures taken," Kelsey added. "If you brought your camera, I'd love you to do a set with Zander, as he's overdue on his eighteen-month pictures. If you didn't, we do have a decent one you can borrow."

Chase laughed. "You don't understand, Kels, Jenna doesn't go anywhere without her camera."

I elbowed him in the side. I was glad he chose to infuse a little humor just then because I was on the verge of emotional overload. My family had never understood my love of photography. It had been discouraged, my cameras confiscated, and my dad would never in a million years approve of me majoring in any form of art, let alone consider it a viable career option, yet these wonderful people I'd just met were basically voicing my dreams aloud and ready to hand them to me on a silver platter.

"I'd love to," I told Kelsey honestly over the lump forming in my throat.

"Great. I know you and Chase are supposed to head back

tomorrow, but if you could squeeze him in before you leave, that would be great," Kelsey said.

"Well." I looked at Chase. I almost blurted out, "We can just stay over a few more days," but I really felt like that was something I needed to discuss with him first. "You're here now," I suggested.

She looked at Zander. He was still relatively clean despite the meal and dressed in a cute little suit that I had been told was courtesy of his obsession with his Uncle Liam, who had taken over as CEO of the Westin Foundation.

"Yeah, okay, but the sun is already setting. Do you have any ideas for indoors?" she asked.

"Mary, may we be excused?" I asked.

"For pictures of my handsome grandson? Certainly," she said, and it was obvious she was head over heels in love with her grandson, both of them actually.

"Can I help?" Oscar asked.

"Sure, come on." I got up from the table and ran upstairs to gather my stuff. I was thankful I had brought the tripod, wanting to take some pictures of the town and local sceneries. Oscar proved to be a great extra set of hands. As I looked out the bedroom window I saw the most gorgeous sunset. There was a cliff not far from the house that would capture it perfectly if we could make it in time.

"Kelsey, I have an idea, but we have to hurry," I told her.

She grabbed Zander and they quickly followed me. The sun was almost down by the time we arrived at the spot I wanted, but the valley below was on fire in brilliant shades of red and orange. I quickly posed Zander near a small boulder and began shooting right away. I only had about five minutes, but he got restless quickly, wanting to explore the surrounding woods. I threw Oscar in with him and got a few good ones of the two of them for Mary.

"Okay, boys, let's head back to the house and see about a few inside shots," I told them. They both nodded, and Oscar helped me carry my gear back while Kelsey carried Zander.

Inside I set them up in the nursery. Zander had just upgraded to a big boy bed and it made a perfect backdrop for his age. A fun milestone. After a few posed shots, I pulled a pair of his PJ's from a drawer and changed him. Kelsey just sat back in the rocking chair, watching. I had never changed a baby before or even been around someone so small, but after a little wrestling match, I managed.

Z climbed into his bed and under the covers.

"Okay, now pretend to sleep," I told him, and he giggled but shut his eyes. "Okay, all done," I said, and he gave me a look of pure mischief. I was grateful I still had the camera raised, as I shot a few candid pictures while he played peek-a-boo with me by pulling the cover over his head.

Last, I had Oscar climb in bed next to him with a book. It was so precious I couldn't wait to see the end results.

When we were done, and I went to pack up, Zander ran over and climbed up on Kelsey's lap. He was talking and pointing to her belly. I pulled the camera back out and started taking a few pictures without them noticing. It was a beautiful moment.

I walked out into the hallway and hollered down for Kyle to come up. When he did, Chase joined him.

"Would you mind?" I asked, pointing to his mate and child.

Kyle grinned and walked over next to them. "Where do you want me?" he asked, and Kelsey and Zander looked up for the first time.

I shook my head at him. "Just act natural. Talk to them like you normally would."

"What are we talking about?" Kyle asked his son.

"Baby," Zander said, pointing to his mommy's tummy.

Kyle probably wasn't aware of it, but he beamed with pride. I was confident I'd gotten several good pictures when I decided to continue with the baby theme.

"How about I take a first pic of the four of you?" I asked.

"That'll still be quite some time off," Kelsey reminded me.

I shrugged. Kyle was kneeling next to the rocking chair, leaning in towards Kelsey. I walked over and posed their hands so that Kelsey and Kyle formed a heart on her still flat stomach. Zander was on her other side and without me telling him, he placed his small hand just below their heart. I snapped a few closeups and then pulled back to get all three of them. Zander leaned down and kissed his mom's stomach as a tear slipped down Kelsey's cheek and Kyle wiped it away. I already knew without checking it was a perfect, one of a kind picture.

After that I really did pack up and take my things back to Chase's room. He followed me, closing the door behind him. I already knew the dampener was on so we were free to talk.

"That was really great what you did back there," he said.

"Thanks. I'm sorry about dinner and putting you on the spot like that. You just have such great ideas for the company; I didn't know you were keeping them to yourself."

He shrugged. "I don't know if I would ever have been ready to speak up and tell them, so I'm glad you pushed me out of my comfort zone to talk about it. Elise seemed excited. I think it's going to work, Jenna."

I hugged him. "I'm really proud of you. And you know that these pictures could take me a few days to format. Would you, um . . ." I bit my lower lip. "Would you want to stay here a few extra days?"

He perked up. "You mean it?"

I nodded. "If you want to, or I can just send these in an email when I'm done."

"No, princess, that's great. I'd love to spend a few more days home, but I knew initially you weren't comfortable coming, so I would never have asked."

"I know. It's just not what I expected. I don't really know what I thought it'd be like, but I didn't expect it to feel more like home than, well, home." The thought saddened me, but it was the truth. "Anyway, if you're sure, I'm fine with staying a few more days, the rest of the week, whatever you want."

I could feel his joy through our bond. It was so intense, but it made me happy, too.

"Do you think I could plug my laptop into the TV in the living room and show Kelsey and Maddie some of the pics I took? I got some great ones of Oscar, too, and of both the boys together."

"Yeah, grab your stuff and come on."

Chase hooked my laptop up to the big screen television and called Kelsey and Maddie in while I set up. Instead of just the two moms, I got the entire family. I didn't mind. I was confident in my work and felt empowered by their support.

Once everyone was settled, I started scrolling through the pictures. There were lots of "oohs" and "aahs." Every now and then someone would ask me to stop and make note of a picture. I reminded them I still needed to do some touch-ups, but they seemed to love the raw photos I had taken.

As suspected, Mary requested copies of the ones I had taken

of both the boys. And when I got to the rocking chair pictures with Kelsey, they were so precious that she and Maddie were both in tears.

"They're really beautiful, Jenna. Chase is right, you have remarkable talent," Jason told me.

I blushed furiously. I think the fact it came from him, Chase's dad of all people, is what pushed me over the edge. I excused myself and rushed from the room as the tears started to fall. How many times had I wished my own father could see me like that?

"She's okay," I heard Chase tell them. "I've told her a thousand times how amazing her pictures are. Our professor raves over them every week, always using her stuff in class, but until this semester, I don't think anyone has ever appreciated her talent, especially not her dad. She's just a little overwhelmed right now by the praise, but I know she appreciates it."

I loved my mate. Truly loved him with all my heart, but I especially loved how he got me even on the things I never meant to share. I let myself have a good cry even if I felt stupid for it. It was like mourning something you never had to begin with.

I fell asleep before Chase came to bed, but it was a restless sleep until he lay in bed next to me, his arms around me, and I could hear his heart beating beneath my ear. Then, and only then, did I allow myself to truly rest peacefully.

Chase
Chapter 27

My parents were thrilled that Jenna and I had changed our minds and decided to stay longer. Life seemed to be moving in the right direction. I felt on top of the world and could clearly see our future planned out before us. It was wonderful . . . and then it wasn't.

On Thursday morning, Kyle called me down to his office. I had never seen him look so stressed before. The Betas and the entire Pack Council were there, but also present were two members of the Grand Council.

The Grand Council oversaw, and sort of governed, all packs. They weren't supposed to be affiliated with any one specific pack, but we all knew they each had their favorites. It wasn't a perfect system. We were all human, after all; okay, well, half human at least.

Being the youngest of the family I had never been invited to even a Pack Council meeting, let alone one that included Grand Council members. I couldn't fathom what they'd want from me.

"Chase, have a seat," Kyle said when I walked in to the room. To say I was nervous was an understatement. These men intimidated the crap out of me and made me feel like a small child again.

"Something's come up," Patrick told me.

I bit back my need to sarcastically reply, "Because, duh, why else would they have asked me to sit in on this meeting?"

"There's really no easy way of saying this," Kyle started. "King Lockhardt has gotten word of your mating to Jenna. He has declared war against the wolves and is rallying the big cats to battle. We've been given warning. They are coming for us and, I quote, 'Humbly request a neutral battle ground.' The battle is to take place in the badlands this Saturday. It gives us very little time to get our own resources together. I think he's underestimated the size of Westin Pack and the wolf alliance."

My heart dropped into my stomach. I knew Kyle had been concerned about this very thing. Neither Jenna nor I thought for a second her father would go through with it, though. I knew it was going to hurt my mate when I told her. As this reality sunk in, my wolf stirred in fury and I growled.

"Keep it cool, brother," Kyle warned. I could feel his Alpha power pressing down on me, trying to control me, and it only pissed me off more. I stubbornly wanted to fight against him, even knowing I shouldn't. I forced myself to calm down.

"What's our plan?" I asked when I felt safe to speak again.

Cedric, one of the Grand Council members, spoke up. "He notified the Grand Council directly, Chase. I'm not going to even bother trying to lecture you on the dangers or mating outside our kind. I can't even comprehend how you managed to convince Jenna Lockhardt, Princess of the panthers, to bond with you, but what's done is done and we have to deal with the threat at hand."

I shrugged. "It was simple. She's my one true mate."

Whispers of disbelief went around the room, but I ignored them.

"That's not even possible," Cedric said.

"Believe what you want. I know it. Jenna knows it. She is my true mate," I said stubbornly.

"At this point, it doesn't really matter," Ambrose, a Pack Council member, added. "What does this mean to the wolves?"

"Can't we just not show up? Force his hand to bring the fight here? See just how serious he is?" I asked.

Patrick spoke up. "I've already put in some inquiries. He's serious, Chase. There's movement on the East Coast. It appears the felines are rallying behind him in force."

"What does he want? I mean, seriously, what does he hope to accomplish from this?" I wasn't one hundred percent sure I wanted to know, but I needed to.

"He wants his daughter back and you dead," Cedric said.

I growled, but Patrick and Cole Anderson held me back when I started to lunge toward the threat, even knowing that Cedric was not the actual threat to me.

"Get a grip on it, Chase." Kyle snarled, letting his damn Alpha power subdue me once again. "He won't get Jenna. I promise you. How many are we talking, Patrick?"

"Hundreds, possibly thousands. Every flight into the area is booked. We'll have to go in on the ground. The area chosen is surprisingly far more wooded than you'd expect. We can plan for an aerial attack as well as ground. The cats will take to the trees, I'm certain of it. It will make it much harder to defend ourselves," Patrick briefed.

"This is not just a Westin threat," Cedric spoke, again. "They directed this to the Grand Council. We do not take lightly to such things. Kyle has agreed to temporarily lift the ban on the Bulgarians and their allies for this. Representatives from the fifteen largest packs worldwide will arrive tonight. We will formulate our plan then. First, we have to unite the packs before we can face an external enemy and hope to survive it."

The meeting ended shortly after. Unbeknownst to most, Patrick and Cole Anderson, as pack Betas and heads of security, had a lodge built just past what we considered our pack line. This was to be a place for visiting packs and representatives, a neutral territory that kept them off Westin land while trying to mend the breaks in the Grand Council alliances caused from the war with the Bulgarians. Our foreign visitors would be putting the place to use while everything got sorted.

I was relieved they would not be on Westin soil. Still too close, but better than the alternative. The Bulgarians had tried to kill Kelsey and had almost killed my father in the process. I was not ready to forgive all that had happened, and neither were most Westins. If they truly accepted the temporary peace treaty being discussed to go to war against the big cats for my mate, I would have to find it in my heart to make peace with them, because I would have an eternal debt owed to each and every one of them.

When I was finally dismissed, I headed out to the living room and found Mom and Jenna with their heads together on the couch looking over the pictures Jenna took of Zander for the hundredth time.

"Princess, can I talk to you in private for a minute?" I asked her.

"What's wrong?" she asked, clearly feeding off my own

anxiety.

"Private," I said.

"It's for the best, dear. We can finish this later," Mom told her. I think that terrified her even more. I had no doubt my father had relayed the information to my mother already through the telepathic connection of their bond. Someday Jenna and I would be able to do that, too.

I led the way upstairs, double-checked to ensure the dampener was still on, and sat her down on the bed.

"You're really freaking me out, Chase," she admitted. "What's going on?"

I didn't want to tell her, but she had to know. "Your father has found out about us."

"What? Already? The girls swore to keep it a secret," she said, starting to cry. "How bad is it, Chase?"

"Worse than we imagined. He's notified our Grand Council with declaration of war against the wolves. He's rallying the big cats together and we're to meet for battle this Saturday in some obscure areas of the badlands in North Dakota."

"Why? What does he hope to gain from that?"

"You," I said simply. "He wants you back and me dead."

She gasped and started to sob. I dropped to my knees before her and hugged her close. "I won't let it happen, sweetheart."

When her initial sobs started to subside, she reached in her pocket and took out her phone. It was too late to stop her when I realized what she was doing. I could hear the phone ringing on the other side.

"Is he insane? Has he lost his mind? Please tell me this is dementia or some onset to Alzheimer's, Mother. What is Daddy thinking, calling a war against the wolves?"

"Jenna?" the woman asked, like she wasn't sure she believed it was really her.

"Yes, Mother, it's me, Jenna. Do you know anything about this?" she asked.

"Jenna, are you hurt, baby?" The woman on the other end was clearly upset and crying.

"Why would you think I was hurt, Mother?"

"We heard the wolves had you, baby. Your daddy says they have you hostage and won't let you come home. I spoke to Tessa earlier, and she admitted you weren't with the other girls in Cabo. Your daddy's going out of his mind trying to get you back safely."

"Mother, listen to me. I am not hurt. I am not being held against my will. I'm free to come home or go wherever I want, anytime I want. You don't need to worry about that."

"Are they telling you to say that?"

"Of course not. Tell me what you think happened," Jenna said, sounding far more patient than I ever could in this situation.

"They said you met a boy at school, a wolf. He became infatuated with you and took you off to his territory over spring break and plans to keep you. We're so worried, baby."

"Mother, listen closely." Jenna's voice became harsher now. "I did meet a boy at school. His name is Chase, and he's my one true mate. Daddy knows this, because he's threatening to kill Chase, take me home against my will, and has threatened war against all the wolves. I don't expect you to understand, but this is my choice. My decision. No one else's. I choose Chase, my true mate, Mother, and I love him."

I heard the gasp and the sobs. I held Jenna close as she shook. The vibes flowing off her through our bond were angry ones. I could understand that. I hadn't expected it, but I knew that if my family threatened her in any way I'd have the same reaction.

"You're too young to understand what's happening, Jenna. Maybe we shouldn't have sheltered you so much, but a wolf cannot be your mate. It's not possible."

"It is actually, and if you and Daddy weren't so racist, you'd understand that. We've already sealed our bond, Mother. To hurt Chase is the same as hurting me."

"For a while, maybe, but it will get better in time. You'll see. Your daddy knows what he's doing to protect you, Jenna. Please don't fight this."

"Don't fight it? Just come home. Let him kill my mate and all will be just fine? Do you even hear yourself?"

"The seer said this would happen," she muttered under her breath.

"What? The seer said what would happen?" Jenna demanded.

"The seer said upon your birth that you and the pride would be the undoing of the panthers. You're going to destroy us all. So, you see, this young man cannot be your mate, Jenna, because your true mate is a lion. We've always known this."

Jenna became very calm. I expected her to be shocked, to cry, to freak out, but the eerie calm that washed through her scared me far more.

"You don't know shit, Mother. Goodbye. I'll see you on the battlefront."

The woman was yelling for someone and crying hysterically as Jenna calmly hung up the phone.

She had a far off look in her eye when she spoke again. "Did you hear what she said—the part about me bringing destruction to the panthers?"

I nodded, but wasn't sure she was actually seeing me. "Yes," I said.

"It all makes so much sense now. They always treated me carefully, different from Tessa—like they were afraid to upset me, even though I never gave them any cause to worry. Never. It all comes back to some stupid prophecy a seer told them. I'm sorry it's coming down to this, but if it's a war he wants, it's a war he'll get. I'll kill him, Chase. I'll kill my father before I let him hurt you."

The lethal tone in her voice would have scared the shit out of a full-blown Alpha, but it just made pride well up within me. My princess was ready to fight for us at all costs. I hated that there would likely be casualties. I hated that others had to go war for us, but when Kelsey had been threatened, the pack rallied behind her, and I had zero doubt they would for us, too. I had proudly fought for my brother and his mate, and I could not take that choice away from anyone else. If they chose to stand with Jenna and me, I would accept the help with gratitude.

Before we had a chance to discuss, my phone started ringing. I picked it up, more out of habit than anything, and saw Matt Williams' face smiling back at me.

"Hello?" I answered.

"Hey man, so I just got a call from my dad and you know what he said?"

"Matt, I got some shit I'm dealing with here, can you either spit it out or I'll call you back later."

"Yeah, that's pretty much what he said, too. All big cats are being requested to stand with King Lockhardt in North Dakota this Saturday. You know why?"

I sat down, feeling a little deflated. “I know, or at least I had heard. He issued war against the wolves. We had a meeting about it a little while ago.”

“Aren’t the wolves already divided in war?” Matt asked. Jenna’s eyes were huge with questions, but I smiled trying to reassure her.

“Yes, but the Grand Council has already called a temporary peace. Representatives from the largest fifteen packs are coming together tonight to discuss. I have to believe it’s going to work out okay.”

“I’m calling the brothers in,” Matt said. “I’m not a panther and he’s not my King, but you are my brother and I will fight by your side to the death.”

“Thanks, Matt. I really appreciate that, dude. Let’s hope it doesn’t come down to that.”

Jenna

Chapter 28

When Chase got off the phone with Matt, he kissed me and left. As much as I loved him, I was glad for a few minutes alone for my meltdown. After a good cry and a shower, I picked up my phone and called Tessa.

"Jenna, are you okay?" she asked. "Mother just called. Daddy's ordering all of us to North Dakota. He says he's coming to get you and bring you home. I swear I didn't tell them anything."

"I know you wouldn't have done that. I just can't believe he's acting like this. Mother didn't even want to hear my explanation. She just started ranting about how Chase couldn't be my mate because the seer said I'd mate a lion and it would destroy the panthers or some nonsense like that."

Tessa was quiet on the other end, and it gave me a bad feeling. "Tessa?"

"She really told you about that?" she finally asked.

"You knew?" I couldn't help the hurt that knowledge caused.

"Yeah, everyone knows. Daddy said that telling you could lead you down the path, that we should never discuss it. He had all of us relocate to the ARC so we could keep an eye on you and take out any lions that tried to come too near you. It's the real reason he's so hung up on this pure bloodline stuff. He's spent our entire lives trying to keep the prophecy from becoming reality. The seer terrifies him—it's why he keeps her close and happy."

I was stunned and didn't know what to say.

"Jenna, are you still there? Hello?"

"I'm here," I said, feeling disconnected from it all.

"I'm sorry. We were sworn to secrecy—never to discuss it

with you. Most of us were relieved when you started showing interest in Chase, though shocked when you mated him. Still, it wasn't a lion, so we thought the prophecy couldn't be fulfilled now, and yet here we are about to walk into war, felines against canines. It's insane, and Jenna?"

"Yeah?"

"I don't care what he says. I know you chose Chase of your own free will. You told me you love him, and I'll support that. If it comes down to it, I won't fight against you. You're my sister. There are others here who feel the same way."

"Thank you, Tessa. I love you," I told her honestly. I didn't know what else to say. Her choosing me meant more than I could ever explain. "I guess I'll see you Saturday on the battlefield."

"I guess so, and I love you, too."

When Tessa hung up, I realized I was numb. So much had happened. I had so much information to digest. It was too much. I curled up in a tight ball and let the darkness take me over, grateful for it.

When I stirred again, the room was dark. I could feel Chase's arm draped heavily over my waist and his warm body pressed against my back. Safety and love washed over me. I pushed aside the thoughts running through my head, threatening to overtake me, and just reveled in my mate. I breathed in his woodsy scent and snuggled back into him a little closer. He was snoring lightly, but his arm flexed protectively tighter around me.

Pain, hurt, and fear were prevalent emotions after all I had learned. Our pack, and from the sounds of it, many other wolves, would be marching into battle for me. I'd have to live with the outcome of that. My parents would do anything they felt necessary to get me back, not even realizing I was right here and if they'd just open up and talk to me they'd see that. But they were too blinded by their own ignorance and assumptions to even consider what impact their actions were having on me, their own daughter.

Somehow I must have fallen back to sleep, because the next conscious thing I remembered was Kyle standing over us. I yelped and pulled the covers closer around me. Looking down, I had my pajamas on and remembered changing before Chase came in. Relieved, I sat up and stretched.

"Hey, man, what's going on?" Chase asked Kyle.

"I think you two should be present for this morning's meetings. Sorry to intrude so early. Breakfast is ready and we'll be heading out in thirty minutes," he said, before turning and walking back out of the room.

I relaxed when the door closed behind him. It wasn't that I had anything against Kyle, I didn't. He had just startled me and set my panther on high alert with the awkward wake-up call.

Chase groaned and pulled me back into him. He started kissing down my neck.

"Today's a big day, we shouldn't keep him waiting," I reminded him.

"You understand what's going on today, right?" Chase asked.

I nodded. "I think so."

"They are going to parade us around to the Alphas of the largest known wolf packs in hopes of garnering sympathy and aligning the wolves. I hate that they are going to put you on display like that—the little panther whose only fault was falling in love with a wolf. We could just leave, you know? Disappear."

I considered that for a moment. "If you had mentioned that a week ago, I'd have been perfectly content and onboard with that plan, but now, it's different. Wolves are pack animals. I would be fine, but after spending time here in San Marco, meeting your family, seeing the connections of the wolves here, I can't ask that of you. You need your pack. You need your family, and for some crazy reason, so do I. Besides, what kind of people would we be to leave and force them all to deal with our crap? Daddy will still come after them. He'll still try and punish someone even if he can't get to us. I can't live with that on my conscience. Can you?"

Relief, that's what I felt when he shook his head sadly. "I know you're right," he said. He kissed his bond mark on my shoulder. "Let's do this then."

Forty-five minutes later we had showered, dressed, eaten breakfast, or in my case picked at it, as I was too nervous to eat much, and then we were on our way down the mountain.

Almost immediately we passed the sign reading "Leaving San Marco," we turned right onto a dirt road. A little ways in, it opened up to a huge lodge. It looked like the kind of getaway honeymooners and families alike would seek out.

Exiting the vehicle, Chase took my hand and squeezed. I

could feel his nerves even while he tried to give me courage. Inside, the lobby of the lodge was even nicer than the outside. A huge stone fireplace was the centerpiece of the room, and comfortable leather chairs and couches were strategically placed throughout.

"This is nice," I commented.

"Thanks," Kyle said. "It was Patrick's idea, and a damn good one. This is the first instance we've had to use the place. In some strange way I suppose we have you two to thank for that."

Chase snorted and shook his head.

"My mate always finds the good in any situation," Kelsey said as she and Patrick walked in from one of the hallways. She gave Kyle a quick kiss.

"Everyone's here," Patrick informed him.

"Everyone?" Kyle asked, sounding a little shocked and maybe a tad uncomfortable.

"Everyone," Kelsey assured him.

"I heard Nikolai was finally chosen as the new Alpha of the Bulgarians. Is that true?" Kyle asked.

"It is, Alpha," Patrick said formally.

"I remember him well. He was always a fair and worthy opponent in the camp games as young pups," Kyle said fondly. "Let's hope that hasn't changed too much over the years."

Chase pulled me over to the side. "Taking Patrick's cue, I think we should stick to formalities here. Anytime you address Kyle, call him Alpha. Kelsey's title is Pack Mother. Can you remember that?"

I nodded.

"You can address me as Beta, as well as Cole, who's around here somewhere," Patrick said as he walked over to contribute to the conversation. "There will also be a lot of other Alphas and Councilmen. You can differentiate the Alphas by adding their pack before their title. Longhorn Alpha. Collier Alpha. Bulgarian Alpha. Do you understand?"

I nodded again.

"Formally for the Councilmen you can call them 'Grand Councilman' then insert their name as you learn them. Same goes for Pack Councilmen. I know it's a lot to take in, and I wish we had more time to prepare you both, but for the most part, just sit quietly and only speak when specifically spoken to. Kyle and I will try to intervene wherever we can."

"Do you have any questions?" Chase asked me.

"A million, but they can wait. Have you ever sat through something like this before?" I asked him.

"No, the last gathering of the packs took place before I was born. It's not an everyday occurrence, and the formalities go a long way to show reverence and respect to our guests. In a setting with so many Alphas, it's especially important. Things can go from friendly to hostile quickly. Should that occur, stay behind me. If I'm not around, Patrick or Kyle will protect you, or stay with Kelsey. Trust me when I say she can hold her own with the whole lot of them."

Patrick led us all down the hall he and Kelsey had come from and into a large conference room. There were sixteen tables throughout the room. It seemed a little odd to me at first, then I remembered how territorial wolves can be. Memories came back of how Chase had to literally mark our territory at the cabin after the tigers had been found there. I assumed the layout of the room was to give each pack, plus the Grand Council, their own space.

Kelsey passed out legal pads and pens to each of us. On the top of mine she had written *Remember, wolves have really good hearing, so write your questions down before speaking aloud.*

I nodded and smiled reassuringly at her.

When we were settled, I jotted down my suspicions about the room, and Chase confirmed them. I looked around at the tables curiously, checking out the people sitting at each. Chase grabbed my arm gently to get my attention and pushed his pad towards me.

Do not make eye contact. Keep yours lowered, or else it could be considered a threat.

My eyes shot up to his and I saw he was being entirely serious. I shuddered at the thought. It was something I did know, I just hadn't really been around the wolves long enough for that to fully sink in, but he was right. In a room full of Alphas, I could start another war without even realizing it, over something so simple. I decided it was best to stay close to Chase and keep my head down. I scooted my chair a little closer to him and linked my arm around his. He leaned in and kissed my temple and smiled.

You're doing great, he wrote on his pad.

I'm so nervous, I admitted on mine.

An older man, short, with a receding hairline, stood and

walked to the center of the room. All eyes followed him, and the tables began to still.

"Greetings, Alphas," he spoke. "It has been far too long since the great leaders of wolves came together for a common goal. I am only saddened that it is for this such reason. Each of you today will have a chance to voice your opinions, ask your questions, and decide for the entirety of your pack where you stand. As you have each been informed, Chase Westin of the Westin Pack has taken a mate. He believes her to be his one true mate, yet she is not of our kind. Jenna Lockhardt is the youngest daughter of King Lockhardt of the panthers. He has rallied the big cats together and issued a formal notice of war to your Grand Council. Had he sent this notice directly to Westin, the decision would be a simpler one to make. He didn't do that though. King Lockhardt has issued a threat to all wolves."

There were growls of anger throughout the room. The intensity of it made me shiver.

Grand Councilman Omar, Chase jotted down on my notepad. I added my own notes to remember which one he was.

"At this time, we know our kind is at odds among ourselves. Do not think for one second that King Lockhardt is not already aware of this fact."

He sat down and a younger, more handsome and distinguishing look man took his place. Since he came from the same table Grand Councilman Omar had just returned to, I deduced he was also a Grand Council member.

"Bulgarian Alpha Nikolai, your predecessor issued a war against the Westin Pack. The Grand Council sincerely appreciates you just being here. That said, the first issue at hand is to determine if the wolves are even capable of setting aside our differences and working together for the betterment of all wolves. Alpha," he said addressing Nikolai, "what say you?"

"I am aware of the grievances my late Alpha had against Westin. My people are not prepared to forgive the loss of our great leader, but I am Alpha now, and his grievances are not my own. I cannot promise an alliance at this time, but I can promise to sit and talk with Westin Alpha Kyle in private and consider a temporary treaty for the good of all wolves."

Kyle began a round of clapping in show of gratitude for his decision. The Grand Councilman Titus—I knew because Chase had once again written it for me—motioned for quiet and thanked the Bulgarian Alpha.

"Am I to assume that those packs aligned with Westin and those siding with the Bulgarians will respect the decision and possible treaty should it be?"

The Alpha at each table agreed. The last one to answer sat directly across the room from us and stared at the Westin table with the look of a thousand daggers. "Aye," he finally said in an unmistakable Irish accent. I glanced between him and Patrick and noticed an uncanny resemblance.

Patrick's dad, Chase wrote. *He's an arse.*

I bit my lip, trying not to laugh.

Most of the remainder of the morning meeting went by in a blur, or more like a snooze. I was quite bored and struggling to focus. When Grand Councilman Titus was back up in the spotlight, he called Chase forward and that brought my attention back faster than a freight train. My heart was pounding in my chest with nerves as my mate left me for the first time that day.

"Chase," Titus said, grasping his forearm as Chase reached for the other man's.

"Grand Councilman Titus, thank you for your consideration, and that extends to each of you present here today. I cannot tell you in complete honesty that had I known King Lockhardt would resort to such extreme measures, I would have reconsidered taking Jenna as my mate, because that would be a lie. Jenna Lockhardt is my one true mate and as such we had every right to complete our mating and begin sealing our bond—a bond that has grown quickly and strengthens more each day."

I blushed when he looked my way. I couldn't believe he was speaking so candidly about our bond to these strangers.

"If you have any questions for me or Jenna, I will be happy to answer them. With the Grand Council's permission, I'd like to go ahead and open the floor for any such questions. If you wish to hold them for private, we will be available over the lunch break, but I do encourage you to bring any concerns, fears, or inquiries forward so that the record can be set straight."

Titus looked back towards the Grand Council table and then nodded his approval. What I assumed was the Alpha, from the table closest to ours raised his hand.

"Collier Alpha Zachary, you have the floor," Titus said formally.

"Thank you. Now Chase, I know that many have doubts and questions regarding the validity of your mating with the Lockhardt Princess."

Chase pulled his shirt over and showed my bond mark on his neck. I bit back a growl of my own in surprise.

The Alpha smiled. "No, son, we realize the bond occurred or else none of us would be here today. What I mean is the validity of her being your true mate. It seems unlikely and to many, inconceivable. I am quite close with your family and I understand the importance of true mates in the Westin Pack. Can you give us some examples or solid reasoning why anyone here should believe that the Princess is your true mate?"

Chase took a deep breath. I could feel his agitation.

"I'll admit that no one was as shocked as me. I walked into my first calculus class of the semester and I smelled her, my wolf stirred, and I felt her presence nearby. For weeks it was a battle of hot and cold every time I saw her. I thought I was losing my mind. How could I feel so much and be so sure one moment, and then look at her and feel nothing the next? I called my Alpha immediately and voiced my concerns, not only that my mate was not a wolf, but that there was something wrong with our bond."

Hurt sliced through my chest and unconsciously my arm moved and I placed my hand over my heart. I then saw Chase wince and rub the exact matching spot on his own chest.

He looked up at me and grinned. "Just hearing me say that caused my mate a great deal of pain. I know this for a fact, because I could feel her pain just now, as fiercely as if it were my own, but bear with me a moment. It wasn't until sometime later that I finally realized Jenna has an identical twin sister. There was never anything wrong with our bond, I was feeling nothing, when looking at the wrong girl. They may be identical, but I could pick Jenna out of a million lookalikes, because I only have one true mate, and that is Jenna."

This time tears of happiness pricked my eyes and he winked at me.

"Now I can't tell you how or why this happened. Until it happened to me, I had no idea that my true mate could possibly be anything other than wolf. I just didn't know. So, for those of you questioning it, I get it. Unless it happens to you, you may always have a bit of skepticism about it, and that's okay. This isn't really about whether you believe the origin of our mating or not, because the fact is, Jenna Lockhardt is my mate. She carries my mark as I proudly carry hers. Our bond is strengthening at an alarming rate. As best as we can figure the panthers and the wolves have different bonding signs, and we are meeting both simultaneously. It's remarkable, actually. You are free to test our bond if need be. We have nothing to hide. Her father doesn't just want her back, trust me, she's tried to reach out to them. They know she's safe. What they want is my head, literally, not figuratively, and not attached to this body."

That caused grumblings throughout the room.

"Rest assured, the only reason King Lockhardt went to the Grand Council was to use intimidation. They don't understand the power of pack. Their kind doesn't form bonds and relationships the way we wolves do. He does not understand that you come after one, you come after all. It's a foreign concept. He expects the Grand Council to hand me over to him, as per his request, because he believes it's okay to cut one, for the good of the whole. Is that how we feel? Is that what we believe?"

"No!"

"He will not win this battle!"

"We fight for all!"

And other shouts came throughout the room.

"Westin Pack is ready to fight. We are large and we are fierce, but the word coming in is that he has rallied every able bodied large cat to come after us. They are already en route to North Dakota, taking up every available seat into the area, because he thinks that will stall our numbers even further, should we have to fight. I do not wish death upon our kind or theirs. It hurts my heart knowing what we're asking here—knowing that some of you, or some of your people, may not make it out of this alive. Westin's been at war against our own brothers for too long. It's time to mend those differences, not just for this, but for good. And if you all choose to turn tail and head home, then I truly pray they kill me swiftly, because living a life without my mate, is far worse than death itself."

The tension in the air was tangible. Chase had angered and rallied an entire room filled with domineering Alphas. My pulse was racing when he took his seat next to me again. Omar came back up, thanked everyone for their consideration, and adjourned us for break.

Several people came up to me and introduced themselves. There were too many names for me to keep up with. The Alpha from Collier pack came over to speak with Chase.

"I'm sorry to have put you on the spot like that, but I'm proud of how you handled yourself, son. That was exactly what they needed to hear. I think you'll have your majority before we reconvene. And in case no one else has bothered to say it, congratulations. It's not always easy to follow your heart. I wish you both many years of happiness."

"Thank you, Zach. I really appreciate that," Chase said before turning to me. "Jenna, this is Zach Collier, Maddie's father."

The mention of his daughter made his eyes glass over. If I didn't know better, I'd swear he was on the verge of tears.

"I know what it's like to lose a daughter. Your father is a fool for pursuing this," he said sincerely. "A damn fool."

Chase

Chapter 29

I couldn't believe it. Zach was right. We had full support of all the packs before recess ended. Kyle and Nikolai came to a peaceful agreement for a temporary treaty. The wolves were aligned and ready for battle.

In a whirlwind of organized chaos, we were settling into North Dakota within twenty-four hours. Those packs that had already known they would align with Westin had sent their wolves on ahead of the meetings. The holdouts scrambled to get theirs in on time. In all, the fifteen largest packs supplied fifty percent of their biggest and strongest wolves for battle. Of course, no one could question or argue if the numbers were legit because packs kept such information tightly controlled, but it equaled out to a whole lot of wolves.

Westin Pack brought in even more. It looked to me like our entire pack was present, but Kyle assured me it was only around seventy percent. I hated knowing he and Kelsey had argued over her attendance. She was pregnant and therefore couldn't shift, but she had been working on her witchy talents and could call upon nature and do other stuff, that I shuddered to think about, even while in human form. Plus, under the code of shifters she could be neutralized, but not killed as it went against the law of shifters dating back to the bible. We couldn't kill a human while in animal form. I mean, technically it could be done, but it went against all shifter morals. We may have our differences from the cats, but everyone agreed that would not be one of them.

It took a heck of a lot of convincing, but in the end, Mom and Dad conceded and stayed back to protect the mostly women and children who remained behind. Maddie, being pregnant, also couldn't go, and after a screaming match with Liam he finally conceded to stay behind, too. He was not happy about it, and I loved him for that, but the reality of the situation was that he was already CEO of the Westin Foundation and that secured the financial future of the pack. If something happened to Kyle, God forbid, Alpha power would transfer to Patrick as Elise's mate until Zander came of age and shifted for the first time. Patrick, as Beta to the Alpha and head of security for Westin, was not going to step down from the fight. If anything happened to him as well, Liam would be next in line for Alpha and we needed him safe to preserve the pack.

North Dakota was still cold despite the spring weather we'd been experiencing in California. What was Jenna's dad thinking? Most of the large cats tended to live in warmer climates, didn't they? I realized I really didn't know all that much about the felines. Since my kids someday had a fifty-fifty chance of being one, I vowed to ask more questions and research panthers when all this was over.

In total there were over five thousand wolves present. Plus, all my fraternity brothers had showed up. They literally dropped what they were doing, canceled their own spring break plans, and came to stand by my side. Even Chad was there, though I wasn't sure what benefit he could possibly be, and I worried the big cats would eat him whole, but there he was, and it meant the world to me.

"You did this?" I asked Matt, looking around at my brothers.

He shrugged as I bro-hugged him. "What's going down is wrong. We're ready to stand by you. Brothers for life," Matt reminded me.

"Brothers for life," I repeated, feeling a little overwhelmed.

Later I pulled Matt aside to make certain he really wanted to go through with it. "I know you were ordered to fight with the cats. I don't want you getting in trouble for this."

"I spoke to my parents, right after talking with you the other day. They respect my decision to stand with the dogs. Enough that they refused to come at all. My family won't stand with them to fight against you. Not all the cats are blindly following him," he informed me.

"How many do they have? Do you know?" I asked, not a hundred percent sure I was ready to hear the answer.

"I don't know. I considered checking in and going all double agent like, but that's just not right. So, I'm gonna stick around over here and get to know as many of these dogs as possible so I'm not mistaken as the enemy when the time comes," Matt said.

I laughed. "Probably a good plan."

Jenna and I discussed trying to reach out to her parents one last time in attempt to stop it all, but the Grand Council forbade it, explaining there would be time just before the call for war began. The King had written in a negotiation period, making it very formal and civilized. We all knew that was up until the point he didn't get what he wanted.

I spent a restless night holding my mate as we whispered until the wee hours of the morning. Exhausted and nervous after awakening, we met with Kyle and the Grand Council. A group of about one hundred would be walking out on the battlefield to meet with Jenna's dad first. If all went south from there, which we expected it would, the remainder of the wolves would present themselves. If the sheer number did not make him stand down, then we'd fight.

"You ready for this?" I asked Jenna when the time came.

"Ready as I'll ever be," she said a little too cheerfully. I could feel her nerves through our bond, betraying the smile on her face.

"Liar," I said, making her laugh and smack my arm playfully just as her parents came into view. I didn't have to ask for verification; the scowl on her father's face gave him away.

Jenna wasn't looking at them though, but she was beaming up at me, still caught up in our playful banter. I heard her mother gasp at the sight. I'm not sure what they had been expecting, but we clearly weren't it.

"Beautiful, they're here," I said, nodding towards her family. As we approached, Tessa shot us both sad, apologetic looks as she stood with their parents.

Titus, as the largest and fiercest looking Grand Councilman, both in wolf and human forms, was chosen as the representative for the wolves.

"Edmond," Titus spoke, greeting the King informally. "I am Titus. We spoke over the phone."

King Lockhardt seemed thrown off by the informality for a

second. "Yes, of course. I see you brought my daughter, but I'm sorry to say that wolf, who has corrupted her, appears to still be alive."

"The Council has met, along with the Alphas from fifteen of our largest packs and we all have heard them out, and deliberated. We have unanimously agreed and found no reason to intervene here. Their bond has been tested, Edmond. They are true mates and we do not interfere with pairings ordained by God himself. That is a sacred bond to the wolves. And we will not do your dirty work for you by killing one of our own and devastating another, because make no doubt about it, Jenna as Chase Westin's mate is one of us. She will be protected by her pack which has aligned with fourteen others ready to go to battle, and fight to the death, if needed, for Jenna and Chase."

"Do not speak of my daughter so informally. She is a Princess of the panthers, part of this royal family, and I will do whatever is necessary to keep our bloodline pure, before she destroys us all," her father spat back at Titus.

"My apologies, Princess," Titus said to Jenna, otherwise ignoring her father.

Jenna nodded. "I thought you were only scared of the lions, Daddy? I beg you, please don't do this. People do not need to die needlessly over this."

"No one needs to die needlessly. Turn the boy over to me for execution and come home, and all of this will be forgotten," he said coldly.

Jenna held tighter to my arm, finding my hand with her own and linking our fingers. "I'm exactly where I'm supposed to be, Daddy. Why can't you see that? He's a good man. Just give him a chance. Please. I've never asked anything of you before, but I'm begging for this."

I saw her father soften. His eyes showed remorse and confusion, but he quickly straightened his shoulders back and huffed his chest in a sign of dominance. It set my wolf on edge and I pulled Jenna behind me, raising my chin to meet his gaze in defiance. The challenge wasn't quite as impactful as it would have been to a wolf, but it stirred the other wolves as they recognized my show of power, something I had rarely ever done. I was an Alpha, too. It ran strong in my blood. As the baby of the family it was often overlooked and unnecessary, but it was a part of me and fueled my wolf's aggressive side.

"Your show of power does not scare me, boy," the King said, but the scent he was giving off betrayed him. He was scared and my wolf was seeing blood because of it.

"It should, sir," I said. Titus glared at me, but I didn't care.

"You show your hands too quickly, Titus," Edmond said. "I have brought ten times this pack of mutts." He scanned the hundred or so people gathered with us. His eyes stopped and confusion, then anger flashed across his face. "You, you're Doug Williams boy," he said, calling Matt out. "You get confused along the way, son? You're supposed to be back at the hill."

"No sir, I'm not. I'm exactly where I'm supposed to be," Matt said, walking forward and placing his hand on my shoulder. "Once a dog, always a dog." Howls broke out throughout the group, causing an eerie noise as it echoed across the land.

"Brothers for life," I said, as he squeezed and side-hugged me.

"Damn straight," Matt said.

"You were ordered to fight with your kind," the King reminded him. "Your father will pay for your insubordination. What an embarrassment you have brought to your family today."

"No sir, my family is proud of my decision to stand with my friends and fight for their right to love. If anyone is an embarrassment here, it is you."

The King started to make an aggressive move towards us, causing a growl to bubble out of me before I could stop it. It halted him on the spot.

"The signal of war has not been given, Your Highness. An act of aggression towards these boys will void all your requests, and my wolves will be forced to act," Titus warned, and even my wolf, already worked up and looking for a fight, cowered.

"Daddy," Jenna tried one last time. "It's not too late to stop this."

"It's not too late for you to come home," he reminded her.

"I can do that, Daddy. I would be happy to come home for a visit and to discuss this like civilized creatures with you and Mother. Just call this off and we can work this out."

Her mother looked up at her mate with tears in her eyes.

"Listen to her, Daddy," Tessa begged.

"The boy dies today," he said coldly.

"Hear my words," Jenna responded just coldly. "Kill my mate, and I will kill you, and then I will kill myself because I will not live without him."

"Jenna!" her mother screeched.

"Get her out of here," Titus said to me.

"No!" Jenna yelled. "This is about his control of me. I will not stand by and allow these people to fight for me while I cower back at camp. I fight, too. I fight for my mate, and I fight for myself."

Howls went up all around us, and more came further in the distance.

"Time's up," Titus said. "What's your word, sir?" He spat out the word "sir" like it disgusted him.

Edmond cried out a high-pitched squeal I had never heard before and suddenly hundreds of large cats began marching towards us. Some took to the trees before they even reached us.

"Shit, they've already shifted," Kyle swore under his breath, speaking for the first time.

Edmond gave me an eerie grin. "Let the war begin," he yelled.

I looked over my shoulder to see a hundred wolves shifting without bothering to even strip their clothes off, and a sea of wolves cresting the hill behind us. I looked back at the shock on Edmond's face as he saw the sheer number of wolves present. I knew he had underestimated us. What he didn't know, is that our wolves had orders to neutralize, to not kill unless it was a kill-or-be-killed situation.

"I've got your back, big brother," Chad told me. He seemed eager and excited to be part of the action this time, as he shifted into his chubby little squirrel form.

"Watch your back, little brother," I told him as he nodded his head, causing his fat cheeks to jiggle, before giving me what sort of looked like a thumbs-up, if a squirrel had thumbs.

As the call of war sounded, I watched Chad take off at lightning speed and hone in on two large panthers by a tall tree. He leaped into the air and landed on one of their heads as he used it to elevate himself into the tree above. The bigger cat roared in fury and they both began climbing after him. I sure hoped Chad remembered that they climb trees, too.

I nodded to Jenna and we shifted simultaneously. As I sideswiped a cougar, and dodged a puma, I was careful to keep Jenna at my side at all times. I couldn't help but glance up every now and then, worried for my tiny friend.

Chad had climbed out to the very tip of a limb. One of the panthers was closing the gap slowly between them as he taunted the cat with squeaky chatter. As the panther tried to pounce at the last minute, Chad bounced on the limb then, like an acrobat, flew even higher into the tree. His abandoned branch snapped forward and smacked the panther in the face, knocking him off balance. Letting out a loud roar, he fell to the ground with a thump.

The next remaining panther gave chase, climbing higher still into the tree after Chad. It was dizzying to watch him climb even from the ground, but he maneuvered the thin branches with grace defying his round body. The panther climbed as high as he dared and began shaking the treetop. It swayed back and forth before Chad went airborne. I stopped and gasped, but he easily grabbed a branch on the top of the closest tree and appeared to be heckling the panther from his new position. Knowing he was safe, I turned back to the fight on the ground.

Kyle and Nikolai were working side by side holding off the King from me. Tessa was at Jenna's other side, both attacking nearby cats while Tessa was protecting her sister. Her mother hissed at them, but moved on to help her mate.

I chanced a look around and saw several fallen, both dogs and cats. A vicious battle between Matt and another jaguar was going on. The large male was getting the upper hand. I yipped, and Patrick's red wolf was immediately by my side. I nodded at Jenna and he took my place as I ran to help my friend.

A black panther joined the fight. I couldn't tell which side she was fighting for. Knocking into Matt while grabbing hold of the other jaguar's tail at the same time, she was then knocked out of the way just as I was coming onto the scene. The cats leapt into the air and massive paws swiped at each other as they both fell hard to the ground.

I watched as my stomach lurched into my heart. I finally reached them and stood over my friend, willing him to get up. He didn't move. The panther that had joined the fight shifted. Anita! I hung my head as she checked him and collapsed across his still body, sobbing. Not Matt, please Lord, not Matt!

I looked towards the sky and let out a painful howl for my fallen friend.

Kelsey arrived seemingly from nowhere. She dropped to her knees, pushing Anita aside and got to work on Matt. It only took a minute before her fist slammed into the ground. She had tears streaming down her face as she raised her eyes to meet mine and shook her head.

"I'm so sorry, Chase," she whispered.

I looked around, sickened by the amount of similar scenes around me. Jenna! I turned and forced my way through a few fights in search of my mate. Patrick had been joined by Cole Anderson, protecting her. Her father was descending on the both of them. I shoved my way into the skirmish and pushed them aside. When they didn't back off, I barked and let go of some of my own Alpha powers. They each took a step back and dropped their head in submission.

Jenna brushed up against my side, her opposite mine, watching my back. Her father began circling us, but between the two of us, I knew we were protected. He was searching out weaknesses and would find none. After several laps around us, he stopped on my exposed side. As he lunged to take a bite, I turned, and Jenna smacked her massive paw at him, hissing. The fur on his back was standing on edge.

Her mother approached as I watched her closely. When she reached us, she shifted back to human form. "Stop. Please, stop this now," Jenna's mother cried, and her father halted and let out a loud roar to call off the cats.

Kyle mimicked him with a howl that was echoed by each of the Grand Council members that brought the dogs to a screeching stop. As enemies faced enemies in a standoff, awaiting the call back to action, she pleaded, "This has got to stop now. Look around you. How many more must die today? The seer was wrong. It has nothing to do with the lions. It has nothing to do with Jenna. Can't you see? It is not the pride that will bring on the demise of the panthers—it is YOUR own pride! Look. See what is happening. Only you can stop this now."

King Edmond Lockhardt shifted and stood beside his mate. He looked around at the devastation. Both dogs and cats lay dead or injured all around. Kelsey was running from one to the next trying to heal as many as she possibly could before it was too late. When she leaned down over a dying panther, Edmond hissed.

"What is she doing?" he asked through gritted teeth.

I hadn't noticed that Jenna had shifted back to human form, too. She was still kneeling on the ground. Knowing how uncomfortable that made her in front of others. I moved to cover her. She wrapped her arms around me and kissed the top of my head.

"Kelsey's a healer, Daddy. She's helping the fallen."

"But that's a panther?" her mom said, astonished.

"It doesn't matter. Every life is worth saving. Kelsey knows that. She shouldn't have been here today. She's pregnant and unable to shift, leaving her vulnerable, but she knew she could still save lives here, and insisted on coming," Jenna told them. "She's my Pack Mother," she added.

Her father tensed, and took a step back when Kyle shifted on the spot.

"Let her do her job, sir. It would not be in your best interest to try to stop her. My mate is very powerful," Kyle told him. He was trying to appear calm, but I could see how tense he was, sensing a threat to Kelsey.

Edmond raised his arms in surrender. "My daughter fights as equal alongside her mate. I realize now that no matter how this plays out, I've already lost her. I am done." He gave another of those awful screeches and the cats that could, turned and walked back in the direction they came.

Kyle barked, followed by the Grand Council as the dogs began to retreat as well. The battle was over. It had been senseless. No one won today. Matt Williams was dead. My best friend was gone. The pain of that was difficult to handle.

Brothers for life, and beyond, I thought.

"Chase, come forward," Jenna's mother said. She looked me over critically. "I do not know how this is even possible. I can't begin to understand it, but I watched you during the battle. One eye on your enemy, and one on my girl. You only left her side once, to help protect your friend, a cat no less, and only after a very strong and capable wolf took your place to protect her. If you had left her exposed for even a second, I would have snatched her up like the cub she once was and been gone in a flash. It will take some time. Old prejudices are hard to overcome, but there is no doubt in my mind that you love my daughter." She began to weep. "And at the end of the day, what is more important than that?"

She then turned to Jenna and, without meaning to, I protectively wrapped my arm around her, pulling her closer to me. I couldn't protect her from all that had happened, but I would shield her as best I could from any further physical or emotional damage that her family could cause.

"My little princess. You grew up when I wasn't looking. He seems like a good man. All I've ever wanted is happiness for you and Tessa. If you've truly found that, then we'll find a way to accept it." She glanced back to where her mate was standing, watching, but unwilling to reach out. "Give him time. He loves you. I know he too will come around."

I was torn as I loosened my grip on my beautiful mate, but as she cried in her mother's arms, a smile lit her face. They said their goodbyes and Tessa grabbed her in a huge bear hug.

"I'm proud of you and I'll see you at home. The girls and I have decided we aren't leaving the ARC. We're ready to take our stand, too," Tessa whispered to her before kissing her cheek and turning to follow their parents.

I held my mate as we watched them leave.

"Do you really think he'll come around?" she asked.

"I think we have to have faith he will."

Jenna

Epilogue

I walked into the cabin, dropped my purse on the table then collapsed onto the couch. My last final of the semester. I was amazed I'd made it. Life had changed drastically upon returning to Archibald Reynolds after spring break, and not all for the bad.

Everyone on campus heard about what went down, and I guess you could say that meant the cat was out of the bag about Chase and me. The gossip and pettiness surrounding that seemed insignificant to me as I adjusted back to life at school. I had only been away from campus for one week, but it felt like a lifetime. I changed, grew up in that week.

Chase took Matt Williams' death really hard. Within a few days of returning to school, he told me he couldn't live in the frat house any longer, and moved into the cabin. It was just too hard for him. I knew he missed his friend and it broke my heart watching him mourn. Anita was still struggling, too, and somehow blamed me for it. We were talking now, but it was always tense.

There was a lot of tension at the sorority house, too. I stuck around for about two weeks before I packed up and moved in with Chase at our cabin. It was truly home now and we were both so much happier. Tessa came by several times a week, and we ate lunch whenever I was on campus. It was strange. With all that happened, I somehow grew closer to my twin than I had ever been before.

Chase might not have lived in the doghouse any more, but he was still very much a Delta Omega Gamma. Brothers for life and beyond, the slogan now went. Those guys had been wonderful through it all. They were family, my brothers too, and they never let me forget it. We had to put some boundaries on the cabin after it became the unofficial second doghouse.

It wasn't the boys who were the problem; it was the girls that followed them everywhere. The cabin was now a mostly girl free safety zone. We especially had issues once the weather turned warm and Chad shed his 'winter fluff' as he explained it. He went from the cute chubby guy you'd want to hook up with your best friend who has terrible luck in guys, to panty dropping sexy, according to more than one girl wiping drool from her mouth. I still couldn't believe it. It actually made me laugh every time I saw him. You would barely recognize him as the same person, yet he was in every way that mattered.

According to Chad, that was normal for squirrels; they bulked up in the winter and slimmed back down during the warm months. It was just what squirrels did. Damon had moved into Chase's old room, unable to stand sleeping in the room he had shared with Matt. According to him, nothing had changed except Chad's looks. He was still hiding food throughout the room and he still talked incessantly, but he had a huge heart and we loved him just the way he was.

The front door opened and closed. I didn't budge. I had heard the Jeep coming up the drive, and I could smell my mate as potent as if he were standing before me. Hey, there were definitely some benefits to being an unofficial wolf.

"Babe, you home?" Chase asked, sounding breathless.

"In here," I said, raising my arm.

He walked over to the couch and looked down at me, smiling and shaking his head. That damn dimple was showing. He knew it was my weakness.

"You up for a road trip?" he asked excitedly.

"What? I just finished my last final. Can't we just chill for a few days?"

"No can do, beautiful. Liam just called. Maddie's in labor and she has already told the doctor that she refuses to have this baby without her photographer there to capture the moment. Both she and Kelsey are still raving over the pictures you took for them during spring break."

I sprung up and ran to the bedroom, throwing clothes quickly into a bag.

"We'll never make it, Chase. It's too long of a drive!"

"Don't you think I told him that?" he said as he grabbed toothbrushes and other toiletries as fast as he could.

A loud noise sounded outside, and my panther hissed.

"Put those claws away, kitten," he joked. "That's our ride."

"What?" I asked as he grabbed my hand and we ran outside. I checked up when I saw the helicopter sitting in our backyard just off my deck. A large logo for Westin Foundation covered the side.

I shook my head as we ran to the awaiting open door. I settled into my seat as Chase reached over and made sure I was buckled in before handing me a set of headphones. He closed the door and signaled to the pilot that we were ready.

"Ms. Lockhardt, Mr. Westin, it's calm skies ahead, so we'll have you back in San Marco as quickly as possible," the pilot said as we nodded our thanks.

I turned to my gorgeous mate. "Will life with you always be such an adventure?" I asked.

He grinned, dimples and all, took my hand in his, and leaned over, kissing me breathless. When I pulled back with a happy sigh, he held up my hand and kissed it. Sometime during that world fading kiss, he slipped a huge princess cut diamond onto my left ring finger. My eyes went wide as I gasped. I looked back up at him with tears in my eyes, and he shrugged.

"There are some benefits to being a Westin."

Dear Reader,

I hope you enjoyed Confusing Hearts. I enjoyed the classic Romeo and Juliet underlying theme of this story. If you enjoyed it too, please drop me a quick review here: https://www.amazon.com/dp/B07BP9XL9W

Now, KEEP READING for a special SNEAK PEEK into LILY'S STORY, the one so many of you have been waiting for. She is feisty and larger than life and has big romantic dreams of her one true mate. She's never understood why mating was so hard for her siblings. But all those opinions and grand ideas come crashing in around her in CAN'T BE LOVE.

For further information on my books, events, and life in general, I can be found online here:

Website: www.julietrettel.com

Facebook: http://www.facebook.com/authorjulietrettel

Facebook Fan Group:
https://www.facebook.com/groups/compounderspod7/

Instagram: http://www.instagram.com/julie.trettel

Twitter: http://www.twitter.com/julietrettel

Goodreads:
http://www.goodreads.com/author/show/14703924.Julie_Trettel

BookBub: https://www.bookbub.com/authors/julie-trettel

Amazon: http://www.amazon.com/Julie_Trettel/e/B018HS9GXS

Much love and thanks,
Julie Trettel

SNEAK PEEK

CAN'T BE LOVE

A Westin Pack Novel

By

Julie Trettel

Coming June 2018

Lily

Chapter 1

Exiting the car, I stretched and smiled. There was something nice smelling in the air that called to me. I liked it. Collier territory was beautiful. I had visited it numerous times in my life, but something felt different this time.

Liam helped unload the car and I was practically skipping with excitement. It was the first time Maddie had been back to her home pack since my twin brother had found her. It was pretty cool that my oldest and dearest friend turned out to be my twin's one true mate. I was really happy for them. All my siblings had found their true mates, and I couldn't wait till I found mine.

Practically skipping with excitement and loving the wide-open space of Wyoming, Liam gave me a concerned look.

"What is wrong with you?"

Maddie laughed, "Leave her alone. This place just has that effect on people."

Madelyn looked happy, I thought.

"Sweetheart, are you okay?" Liam asked her, and I knew he was worried about being emotionally overwhelmed from this trip. That's why he had asked me to tag along. I had a way of pulling her out of her shell.

Madelyn Amanda Collier Westin, also called MC, was my very best friend in the entire world. We had met at summer camp when we were six years old and practically inseparable every year after, until the dark day that she had disappeared. Eight years later, my brother would find her living a new life in the human world and bring her home.

Oscar, MC's son bounded out of the car. He was clearly as excited as I was. It didn't take long before her sisters swarmed. Maddie had five sisters, and 1 douchebag brother. I hadn't seen Thomas in years. He was a year young than Maddie and me, and had been a pain when we were kids, but had disappeared and pulled away from the family after Maddie's disappearance. Asshole.

We headed for the alpha house that Maddie had grown up in as everyone started grabbing our things and a round of welcome hugs.

There was something so familiar about the Collier alpha house. It made me happy just to be there.

Cora and Zach Collier were good people. Zach was a great leader and alpha of the pack. Both being alpha brats had helped Maddie and I become fast friends so many years ago. Few understood the pressures of that role, so it was a unique bond we had formed.

They had visited Westin a few times but seeing Madelyn home was starting a chain of tears and high emotions.

Sorry girl, I thought to myself. *I'm out of here!*

Leaving them to their reunion, I headed back outside. I breathed in the crisp mountain air and it made my whole body start to tingle. *Mate,* I thought to myself.

I didn't want to freak out, but I just knew my one true mate was here. He had to be a Collier. I could live with that. I had waited my entire life to feeling the tingly sensation that had the hair on my arms standing up. I could barely contain my excitement.

My siblings had all fought their bond in some way, but I knew that would never be me. The magic of true mates was so romantic and something I had longed for and dreamed about my entire life.

There were several groups of people around. Unlike the Westin alpha house that I was raised in that sat back in the woods away from town, Collier's alpha house literally sat on Main Street.

People had obviously heard of Maddie's visit ahead of time and were anxious to catch a glimpse of her. I started walking around and saying hello to people I passed, trying to make eye contact with every male in the area. I knew the moment I our eyes met, I'd know and everything was going to be perfect.

My senses were on full alert and I imagined my wolf was wagging her tail happily. He was here, this was it! There was even more spring in my step as I anxiously honed in on my mate, my one true mate! It took everything in my power not to "eek" out loud in excitement.

I channeled a little more of my wolf and let her guide me. We rounded a corner and I saw a group of young men standing around talking. Every single one of them was super sexy hot. *Yes please!* I was getting a super sexy hot mate. It was the greatest day of my life.

I looked at each of them wondering which one he was. They all smiled and nodded as attention turned to me. I was careful to make eye contact with each of them. Nothing. Then I noticed the one with his back turned towards me stiffen. His shoulders sagged, and he took a deep breath. I was acute aware of how his heart rate sped up and I was a million times positive this was him, the man I had longed for my entire life.

I took a moment to check out and appreciate my mate. The thought alone had me grinning from ear to ear. He had close cropped, brown hair. He was wearing a black flannel shirt tucked into tight jeans with a wide belt, completing the package with a pair of black cowboy boots. *My very own cowboy*. I quickly admired just how well his ass filled out those jeans too. I already knew he was hotter than hot and he was all mine.

He slowly turned around and our eyes locked. It felt like my entire world tilted and he was the new gravity holding me in place. Wow, I thought. He had the most alluring chocolate brown eyes. I was mesmerized. It was everything I had ever dreamed it would be.

Recognition flickered in his eyes, breaking the fog I had found myself in.

"Lily Westin?" I heard him say in a deep sexy voice that had my body trembling.

Surprised he knew my name, I shook my head and took a closer look. Revulsion immediately set in. I couldn't believe what my eyes were telling me. I couldn't believe what my heart was telling me.

"Thomas?" I spit out, disgusted at the very thought. "Oh, hell no!"

I turned and ran as fast as I could. I had to get away from there. God was a good, loving, and kind God, there was no way he could possibly be evil enough to condemn me to Thomas Collier as my one true mate. I had to have read things wrong. This could not be happening to me.

Check out more great books by Julie Trettel!

The Compounders Series:

Start with Book 1!

In the wake of terrorist attacks, economic collapse, and martial law, America has become a nation at war and a country at odds. Mike Jenkins was well prepared, and moved his family and friends to his totally secure compound on a remote mountain in western Virginia.

After several years, Holly Jenkins couldn't wait for the elders to open the bunker doors, allowing her to roam at will, and feel free once again. Escaping to the sanctuary of her hidden cave would set in motion changes in her life heretofore unknown.

The AMAN presented a threat to the compound and the nearby towns; a threat that could not be ignored. They were prepared for war, but nothing could prepare Holly for her own battle between the two men she had grown to love… and the third she might be forced to marry.

Chaos will reign! Will love survive?

The Compounders: Book1
http://www.amazon.com/dp/B018HKIU7O/?tag=kp-jtret-20

DISSENSION
http://www.amazon.com/dp/B01N6FSGLE/?tag=kp-jtret-20

DISCONTENT
http://www.amazon.com/dp/B07215QYL1/?tag=kp-jtret-20

Westin Pack Series:

Start with One True Mate

Kelsey Adams is alone, and has been since childhood. Running away is all she knows and necessary to preserve her deepest, darkest secret. She can not afford for anyone to get close, or know about the monster within. But when she lands a lucrative job as an administrative assistant to Kyle Westin, CEO of the Westin Foundation, her life changes and everything's at stake. Can she conceal her growing feelings and her true self from this enigmatic, strong willed man, or will her world fall apart?

Kyle Westin, an alpha male who always gets what he wants, has watched and waited for the little she-wolf he knows is his perfect mate to show any signs of recognition. For two years he endures her unnecessary formality and daily rejections with a patience he did not know he possessed. But even Kyle has his limits.... Can he make Kelsey notice him as someone other than her boss and break down the walls she built around her heart? Or will Kelsey do what she has always done --- run?

One True Mate
https://www.amazon.com/dp/B071HXL3R2

Fighting Destiny
https://www.amazon.com/ dp/B07575HC9T

Forever Mine
https://www.amazon.com/dp/B077V9WHMG

About the Author

Julie Trettel is author of the Compounders and Westin Pack Series, a full time Systems Administrator, wife, and mother of 4 awesome kids. She resides in Richmond, VA and can often be found writing on the sidelines of a football field or swimming pool. She comes from a long line of story tellers. Writing has always been a stress reliever and escape for her to manage the crazy demands of juggling time and schedules between work and an active family of six. In her "free time," she enjoys traveling, reading, outdoor activities, and spending time with family and friends.

Visit
www.JulieTrettel.com

Printed in Great Britain
by Amazon